'This book is bliss.' HILARY MCKAY

'What an absolute hoot! Set in 1924, and galloping with coming-of-age giddiness, and the promise of parties and life-changing romance, Joanna Nadin's *A Calamity of Mannerings* simply brims with vim.' *LOVEREADING4KIDS*

'Flawless. Fabulous.' RACHEL DELAHAYE

'If Louise Rennison had written *I Capture the Castle* it would be this book. Witty, totally charming and proper laugh-out-loud-several-times-on-each-page funny, it's just a joy from start to finish and I felt sick with envy over the writing.' LAURA WOOD

'A real roaring 20s romp of a read. Delightful.'
WRD ABOUT BOOKS

'A storyline that tips a cap at *Love in a Cold Climate*, *I Capture the Castle* and even *Bridgerton* make this a must read for ages 16–106!' CATHY CASSIDY

'I couldn't put it down.' EMMA CARROLL

'So much fun! So clever, with such wonderful characters who I can still feel breathing and
I kept on guffawing with

HAVE YOU EVER WONDERED HOW BOOKS ARE MADE?

UCLan Publishing is an award winning independent publisher specialising in Children's and Young Adult books. Based at The University of Central Lancashire, this Preston-based publisher teaches MA Publishing students how to become industry professionals using the content and resources from its business; students are included at every stage of the publishing process and credited for the work that they contribute.

The business doesn't just help publishing students though. UCLan Publishing has supported the employability and real-life work skills for the University's Illustration, Acting, Translation, Animation, Photography, Film & TV students and many more. This is the beauty of books and stories; they fuel many other creative industries! The MA Publishing students are able to get involved from day one with the business and they acquire a behind the scenes experience of what it is like to work for a such a reputable independent.

The MA course was awarded a Times Higher Award (2018) for Innovation in the Arts and the business, UCLan Publishing, was awarded Best Newcomer at the Independent Publishing Guild (2019) for the ethos of teaching publishing using a commercial publishing house. As the business continues to grow, so too does the student experience upon entering this dynamic Masters course.

For my union sisters: Carrie, Lucy, Lucy, Celia, Rachel and Eliane – we fought a good fight

A Calamity of Mannerings is a uclanpublishing book

First published in Great Britain in 2023.
This edition published in 2024 by
uclanpublishing
University of Central Lancashire
Preston, PR1 2HE, UK

978-1-915235-09-1

3 5 7 9 10 8 6 4

Set in 10.5/17pt Kingfisher by Becky Chilcott.

A CIP catalogue record for this book is available from the British Library.

Printed and bound in Great Britain by Clays Ltd, Elcograf S.p.A.

JOANNA NADIN

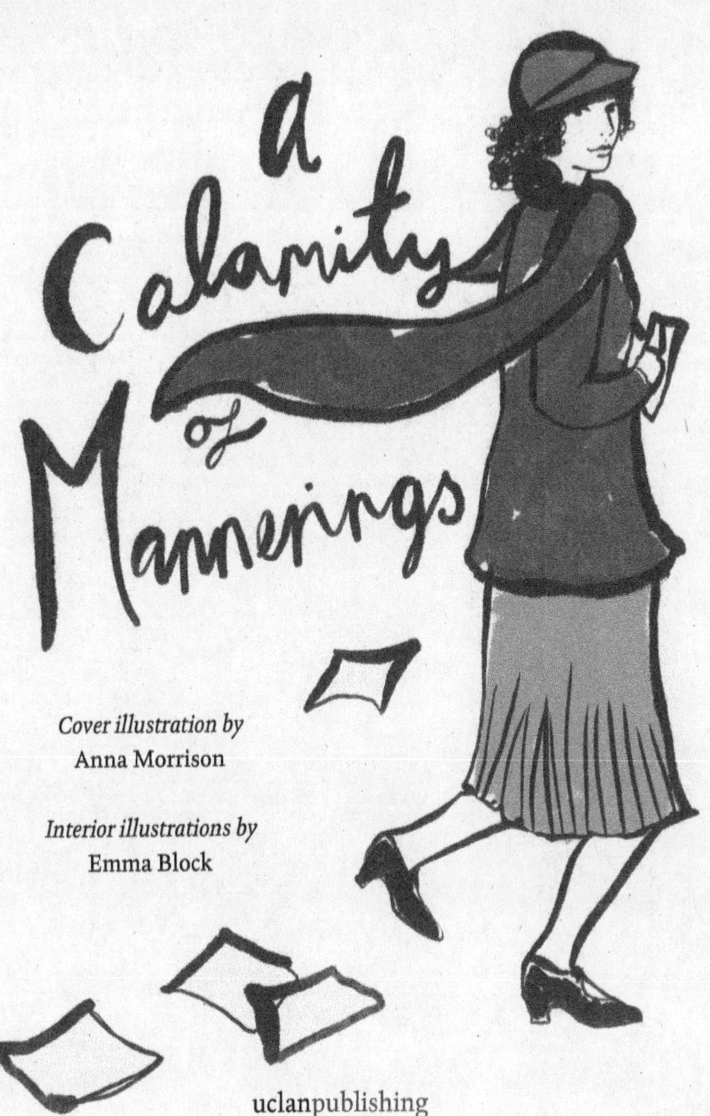

Cover illustration by
Anna Morrison

Interior illustrations by
Emma Block

uclanpublishing

'Sisters are a shield against life's cruel adversity.' Nancy Mitford

'But sisters *are* life's cruel adversity!' Decca Mitford

The Mitford Girls by Mary S Lovell

JANUARY

FRIDAY 25 JANUARY

11 A.M.

It is a curse to be born a girl.

There, I've said it. If not out loud, then on paper, and in crimson Indian ink. Aster says the shade is tasteless, but I say it is just the thing for chronicling the downfall of us Mannerings, and Marigold agrees. Aster said Marigold *would* agree, being ten, and strange, but I am ignoring her, just as I am ignoring her belittling my very endeavour, which *is* an endeavour because, since Siegfried got in and chewed the electrics, the light in the morning room has been exceedingly dim.

'What on earth is the point, Panther?' she demanded. (Panther is not my real name, but the less said about that for now, the better.)

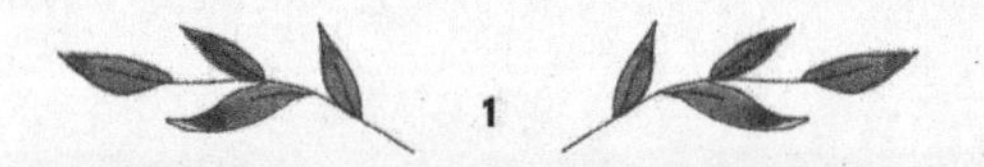

'So that I may look back in years to come and weep at the sorry state of the nation,' I replied. 'That, in 1924, merely being in possession of a P-E-N-I-S still seems to guarantee one supremacy, regardless of talent or even aptitude.' (I had to spell the p-word out because of Marigold.)

'You're hardly Pepys,' Aster pointed out needlessly, and somewhat aspishly I thought. 'Anyway, it's tradition, however much we may regret it.'

'Tradition *is* a penis,' said Marigold, making a mockery of my spelling attempts, and everyone's attempts to render her language and behaviour more ladylike, all while barely looking up from one of Daddy's old farming manuals. 'And I bet Pepys was as well.'

Aster made a noise of utter disgust.

For once, I am with Aster and Grandma: it is Daddy's fault Marigold is so uncouth, on account of him allowing her unfettered access to *Gray's Anatomy* and *The Daily Mirror* (Grandma says she doesn't know which is worse). Just as it is Daddy's fault that I am so despondent about the state of the nation and its ludicrous laws, because it was he who pressed the *Hansard* parliamentary debate report on to me after I asked him what on earth he did all day.

But then it is also Daddy's fault we are in this wretched position in the first place. If he hadn't gone and died, then the future of Radley Manor and the Mannering clan wouldn't be in doubt. It's not as if it were even in the Great War, which would at least have had an element of heroism about it. As it is, there is nothing remotely heroic about getting run over by a dustcart on Whitehall, especially five years into peacetime.

I realise this all makes me seem utterly unfeeling, which I must insist I am not. Not a day goes by in which I don't find myself practically weak with grief. Daddy was the very heart of the house, and, even though he *did* have the essential appendage, he didn't wield it with any authority. He preferred art to archery and gardening to blood sports. He never once shouted at us unless we were in mortal danger (though in Marigold's case this was rather often). Mama said he was a fool for us three girls and would have given his right arm for us, if he could. He certainly went without cigars one Christmas so that Marigold could have sheep feed, Aster a new canvas, and I a pair of pink kid gloves. Which, now I consider it, was rather greedy and conceited of me as I promptly lost one, so have never even worn them. Poor Daddy.

But still, he did get us in this terrible mess.

I suppose I should be grateful that at least he left Mama pregnant, so there is one last-gasp chance of an heir (and any moment now, judging by the sounds upstairs). Otherwise the house, estate and title will all go to Cousin Valentine, much to our great sadness, and Grandma's rather greater anger. It is because Valentine is half-Italian and an actor and both are equally unsavoury in her book – to be avoided like nits or dysentery, as if they might be catching. It is lucky that she doesn't yet realise he is also homosexual, which would be the very cherry on her cake of menace. She has still not forgiven Daddy for becoming a socialist, which is on a par with treason and murder as far as she is concerned.

'Can't we pretend?' said Marigold then. 'If it's a girl, I mean. We could call it one of those vague names that can be either, like Vyvyan, or Evelyn, and dress it in blue?'

'Won't they want to inspect it?' I suggested, unsure though I was as to who 'they' might be.

'Oh,' said Marigold, deflating like a tired birthday balloon. 'I hadn't thought of that.'

Which only goes to show how ridiculous it is that a bit of skin and whatnot, a mere few inches of flesh, should change one's life so drastically – alter the course of history, even. It's not like it's a magic wand. Not that I've seen one, unless you count Bobby's. But Bobby is a dog, and smelly and ancient, and I'm not sure he's ever really used it for its intended purpose anyway. I suppose Siegfried has one, but with sheep it is hard to tell what's what, with the wool. We all thought he was a ewe for months until Rapsey (the yard man) put us right when he caught Siegfried trying to harass a hay bale.

Though I expect at some point I shall have to face up to one – a penis, I mean – and quite literally. Books don't really prepare you for the anatomical aspect. Only for the romance, with which, I have to say, I am slightly more eager to engage. I have read *The Sheikh* several times now, and am already quite

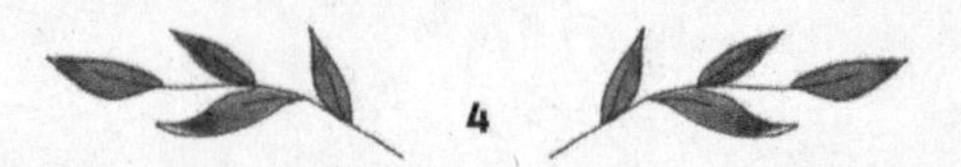

au fait with the savagery of love: the mouth 'bruised by brutal kisses', the waist 'gripped by manly hands', the cheeks 'scalded by hot tears', all of which is vaguely anatomical, I suppose.

As Margot, my best friend since Hedingham Prep, would say, 'Sigh'. This is because Margot is perpetually in love. Although mostly of the thwarted, doomed or unrequited kind, not least because the men she falls for are invariably poetic, foreign or louche. I wouldn't mind being in love, even thwarted, doomed or unrequited, but so far the closest I have come is the fictional sheikh.

Aster says the novels are nonsense, and merely perpetuate the patriarchy and our thrall to the swarthier sex. But then she would, as she is twenty-three and has still to kiss a single soul, instead spending her entire time disappearing down darkened corridors with Daphne Balfour or playing the cello with an air of contrived melancholy that verges on the terminal. Whereas I may be merely sixteen, but I have at least held hands with a man. Admittedly, it was Freddy Spencer, whom I have known since I was seven, and it was almost certainly accidental, as he grabbed me as I was about to fall off the stile at Badger's Copse, but still, it is something.

I feel sad for Mama that all that sort of thing is in the past for her, being so very old, and widowed to boot. Though she probably hasn't the time, what with us three, another on the way at this very moment, and Grandma in the Dower House to worry about as well. Perhaps that is the way with love, and torrid kisses must be replaced with napkin changes, and bottles, and colic. (I am referring to babies here, not Grandma, though she once threatened to become incontinent just to spite Mabel, her housemaid, when she allegedly wronged her with an underdone crumpet.) And yet, Mama and Daddy did seem blissfully committed, and visibly kissed at least twice a year: once on their anniversary and once under the mistletoe in the long hall at Yule.

This Christmas was spent in somewhat less celebratory circumstances, with one of Marigold's hens on the table because we couldn't afford a goose, and a bent thimble in the pudding because no one could muster a sixpence. It was all terribly Dickensian. And of course all anyone could think about was the empty chair at one end of the table, and Mama's swelling belly at the other. A belly that is currently so distended as to be barrel-shaped, and yet is stubbornly refusing to relinquish its guest, despite poor Mama being in labour for four hours now.

It is rather like waiting for an omnibus to arrive. Only in this case, the omnibus is penis-shaped, and will dictate the rest of our very existence.

3 P.M.

Our fate is still unsealed, Mama is still sweating and restless, and Doctor Spencer has been sent for to speed things up.

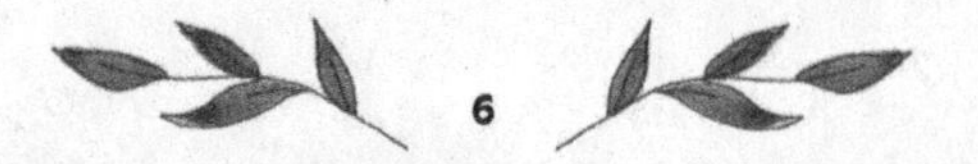

Meanwhile, Aster and Marigold have been finding new and evermore depressing ways to pass the time.

'That howl,' said Marigold, upon hearing an awful mooing noise escape from upstairs, 'is caused by the agony of the cervix opening so that the baby can make its way down the vaginal canal.'

Aster went positively pale, as well she might. On the only previous occasion on which we have caught glimpse of a canal, it was a dubious sort of brown and there was a dead dog floating in it.

'Once the cervix is fully dilated, then she can start to push,' Marigold went on. 'Though that can take hours, days perhaps, and even then forceps—'

'Shall we play a game?' I said quickly, for fear more vivid description might put me off babies for life. Which, while I am not hugely keen on the prospect, is my 'only purpose on earth', according to Grandma.

'Would you rather be dead or pregnant?' said Aster. 'I know which I'd prefer and it doesn't involve being shackled to a wailing baby.'

Even Marigold pulled a face at that.

'How cruel,' I said. 'What if Mama were to perish right now?'

We all went silent then, and prayed for Dr Spencer to hurry up, though he has to come all the way from the other side of the village and the roads are perilous at the best of times, and positive death traps in January.

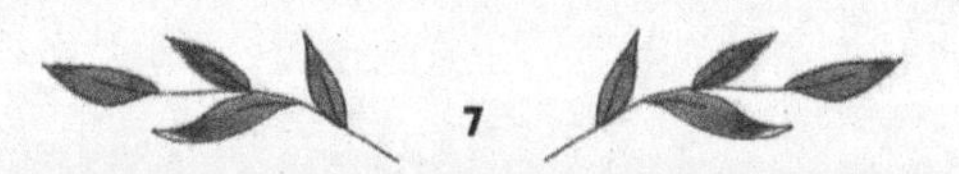

'Would you rather have one leg or one eye?' I questioned instead.

'One eye,' said Marigold. 'I'd wear a patch and carry a parrot and make anyone who was beastly walk the plank.'

'And what would Siegfried do?' I asked. 'You can't keep a sheep on a ship.' (Which is horribly tricky to say. I bid you: try it.)

'Why not?' demanded Marigold.

'No grass,' snapped Aster.

'He eats biscuits,' Marigold snapped back.

Which we had to concede was true, as he had cleaned us out of the last batch of fairings. Not that any of us complained particularly; they were desperately leaden things, as are most of Cook's conjurings these days. Cook says it is the diminished means with what (she means 'which') she has to shop. Aster says it is diminished ability, or possibly no ability in the first place. I say at least we *have* a cook. I suppose we may have to fend for ourselves kitchen-wise if this baby doesn't come out right. Heaven knows where, however, for how can we possibly pay rent, and who would be fool enough to take five of us in?

Oh, I'm afraid I shall find poverty intolerable. I know there are people far worse off, but, really, Radley is all any of us have ever known. And though it is held together largely by wallpaper paste and faith; though frigid winter has slid into the brickwork and will cling still in July; though it is hardly Balfour

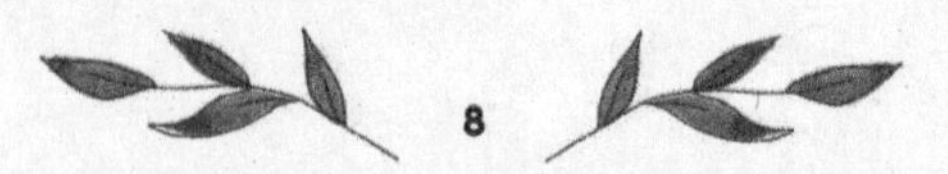

Manor, let alone Buckingham Palace, we are, all of us, so very fond of it.

'Would you rather eat Siegfried or Grandma?' asked Aster eventually, ever the pessimist.

'Grandma,' Marigold and I agreed in unison. 'Though she'd be stringy, and tough as mutton,' I added.

'Hush!' said Marigold. 'Or Siegfried will hear you!'

'He's not in the drawing room again, is he?' asked Aster.

'Scullery,' said Marigold.

'Marigold!'

'What?' she protested. 'It's ghastly outside. I'd like to see you try to get a wink of sleep in the wretched elements.'

'I'm not wearing the equivalent of forty Fair Isle sweaters,' said Aster.

'Even so.'

'Would you rather be Marianne Dashwood or Elizabeth Bennet?' I changed the subject, rather cleverly I thought.

'Neither,' replied Aster. 'I'd rather be Darcy, or Willoughby. Though Willoughby is a swaggering cad, and Darcy a prig.'

She is right, of course. I thought of the sheikh then, who is so very dashing (if brutal), and evidently accomplished, love-wise, but unlikely to pass any of Aster's vigorous tests of mettle and manners. But I put it out of my mind quickly, realising that I'm not sure any man would.

'Perhaps we can call the baby Darcy,' suggested Marigold. 'If it's a boy.'

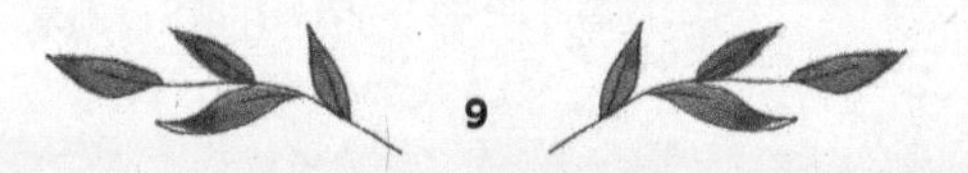

'Don't be absurd,' said Aster. 'Darcy isn't a first name.'

'Nor is Aster,' retorted Marigold. 'It's a flower. Just like Marigold and Ag—'

'What *will* we call it?' I asked quickly.

'Calendula, I expect,' said Aster grimly. 'Or Primrose. Or Pansy, perhaps.'

'What if it's a boy?'

'Lupin,' she said, so decisively that neither of us dared argue. 'But it won't be.'

'We could just call it Baby,' said Marigold, clearly still enamoured of her master disguise plan of turning any potential girl into the requisite gender.

'Baby is a ridiculous name,' I said.

'And Panther isn't?' Aster raised an eyebrow.

'Well, that's your fault,' I snapped, smarting somewhat. 'You couldn't pronounce the real one.'

Trust Aster to saddle me with something so absurd and, worse, ill-fitting. Panthers are long and sleek and elegant – like Aster – whereas I am short and curved in decidedly irritating places while my eyebrows are unruly and my hair untameable. Mama insists the latter is my crowning glory, but she is only being kind because I am the one who inherited Daddy's tendency to curls and redness, plus she is not the one who has to untangle the mess in the morning.

'More importantly,' I carried on, 'if it *is* a girl, then what will become of us? Will we be destitute?'

Aster snorted. 'Hardly.'

'We shall have to turn to vice,' said Marigold decisively. 'Or rockhopper penguins.'

'Not more animals,' I pleaded.

'Not animals; penguins – rockhopper ones. And they're all the rage,' she insisted. 'I read it in *The Tatler*. Thingummy Sassoon – that poet – has a whole flock. We could breed them and sell them to the rich.'

'To fools,' corrected Aster. 'And you shouldn't be reading *The Tatler*, it only encourages things.'

'What things?' I demanded, as well I might, given that *The Tatler* is my and Margot's bible. (Margot doesn't know about *Hansard*, or she would accuse me of being a bluestocking (i.e. literary and tedious), which would mean no hope of romance – look at Aster.)

I could see Aster grasping for something. 'Frippery,' she said finally. 'Pointless pursuits.'

She meant champagne, and fast cars and short dresses, all of which Margot and I worship, of course. Or the idea of, as I have only seen champagne at a distance, Grandma's motorcar is so slow as to be glacial, and my dresses are defiantly ankle-length, all of which is thoroughly gloom-making. As was the ridiculousness of Marigold's plan.

'Where would we even get a penguin to breed?' I said. 'There must be something else.'

'Ambergris,' said Marigold, trumping herself quite

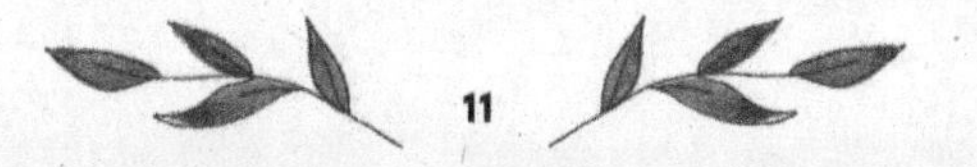

spectacularly, given that ambergris is, effectively, whale vomit.

'Repulsive,' said Aster.

'Agreed,' I seconded.

'It's not!' said Marigold. 'It's ever so precious.' She then went on to explain how its benevolent discovery would secure not only our fortune, but our fame. Though, as I pointed out, this in itself is highly unlikely, given that we live a hundred miles or more from the sea, and, on the few visits we have made, I am yet to see a whale bask off Great Yarmouth, let alone vomit there.

'Perhaps,' I said, keen to assert my usefulness, 'my chronicle will prove to be of financial benefit.'

Marigold actually laughed, and Aster said that unless I write the dictionary, the Bible or a best-selling romance then I shan't make a shilling. And as two are already done and the other I may have read about but have never actually experienced, then the whole plan is as pie in the sky as whale vomit and vice, and I am more likely to marry the Prince of Wales.

'Perhaps I *shall* marry the Prince of Wales,' I snapped then. 'Or a duke, at the very least. Then you shall both have to come begging to me to be spared the workhouse. Or Grandma's, which is possibly worse.'

'Don't be absurd,' said Aster. 'I shall never beg for anything from you. Besides, how will you find someone to have you? You're not even "out" as a deb.'

'And whose fault is that?' I snapped.

'Hardly mine,' said Aster.

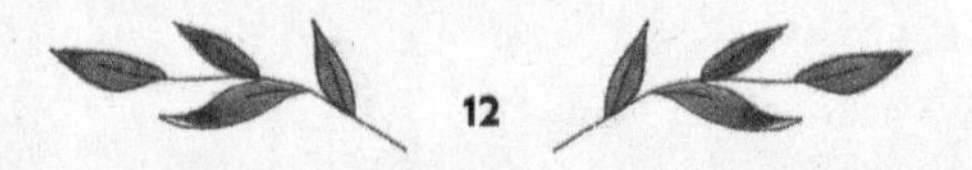

Which is, strictly speaking, correct, though I did not give Aster the satisfaction of admitting it. The truth is, it all comes back to Daddy dying in an untimely fashion, and before that being too poor to present me as a debutante. There wasn't even enough money to run to a new dress, let alone hire a flat for the London season. Mama said I could let out Aster's old gown but I said I would rather die in penury, which isn't absolutely true, but the dress was woefully outmoded even a year ago. Besides, it had hardly worked for Aster. As Grandma says, there is a fine line between exuberant youth and bitter spinsterhood, and my sister crossed it and left it for dust several years ago.

I don't suppose there's much chance of me becoming a deb at all now unless we do find whale vomit or I write a bestseller, so the Prince of Wales is off the list before he was even on it properly and it is back to more realistic prospects, i.e. men who actually dare venture to Ickthorpe and its environs.

'You could marry Reg Nesbitt,' added Marigold at that point, as if she could read my thinking, at least partially.

This is because she and her friend Harriet Ponsonby, otherwise known as Bad Harry (following an incident with some table fireworks, the less said about which, the better), have taken to mooning around after Reg, the farrier's boy, who is short and gormless and spits in the forge, which makes an irritating hissing sound. Marigold says this is manly behaviour and to be admired. Neither Aster nor I agree. Though I have suspicions that Margot might approve. In any case, Grandma has forbidden any more lurking near the blacksmith's, for fear of burns or, more probably, learning to spit, or speak with a glottal stop.

Aster then declared she would rather die than marry Reg Nesbitt. I said that was a lie and a bad one, and Marigold expanded into the precise manner of death, with Aster eventually agreeing she would happily be shot or garrotted, but if it were a matter of laudanum poisoning, dysentery, or being chewed to pieces by rats over a matter of weeks, she might reconsider nuptials.

It strikes me that taste is strange. I wonder what man I shall fall for? Margot and I made a list of requisites in a suitor once. We decided they must:

- be terribly good-looking (obviously)
- have a good head of hair, with no signs of receding (check the father for likelihood of this happening at a future date)
- be preferably five foot eleven or above (or at least three inches taller than us if all other requirements fulfilled)
- be able to recite at least two verses of *Kubla Khan* (or another poem of their choice approved by us)
- have appeared in *The Tatler*, only preferably not with Evangeline Balfour, because neither of

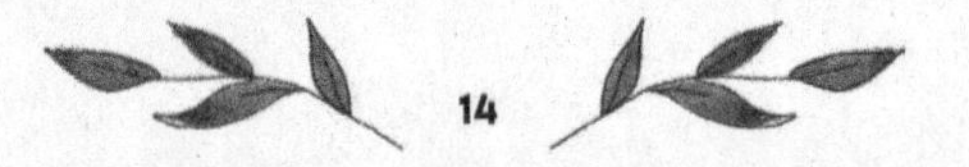

us want her cast-offs (of which there are many)
It would be too, too shaming

- not 'smell of trade' (this is actually Grandma's criterion, but we have adopted it, because trade surely discounts marriage).

So far I am yet to meet anyone who fits all of these, and the likelihood grows less by the day. Daddy always said there is someone out there for everyone, even Aster. Though it is hard to imagine who in her case.

Oh! That is the door. I must go and let the doctor in. I feel quite sick with anticipation. By the time I return to these pages the Mannerings may be utterly destitute and my life irrevocably altered.

5 P.M.

Life is not quite yet irrevocably altered, and the Mannerings not quite yet destitute. Rather, the hideous limbo continues upstairs, still loudly, but now with the added audience of Dr Spencer *and* Freddy, who has apparently come to gain practical experience, now that he is studying medicine.

I have to say I am most uncomfortable knowing that not one man but two are party to Mama's most private moment, not to mention anatomical parts. It is a great pity that the greatest qualification for a medical career, far greater than any amount of scholarship or 'practical experience', seems to be, yet again, a penis.

It is also a pity the state of Radley. I suppose we have become used to its faults and fissures (literal and otherwise), but neither the doctor nor Freddy have stepped foot inside for nearly a year, and suddenly I am forced to see it through their surely disapproving eyes. Oh, it is imposing – ten bedrooms, two bathrooms, a stone staircase just made for grand entrances – and larger by far than their own Bridge House, which is Arts and Crafts, and a dear thing. But I would wager Bridge House doesn't have mildew in the kitchen and up the walls of the long hall, or a patina of pin mould on several Persian rugs (luckily, it is easily camouflaged, or trodden in), or more rodents than human residents.

But I cannot concern myself with that right now as, firstly, there is nothing we can do about the state of anything, given our finances and abilities – or lack thereof – and secondly, the noises from Mama are becoming far louder and far more frequent, which Marigold says sounds promising, vaginal canal-wise. I do not think it sounds promising at all. It sounds quite miserable. In fact, I am suddenly minded that our family motto, 'Fortiter gerit crucem', or, 'He bears the cross bravely', is not at all apt. For, there is no 'he' bearing much at all round here; it is always a 'she'. First there is all the frantic plaiting and pulling of hair to endure, then the indignity of monthlies, then, to cap it all, childbirth. Not to mention accommodating the you-know-what in order to get to the childbirth stage in the first place.

Men just cannot possibly understand the trials women must go through. To hear them talk in Parliament (not that I have heard them, but thanks to Daddy's *Hansard* I have read it all written-up word for word) you'd think we barely even existed.

Perhaps they wish we didn't.

'You could marry Freddy,' suggested Marigold, finally tiring of *Goats Today*.

I felt my cheeks flame, which was strange. But I told her I was more likely to marry the Prince of Wales or the spitting farrier's boy. 'He's not *bad* looking,' is all I would admit.

Which is true. He's tallish (almost five foot eleven, I would say) and blondish and in a certain light one might even say he had a kind of nobility, which is ironic as he's not at all *Debrett's* material (though *we* are only just in said guide to the British aristocracy, and possibly not for long). Anyway, he's away at Cambridge most of the time so even if I did have an urge to marry him, or just moon over him, which I do not, he wouldn't be around for said mooning. And besides, his current first-hand experience is probably putting him off marriage and all it entails for life. It certainly is me.

At which point, as if to confirm my very thought, Freddy descended the stairs, red-faced and sweating, with his shirt sleeves rolled up and a disconcerting blood stain on his right forearm.

'What's happening?' Aster demanded. 'Is Mama all right?'

'Is it born yet? Is it a boy?' asked Marigold. 'I wish it were a rabbit.'

'You have ten rabbits,' I pointed out. 'At least.'

'I'd like another.'

For someone who has an anatomical knowledge of reproduction both human and animal, she can be terrifically whimsical at times.

'It's neither,' replied Freddy, thankfully immune to Marigold's whims. 'That is to say, it's not quite out yet.'

'Oh, for heaven's sake,' Aster complained. 'How much longer?'

'She's thinking of Mama,' I said quickly. 'She does sound in terrible pain.'

Freddy reddened further, so as to be verging on beetroot. 'Birth can be frightfully tricky at times, and the baby is breech.'

'That means backwards,' said Marigold. 'Bum first.'

'Marigold!' snapped Aster.

'Oh, heavens,' I said.

'It's quite all right,' said Freddy. 'I'm not easily shocked.'

'Poor Mama,' I said quickly, before Marigold could prove him wrong. Then, 'Why *aren't* there women doctors? I believe it would be so much less distressing.'

He frowned, causing his hair to flop over one eye, which, I

have to admit, was a little dashing. 'Oh, but there are,' he said, pushing it back. 'Just very few. Why? You're not thinking of studying medicine, are you?'

I myself reddened. 'Don't sound so mortified. But no, I wasn't particularly thinking of studying at all.' I did not add that this was because we couldn't afford it.

Aster smirked. 'She's already wasting the education she does have. She doesn't need more to squander.'

'Shut up, Aster. It's not as if you're using yours much either. What do you even do all day, you and Daphne?'

Well, that set Aster into a terrifically Dark Mood. Though that is nothing unusual. She is always in Dark Moods these days and either skulking off on solitary walks to heaven knows where or sulking in the morning room with the wretched cello, which, given the inclement weather, is what she immediately took up at that very point.

Freddy's face became pained, to add to the puce.

'Tea?' I said hopefully.

'Thank goodness,' he said. 'Yes. That's what I came to fetch, actually. I think everyone could do with one.'

This was surely an understatement. Brandy or a hot toddy sounded more in order, but perhaps that would come later.

'You *could* study, you know,' he said, as we made our way to the kitchen. 'Find a . . . a purpose.'

I felt a prick of something then. The sudden hot shame of being tested and coming up wanting. I turned my head away.

'A purpose?' I scoffed. 'Am I allowed one? Isn't my purpose to be in Mama's position?'

'Well, I suppose. If you want that. But there's more to life than babies.'

For you, I thought. I am no more likely to be able to choose my purpose than I am my name. Perhaps if I were a Pankhurst I might stand a chance, but she has the luxury of university behind her, and money, *and* a husband willing to back her. I have none of these.

'Not in Ickthorpe,' I said.

'In Cambridge then,' he said. 'Or Oxford,' he added, 'if Cambridge is too close.'

My insides billowed, a brief burst of hope blowing them out like pillows in the wind. Though this, now, was torment. Cambridge may well be only twenty miles, which *is* quite close, I suppose, if one has a car. But he might as well have suggested Timbuctoo for all my chances of seeing it. I may not be a fool, however I am hardly scholarship material like he. I snapped to.

'Chance would be a fine thing,' I said. 'Anyway, why would I want to suffer endless lessons?' Thus putting what I hoped was a firm end to the discussion, I stomped the rest of the way down the long corridor and down the stone stairs in the east wing, Freddy trotting awkwardly behind like a dog.

Assembling tea was a more arduous task than I had imagined. Partly because Cook was upstairs acting as nursemaid, as we cannot afford both (or a housekeeper, or stable man, or any other servants bar Rapsey, who is actually officially Grandma's Odd Man, but does for us as well when he has to, despite being heaven knows how old); partly because finding sufficient china, let alone matching, is daily more difficult since Marigold and Bad Harry borrowed it all for a menagerie tea party; and partly because Siegfried had butted open the scullery door and was on the kitchen table eating the ham sandwiches Cook had set aside for our supper.

'I'm so sorry,' I said, hotly embarrassed. 'Marigold lets him in and he makes a beeline for biscuits and things the minute her back is turned.'

Freddy laughed. 'Don't blame her,' he said. 'It's bitter outside. I'd want to be in here too. Though I'm not sure sheep are supposed to eat meat,' he added.

'He ate a stair once, so I don't suppose it will hurt him,' I replied, shooing the disappointed Siegfried swiftly on to the flagstones and back into the scullery, firmly latching the door this time. I heaved a sigh of relief. But it was to be short-lived.

'What *will* you do?' asked Freddy.

'If it's a girl, you mean?'

'What? No. I mean with your future.'

I found myself faltering again, oddly awkward in front of my oldest friend. 'I hadn't thought,' I admitted eventually. 'I've just been waiting on the baby. All of us have been.'

'A baby shouldn't stop you doing things,' he said, pouring milk from one shamefully cracked jug to another, smaller one.

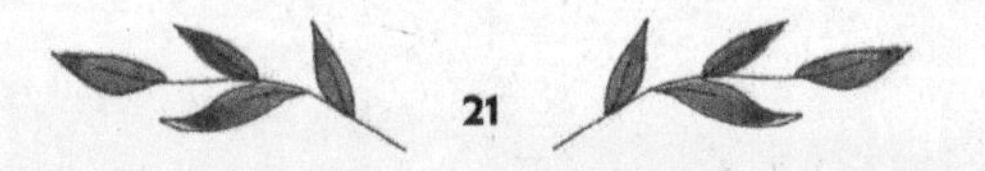

If only that were the case, I thought bitterly, and said so, or attempted to.

But Freddy could not be dampened. 'You could do anything,' he continued.

His zeal flickered bright as a struck match, its flame catching that kindling in me I had tried to deny was there. Heat thrilled through me for a brief, brilliant second.

'You could–'

But I never found out exactly what he thought I could do, because at that point came the most ear-shattering caterwaul yet, and tea seemed suddenly so pointless, like using a flannel to mop Noah's flood, or a sticking plaster on a broken leg. Instead, Freddy fled upstairs, and I back to the morning room where we sit, all three of us now, on tenterhooks, and the brink of misfortune.

8 P.M.

It was only minutes before Freddy came back downstairs, ashen this time, and trembling heavily, but hours before I could muster the courage to pick up my pen again.

I shall get straight to the fact of the matter, for this is no time for Pepysish description or Dickensian wit: the baby does not have a penis.

'It's a girl,' said Freddy. 'Quite alive and well.'

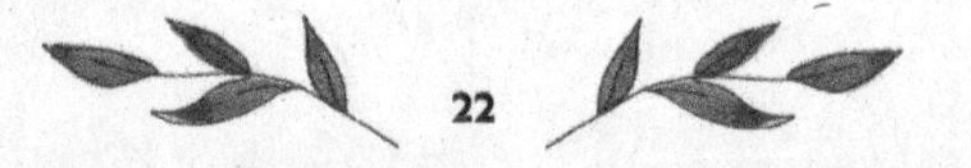

I must admit that this news was almost a relief given his demeanour, which had suggested the morgue might be in order, not the baptismal font. But then I had another awful thought, as, clearly, did Aster.

'Mama?' she asked, quite pale herself.

'She's well,' he said. 'Or as well as expected after . . . that.'

It was suddenly and patently clear that Freddy's whey-face was the result of 'practical experience' and that perhaps he was better suited to textbooks after all, at least for now.

'She'll be in bed for days, I imagine. So . . .' He looked at me expectantly.

I got his point. We were to muster, and soon. 'I suppose one of us will have to telephone Grandma,' I said.

'Well, I shan't,' said Aster.

'I'll telephone Grandma, if you telephone Valentine,' I said.

Aster paused in thought. Then, 'Fine,' she said.

'And I will telephone Bad Harry,' said Marigold. 'Because she owes me a shilling for betting it would be web-footed.'

'Marigold!' scolded Aster and I, united, if briefly.

'You're to telephone no one,' continued Aster. 'It's far too dear. You can go round in the morning and collect on whatever terrible bet you've made.'

As such, the call to Grandma was brief and to the point.

'Well, that's that,' she said, as hard and final as a full stop.

'I suppose,' I replied.

'There's no "suppose" about it. I shall visit in seven days.

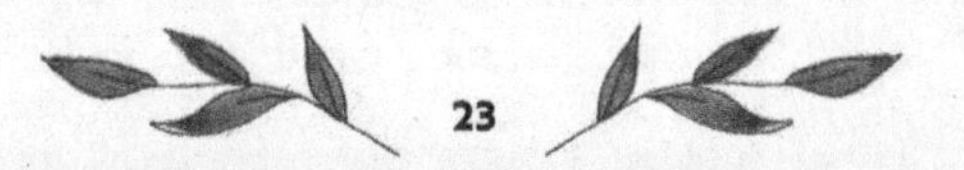

Even your mother should have recovered by then.' Then she hung up abruptly.

Seven days makes it sound like *she* lives in Timbuctoo, when in fact it is merely the end of the drive. But she does like to be dramatic. Which is where Valentine gets it from, not that anyone will tell her. She is convinced everything poor comes from this mother, who is admittedly prone to over-emoting. Grandma says she is a mesmerist, like all Italians, and it is best to avoid eye contact.

That said, Aster's exchange was no more verbose.

'Hullo, Valentine,' she said, when he finally answered.

'Who *is* this?' came the reply (for both Marigold and I were huddled at the receiver to hear every word).

Aster sighed. 'It's your cousin. Aster,' she added, lest he had muddled us, or even forgotten our names.

'Oh,' he said. Then a stretched echo: 'Ohhhhhh,' as the significance hit him. 'Is it . . . What is it?'

'It's a girl,' she replied haughtily, before her tone dropped to ominous. 'Radley is yours.'

And then, as mannered and angry as Grandma, she hung up and stalked from the room, leaving Freddy and me, and Marigold and Siegfried (quite the Houdini of creatures) in abject silence, bar the tinkling trickle of sheep's urine onto Persian rug.

*

The queerest thing is, I know I should be celebrating. I have

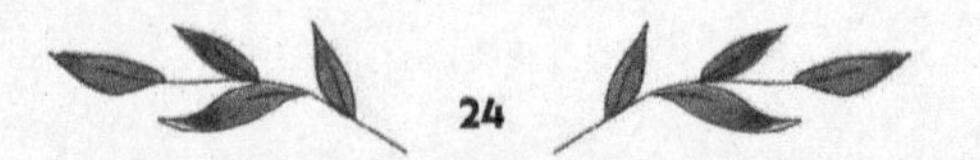

a sister. Ten fingers and ten toes (none webbed). A dear little creature, really. But instead, I feel desperately empty. Bereft, in fact. As if it's not just Daddy who has died, but something much larger, more profound and yet ephemeral. An era, perhaps. Hope, even.

Or a purpose. *My* purpose. Something I'd not even paid two seconds of attention to, not really. Not until today and Freddy's pressing. But how can I have one now? How can I think of anything other than our terrible fate?

So you see, I knew I was right to choose crimson ink. Though perhaps black is now more appropriate. For, though it may not be a funeral, we are all in mourning. No longer just for our poor dead Papa, but for the entire Mannering family.

And all for want of a P-E-N-I-S.

FEBRUARY

FRIDAY 1 FEBRUARY

11 A.M.

In keeping with my new shade of ink, and the general air of doom at Radley Manor, Marigold came down to breakfast this morning in black from head to toe, complete with Mama's lace veil, gloves and a funereal expression quite as sombre as Mr Sowerberry's. Given that we are all still officially in mourning for Daddy this might not sound so very odd, but the fact is none of us had much black nor the money to run to it, so we have made do with crepe armbands when we remember, and a general air of sadness if we have to go into the village. So this was, actually, quite the sight.

'Oh, dear. Who has died?' asked Mama (who is up now, and quite revived, though she has to sit on a rubber ring left

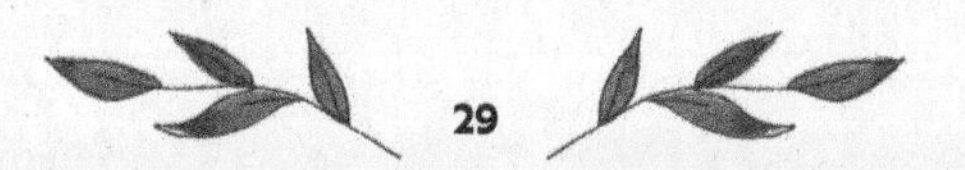

over from swimming in the river last summer, which is rather alarming when one fathoms why). 'One of the rabbits?'

'Lenin,' replied Marigold.

'I don't remember a Lenin,' Mama said.

This is because there isn't one. There is definitely a Jack, a Nancy, and, inexplicably, two Aneurins, but no Lenin. Though how on earth Marigold can tell them apart anyway is a mystery. Rabbits all look the same to me. This Lenin was not of the rabbit variety in any case.

'No. *Lenin* Lenin,' said Marigold.

'There's a rabbit called Lenin Lenin?' Mama seemed surprised, as well she might, for that would have been extreme even for Marigold.

'For heaven's sake,' snapped Marigold, flipping up her veil. 'Lenin. The Russian one. He has died and Harry and I have decided we are quite distraught.'

'Oh, for crying out loud,' lamented Aster.

'What?' demanded Marigold. Then, in a clever parry, 'Daddy would have approved.' (The mention of whom is usually enough to shut everyone up. Though not today, it seems.)

'He would not,' said Aster.

'Would too,' Marigold came back. 'He was a very committed Communist.'

'Socialist,' I corrected. 'There is an enormous difference.'

'Is there?' asked Mama. 'What is it exactly?'

It is fair to say Daddy tried several times to educate

Mama as to the difference between the political parties, but her understanding has always been limited to the necessity of hating the Tories, and thus Lord Balfour (which made Aster's inseparable friendship with Daphne Balfour a bit sticky at times). I was about to gallantly step into the breach to continue Daddy's valiant efforts when Dinah (more of whom in a moment) decided this was the precise time at which she needed to defecate quite loudly and malodorously and so Mama and she vacated the room none the wiser, and Marigold flipped her veil back into place and sat down to her egg with renewed gloom.

*

So: 'Dinah'. For that is the baby's name, and a very good name it is. Sort of solid and spherical; almost egg-like in its perfection. Not that Marigold is entirely enamoured of it.

'But why Dinah?' she demanded. 'Why isn't it a flower?'

'She,' corrected Mama, 'not it. And because, well, I like the name.'

'Daddy wouldn't have approved,' said Marigold, her eyebrows quite beetleish and menacing.

What she meant was, Daddy isn't around any more to inflict horticultural monikers on us all, and I expect Mama is quite relieved in that aspect.

'Well, perhaps you would like to choose a middle name then,' said Mama, ever keeper of the peace.

'I'm sorry?'

It was Aster's turn to furrow her brow, and well she might,

for Marigold perked up substantially and immediately began reeling off possibles, of which 'Laburnum' was the worst, and 'Begonia' hardly better. Though neither come close to the monstrosity Daddy bestowed on me. In the end, after consultation with Bad Harry, and a voting process involving two sheets of paper and a complicated points system, she settled on 'Marguerite', which is beautiful but terribly French, which will no doubt upset Grandma, as being French is almost as bad as Italian in her book.

Perhaps we shall just not tell her that bit. I shall suggest this to Mama before Grandma comes for tea later. Though I shan't remind Mama of that appointment for another hour or so, as I don't want to dampen the happy atmosphere (Marigold's mourning not withstanding). It is strange how hard it is to maintain a sense of melancholy with a baby in the house. I realise this is rather ostrich-like behaviour as far as Radley Manor is concerned, but the longer we can fend off our terrible fate, or at least forget about it, the better.

Only now of course, it is uppermost in my mind, hotly followed by the impending arrival of Grandma Mannering, whose pessimism makes Lenin look like Father Christmas.

10 P.M.

On a scale of one to ten – one being Grandma telling Daddy

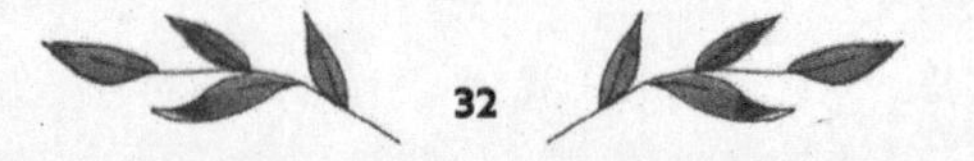

he had blackened the Mannering name for eschewing the Ickthorpe hunt (Daddy was rather fond of foxes) and ten being the time Marigold was sick on Grandma's shoes – today's tea visit was a mild five.

She arrived already in a subdued mood. It was because Ramsay Macdonald was elected Prime Minister last week, and he is Labour. Which is on a level with being French, etc.

'Daddy would have approved,' I pointed out, though failed to mention that I would agree with Daddy. In Grandma's book, ladies are not permitted political opinions, unless they are, firstly, sufficiently vague, and secondly, in line with her own.

Grandma raised a practised eyebrow above her lorgnette. 'Precisely,' she said. 'He never backed the right horse.'

'He never backed horses at all,' Aster replied, snidely. 'He thought racing rather brutal.'

'Racing is the sport of kings,' snapped Grandma, for whom Cheltenham is the highlight of her calendar. Not that she goes. She barely leaves the Dower House, let alone the village. She just greets the newspapers rather more eagerly.

Thankfully, at that point Marigold arrived in the drawing room, still in black, but with added straw and a faint smell of stable.

'Who has expired?' demanded Grandma.

'Lenin,' explained Marigold again.

'Lenin,' repeated Grandma, as if the very word were dirty. 'I suppose he is one of your rodents.'

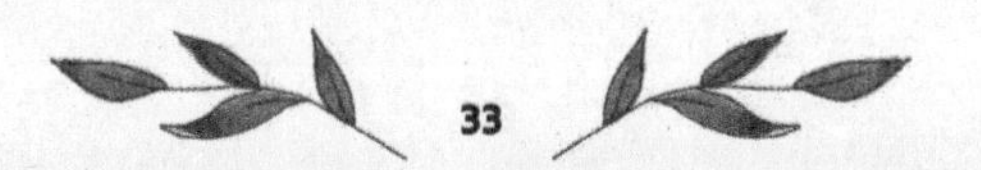

'Yes!' I got in quick, before giving Marigold a hard stare.

But Marigold was not to be stared at, at least not by me. 'If you mean rabbits,' she said, 'then rabbits aren't rodents, they're lagomorphs. Which also includes moles and shrews. And no. Although I think one of them may have got stuck down the back of the sink in the scullery cupboard. I shall have to see later when Rapsey does something with the U-bend.'

'You keep rabbits in the scullery?' Grandma appeared on the brink of a conniption.

'Don't be silly,' said Marigold. 'We keep Siegfried in there. The rabbits are in the blue bedroom but they are terribly good at escaping. And breeding. They breed like, well, rabbits. They're fertile at three months. Imagine that! Though luckily they eat some of their young so it never gets too crowded—'

'That's quite enough, darling!'

Mama had entered, accompanied by Dinah, who looked especially bizarre in a bonnet that Marigold had knitted from an unravelled sock, and which I strongly suspect Mama had chosen deliberately to irritate or at least baffle our guest.

'Oh,' said our guest. 'The child.'

'Dinah,' said Mama, seating herself gingerly on her rubber ring at the good end of the chaise (the other has been got at by moths and Bobby the dog, and even Siegfried, and so is fairly chewed).

'Dinah,' repeated Grandma, in the same tone with which she had spat out the name of the Russian leader/rabbit, then proceeded to peer at Dinah as if she might be a newfound species, or dreadful specimen of some sort. 'What's wrong with it?'

'What do you mean? Nothing.'

'It's awfully swarthy. Has the look of the French about it. Or' – she paused at this point to steel herself – 'an Italian. In fact it barely resembles Henry at all.'

'Well, *she* is a *girl*,' said Mama. 'So it's surely to be applauded that she doesn't resemble a forty-year-old man?' *And a dead one at that*, she didn't need to add.

But Grandma is not the applauding sort, not even at the best of times. 'She has your chin,' she said, with the distinct tone that this was not a compliment.

'And the Mannering nose,' batted back Mama. 'More's the pity.'

I could have applauded Mama right then, for Grandma did not say another word about Dinah's demeanour after that. Though she failed to turn to lighter subjects.

'So when does the axe fall?' she said next.

'What axe?' asked Marigold, all ears suddenly. This is because she had begged Daddy for an axe, or preferably a machete, in order that she and Harry may better defend Badger's Copse against the marauding Launceston twins, Hugo and Julian, who claim it is half on their land. It is not. But they are quite insistent, and prepared to 'fight to the death' over it, according to Marigold.

But Marigold was to be disappointed, and the twins to live another day.

'The axe of doom, I assume,' said Aster.

'You assume correctly,' said Grandma. 'I suppose Valentine is moving in any minute, with a troupe of useless minstrels in pursuit, no doubt. Heaven knows what will become of Radley under his watch. Your grandfather will be turning in his grave. And your father.'

'Daddy won't,' I said. 'He was rather fond of Valentine.'

'Well, he should be spinning,' said Grandma. 'Though if he'd managed to produce the goods, you wouldn't be in such dire straits.' Which as you know we have all thought, but try not to say out loud, at least not too often.

'Well, we don't know exactly what straits we are in yet,' said Mama, diplomatically. (Though it is hard to be anything but diplomatic when you have to sit on a rubber ring for fear of bursting stitches.) 'I'm to visit Hubert and Briggs next week to sort it all out. Valentine too. And you are quite welcome of course.' She smiled at Grandma.

Grandma's lips went so thin as to disappear. 'I'd rather picnic in a cemetery. And what are you doing traipsing off to town in your condition?'

'I've had a baby, I'm not ailing,' replied Mama. 'And I'm perfectly capable of going up to London and listening to solicitors.'

Which is rich, as Mama never goes to London if she can

help it, and solicitors are on a par with dentists in her thinking. But I knew what she was doing.

'Cake, mother, dear?' she suggested then, gesturing at a plate of Cook's fruit loaf, which is notoriously heavy and has previously concealed such rogue ingredients as non-stoned cherries, pickled walnuts and, once, a tin zebra from Marigold's zoo.

Grandma narrowed her eyes. 'No, thank you. I'm not entirely sure it's edible.'

She was right, of course. This version came with an inexplicable cheese layer. But, never ones to lose a battle with Grandma, we, all four of us, chewed through two slices each to make a point.

And now, I lie in bed, under my fading cabbage-rose counterpane, my stomach solid as a hockey ball, and the axe of Mannering doom hovering above my head like the Sword of Damocles: suspended by a single thread, and apt to fall any minute.

The worst of it is my abject helplessness. It is as if I have drifted through life like a dandelion seed, enjoying the view and letting the wind take me where it may – to a Queen Anne manor house with an earl for a father; to the splendid Hedingham to meet darling Margot; even to the village in the long hot summers, Freddy and I dropping sticks in the river then rushing to the other side of the bridge to see whose emerged first. And how lucky I have been– no, *we*, all three of us have been, until Daddy left. For his was the generous breath that let us fly. And now we seem to lack the will or whereabouts to direct ourselves, falling instead to the sharp huffs and puffs of solicitors, of wills, of hereditary law.

Oh, heavens, how I miss him. Not just his benevolence but his belief in us. At times like this I feel his absence not just as a lack, a gap in the atmosphere that he should fill, but a wound, red and raw, that smarts at every memory, every mention. Reminding me how bereft I am; telling me I am nothing without him.

Asking me on how on earth I am going to do anything, achieve anything in life, alone.

THURSDAY 7 FEBRUARY

9 A.M.

The dangling sword has managed to stay itself for six days, but must surely fall this morning, for we are due at Hubert and Briggs at eleven forty-five promptly. Or rather, Mama is. We are all accompanying her, as, despite what she claimed to Grandma, she has a terrible tendency to get lost in London, plus wrangling Dinah's pram is not a one-woman job, especially not on a train, not even now Rapsey has fixed the wheels (Marigold and Bad Harry 'borrowed' them to make a dilly and obviously hadn't bothered to screw them back even vaguely tightly so they had a habit of falling off at inopportune moments).

We will make quite the spectacle I fear, us four Mannering girls – five if you count Dinah. Perhaps there should be a

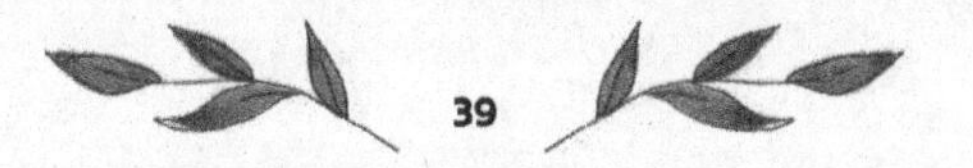

collective noun for us, like a 'gaggle' of geese, or 'murder' of crows. Though there won't be enough of us to muster any sort of noun if Aster doesn't shake herself out of her slump and Marigold doesn't hurry back from the stables. She is shutting Siegfried in, much to her annoyance and his disgust. Mama says it is for the good of Cook, who cannot be expected to add sheep-rustling to the roster of duties she must perform in the absence of any other house servants.

I have no idea why Aster is in a Dark Mood again, other than the obvious. Nothing untoward or even unusual has happened since I last wrote. Daphne Balfour came to tea yesterday, sporting a rather ugly camel sweater and ill-advised haircut (she doesn't quite have the bone structure for a bob, unlike her sister Evangeline, who could shave her head completely and still elicit whistles). But Daphne calling isn't unusual. Though it has been less frequent of late, and, after battling with sandwiches of unidentifiable content, they did spend several hours closeted in the morning room in hissed whispers.

It is probably about a man. Daphne was in *The Tatler* again last week on the arm of the Earl of Beaulieu's eldest, Nigel who, if you ask me, is entirely vapid, with the bland face of a wheel of cheese, but sadly Daphne hasn't – asked me, I mean – and Marigold claims he is going to propose any minute. They were probably discussing the impending wedding night and all the terror it entails. I tried to listen in at the crack in the panelling but I got distracted by a rabbit that was trying to burrow under the runner and had to return it to the blue bedroom before Cook caught it and stewed it. (We have had rabbit several times for supper this year already and Marigold is still to catch on.)

Besides, if anyone is allowed to sulk it should be me. I begged Mama to let me call on Margot this afternoon, as she is bound to be in the Glasshouse Street apartment, given its proximity to Piccadilly. She is passionately in love with a Yank band leader at the Button Club. He is called Brilliant Baker and, according to Margot, looks set to love her back just as passionately. Though even if this were true (it probably isn't) it would be impossible: at eighteen she is underage and Margot's mother will never agree to a match with an American (Mrs Forbes-Rawlinson has more than a touch of Grandma about her. It is lucky her younger daughter Deborah is the very model of modesty, though Margot says she would have to be with those teeth). Anyway, Mama said no, as she had no idea how long the consultation would last, and in any case we would need to eat straight after. I suggested packing a sandwich, but Mama says she is not taking egg on a train, not after last time, and we can run to a Lyons Corner House for once, even in our impoverished state. Aster said we should make Valentine pay, and I agreed – by the time we sit down to luncheon, he will be an earl, with his hands on a hundred acres and a once-majestic manor house. But Mama, who is as generous as she is patient, said we would do no such thing and that she had two pound notes in her purse left over from paying off Mrs Gibberd at the shop last quarter, as well as several shillings that she had found down the back of the chaise. I felt rather guilty then and offered her the tuppence left over from buying a quarter of fruit drops, and Marigold gave her a bent penny from her collection. Aster offered her nothing, I noted.

I then suggested I could see Margot after lunch, but Mama says we must get the train straight back for Dinah's sake (and Siegfried's, I suspect) and no I may not stay and catch a later train as I cannot be left in London alone, especially not with Margot. Not since the incident with the doorman at the Savoy, which I have explained several times was Margot's fault not mine, but Mama remained resolute.

And so it is now a matter of mere hours before the sword drops, with not even the pleasant diversion of Margot's forbidden love to mop up the sorrow afterwards. I shall have to take *The Sheikh* with me instead. I am quite in need of some savage romance and at least the fictional kind does not come with the problems of how to get him past one's mother.

9 P.M.

The best I can say of today is that the train journey was less arduous than I imagined, with calamities limited to a spilled cup of tea in the station waiting room, which Bobby saw to in

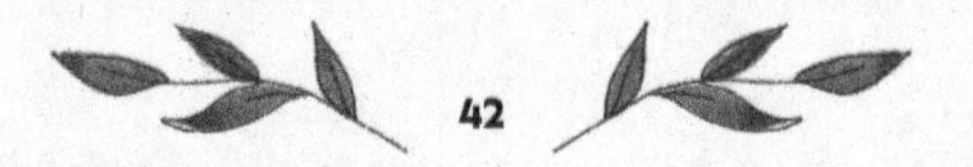

any case, and Dinah's untimely toileting, which required rather more attention than a dog can offer. There was a moment that teetered on the brink of difficulty, when Marigold suggested a taxi from King's Cross.

'Oh, no,' replied Mama. 'Your father never took taxis.'

At that, we all paused, as if waiting for a pin to drop, for we all knew that if Daddy had taken a taxi that fateful day then it wouldn't have been fateful at all, but dull and humdrum. Wonderful in its mundanity.

It was Aster who saved us. 'Actually, let's walk,' she said swiftly. 'It's such a fine morning.'

And it was, and we did. And the walk, though long, was oddly jolly, as Marigold has become quite taken with the idea of a collective noun for the Mannerings, and educated us in many other terms of venery. For example, according to Marigold, herons are a 'siege', hawks a 'kettle' and hippopotamuses a 'bloat'. Though I have my suspicions that she made the last of these up.

So taken was she, and so desperate for diversion we, that we rather dawdled down Dover Street as she offered up 'gulp' (cormorants), 'creche' (penguins), and, somewhat horrifyingly, 'business' (flies), not watching where we were wheeling Dinah. Which Aster says is my fault, because I had the pram handle, but I say is hers because she was in front and therefore lookout. But in any case, we hit a missing cobble and one of the pram wheels spun off at pace down the street, coming to a halt only when it crashed into the ankle of a rather angry man, who was not at all placated by Mama's apologies, Marigold's offers of a gum drop, or Bobby's keenness on rubbing himself over his trousers, adding insult to injury in the form of a layer of yellowing hair.

This was the point at which it all began to sink, quickly and inexorably, into a predictable mire. Not only did we now have to wrest a hefty and now three-wheeled contraption up two flights of stairs, the solicitor's office was excessively drear – dark-panelled and sallow-painted, not at all as grand as in my imagination (though life does have rather a habit of coming up short in that respect) while Mr Briggs himself had quite the look of the cadaver about him – thin and grey and desiccated, and not at all amused that our arrival was several minutes past the allotted slot. Thank heavens for Valentine, late himself, who burst in like the first spring crocus in a lavender cravat and two-tone Oxfords, just as fabulous as the version from dim Christmas memories, in the days when he still visited.

'Oh, my darlings,' he cried, and made to fling his arms around all of us at once, which, as you may have guessed, is a nigh-on-impossible task, especially given Marigold's tendency to wriggle and Aster's to slap.

'Valentine,' said Mama, extricating herself. 'Thank heavens, they're waiting.'

'Unto the breach, dear friends,' declaimed Valentine dramatically, before patting Marigold on the head as if she

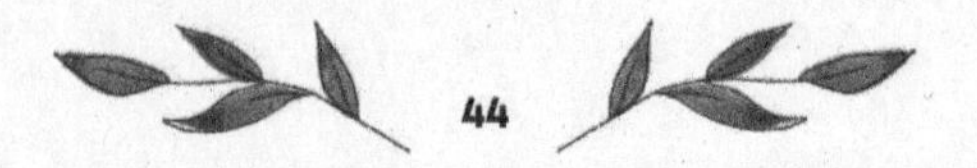

were the dog, not Bobby. Not that she minded. I think she was rather taken by him, as am I. It is only Aster who sees him as sworn enemy, on grounds of being, as she put it, 'a thief and swindler', when in fact he is no such thing. His only sin is being a man (though Grandma might argue he is hardly that).

'If only Papa had lived another year,' Aster hissed, after Mama and Valentine had been ushered into an anteroom painted the exact shade of Dinah's very worst emissions. 'They could have tried again.'

'He might have lived ten years and Mama had ten more babies,' I said. 'But if they were all still girls, then we'd still be here, but with more mouths to feed.' Which I thought was a terribly measured and clever response, and evidence of my increasing maturity.

'If they had had ten more babies, we could form a travelling band,' replied Marigold, revealing her entire lack of it. 'The Mannering Racket. We'd be famous. Siegfried could do tricks.'

'Oh, for heaven's sake,' snapped Aster.

'Don't blame me,' Marigold snapped back. 'It's not my fault I don't have a penis.'

Aster winced, and the secretary at the desk in the corner – all limbs and rigidity – looked up in alarm, as well she might.

'Let's play a game,' I suggested, desperate to divert attention from penises, and to distract myself from our impending fate, which had sent my stomach swirling murkily like Cook's soup. 'I spy, with my little eye, something beginning with "b".'

This went on for an hour, with Marigold and I determinedly chin-up and sporting, and Aster deliberately gloomy and obtuse, opting for the ephemeral and impossible, including 'dead' (which didn't exist, except in a fly which lay on its back under my chair), 'stain' (which did exist, on Marigold's stocking, but was so minute as to be irrelevant), and 'misery' (which she insisted existed in her, only Marigold said in that case Aster wouldn't be able to spy it, but Aster countered, claiming she had caught her reflection in the glass on a painting of a murderous-looking cow, and thus had won).

It was almost a relief when Mama and Valentine emerged from Mr Briggs's faecal-toned chamber, both pale and somewhat troubled.

'What is it?' I asked. 'What's happened?'

'I feel rather faint,' said Mama. 'I think I need to eat, and quickly.'

And so, we six of us, seven with Bobby, wrangled the pram and ourselves to the nearest cafe in near silence, which, for the Mannerings, is almost unheard of.

'So?' demanded Aster, the moment Mama had swallowed a spoonful of stew.

Mama took a breath, and seemed to settle herself. 'It is as we thought,' she said.

Immediately, my stomach, though terribly empty, set to swirling again, and I put down my ham sandwich for fear I could not swallow a bite if I tried.

Mama took another deep breath. 'Valentine will inherit.'

I don't know why I felt such a sudden wash of horror, of shame almost. I knew this was coming, we all did. But perhaps only ephemerally, as if it were a wisp that might yet dissipate. And now it was upon us, hard and sharp and real.

'But it's rather more complicated than that,' Valentine got in quick, possibly wary that Aster, in possession of a rather sharp-looking knife, might be about to launch herself at him. 'What with death duties and everything else there's no money for the estate.'

'What does that mean?' I asked.

'It means,' said Mama. 'That even if Radley had remained ours, we couldn't have afforded to keep it anyway.'

This was gloomy news on top of brutal, but hardly a surprise. Everyone is struggling, these days, and those who aren't entailed are selling up. As Grandma has said, 'England is changing hands'. Even the Balfours have put the castle on the market. Though that still leaves Balfour Hall, the flat in Mayfair, and the villa in Nice.

'So now what?' asked Aster.

Mama smiled, but rather thinly. 'Well, they say Valentine must let it out, until the law changes.'

'Briggs reckons there's hope for that soon,' added Valentine. 'Then I can sell, and there'll be a pay-out for all of you.' He smiled then, wide and sincere. 'But, until that happens, renting is the best we can hope for.'

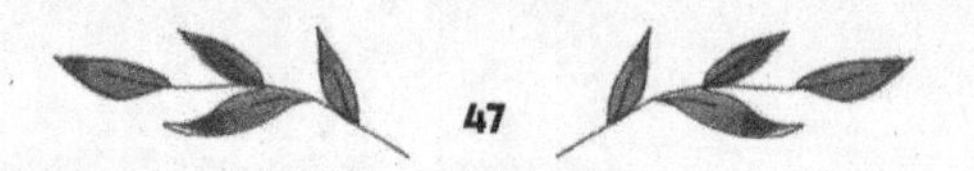

'But what about us?' asked Marigold. 'Where will we go? *Will* we be destitute?' This with a worrying touch of keenness, as being destitute has been one of her greatest wishes since she was six, along with being an orphan and forced to join Fagin's gang, or having an interesting birthmark, all of which Mama has explained are probably not all they are cracked up to be, to no avail.

'It's yet to be settled,' said Mama.

'You can always stay with me,' said Valentine, kindly I thought.

Clearly Aster did not agree. 'I'd rather die,' she said.

'I wouldn't,' I retorted, my eyes smarting with salty tears which I hurriedly rubbed away.

'No one is going to die or be destitute,' said Mama, with a snap about her. 'Something will be sorted. There's no need for any of us to worry.'

Though at this point her own eyes brimmed and of course we all set to worrying even more than we already were.

'I'm so sorry,' Valentine said, for about the tenth time.

'No, don't be.' She put her hand on his arm. 'This upset isn't because of you. Or even Radley. It's Henry. I miss him. More than ever on days like this. Solicitors were his bag, not mine. And now, I'm, I don't know, unruddered. Is that a word?'

'It should be,' said Aster, softly now.

I nodded, knowing just what she meant. We are all unruddered without Daddy. Left to the mercy of whatever tide takes us, whatever storm. And what a storm this was.

Marigold frowned. 'And all because of a penis,' she said loudly.

The entire Lyons House fell silent, but for the clatter of cutlery as it was dropped on the table in shock, and the smack of Marigold masticating an egg sandwich, for which we all paid later .

It wasn't until the train journey home that any of us began to talk again, though for the most part the conversation was so futile as to be impossible to recall in any detail. Except for the moment I mentioned that the guard had a face almost exactly as wide and flat as Nigel Pakenham's, that is to say, Daphne's man. At which point Aster fell into another of her Dark Moods and still hasn't spoken a word to me other than to tell me to 'shut up' when Marigold and I started up with 'Ten Green Bottles' to pass the time waiting for Rapsey to fetch us from the station.

But, singing aside, we are all utterly subdued now. For it is certain: we are to leave – and by the end of the month, as Briggs suggested, so that the manor is free to let in spring. But with no idea where we might end up, or what kind of a life is in store for us. Other than it shan't be at Radley.

*

Unruddered is exactly the word.

I sat, this evening, on the landing, shivering in my nightdress, my heart in my mouth, my legs dangling through the banisters as they had when I was a small girl. Tears streamed down my face, in great rivers it seemed, as I looked down on the portrait of Daddy himself as a boy.

'What shall I do?' I asked it in desperation.

I felt, then, a tickling at my fingers and gasped, sure it must be a sign. But when I turned it was only a rabbit – Nancy, perhaps – nudging me as they do for food.

I clutched the creature to my chest, felt the warmth of its fur, felt its whiskers twitching. 'What will become of me?' I asked.

But the rabbit, of course, remained silent, and so I remained snotty, and cold, and none the wiser.

I have realised something definite, though. We are not a gaggle of Mannerings. Not a business. Not a siege, nor a creche, nor a kettle.

We are a calamity.

I think it is rather fitting, given everything: a calamity of Mannerings.

And homeless ones at that.

SUNDAY 24 FEBRUARY

11 A.M.

If I were a positive sort of person, which I am endeavouring very much to be, however trying life might turn out, I would say that at least now our destiny is set. Though, it is difficult, on reflection, not to be Asterish and angry about it. She had worked so hard to come up with alternatives, after all.

'Doesn't one of your cousins have a place in Wales?' she pestered Mama.

'Wales.' I shuddered in disgust, though only because of its distance from London, I should add. I have nothing against the Welsh. Siegfried is of Welsh heritage, after all.

Aster ignored me anyway. And Mama dismissed it as too small to swing a cat, not even our tiny but recalcitrant one

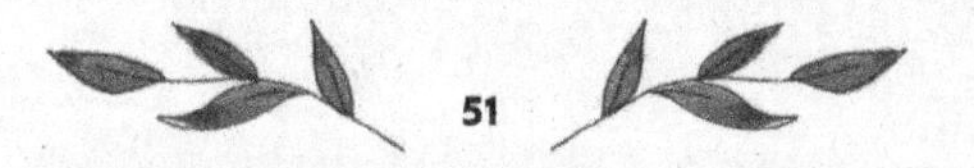

(which isn't even ours – no one has yet deduced its origin – but which slinks in every evening, demands supper and then sits on the mantelpiece, eyeing us all with an air of malevolence), plus we'd also need to be able to swing a dog, a sheep, and an unidentified number of rabbits.

'What about your brother?' Aster tried.

'What about my brother?' asked Mama, preoccupied with Dinah, who was refusing to release any wind, despite several attempts from both Marigold and I.

'Doesn't he have room for us above the shop?'

'Well, he might,' admitted Mama. 'But he also has your aunt, of course.'

We all shuddered then at the thought of iron-faced Aunt Brenda, whose hair resembles a helmet, and whose kippers rival Cook's for smell and inedibility.

'And it's in Birmingham,' lamented Marigold. 'They don't have sheep in Birmingham.'

'I'm not sure that's true,' I said. But Marigold was having none of it. Besides, even if Birmingham was sheep-friendly, Aunt Brenda certainly wasn't.

It is a shame in a way that Mama is not from a rich family. Daddy said her normality was half her charm, and I agree. But Grandma has always insisted he married beneath him and it will come back to haunt all of us one day. Daddy said that day would never come. But perhaps, after all, this is it. For, in the absence of any benevolent relations on the maternal side, there is, it seems, only one place for us.

We are moving in with Grandma.

This has not gone down well in any quarter. Aster said she would rather die, of course. And, though it was Grandma's suggestion (on the grounds that Valentine is less likely to evict her from the Dower House if she has back-up), even she has made clear it is not to be considered a permanent arrangement, and that there will be 'rules'. These rules are, as yet, unestablished, however there are already several strict regulations in operation, for example who is allowed to sit where in the drawing room (never the velvet wingback; only two at a time on the pale pink chaise), what precise time luncheon is served (one on the dot, and if you are late then you must sit in the kitchen with Mabel and eat there), and what that meal must consist of. (Inevitably something in aspic. I do not understand old people's fascination with aspic; I am sure they would preserve their very selves in the stuff if they could.) So needless to say, we are verily quaking in terror.

Mama says we must muster, and at least pretend to be grateful. Marigold has taken this to heart and has pasted a fixed grin on her face ever since, which makes her look even stranger than usual. Aster is resolute in her refusal to smile, even for a minute, and is instead taking an inventory of which paintings are hers, and which may be left for Valentine. Mama says there is little point in us packing too much as there shan't be room at the Dower House, but Aster has already earmarked the sub-Stubbs thoroughbred from the Great Hall, the two bleak seascapes from the landing and the one of the wonky kettle from the morning room, which she insists is striking in its modernity but which everyone else thinks looks like something Marigold might daub. Then there is the enormous portrait of Daddy, which we all agree must come, plus Aster's myriad canvases of Daphne stacked in the morning room, not to mention the sketchbooks, which must run if not into hundreds, then at least into tens.

Marigold is mainly concerned about the stabling of her menagerie. Mama says the rabbits will have to be hutched and Siegfried must make do in the garage. Marigold complained that it has the motorcar in it, but Mama says she is sure he won't mind sharing. Though the car and Rapsey may well complain.

I shall travel light, and take only my good dresses, of which there are few, and even their usefulness and beauty is in doubt according to Margot; my novels, of course; and this journal, which is of far greater weight than it appears, for I believe it contains the very essence of me, and indeed the entire Mannering family.

Plus, somewhat cunningly, I have written to Margot to tell her we are off, and that I shall likely expire from boredom. I am hoping she will see fit to immediately invite me to London for a week, if not the season.

And if that isn't mustering, then I don't know what is.

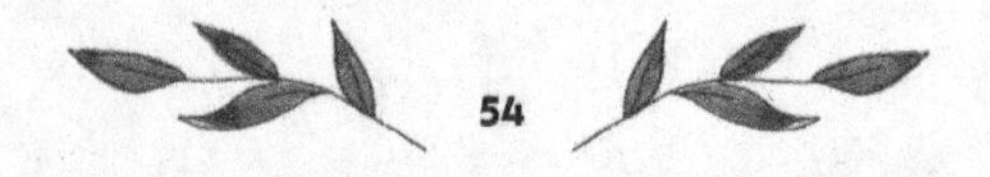

5 P.M.

My mustering has stumbled a little. It is Aster's fault, really. She had an argument with Mama about the portrait of Great Uncle Hawsley, which Aster insists is worth something, but Mama says gives her the shivers and it is bad enough that Grandma's house is so full of grim depictions of the deceased without adding to them. Thus, it is best left to Valentine, whom she is worried might be put out by the fact that, on top of the temperamental electrics, Daddy let us paint the morning room one wall each and the overall effect is having been decorated by someone drunk or colour-blind or quite, quite mad.

Anyway, Aster stormed out of the house, not even bothering with a coat, which she will regret later as it may be crisp and clear but the temperature is still barely above freezing; even inside the house we are wearing several layers and gloves at all times. (I suppose that will be one advantage of being at Grandma's: her boiler manages to raise room temperature above the Arctic. It is quite the acme of comfort in that sense.) But, fearing a chill, possibly pneumonia (she has already lost one Mannering and is loath to misplace another), Mama sent me after her, which was a lost cause as Aster had disappeared into the distance quicker than one of Marigold's rabbits. But, as I turned to come back inside, I caught sight of Radley – the tilt of the weathervane on the west wing, the sun glinting off the diamond glass of the mullioned windows, the chimneys

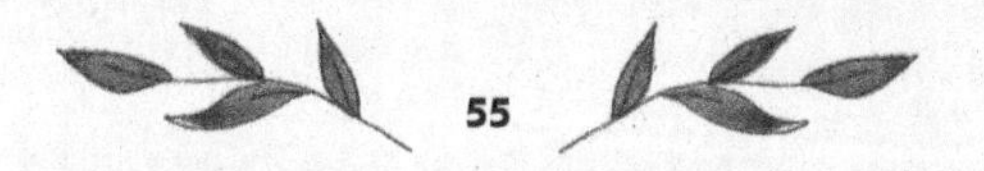

stacked in their ranks like forthright soldiers – and felt a sudden surge of something, almost like nausea, but mixed with wonder and love and regret.

For it is a little shabby perhaps, a little behind the times, but on a bright day, in the right light, it is the absolute embodiment of English splendour. And more: it is our playground, our wonderland, our turreted castle with dragons in its grounds. There is the lawn on which we played at ponies with coconut halves and string for reins; there is the ha-ha over which we flung ourselves, imagining we might fly like Tinker Bell; there is the oak tree we climbed, believing at the very top we might touch the sky.

Of course, we never did. But, absurd as it sounds, I never lost hope, not until now.

For now the oak, the ha-ha, the lawn are all for other, luckier, children to explore.

Because Radley Manor – oh, I can hardly bear to write it! – Radley Manor is no longer ours.

FRIDAY 29 FEBRUARY

11 A.M.

Our last dawn at Radley, and on a Leap Day, at that. I suppose, under such circumstances, some sort of desperate attempt at rescue was inevitable. Though I hadn't imagined it might be Marigold who would try it.

'Aster could marry Valentine,' she suggested at breakfast, still very much with her out-to-please face plastered on. 'Or Panther could. Or even I. Harry says their butler's uncle is married to his cousin and their children are quite normal, apart from their foreheads.'

'It would be a solution,' I agreed. 'If you could ignore the reckless spending and questionable company. And the royals positively encourage that sort of thing – cousins and whatnot.

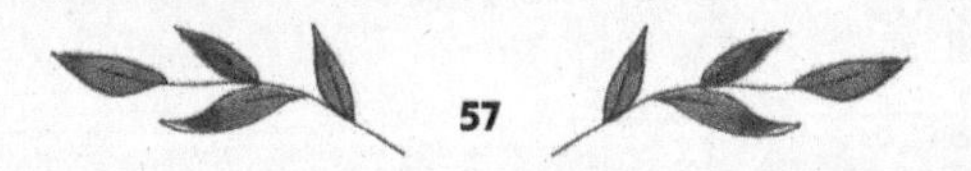

You could propose on the telephone. Right now.'

'Yes,' agreed Marigold. 'And if he refuses, at least you'll get a set of gloves come Easter. It's how leap years work. Harry told me. Oh!' Her face lit up further. 'Do you think he'd give me a pony— no, an axe, if I proposed and he said no?'

'No one is proposing,' snapped Aster. 'It's not any solution. We'd still be poor as church mice. Anyway, none of us is his type.'

Even Mama mustered the ghost of a grin at this.

'Well, one of us will have to marry soon,' I said. 'And you're the eldest. Perhaps Daphne's man can find you someone.'

At which point Aster's mood dimmed considerably. And yet it is not that which has set all Mannering women, including seemingly Dinah, who has been caterwauling since dawn, into a state, but the post.

Mama is in a panic because she has been reminded she must instruct Mrs Gibberd to instruct the postal service to redirect everything to the Dower House from now on.

Marigold is in raptures of potential fame and fortune because she has had a letter from Mr Goggins, who is in charge of the Ickthorpe Summer Show, and Siegfried has been accepted as an entrant in the 'best ram' category, as well as 'pet the judge would most like to take home'.

'But the judge for that is Mrs Gibberd,' I reminded her. 'There isn't even a sliver of a chance she'll want Siegfried in her parlour. She barely tolerates dogs.'

'One wonders why she was given the position,' pondered Mama.

'Quite,' I agreed.

'Well, I think he's charming,' insisted Marigold, 'and that you're all completely beastly.'

She is deluded, of course. Siegfried's habits are not at all charming, mainly involving as they do: urinating on things he shouldn't, defecating on things he shouldn't and eating things he shouldn't. But Marigold refuses to see anything but good in him and is in giddy fits about the rosettes, shilling prizes, and subsequent flood of stud fees she is confidently expecting. She has gone to see Bad Harry to share the happy news, and, I suspect, to lurk at the farrier's. I fear a proposal to Reg in the offing. Possibly two.

Whatever was in Aster's letter (black ink, cream vellum, very feminine tilt to the 'g's) sent her dim mood plummeting into the Darkest I have ever seen – positively pitch and inky, in fact. She fled to the morning room and is now playing her cello loudly and aggressively, but to make matters worse the G string has gone and she cannot afford to replace it, so the tune no longer even makes sense. Though on the positive side, if the other strings go, soon she will be reduced to bowing the air in silence.

Meanwhile, I have had a reply from Margot, agreeing that it is terribly wretched about moving and that the prospect of endless Grandma is ghastly, but with no mention at all of possible respite at the Glasshouse Street apartment.

This, though, is not what has befuddled me, post-wise. No, it is that I have also received a letter from Freddy Spencer. Which is strange, as he has never written before, not unless you count clues in the stump of the dead elm when Aster ran a paper chase one summer, which I do not. Also strange is that he didn't mention he might when I saw him last. Though I suppose he was rather bloody, and I somewhat startled. Anyway, it is mostly details of college life at Magdalen, and the escapades of someone called Egg, who is the sort of boy whom Aster would say is a pest and a menace, and whom Freddy would be better off without, but to me he seems rather amusing and Margot-like.

I wonder why he has bothered. Freddy, I mean. Unless it is to lure me into ideas of more education. Frankly, the sight of his forearms during Dinah's birth, and the state of Mama after (she is still sitting on a ring) is enough to put me off medicine for life, as well as motherhood. Anyway, I shall only bother to write back if I have time. On top of this journal, there is a party to prepare for.

Mama is determined to make something of our last night. And it gives Cook something to do other than weep. She is quite beside herself at our departure, even though Mama has given her a very generous (and thus somewhat misleading) reference. You'd think she'd be relieved at the prospect of no more Mannering tantrums or sheep in the kitchen. Not to mention the endless vats of rabbit she's forced to stew.

'I can't credit it,' she said, wiping her face of what might have been tears, or sweat, or the consommé, contents unidentifiable, she was cooking for supper. 'What will I do without you?'

'And we without you,' I placated. Though, along with the heating, I must admit I am rather looking forward to the catering at Grandma's. Mabel may be young, and jabbering, with a gait that Grandma describes as 'apeish', but her flan is incomparable and the very fact she tolerates Grandma at all makes her a saint. 'Shall I make a start on the pigs in blankets?' I suggested.

'That'd be kind,' said Cook, still dripping into the thin soup. 'Only, there's no pigs, as such, not unless someone pays off Goddard's sharpish, so it's rabbits in blankets and be glad about it.'

I didn't dare ask which this time. No doubt there'll be another seven along in a minute anyway. And the fewer we have to decamp to Grandma's the better.

11 P.M.

It is late, and I must go to sleep soon, not least because Rapsey wants to get an early start on moving the tea crates down to the Dower House. Mama has told him to hire some local brawn, but he is insistent that he can manage it. I think he's worried he might be for the chop along with Cook, but, as it's Grandma who pays his wages, that's highly unlikely, as having fewer than two servants is seen as positive poverty in her bridge circle. Hermione Lightfoot hasn't invited Celia Rigby to play so much as a rubber since she had to let go of her Odd Man. One can only hope Hermione doesn't shun Grandma because of us. Now that we have nobody at all.

Still, I am refusing to be blue about it, because I have had the most marvellous night in spite of it all.

Cook drank too much sherry and sang a terribly blue sea shanty her father had taught her (he was a mackerel man, apparently, lost off the coast of Falmouth in a frightful north-westerly, and also nifty with his fists, so no great loss to Cook or her mother, but he could sing at least). Next, Marigold, cheered since her return from the village (Reg did not agree to marry her, for she was too shy to propose in the end, but he did spit frequently and voluminously, which she and Bad Harry agreed meant a definite yes for future years) sang a song about 'manatee plop' that she and Harry had made up, which was disgusting but funny, and of which Daddy would have approved. Then Mama joined in and soon we were all singing a chorus of 'Mannering gals!' to the tune of 'manatee plop'. Even Aster sang along (thanks to the sherry). I think it's the first time I have seen her smile properly in months. Though it was short-lived and she scurried to bed by ten, quite outdone by Marigold, who is still singing (about green bottles now, not 'plop'; she started at two hundred and is now down to seventy-two) and Siegfried, who has also drunk some sherry, but has evacuated his already in the form of his own 'plop'. Marigold said it was lucky, and was his gift for Valentine. Mama said she no longer had the energy to deal with it, and Cook fell asleep on the chaise hours ago and will most likely have to be carried out by Rapsey along with the crates.

Anyway, I have decided to relay all this to Freddy in the hope it will at least make him laugh, as Egg did for me. He won't be offended by the drink or the 'plop'. After all, he has seen us at our worst.

I have already given the letter a heading. It is 'The Calamity of Mannerings'. But it is a term of venery I no longer feel bleak about. Instead, I sincerely believe we 'gals' might have a bright new life in store for us, starting tomorrow. And to hell with penises, to boot! Perhaps I shall, after all, find myself a purpose! That would shut Freddy up, and no mistake.

Heavens, I think it is the spirit of Daddy seeping into me somehow from the very walls of Radley, filling me with his conviction that somehow, one day, everything will come good.

Either that, or it is the sherry talking.

I suppose we shall have to wait to find out which.

MARCH

WEDNESDAY 12 MARCH

5 P.M.

The persistent inclement weather that has dogged us since we arrived at the Dower House, as if to remind us of our circumstance (the sky has been a stubborn wash of grey for days now), was brightened slightly by the arrival of post, soggy though it was, and with slightly chewed corners that looked decidedly as if Ralph Gibberd, the post boy, had let his terrier at them.

'Snails, miss,' he said.

'Snails what?' I asked, none the wiser.

'At the letters.' He nodded at the brutalised beige envelope in my hand. 'They lives in the postboxes, miss, and eats 'em.'

This seemed far-fetched to me – not unalike the time

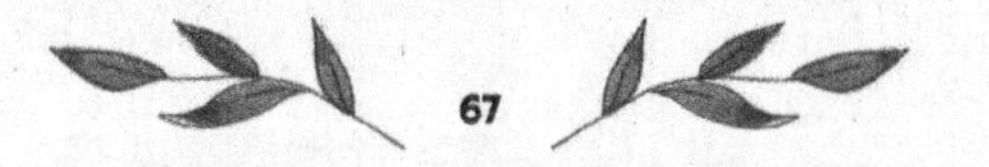

Marigold tried to blame a missing honey sponge on bees – and I said so.

'It's true, miss. Scourge of the postal service, they are. Devils. Worse than badgers.'

Again I raised a doubtful brow, both to the assertion and the relevance of the latter animal. 'But how do they get in in the first place?' I demanded, expecting this to put an end to it.

'They climbs. Or kids bungs 'em in.'

Given Marigold's and Bad Harry's antics, this did, in fact, seem awfully plausible.

'Oh yes,' he went on, 'you'd be surprised what we find. Old socks, keys, faeces.'

'Oh, golly.' I held the letters slightly more gingerly than previously.

'Oh, we throws them away,' he said. 'The heavily soiled ones. Not supposed to, mind. But would you want a bill covered in doings? Insult to injury that is.'

'I see.'

'Oh, yes. Anything and everything gets shoved in those slots,' he continued. 'Even a vole once.'

'Dead or alive?' I hesitated to ask.

'Alive. And feisty and all. No match for Mr Gibberd though.' He was referring to his father, senior postmaster.

'Well, quite,' I said, minded to end the conversation before Marigold could be actually incriminated and Mr Gibberd called for, as he makes Mrs Gibberd look half-hearted.

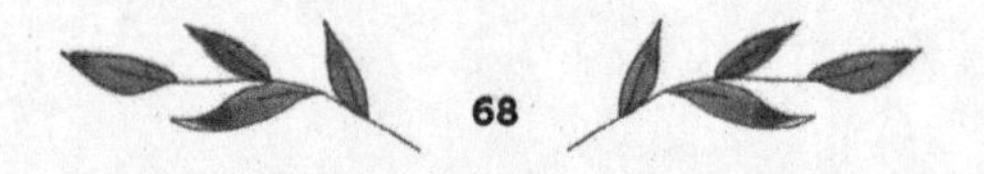

But Ralph continued to slouch there in the drizzle, his moustache dripping so that it itself resembled a slug. 'Got a letter there, then,' he said. 'From young Mr Spencer.'

I felt myself bloom then shrink under sudden scrutiny. 'What?'

Ralph nodded again at my hand. 'Freddy Spencer.'

'How on earth do you know that?' I demanded, wondering if he had some sort of sixth sense. Margot is terrifically taken with psychics and has been to see several in the pursuit of romantic knowledge, though none have yet predicted her past or future with any flash of accuracy or indeed possibility (she has never been in love with anyone called 'Loz' and tall dark strangers are two a penny in the Café de Paris).

Ralph was no more mystical. 'Written on the back it is. Bit smudged mind.'

'Oh, well, right. Bye then,' I blustered and shut the door swiftly, horribly aware my cheeks had got hot, though they had no business doing so. Still less once I had read what Freddy had to say.

Dear Panther,
There is little to report from Magdalen. It is all rather books open, head down in Lent term, and the rain has kept even Egg at bay, which is a good thing as the porter almost caught him shinning in past two a fortnight ago. He'd gone back to a

flat with a girl from Fitzbillies whom he claims has been giving him the eye since Michaelmas and finally slipped him 'the wink' in a bag with his Chelsea bun. He could charm the dead, could Egg. Though I feel sorry for his 'charmees'. When he finally leaves the college lawns for the gold-paved streets of London, the line of broken-hearted shop girls will doubtless stretch all the way to Trumpington.

On a more serious note, it is heartening to hear that you are embracing fate (or rather the absurd laws that still pervade our antiquated peerage system). But you do know, don't you, that you don't have to pretend to be brave with me? So, tell me, Panth, what it is really like? We have known each other for far too long for false fronts.

'False fronts?' I thought. I wasn't pretending to be brave when I wrote to him; it was a heady mix of hope and Oloroso sherry. Both of which I am sorry to say have been completely lacking in recent weeks. The truth is, life at the Dower House is far from the bright, shining one I had conjured up for myself. Conditions are cramped, to say the least. Our bedrooms are adjoining, with no corridor at all, so that Marigold and I are forced to walk through Aster's to get to ours. On top of that, we have twin cot-beds, once belonging to Daddy and Uncle James,

while Aster has the luxury of a four-poster bagsied on grounds of being the tallest (it is a curse being small) and eldest, thus requiring more privacy and fewer idiotic conversation about otters. Mama said we must take it in turns and if Aster does not agree she will devise a rota so we can each have a go. Aster says she will adhere to no such thing and if she is forced to move, she cannot be held responsible for the consequences.

Hopefully she will tire of us traipsing through soon (Marigold has developed a particularly elephantine tread) and will be induced to find a fiancé, thus at best securing our financial future, or at worst ridding us of one resident. If the stamping doesn't do it, then the dust surely will. Mabel has clearly not ventured into half the rooms in a year (nor Grandma, or words would be had there). Or, if she has, her dusting is as lacklustre as her pot washing (Grandma had to send a spoon back this morning, as yesterday's egg was clearly still congealed on it). Though her job is not aided by all manner of bric-a-brac that Grandma insists on piling on or having hammered in to every surface by Rapsey. There are porcelain figurines, paintings and Uncle James's plaques (rugby, running, cricket), and a whole set of his war medals in a display box.

Daddy never won a plaque or a medal, though he did get a collection of Wordsworth as a school prize for poetry. I suspect it's in one of the boxes still. Perhaps I shall ask Mama for it later. And for his *Hansards* back. I might as well make use of all the idling time I have here and I cannot read *The*

Sheikh any more as Marigold has nabbed it and she and Bad Harry have been taking it in turns to read it aloud to Siegfried. I don't know who finds this more alarming: the sheep or Mama.

To add to the mayhem, Marigold's menagerie is on some sort of protest. The hens have stopped laying, and Siegfried, who is now corralled in the garage, has become doubly destructive (hence the recitation of romantic literature). He has already kicked several dents in the motorcar and eaten a chunk out of a tyre. And when he's let out, he's no better, inevitably making a frantic dash for freedom with Marigold and Rapsey in hot pursuit. Marigold has begged to let him into the Dower House, if only to the vestibule by the back door, but Grandma says it is bad enough she has Bobby and the cat in close proximity to her Chippendales, and it will be the vestibule one minute and the chaise the next if he's given half the chance.

It is a good thing she is yet to realise the rabbits have decamped to the attic.

I suppose I should be generous and say that the food, as predicted, is a marked improvement. Though, with six of us, dinner is quite a clattering affair. So much so that on several occasions I suspect Aster of being deliberately late so she can eat in peace with Mabel.

Poor Cook. I wonder who is suffering her meat loaf now.

Another small positive is that Grandma gets *The Tatler*, meaning I save a shilling. Ralph delivers it on Wednesday along with her other weeklies.

'You read *The Tatler*?' asked Aster, aghast, when Grandma informed me of this fact.

'I like to keep on top of current affairs,' she retorted, using affairs in the loosest sense of the word. She means she likes to know who to be disgusted with. 'You'll have to be quick though,' she added. 'Mabel takes possession after me. Heavens knows what she does with it.'

'Reads it?' I suggested.

Grandma pulled a face that suggested this was an impossibility. 'Such a strange thing,' she continued. 'Sometimes I hear voices from the kitchen. I think she talks to herself.'

'She's probably possessed,' said Marigold. 'Probably the dead spirit of someone who used to live here takes over her mortal body and forces her to talk in tongues.'

'Where on earth did you hear such nonsense?' asked Mama.

'Bad Harry?' I suggested, though it was gullible Margot who came to mind first of all.

'No, *The Daily Mirror*,' replied Marigold. 'Anyway, it's probably only Grandpa.'

Grandma looked alarmed. 'Your grandfather never discussed handbags,' she snapped.

At which point I left the room to write to Margot as a matter of urgency.

I have told her conditions at the Dower House are verging on purgatorial, with ancient dust and possibly ghosts, not to mention that with so many people under one roof it is a positive breeding ground for bacteria and a wonder that I don't die from tuberculosis. So now she positively *must* invite me, as it will be an act of kindness, if not actually life-saving.

I am less sure what to say Freddy. There was more, you see, after the bit about false fronts.

> Do you miss Radley? Do you miss him?
>
> I know you must. I miss my mother, too. You probably don't remember her at all. But she was everything to me when we were little. I was a mummy's boy, I suppose, just as you were a daddy's girl. I think everyone assumes I take after my father, because of the medicine, but it was she who encouraged it. She was the one who delivered Aster, in fact, and you too.
>
> But I'm wittering about midwives now. I just wanted to say, I do know what you're going through. A little.
>
> Anyway, goodbye from a sodden college. And do write back. I welcome the distraction.
>
> Yours,
>
> Freddy

A distraction? Is that what I am?

And he's wrong about his mother. I remember her vividly.

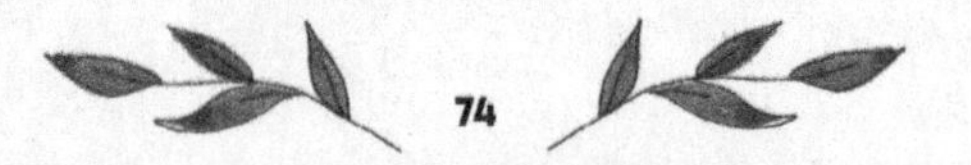

Snippets at least. She was different to Mama: sturdier, but softer somehow too. And she was how Freddy and I met, I should guess, because she always brought him when she checked on Mama. Then, when she died, Mama sometimes took Freddy for the day, and nights when Dr Spencer needed. We slept top to toe in my room, then on a makeshift bed on the floor when we got too big. And we'd sing silly songs, like Bad Harry and Marigold, and make up glittering futures for ourselves. Once – heaven knows why – we even said we'd get married.

Though I don't suppose he remembers that, daft as it was.

Anyway, then Dr Spencer met the new Mrs Spencer, who, defying all stepmother stereotypes, isn't a spot wicked, and so Freddy didn't need Mama any longer. Nor me.

I wonder if Freddy has a string of women who will mourn his departure. Though I can't imagine so. He's hardly the heart-breaking type.

Unless that's what I'm a distraction from.

Perhaps I should ask him.

Perhaps I should tell him that I still cry for Daddy at night sometimes, when Marigold and Aster have gone to sleep. In the first months, back at Radley, Mama would come in to comfort me. She'd lie on my bed and sing 'Green Willow', which was always my favourite. But now she has Dinah and, besides, they're in the room with the rose wallpaper, which is far too far to hear me.

Though perhaps, after all, that is not the sort of thing

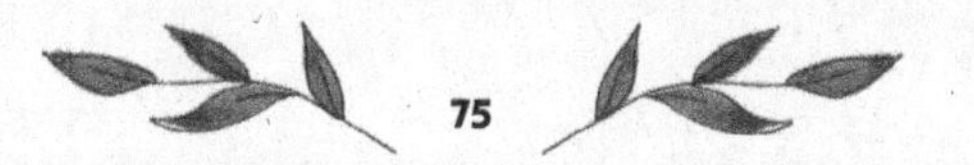

Freddy, or anyone else, needs to hear. It hardly paints a pretty picture, does it?

No, now that I think it, I am determined that in this reply I shall remain defiant in the face of adversity. Because I am a Mannering. And Mannerings, as Daddy was fond of saying, can make a feast with a farthing.

And now that, thanks to Grandma, I no longer have to fork out for *The Tatler*, I have at least two.

MONDAY 17 MARCH

11 A.M.

Margot has yet again ignored my not even subtle hints at rescue and managed to segue to her own pressing plight, to wit:

> *Dearest Panth,*
> *Oh, how beastly it all sounds in Ickthorpe. And what poverty! It is all very Hard Times. But things are no calmer on Glasshouse Street. Mummy is in fits because Cynthia Chivers (remember her from Hedingham? She once stuck a rubber up her nose and Nurse had to get it out with tweezers?) has run off to Paris with a photographer she met at the KitKat called*

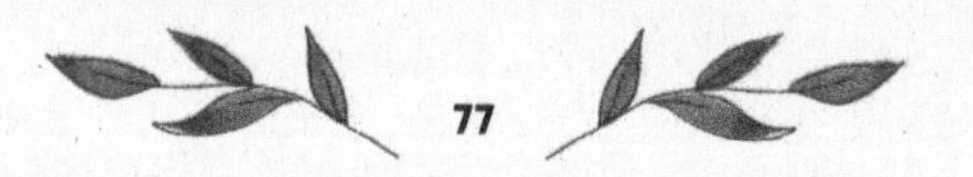

Gaston DuPont. Only, that isn't the worst of it. Apparently he snapped her naked as well! Can you imagine? Oh, I would die to run off to Paris or even just Manchester if I could be snapped naked. Anyway, Mummy says I must never be seen at the KitKat again in case I am lured into the clutches of such a fiend.

I am unperturbed. The only luring will be by Brilliant, who definitely winked at me from stage last Saturday. Or at least I think it was at me. I suppose it could feasibly have been at Lettice Chamberlain, but she's engaged to Jonty Newbold, so that makes no sense at all.

Anyway, toodle pip, Panth. Hope things duly improve. Love to Dinah! Is she adorable?

Margot

How dare she. It is nothing like *Hard Times* here. For a start, the Gradgrinds were forbidden from fanciful pursuits, and so far today Mama has already allowed Marigold to take Siegfried for a walk to the village so that he can get used to 'crowds' for the village show. The only crowd is Mrs Gibberd at the shop and Reg at the forge and I can guess exactly which she is headed to. I do wish my life were more like a novel though. Not Dickens, obviously. But more *The Sheikh*. Or *The Highwayman*, which is Margot's latest, and which, in postscript, she says is 'very bosomy with a lot of mud'. I have asked her to send me her copy as Mrs Gibberd has nothing bosomy of any sort in stock and Grandma only has *Mrs Beeton's Book of Household Management* and *Wisden's Cricketers' Almanack*.

Perhaps I shall write one of my own. A romance, that is. At least it would bide the time until something happens here or one of us finds a husband. Though then there is the matter of how one would go about it without any actual experience? I don't even know to kiss properly. I once tried on a picture of the Prince of Wales I'd snipped out of *The Tatler*, but it just got soggy and my lips inky. Then I tried it on a stuffed toy bear called Gerald, but Aster walked in and asked me if I was ill so I just said yes, because it seemed the easiest answer. And I could hardly ask her the truth of it, because she is as unskilled as I.

I did ask Margot, because she once kissed her cousin's friend Ginger Wyndham, with whom she got stuck in a wardrobe during a game of sardines on the Isle of Wight. She said his lips were chapped and his tongue enormous so it was both scratchy and wet, and overall a bit eel-like, but that's because he was not her 'destiny'. She has kissed several men since, all of whom she has insisted are her destiny for at least a week. But she has yet to satisfactorily explain kissing. All she can muster is 'you will just know when you're doing it right'. Which is exactly what has been said to me about knitting, the quickstep, and beating egg whites for a soufflé, none of which I have ever come close to mastering.

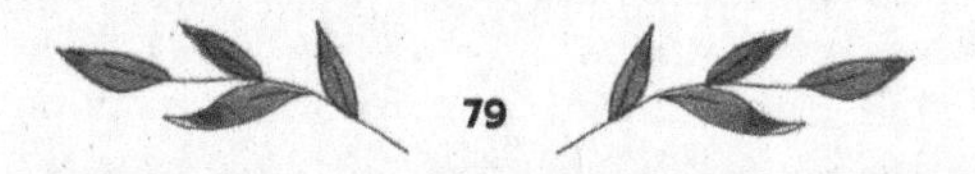

I suppose I could borrow one of Margot's many liaisons for material, but, like the current infatuation with Brilliant, those are more often in her head than actual tangible relationships, and, when they are real, they tend to last only a matter of days.

Perhaps I should befriend Evangeline Balfour. She is the epitome of racy romance, after all. So far she has been engaged to two dukes, an earl, and the purser on a ship she was sent on to get over the earl. Unlike Daphne, who has already settled (in every sense of the term). At least their older brother is already married with children (including two boys, so no worries about heirs there, even if they do have heads shaped like helmets).

Grandma suggested at breakfast that perhaps if we went to church more often, or in fact at all, we might meet a marriageable man or at the very least improve ourselves. Only, we haven't been since Daddy had an argument with Lord Balfour about God's opinions on poverty and whether or not Jesus was a beggar, and renounced both Lord Balfour and religion itself.

'If we showed up now the vicar might have a fit,' Mama admitted. 'I doubt he'd even recognise us.'

'Is it a vicar?' I said, realising as I said it that I have no idea what religion we all are. 'Perhaps we're Catholic,' I added.

'Perhaps we're Jewish,' said Marigold. 'We had a Jewish girl at choir once. She could sing and burp at the same time.' This said in tones of awe.

'I don't think we're Jewish,' I said. 'Or Catholic, actually. Don't the Catholics have incense?'

'And guilt,' added Aster.

'Honestly,' snapped Grandma. 'We're Anglican.'

'I'm going to believe in all the gods,' said Marigold, ignoring her.

'When will you find the time?' asked Mama.

'And what on earth for?' I demanded.

Marigold frowned, as if we were the fools. 'Because that way I'll have the best chance of getting into heaven.'

Mama hooted. Grandma closed her eyes in despair.

'I don't think it works like that,' I said, as kindly as I could muster.

'Well, it should,' snapped Marigold. 'I thought God loved a trier. Didn't Daddy say that?'

'He did,' said Mama. 'Once upon a time. But I'm not at all sure any god would love someone who eats jam from the pot with a spoon and then lets Bobby lick it.'

Grandma pushed her toast away. 'Really, this is the limit,' she said, addressing Mama. 'You must try harder to shape your girls into ladies. Heathens is what they are at the moment. Heathens! What chance of marrying any of them off if they share spoons with dogs, sheep and who knows what other unsavoury creatures. They'll be gallivanting with the French next!'

'Oh,' said Mama, as well she might. No one had said anything about marrying any of us off before today except amongst ourselves, but it now became blatantly apparent that it was at the top of Grandma's to-do list.

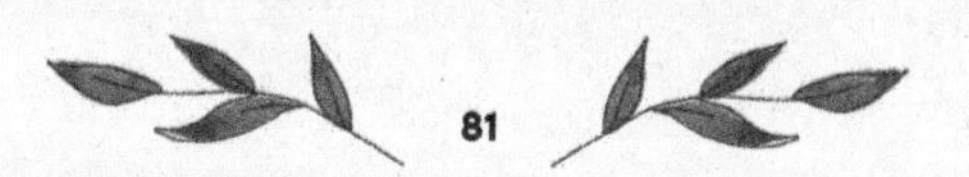

She will be wasting her time. As I have explained before, we should be so lucky as to meet a Frenchman, let alone anyone eligible. Ickthorpe is bereft of men of any type, least of all suitable ones, unless one considers Reg Nesbitt a catch. It is as if all life goes on outside the village perimeters while we are stuck here in some sort of waiting room, or quarantine. As if there are two worlds almost. One low-ceilinged and close-walled, with the kind of lighting that barely reaches the dusty corners, and the other a vast ballroom hung with expansive chandeliers that dapple the backs of the bright young things while the band plays rackety jazz.

Oh, how I wish to be in that bright-lit world. To dance under that glinting crystal, to that tooting music, with those brilliant, terrible men!

Or rather, I'd like to at least try it. Because right now I'm not really sure what I want, or who, if anyone at all.

I just know it isn't this.

THURSDAY 20 MARCH

8 P.M.

There is news. Of the minor and major types.

In minor news, Marigold says Mabel says Mrs Gibberd says that Cook put an advert in the shop window and has been taken on by the Balfours. They are probably cursing our very name. Or at least they would be if their teeth were not likely stuck together with questionable gravy. Honestly, it is a wonder Lady Balfour has not rung and demanded some sort of refund. They must be hitting harder times than I thought if they are stooping to Cook.

But that is, as I say, of only minor concern, because, more worryingly, Grandma has, as promised, taken it upon herself to secure Aster and I husbands. She says if we are so transparently

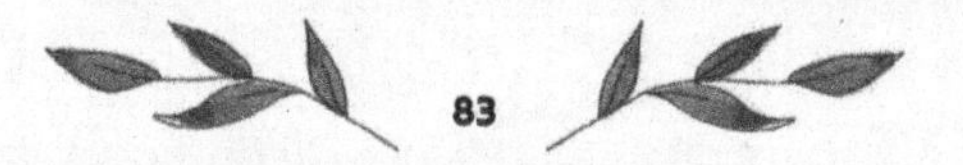

incapable of finding them ourselves, and Mama seems disinclined to involve herself with anything but Dinah and endless sheep misdemeanours (which are a daily occurrence), then she will have to take matters into her own hands. She has sent Mabel to fetch *Debrett's* and her address book and is going to send off a series of invites.

I dread to think whom she will deem suitable. As does Aster, clearly.

'What makes you think I even want a husband?' she demanded in anticipatory distaste.

'It's not a question of *want*,' replied Grandma, 'but the done thing. You *have* to have one. Unless you're a nun. Are you a nun?'

Aster ignored her. 'Half the men my age are dead anyway.'

Grandma steeled herself. 'There's no need to be macabre as well as petulant. There are plenty of men if you know where to look. What about Ludo Foulkes, for example?'

'Ludo Foulkes?' snapped Aster. 'That friend of Daddy's? He's ancient. At least forty-two.'

'I'm forty-two,' said Mama.

'Precisely,' said Aster.

'Well, perhaps not him,' said Grandma, uncharacteristically conceding a small defeat. 'But there will be someone. Somewhere. For you *and* your sister.' She glared at me at this point, as if my very presence were as tormenting as a fly. 'And I will wheedle them out.'

The image that sprung to mind was of a long-fingered

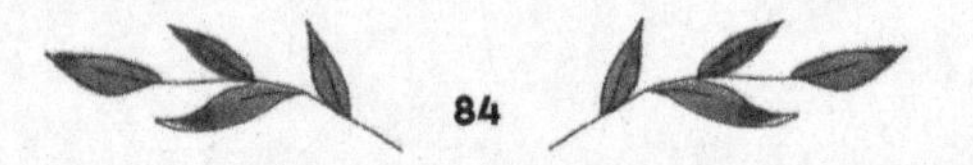

monkey with a weevil I had seen in *The Times* once, but I said nothing, too busy baulking at the thought of interminable teas with weak-chinned Charleses and Arthurs. But what other hope was there, unless–

'What if someone – a man – rents Radley?' I said suddenly. I had walked there only yesterday, and had had to rally myself when I saw it standing shuttered, like a closed eye. To think of it wasting away, unloved, unlived-in, was almost worse than it being out of our reach. But if a man, a suitable man, came to live there, well, that might change everything.

'Who on earth is going to rent Radley?' demanded Aster. 'You know as well as I that everyone the agent has found has run a mile as soon as they've seen the state of it.'

Mama made a small squeak, like a guinea pig, or Dinah at times.

'That's unfair,' I said quickly. 'It's not . . . it's not a wreck, at least not yet. And anyway, Valentine says he will take matters into his own hands if the agent fails.' Though heaven knows what that means. Perhaps minstrels will move in. Though it might be worth it just to see Grandma's face if they did.

'Enough hoo-hah,' she said then. 'Whether Radley is let or not is moot, as anyone who would want to take that place on must be either a fool or American. And you don't want either of those mixing with Mannering blood. No, I shall find a nice English man for each of you. Sensible. Sane. Godly.' She looked at me in particular at that point. (Though possibly only because

Marigold was in the attic giving carrots to the rabbits. Grandma is still none the wiser as to their presence in the house, which is frankly the kind of miracle that would make one believe in a higher being. Either that or she is pretending they don't exist.)

'A week on Saturday,' Grandma said then. 'Tea at three. I expect all of you to be there.'

*

So now Aster and I are in absolute dread as to who will meet Grandma's exacting standards, and whether those standards will include good looks and romance potential or are purely set to take into account bank balance, familial birth defects and a tendency to divorce.

Though I suppose even if they're not marriage material, they might prove fodder for a novel. At the very least it will be something to tell Margot about.

And Freddy.

Or, I *would* tell him if he would only write back to me. It's been eight days now and nothing! And I'm not sending him two letters in a row because that absolutely smacks of desperation.

Not that I am desperate for anything from Freddy.

It's just . . . I don't know. Sometimes I think Margot isn't really listening. While Freddy wants to do nothing but.

And for that alone, I long to hear from him.

SATURDAY 29 MARCH

11 A.M.

There is still nothing from Freddy. Obviously I am not distracting enough. Or he has found something far more fascinating – probably Egg's queues of smitten women.

Not that I don't have distractions of my own. Margot at least has replied, with a parcel including *The Highwayman*, as well as a bar of chocolate and half a pound of gumdrops she says she needs to get rid of lest they prove too tempting. Though she has again failed to offer the best distraction of all – a trip to the city. Anyway, the book is as riveting as promised, though the eponymous hero, whilst indeed thrillingly dashing and handsome, does tend worryingly towards thuggery. It is both fascinating and disturbing to find that, whilst deep in reading,

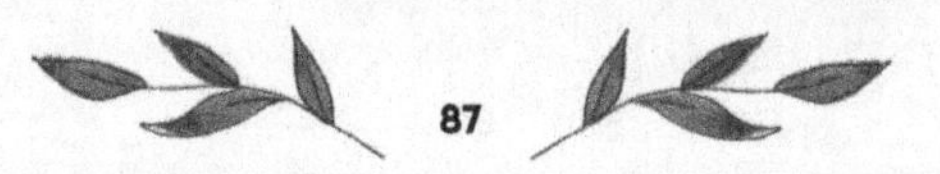

I am ready to fling myself at the feet of a man who is, at best, a rather better-looking and less phlegmy version of Reg, and yet, several hours later, a more objective outlook having descended, I wonder what on earth we'd have to talk about bar horses and gold. Though perhaps small talk isn't what one should want for in a man. Perhaps that is what sisters are for. Except, now that I think of it, Mama and Daddy never wanted for conversation; they could (and did) discuss anything and everything from the state of the dahlias to the plight of cotton workers. Oh, why is it all so complicated? What with this kind of conundrum and the p-word, it is a wonder anyone bothers at all. I sometimes think nuns have it right: at least they have purpose.

Though Grandma has made clear that Aster and I must bother and soon, as, in another rather more pressing distraction, one Brandon Attlesey and his mother, Lady Melcham, are set to call at three o'clock precisely for what has become known in the Dower House as Fortune Tea.

Oh! Seeing it written in ink, so definitively, has made my insides swill.

What if we both loathe him? What if he loathes us? I can't imagine having Grandma present is at all alluring. I mean, it is all very well if we turn out like Mama, who is, as I have said, still a beauty despite advancing years, but Grandma has a hard stare that could curdle custard. Plus, this mercenary approach feels rather as if we're the Bennet sisters, instructed to ravage anyone of male persuasion who happens to wander into our vicinity, bidden or unwitting. Which is the sort of behaviour Margot goes for, not I, and still less Aster.

On top of that, the drawing room is awfully maudlin – not at all conducive to the sort of gaiety one might hope would accompany a prospective pairing. This is not aided by the enormous still life of four oranges and a dead heron that Grandma has hung above the mantel after Aster snaffled it from Radley. Grandma says she has had her eye on it for decades. Heaven knows why; it is gruesome and inexplicable. Marigold has offered to daub something of her own, if Grandma is that way inclined. Grandma said, 'How nice,' in a voice that very much indicated she did not think it nice at all, but Marigold ran off to borrow Aster's brushes and paper (Aster's absence meaning no permission was needed, as it would most certainly not have been given).

Where Aster actually is at this moment is anyone's guess. She went out straight after breakfast without saying a word. Marigold said for a shilling she can ask Mabel to ask Ralph to ask Mrs Gibberd as she knows everything that goes on in the village but I said that rather sounded like extortion and in any case, if anyone is going to spy it should be one of us. As long as Aster is back by the time this Attlesey chap arrives then I suppose it will all turn out. I'd go myself but I have rather more urgent concern: what to wear!

Oh, I wish I had Aster's figure. At best I think one could say I was satisfactory, looks-wise. Until fifteen I was all teeth and knees. Now I have sort of grown into those, however other areas have done growing of their own, most notably the chest, which Margot insists will be a magnet for men of a certain persuasion, but frankly is an awful bore as it makes fitting into my own clothes, let alone Aster's cast-offs, almost impossible. As it is, the dove-grey crepe has had to be let out twice, once with fabric from some curtains, so I now have horrible orange stripes down my sides. Mama said I should be grateful Aster is a dab hand with a needle. I said I'd be more grateful if she married a shipping magnate and just bought me a new frock.

Though I suppose it reveals that Aster at least stands a better chance of winning over Brandon. Her hair does what is asked of it, she can sew and cook, and her room, bar her art, is meticulously clean. Whereas I cannot even boil an egg, my room is strewn with books and newspapers and, at times, a sheep (though this is not my own doing), and my sewing is woeful. I suppose I can name every prime minister from Walpole to Baldwin – oh, now MacDonald! – and recite both *Ode on a Grecian Urn* and *The Rime of the Ancient Mariner*, which is quite the party trick, though of questionable use, marriage-wise. I fear any husband would demand a refund.

But, back to matters sartorial: my second-best dress – the blue wool – is frighteningly tight on the top, but at least lacks the gravy stain that is still stubbornly blighting the primrose silk. I suppose as long as I don't eat too much or breathe too much I shall manage.

2 P.M.

Too late! Too late! The pork chop and potatoes at luncheon tipped the stitches the wrong side of chest containment, and my wretched dress has rent down one seam. Mama says I should never have worn it to the table, but I said in fact it was essential practice for not breathing at tea, and wasn't it a better thing to happen now, than to have my undergarments exposed to Lady Melcham?

Mama agreed reluctantly. Grandma just sighed and sent me off with Mabel to find something suitable from her own wardrobe. Unfortunately, Grandma's idea of 'suitable' does not really equate to any of her dresses, all of which are in gloomy hues that suggest death or, at best, misery, rather than anything I am supposed to be mustering on this allegedly happy day. But, in what I think is a terribly clever ruse, Mabel unwrapped the furs, so now I am splendidly draped in several dead beaver.

Oh, I could get used to this. It is somewhat hot of course (the weather today is surprisingly clement), yet terribly glamorous. I can almost imagine I am Evangeline Balfour, or an American actress – Tallulah Bankhead herself – swathed as I am. Of course, Daddy thought fur cruel, so Mama never owned one – not that we could have afforded it in any case. But Grandma has several – a mink; this, the beaver; and something that looks alarmingly like all the rabbits stitched into one, which I rejected on the grounds that Marigold might get upset, or, worse, ideas.

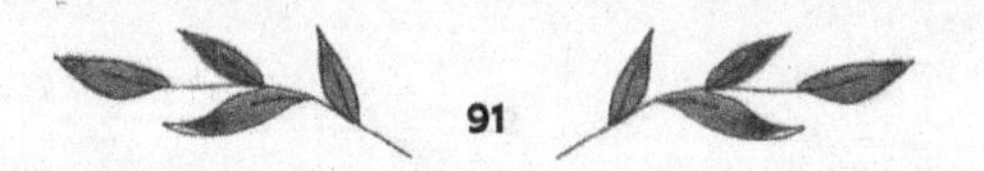

'I'm not sure what Grandma will say,' I worried to Mabel as I turned to and fro in the cheval mirror.

Mabel shrugged. 'Probably, "Is it snowing in here? Is it winter?"' These said in such an extraordinary imitation of Grandma I was struck dumb for a second.

'Heavens,' I said eventually. 'That was uncanny. Can you do anyone else?'

Mabel stared at me, unwavering. 'Everyone,' she said.

'Even me?'

She nodded solemnly. 'Everyone,' she said again.

I suppose I could have asked for a demonstration but I was too concerned at what unflattering manner of portrait she would make of me. And besides, I had Aster to chivvy (who would surely come off worse, as portraits go).

She had slinked in, akin to the cat, just before lunch, eaten two potatoes and a mouthful of meat in abject silence, then stalked upstairs to start on the cello. Grandma immediately threatened to have Rapsey snap the three remaining strings. She said if Aster continues to inflict this dirge on us any longer, she might be forced to emigrate.

I shan't tell Aster that. I shouldn't give her the hope.

No, that is terrible thing to say. Grandma is difficult to love, but still I manage it. I just wish Aster would seek solace from whatever it is by taking up painting again, but as it is she hasn't so much as opened a tube of gouache in months.

Anyway, I am sent to fetch her. Mabel has gone back to

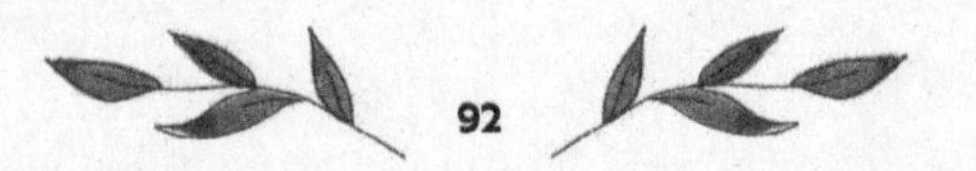

turn out the salmon in aspic (of course), and Marigold is still occupied with her own art. Mama advised it might be better if Marigold was excused from tea entirely and left to her own devices instead. Personally, I think this is like choosing between a rock and a hard place as there is no knowing what manner of madness she might get up to left unsupervised. But Grandma agreed and so it is only Mama, Grandma, Aster and I at the party.

Oh, wish me luck, dear journal. Perhaps, in a few hours' time, I will have found a fiancé. Or, better, will be wishing my sister felicitations on her impending name change to Aster Attlesey.

See? It even has a ring to it.

7 P.M.

It is hard to know where, exactly, to begin.

Suffice to say that the least of evils is the fact that the beaver coat is now liberally decorated with both oil paint and salmon in aspic, neither of which have succumbed to Mabel's attempts at erasure. I suppose I should have known from the very off that it was all going to go scones up. For a start, Grandma was lamenting the disappearance of her best gilt tea tray, so that we were being forced to use the silver, which was scratched from the time I tried to monogram my initials into it with a fork aged four. Then there was the matter of my outfit.

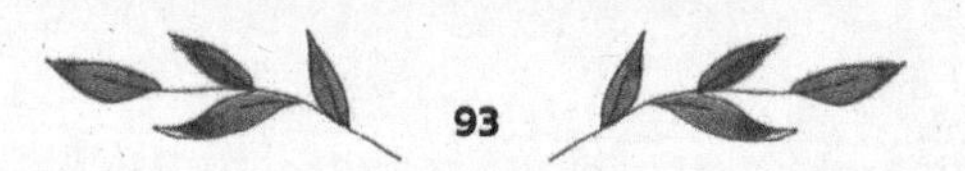

'You look like a bear,' said Aster cruelly.

Grandma frowned in what seemed to be agreement. 'Is it snowing?' she asked.

Ha! I thought, remembering Mabel, but dared not say it. 'It makes me look important,' I said. 'Besides, I am a little chilly.'

I was not in any way chilly – in fact, the armpits of the blue wool would be soaked, were they not already gaping under their camouflage – but I was not going to let Grandma win. Besides which, there was no time to change as the Attleseys were already impending, and Grandma had rung a bell to summon Rapsey to the door. The first of which was absurd as usually she just calls for him or Mabel in a voice so loud and shrill it could crack ice as far away as the Arctic. The second, though, was alarming, as Rapsey had somehow been persuaded into butler's tails, which were a little too tight about the trouser, giving him an awkward walk that made him look as if he had had an accident.

'Why can't Mabel just answer?' I asked.

'One must keep up appearances,' said Grandma. 'Hard as I know that is for you.' She eyed the beaver coat again pointedly.

I hardly think a limping Odd Man who smells of sheep is an appearance of any positive sort, but I was hardly going to argue. Unlike Aster, whom I could tell was readying herself for contrariness of every kind.

It only went downhill from there.

The Attleseys were ushered in by a staggering Rapsey: Lady

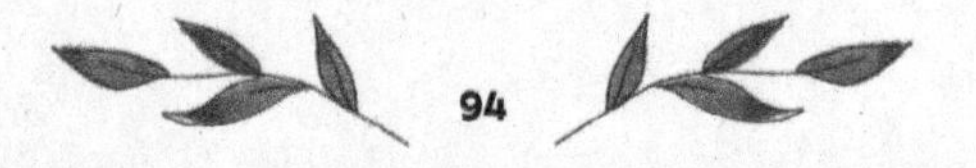

Melcham managing to combine disturbing nervousness with a voice like a gull (and a nose already turned up so that any further distaste would render the view of her nostrils almost forensic); Brandon in turn cursed with a similarly pitched vocal tone along with a constellation of pimples across his unfeasibly high forehead that gave him the appearance of an overgrown schoolboy rather than a man of marriageable age, let alone appearance.

Aster wasted no time in making her distaste at the situation known. 'How old *are* you?' she asked.

'He's twenty-seven,' said Lady Melcham, before poor Brandon could think to open his mouth.

'And not yet married?' said Aster, leaving the accusation obvious, if unsaid.

'He was engaged, once,' cawed Lady Melcham. 'But it didn't take.'

'Oh dear,' said Mama. 'Did something happen to her?'

'Yes,' said Lady Melcham. 'The fifth Earl of Winchcombe.'

'Oh,' said Mama hurriedly. 'Is that . . . ? I think I hear Dinah.' And rushed from the room, leaving us flailing. Or me, at least. Grandma never flails. Nor Aster.

'I've always thought the obsession with aspic is a metaphor for society's determination to preserve patriarchal dominance,' said my sister, eyeing Brandon's plate of insipid salmon.

Grandma narrowed her eyes.

I winced. 'Oh, I don't mind it,' I said, digging in heartily and

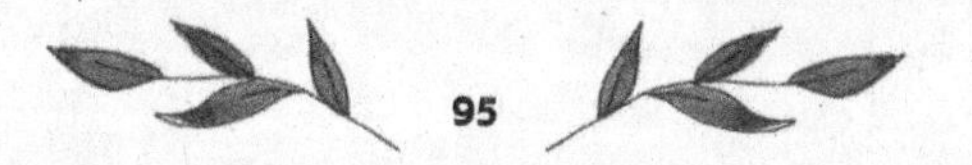

immediately dropping a blob of the meaty jelly on the beaver. 'Oh, damn,' I said. 'Sorry, I mean, oops-a-daisy.'

Lady Melcham's nose tilted skyward.

'I'm just so terribly clumsy,' I said. 'Once, I tipped a whole bowl of oxtail onto Daddy's lap. Luckily it was only lukewarm or heavens knows the damage. Dinah might not even be here!'

I was blathering but, far from the designed effect, Lady Melcham's nose now appeared to gape. Thankfully, or so I thought, Marigold chose that moment to appear in the drawing room with her masterpiece, swiftly followed by Mama (and Dinah) who appeared to be beseeching her to stop. Why, exactly, became painfully clear when she presented the painting.

Grandma sighed and closed her eyes.

Lady Melcham leant forward, her nose normal for at least a second. 'Good heavens,' she squawked. 'Is that–'

'A dead rabbit,' finished Brandon, uttering his first (and last) words of the afternoon.

'It *is* terribly lifelike,' I said, rather generously, grabbing it and accidentally smearing it on the sleeve of the beaver. 'Oh, lawks,' I said.

'That's because it is,' said Marigold, vivid with pride, before leaving the room and rushing back with Grandma's gilt tea tray, on which was lying one of the rabbits in a state of some savagery.

'Great Scott!' said Grandma.

'What happened?' I asked.

'The cat I think,' said Marigold with a sigh. 'Still, waste not, want not.'

'I think I may faint,' said a pale Lady Melcham, while her son went positively green.

'He's going to be sick,' said Marigold matter-of-factly.

No sooner had she uttered the words than a plume of fish-pink vomit arced across the tea table and onto the carpet, at which point Lady Melcham did faint, as well she might.

'See?' said Marigold.

'This is hardly the time for claims of victory,' said Grandma, before shrieking for Mabel, her bell quite abandoned.

'Someone fetch a bucket,' said Mama. 'I think he might go again.'

Which of course he did, this time at least into the aspidistra pot.

The Attleseys departed soon after; Grandma retired for the evening, claiming faintness of her own, leaving Mabel and the staggering Rapsey to clear the crime scene while Mama and us girls sought refuge in our rooms.

'Well, who wants a husband who's sick at the sight of a dead rabbit?' said Marigold. 'Not I. Imagine what would happen if he came across a severed head.'

I dared not ask under what circumstances she imagined that might happen.

'Who wants a husband at all?' added Aster, as briefly cheery as I have ever seen her.

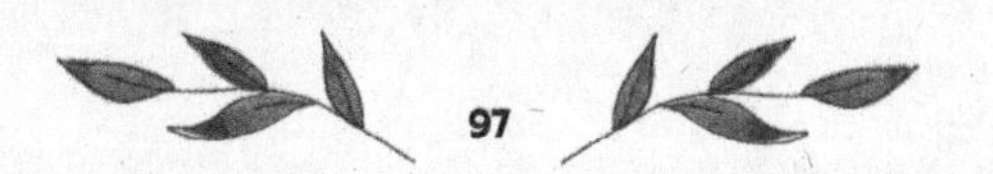

But, relieved as I was to have avoided Brandon Attlesey, who was as far from the brawny highwayman or, indeed, a man of words as is physically and intellectually possible, I felt something odd in me. A loss, I think. Not for Aster or me, specifically, but for the Mannering family. For it seems, with this latest calamity, that the candle of hope itself has, if not been snuffed out, then at least guttered. For if this was the best Grandma could do, and given our limited circumstance, then perhaps Daddy was wrong. Perhaps there isn't someone for everyone.

Perhaps there isn't anyone for me after all.

APRIL

TUESDAY 1 APRIL

8 P.M.

Spring, and with it, something to cheer at last.

Mama has finally given in to Grandma and agreed to get Dinah christened. On the down side, it means we will have to brave the vicar and several stern pairs of eyes across the pews, I imagine. Plus, she has asked Valentine to be godfather, which has set a cat the size of an elephant among Grandma's already cantankerous pigeons. Though, given godparents are surely only there to dole out shillings every so often, and bigger things at Christmas, it's hardly condemning Dinah to the devil. And anyway, a christening, and a spring one, is optimism itself, isn't it? We can fill the church with cut flowers, and perhaps Aster can fashion some sort of floral arrangement to cover the gravy

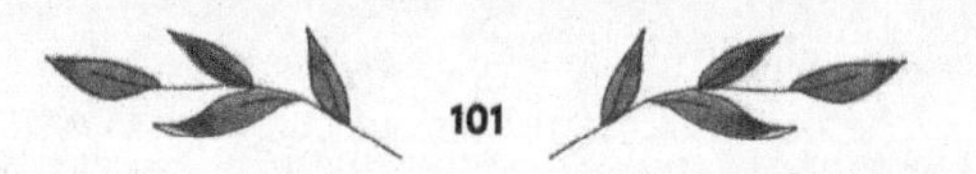

stain on the primrose silk. I should probably have thought of that before, instead of the beaver, which ended rather messily. But all we had back then were a few desultory daffs, and that would have been distracting in all the wrong ways.

The longer days will be a pleasant welcome as well, if only for the opportunity to escape the Dower House at greater length. Evenings at Grandma's have become terribly desperate. Mama has taken to knitting with renewed vigour and is currently on her eleventh matinee jacket for Dinah, all with wool from Daddy's unravelled socks and sweaters. Though when Dinah is going to have the opportunity to wear a sludge-green ensemble, let alone eleven of them is a mystery. And as for Aster, when she is not on her cello she lies on the chaise in some sort of torpor while Marigold recites surprising facts from farming manuals. Her latest discovery is that horses cannot vomit and she is worryingly keen to test the theory. Thankfully all our ponies were sold long ago and Bad Harry's roan is likely to bite anyone who tries to force it do anything it doesn't fancy. Grandma, meanwhile, has taken to retiring as early as possible, claiming headaches. If she *is* pained, it is either at Marigold, or Daddy's radio, which Mama has installed in the drawing room, and which she largely regards as some sort of inexplicable trickery and likely to catch fire or convert us to savagery.

As for me, I am so awfully bored I have finally started on a romance novel of my own. So far, I have a setting – a once majestic but now crumbling country manor – and my leading lady – the daughter of a duke who is desperately down on his luck. I am yet to settle on a hero, though. I cannot decide if he should be foreign and unable to communicate except through the language of love, or a high-ranking army officer who went mute in the war (which he almost single-handedly won) and is now unable to communicate except through the language of love. Being mainly able to communicate solely through the language of love seems to be key. And women's tongues must not be smart at all but silent or sighing. I suspect I will fail spectacularly at that part, on paper and in actuality. Daddy always said we girls couldn't help blurting out what we were thinking. He saw it as a good thing, and said he wished politicians were more honest. I doubt Grandma would agree.

Lately I have been feeling especially bereft as far as Daddy is concerned. It's nearly a year since he left us and I woke with a start this morning, suddenly worried I couldn't picture him properly. But then a wash of something warm and glorious came over me and I recalled it all: his face, his voice, the smell of him – cigar smoke and gardens. The feel of him too, when he hugged me after I'd fallen off Socks (our last Shetland) or scraped a knee trying to climb up a tree or down a riverbank. He wasn't at all like a normal papa: those men who spend no time with their children at all, believing them better seen only briefly and never heard. He loved nothing more than all of us crawling on him, singing him ridiculous ditties or letting us fashion plaits into his leonine hair. And I don't mean he

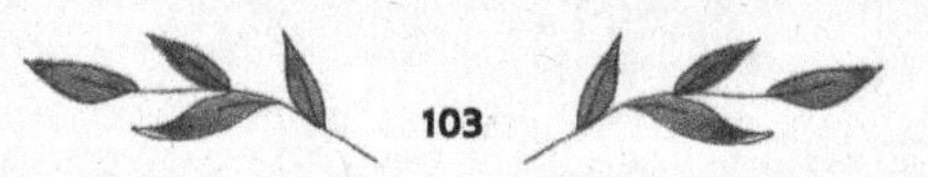

tolerated it, but positively wanted it.

'Do you still miss him?' I asked Aster as we lounged on the drawing room floor waiting until sleep summoned us upstairs.

She didn't even have to ask who. 'Every day,' she said.

I had a thought then, wondrous and mortifying at once. 'Do you think Mama will ever meet another man again?'

Marigold, who, unbeknownst to us had been under the chaise with a contraband rabbit, took this opportunity to make her presence known. 'Statistically, only fifteen per cent of women over thirty-five remarry,' she announced.

I, and surprisingly Aster, burst out laughing, at her brashness rather than her words, depressing as they were.

'Where on earth did you hear that?'

'*The Daily Mirror*,' said Marigold. 'You should read it. It's thrilling. Far more informative about the facts of life than *The Highwayman*.'

'What would you know about that?' I blurted (see – we cannot help it).

'I know that "succumbed to his urgent advances" means he did that thing with his willy.'

'Marigold!' snapped Aster, her smile wiped off in an instant.

'What? It's true, isn't it?'

'Even if it is, you shouldn't be reading it,' I said firmly. 'Stick to sheep and chickens. And horse vomit.'

The thought of Mama ever succumbing to anyone again had sent happy thoughts of Daddy packing. The thing is, even

if Mama did meet another man, he wouldn't be half as good as the one she— no, we all, had.

Perhaps that is Aster's problem. Perhaps she thought Nigel Pakenham was some sort of replacement, a match even, for Daddy. And now that he's marrying Daphne Balfour, all hope is gone. Though heaven knows why. Daddy was a fascinating man, if a little strange to some, and Nigel is, at best, a conformist, and one with a cheese face at that.

On the subject of men, there is no news from Freddy. Not that I care. This is mere statement of fact. Though I do wonder that women try to rely on men at all. They either fail to do whatever it is they have stated they will do, or die and leave you thinking you can't possibly go on without them.

And yet, again and again, we have to, and do.

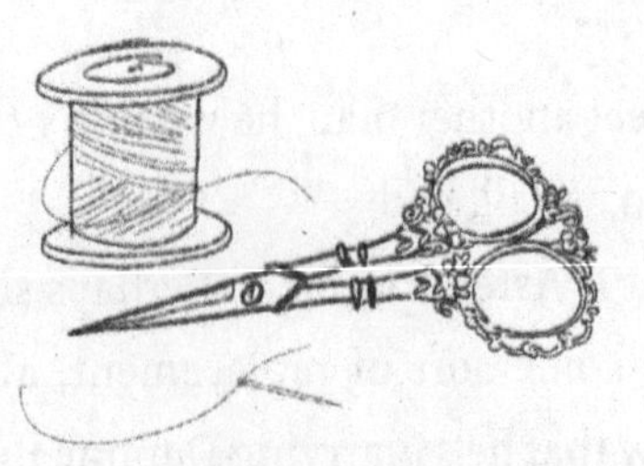

MONDAY 7 APRIL

7 P.M.

From drought to abundance in a mere week! I now have three things to report, all of utmost interest to members of the Mannering household, though varying in their import to wider society.

Firstly, of admittedly less pressing interest, the cat has a name.

It was Grandma's idea. She said if she must continue tolerating its malevolent presence then she at least needed a moniker with which to scold it. At which point, all of us began to offer suggestions so vociferously Grandma clanged the teapot with her cake fork and told us to please stop all talking at once because we sounded like a gaggle of marauding gannets.

'Plunging,' said Marigold.

'Pardon me?' asked Grandma.

'It's not a gaggle of gannets,' Marigold explained. 'It's a "plunging".'

'Well, whatever it is, it's making me wish for ear muffs,' snapped Grandma, who then proceeded to dole out strict instructions as to the rules for the Grand Cat Naming: we were to each write a single name on a slip of paper then put it in the tea cosy, whereupon she would pull one out and that would be the cat's name whether the rest of us liked it or not. Unless she didn't like it, in which case she would keep on drawing names until she did. Which Marigold said was unfair as Grandma could just keep on drawing names until she picked her own. So we agreed that Grandma couldn't write a name, just the rest of us and Mama and Mabel.

Anyway, as a result of this unnecessarily complicated process, the cat is now called Hamilton (Mama's suggestion – she cannot explain why, she just liked it). The best I can say is that it could have been worse, for Marigold had put in 'Isambard', Aster 'Iolanthe', and Mabel 'Derek', none of which are suitable for a cat, especially one whose gender we are yet to satisfactorily determine (no one can get near enough to attempt it). I am trying not to sulk that 'Tallulah' (my suggestion) was rejected out of hand. The cat is less able to conceal its disappointment. It is absolutely refusing to answer to its name, merely regarding Grandma with complete disdain whenever she mentions it, before skulking off to the scullery.

The second, rather more weighty report, is that this morning Ralph (along with a lengthy musing on whether or not squirrels should be classed as vermin, and their menace-ranking against the snail scourge) delivered our invitations to the Balfour wedding.

'How thrilling!' I said (once I had rid the doorstep of the pestilent post boy by sending him round the back to see Mabel, who insisted she had something to ask him about buttons). A christening and a wedding in the space of mere weeks was almost too much excitement to bear (which says a good deal about the paucity of entertainment in Ickthorpe). Only then, of course, I immediately set to worrying about what I might wear. 'Perhaps we could let out the blue wool,' I suggested.

'You can have anything of mine and alter it all you want,' said Aster then, strangely generous. 'I shan't go.'

My sartorial ponderings stopped as if snipped in two.

'Don't be ridiculous,' said Mama. 'Of course you're going. We're all going. She's your best friend.'

'Not any more,' snapped Aster.

This was news almost as shocking as when Marigold said she was giving up cake for Lent (she lasted two days).

'But you're always thick as thieves,' I pointed out. 'You were round at the Balfours' only yesterday.'

Aster blanched (which for someone so pale is quite an achievement). 'How on earth do you know that? Have you been following me?'

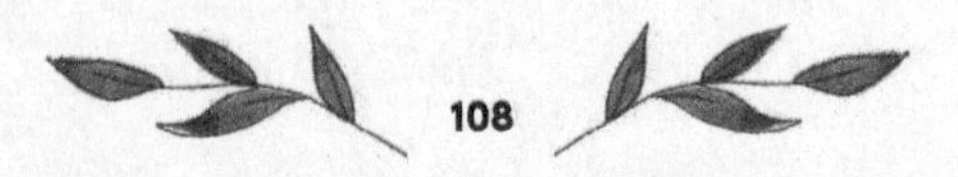

I, in contrast, reddened, and did what any sister would do: blame someone else. 'Marigold said Mabel said Ralph said he saw you.'

Aster visibly bristled. 'Well, perhaps I was,' she admitted. 'But it will be the last time I set foot there again.'

'But if you don't go to the wedding, we can hardly go,' I said. 'That's unfair.' For where else might I meet a silent aristocrat who might talk to me solely in the language of love? Or, as Grandma has put it: someone rich enough and fool enough to take me on.

'Panther,' warned Mama, uncharacteristically forthright. 'This is not about you.' But then she turned to Aster. 'I don't know what has happened between the two of you, but even your father would attend and you know how he felt about Lord Balfour. So, you are going and that is that. And we can discuss dresses nearer the time.'

At the mention of Daddy, Aster demurred, at least for now. I kept entirely quiet, but I do hope the dress discussion comes soon. June will be far too hot for fur and heaven knows how else I am supposed to look respectable, let alone a catch.

Which brings me roundabout to my third item of news: Freddy Spencer has finally replied. It seems he was distracted, though not by Egg's women, or any other women. Though Egg was, indeed, at the very centre of things.

Dear Panther,

I'm sorry not to have written sooner, but vac had already begun by the time your letter arrived and Egg had generously offered his father's apartment in Venice for a fortnight.

Oh, Panth, you should see it here! The boats – gondolas, they're called – fill the waterways like traffic on Pall Mall. It's as if we're living in a river; what bliss! Though of course we cannot swim in it. And I don't suppose it would be the same as our own.

Ickthorpe feels terribly far away at times like these, almost as if I'm trapped in a fever dream. I miss it, you see, in all its mundanity: England, the village, the simpler things. Though by the time you read this I shall probably be back there and wishing for Italy. Such is life.

I'd write more, but dinner is calling. Heavens, the food. You've never tasted anything like it. Not even my stepmother's lamb casserole comes close. And certainly not your cook's stew.

Talking of which, I do hope I'll see you at Easter. I assume you're not going away?

Yours,
Freddy

'Yours'?

He's not mine. And, what is more, the farthest I have ever ventured, aside from school (which was fewer than thirty miles in any case), is Yarmouth and then the trek to terrible Aunt Brenda's in Birmingham, so of course I'm not going away. Where in heaven would I go *to*? Not to Margot's, that's for sure.

Though, perhaps, now that I think of it, if I were to invite Margot here for Easter, then she should have to return the favour. I could tell her an eligible man is in the offing. Freddy, I mean. Not that he's terribly eligible, and nor do I expect her to fall for him for a minute. He's not nearly unsuitable enough. Far too ordinary. But the mere mention will be sufficient bait.

I've just realised, he's probably already back. The letter has taken two weeks to fetch up here, according to the date, so he may as well have hand posted it. Not that I feel any desperate need to see him; not until Margot is here. Though at least he wouldn't have wittered on about squirrels, I suppose. Or snails. Not unless they were medical ones. Or served some greater purpose.

That question of purpose again. Why does it rattle me so? Does life require purpose beyond mere existence? If we're only going to get run over by a dustcart as we hurry back to Parliament to argue for the poor, or have our lives snuffed out in their thousands by disease or war or worse, then why strive at all? What can God, if indeed there is one, possibly be thinking? And yet it is almost as if there is a space in me now, ready to be taken by whatever it is I choose for my own great toil. Whether that be the general expectation of women – babies, sewing, doting on a husband – or something else. As if Freddy has rent open an emptiness that must be filled lest I suffer in some sort of endless purgatory.

I should get back to the novel. It may not be a purpose, but it occupies otherwise idle time. Perhaps I will add a minor character who is studying to do something useful and talks a lot. He can serve as stark contrast to the hero who will say nothing and everything with one flash of his dark eyes.

Oh, and there is a line! This novel lark is not as arduous as I thought. Perhaps by the christening I shall have a whole chapter down!

Or at least have found a model for my leading man.

FRIDAY 11 APRIL

10 A.M.

Success! Margot is charmed by the idea of Freddy, for, what, she replied, could be more romantic than 'the boy next door'? I haven't bothered to point out that he is not technically 'next door' and that almost anything could be more romantic. Instead, I have informed her: which train gets in when; not to sit in a carriage with Mr Hendry (squat, cross, face like one of his Tamworth pigs) if he happens to be catching the same service, as the smell will only get worse; and that I will see her on Good Friday.

Perhaps my purpose after all is to play matchmaker. I could be like the eponymous Emma and find suitors for even the most ineligible of men. Even Mr Hendry, if he wasn't already

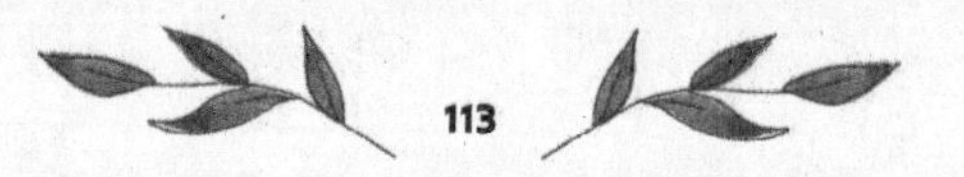

wed to Mrs Hendry, who, luckily for her, lost her sense of smell in an incident with a crochet hook. Yes, in fact perhaps I can start at the christening later! Though as the main guest is Valentine, perhaps not. Ickthorpe is notably narrow in its outlook, and 'theatricals' are limited to Mrs Gypp's annual operatic and the under-elevens ballet (elephantine, I fear). Besides, it is not actually Valentine who is in need of a man, but his mother, whose marriage is apparently in tatters after her second husband, one Frank Buttle (very much smells of trade), was found in flagrante with a Fortnum's shop girl.

'Where *is* Aunt Valentina?' demanded Marigold, who has always regarded her as a role model both in absolute frankness and ability to faint.

'Busy getting D-I-V-O-R-C-E-D,' said Valentine.

'Pointless,' I sighed.

'Divorced,' deduced Marigold, proving my sigh right.

Grandma's intake of breath could have sliced tough mutton. 'The Replacement didn't take then?'

Valentine shrugged. 'He says she's too inscrutable. And she says he can't dance. And then there's the matter of the meat-slicing woman. I just wish they'd hurry up and get it done. It's not as easy as you think, this D-I— oh, to hell with it, this divorce business. One has to prove cruelty as well as adultery.'

'Isn't being Italian enough?' demanded Grandma quietly, but definitely perceptible. 'Or naming a child after oneself?'

Valentine adopted a pained expression, quite successfully I

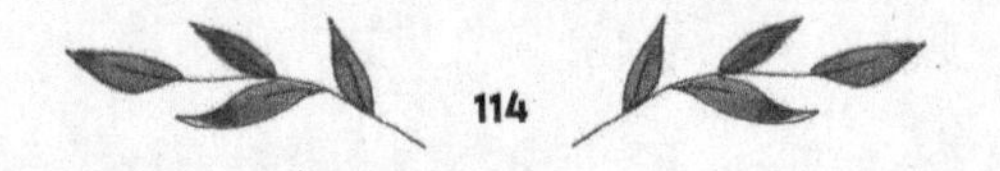

thought. 'I meant on his part. Though swapping a countess for someone who doles out ham for a living is surely cruelty itself.'

'How modern,' was all Grandma could muster.

At which point we were all thankfully distracted by Marigold's sudden demand to bring Siegfried to the christening.

'I can festoon him in anemones,' she suggested. 'Rapsey says there's plenty. And anyway, the greenfly will only get them if I don't, the buggers.'

'Marigold!' Mama came to her senses.

'It was only what Rapsey said,' Marigold defended herself. 'So, can I?'

'Absolutely not,' said Mama. 'It's not . . . the done thing.'

'Daddy would have approved,' Marigold tried.

'Daddy wouldn't have approved of the christening in the first place though,' I pointed out.

Grandma made a noise like a horse.

'No one is taking any animals to church,' said Mama firmly then. 'We don't want to alarm the vicar any more than is necessary. He probably still hasn't recovered from the "was Jesus a beggar?" argument with your father and Lord Balfour.'

'Well, *was* he?' asked Marigold.

'Not now!' prayed Grandma.

'Hurry along,' added Mama swiftly. 'Leave the rabbits and Siegfried to Rapsey for the morning. I'm sure he's eminently capable of—'

'One minute,' interrupted Grandma. 'Where is Hamilton?'

Grandma is the only one bothering with the cat's name. Or indeed, its whereabouts. If I didn't think she had a heart as cold as a dead herring, I'd suspect her of growing fond of the creature.

'On the credenza,' said Aster.

We all looked over and shuddered as it glared at us like some brindled homunculus.

'Oh, yes,' said Grandma. 'There he is, the wretched fellow.'

And, satisfied as Hamilton himself, she led us out the door.

4 P.M.

It turns out we needn't have worried about taking Siegfried to church. In fact, it might have saved everyone a deal of bother.

For a start, the old vicar has gone, to be replaced by one who is rather young and thrusting. Grandma, predictably, is not enamoured of him at all. It is mainly because he has a beard, which she says is a magnet for bacteria, as well as an obvious cover-up for a weak chin. He, though, seemed rather taken by Aster. Perhaps they may make a match! Though I can't really see her as a vicar's wife. She is not good at obeying the word of anyone, least of all God. As it is she refused to sing 'Ride On, Ride On in Majesty', though that may have been down to the presence of Lady Balfour, and Daphne, who stared at her pleadingly across the pews, while Aster pretended not to have even noticed. I would have paid more attention to deducing why, except that I was thrown by an unexpected guest of my own: one Freddy Spencer.

'Well, I helped deliver Dinah,' he explained, 'so it only seemed right.'

'Of course,' I said, suddenly scrabbling for something – anything – to say. 'It's . . . good to see you.'

Which it both was and wasn't. I can't explain it, but I felt somehow out of kilter with him. As if he no longer belonged here, as an Ickthorpe boy, but rather as a man out there in the world. Perhaps it was Venice. He had caught the sun even in April and, though not unattractive, it looked strange on him, almost painted-on.

'Your mother has invited me back for lunch,' he said then. 'I hope that's all right.'

'Of course,' I replied, rather too forcefully. 'Why wouldn't it be?'

'I just . . . It's good to see you.'

I nodded for want of reply. 'We'd best be off. Grandma doesn't tolerate lateness,' I said. 'Or much else, to be honest.'

Which was true. At that very second, she was lamenting the absence of Rapsey, who was supposed to collect her in the car directly after the service, at half twelve sharp, and it was twelve thirty-five at least and there was no sign of either man or motor.

Freddy laughed. 'She must struggle with a house of Mannerings.'

I wanted to snap at him for that, but then he broke into such a grin and the tan seemed to pale and he was Freddy again. Just plain old Freddy.

'She does.' I summoned a smile. 'I pity her. Still, let's do our best. It's a bit of a walk. But we'll beat her if we're brisk.'

It *is* a walk – past the shop and beady Mrs Gibberd, past Bridge House, where the doctor and Mrs Spencer took their leave (afternoon calls), over the bridge itself and then along the brimming river to the very gates of the Radley estate. It was tempting, then, to carry on, to stride back up to Radley and walk through the door as if it were mine by birthright. But the Dower House, or rather, the clatter of Rapsey, was calling. Quite literally.

'What on earth is it?' I asked. 'You look positively mortified.' Which he did. His face was red and sweating and his hair in wilder disarray than ever.

'It's that bleedin' sheep,' he declared. 'Made a run for it when I went to get the motor out, he did, and now he's clean gone.'

'That's hardly your fault,' I reassured. 'He's a beast. He does this all the time.'

'I don't think her ladyship will agree. Not when she finds out he's had the ham and the duchesse potatoes and all.'

'Ah, well, perhaps Mabel can manage some sandwiches for now,' I suggested. 'And in the meantime, Freddy and I will have a hunt for him. He can't have gone far. You fetch Grandma and

we'll head up the main house drive. Marigold and Valentine can help you check the garden again when they get back.'

'That was all terribly sensible of you,' said Freddy as we marched in the very direction I had hesitated to take only minutes earlier.

'You say that as if it's a surprise,' I replied.

'Well, perhaps it is,' he said. 'A little. The Panther of old would have sulked at sandwiches and made up an adventure for Siegfried instead of stopping him.'

'I may still be doing that for all you know,' I said. 'He's probably been captured by pirates. Or an errant collie dog who's herded him halfway to Larkham.'

'Touché,' said Freddy. 'I just meant . . . you're so very grown up. In a good way,' he added.

I didn't know what to say to that, so erred on nothing. Instead, we stamped on in companionable silence, across land as familiar to me as my own hands.

And what land! Acres of pasture, farm and garden, and across all of it spring had spread its benevolence: the trees in blossom, the drive flanked by daffs and bob-headed narcissi, the excitable sparrows almost heralding a welcome. Then, to the side of the manor, the flint and brick of the walled garden, behind which I knew would soon bloom lupin and larkspur, lilac and hyacinth. I only hoped whoever moved in had Daddy's green fingers.

It was then, at that very thought, that something rather

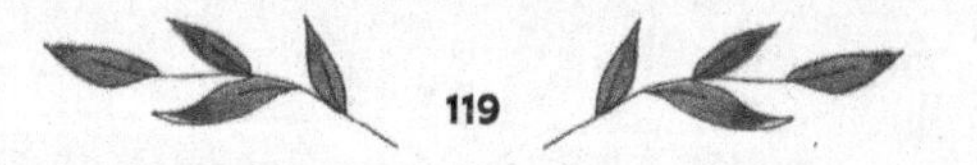

rum caught my eye. It was Radley itself. When we had left, the drapes had been drawn, everything shuttered to keep out the weather and intruders – man and mammal – but now the windows glinted and I could make out shapes in the rooms beyond: the ceiling-high bookcases in the library, the standard lamp in Daddy's study, and, in the drawing room, the chairs and chaises, which were no longer ghosted with white sheeting but newly velveted, it seemed, and readied for whomever might require seating.

'Freddy,' I said. 'Look.'

He took a moment to add it up, but then got it without prompting. 'Oh, Panther,' he said in tones of condolence. 'Well, I suppose it had to happen.'

'I'm perfectly fine,' I replied, as snappy as I could manage. 'It's a good thing. The house needs care, and whoever is coming must have money which, let's face it, we never did. Or not the sort that Radley requires.' I was blathering, and he knew it.

'Panth—'

'Don't,' I said then. 'You mustn't.'

And then the oddest thing happened. Freddy squeezed my arm. Just gently, and only momentarily, but the feel of it, the sweetness of it, brought tears brimming, and I had to wipe my eyes. 'The wind,' I said swiftly. Then, desperate, 'Come on. Siegfried *will* be halfway to Larkham if we don't hurry up.'

Freddy smiled. 'I bet he isn't. I bet I know exactly where he is.' And without waiting for my retort, set off towards the back lawn, where he dropped down the ha-ha and headed for the domed, stone building on the far side of the pond.

'The folly!' I called as I hurried after him. 'Of course.'

Each of us had claimed the absurd circular summerhouse at one time or another, playing 'house' by day and daring each other to sleep there by night. Pride prevented us from ever backing out, though Daddy sometimes had to come in with us to fend off tigers, or lions, or the wretched cat, who had a habit of slinking in then hovering at the edge of the bedding as if it might molest us at any moment. Aster and Daphne spent a whole weekend in there once, only coming back to the house to fetch provisions and for the lavatory. What they did all that time is a mystery. Conspiring, most likely.

Poor Aster, I thought. We'd all lost Daddy but she'd somehow misplaced Daphne too, while Marigold still had Bad Harry, and I, Margot.

And Freddy, it seemed.

'He's here,' he called. 'Siegfried, I mean.'

Of course he was there. Whoever had opened up the house must have left the folly door off the latch. I don't suppose they'd ever had marauding sheep to consider before.

'How did you know?' I asked.

'I didn't,' he said. 'I just thought about where I would go, if I wanted to hide on Radley land.'

'If you were a sheep?'

'Or a boy. Remember?'

I did remember, then. Hide and seek one summer, and I the first sardine in the folly, Freddy next, the pair of us waiting breathlessly for Aster and Daphne to find us, which they never did, distracted by something else, or each other. 'Too big for those games now, I suppose.'

'Never,' said Freddy. 'Though not sure I fancy camping out in here with him.'

'Good point,' I said. Then, to Siegfried, 'You wretch,' as Freddy threaded his neck tie into the jaunty dog collar we'd all mocked Marigold for at the time but now rather saw the point of.

Siegfried harrumphed in seeming disgust, and continued harrumphing on the long walk back to the Dower House, topping it off with a positively vicious bleat once he got back.

'Where on earth have you been?' demanded Grandma. 'You've missed luncheon. Not that *that* was anything to get excited about.' She stared pointedly towards the door, as if her very gaze might fell Mabel at twenty paces.

'We were fetching Siegfried,' I replied.

'Oh, good-oh,' said Marigold, which was less enthusiastic than I would have expected, given our endeavour.

'Didn't Rapsey say where we'd gone?' I added.

'He must have forgotten,' said Mama. 'Anyway, well done. Rapsey is far too old to be chasing sheep around.'

'He must be a hundred,' agreed Marigold. 'I hope I live to be a hundred.'

'I very much hope I don't,' said Aster, who was darning a stocking.

'And I,' said Grandma. 'And in any case, he's seventy-two and it gives him something to do. Otherwise he'd have to spend all day with Mrs Rapsey.'

Freddy and I exchanged glances that suggested Mrs Rapsey must be an absolute harridan if he chose Grandma above her.

'Where *was* he?' asked Mama.

'The folly,' I replied.

Aster snapped up, then looked swiftly down again when she saw I'd caught her.

I turned instead to Valentine, who was slumped at the piano, Hamilton seated resolutely on the fallboard, as if man wished to play but cat wished he would not. 'Has something happened at Radley?'

'Oh yes!' He revived brightly. 'I forgot to warn you. I've only gone and let the house!'

'To whom?' asked Grandma. Then, in a distinct tone of concern, 'Is he French?'

'Oh, even better. He's American.' Valentine smiled. 'So he'll find the cracks and the cold and the tricky plumbing all terribly quaint.'

'He hasn't seen it?' I asked.

'Oh, no.' Valentine shook his head. 'That's the trick, you see. I worked it out. You just tell someone, preferably someone drunk, that you've an enormous manor going for a song.

And you get them to shake on it then and there.'

Grandma made a face that bordered on the murderous. 'So who *is* he?'

'Oh yes, sorry. I met him at the Savoy. He's a friend of a friend.'

'What friend?' Grandma demanded.

'Topaz.'

'Who's Topaz?' snapped Aster.

'Topaz Attlesey,' he replied, as if everyone must know that.

'Wait,' I said, adding it all up. 'Topaz. Is she related to Brandon?'

'Sister,' said Valentine.

'Another wet, then, I assume,' said Aster.

'Hardly,' said Valentine. 'She's quite the gal.'

But I had allowed us to be diverted from the key point here. 'So who is *he*?'

'Oh, yes. He's arriving for Easter weekend, I think.'

'His name!' I practically yelled.

'Oh, yes. Buck something. Anyway, you won't know him,' Valentine dismissed. 'Not your circles.'

Yet, I thought. Then immediately felt something plummet in me. For this was it. While Radley had stood shuttered, though it was a waste, it was still staving off fate. And now? Now we had to face a future with someone else in our bedrooms, our kitchen, our morning room with the odd walls and the smelly carpet.

I grasped the back of the chaise. 'I think I might have to lie down,' I said.

'Are you quite all right?' asked Freddy. 'Shall I fetch my father?' He thought for a moment. 'Or my stethoscope? I could—'

'No,' I said quickly. 'It's all the walking. I'll be right as rain later.'

And I left before he, or anyone, could check me over or change my mind, and am now lying in Aster's canopied bed (mine has a rabbit in, and I dread to think what else) wondering when, or indeed if, I will ever be quite 'right' again.

10 P.M.

Mama came up in the end and had one of her 'talks', telling me only what I had told myself earlier: that it *had* to happen, and it was for the best, for Radley, anyway. But sometimes one needs to hear one's thoughts and words echoed back from those wiser than oneself. And Mama is so terribly wise. As wise as Daddy, if not more so, for she is here, and he is . . . not.

But I have mustered, and not a minute too late because Aster then stamped in and demanded I get out of her bed that instant on pain of torture.

I suspected that would involve the cello so I moved swiftly, if only to the door.

'I wish you'd tell me what happened with Daphne,' I said

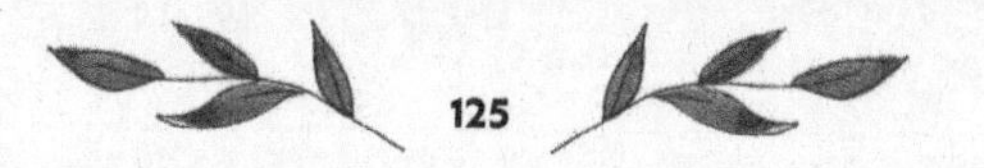

then, summoning wise Mama, as well as the sensible Panther that Freddy had seen in me.

Aster flounced back on the bed, her hair fanning out as if she were Millais' own drowning Ophelia. 'Well, I shan't,' she said. Then, softer, 'I can't.'

'You can,' I insisted. 'You can tell me anything. If it's about Nigel, if you're jealous, then perhaps I can even help with finding someone else. I'm going to be a matchmaker,' I added for clarification.

'Nigel?' She snorted. 'I'm not jealous of Nigel! At least, not in the way you think.'

She then proceeded to remind me that Emma is not at all a favourable character on which to base my endeavours. She said if I were to reread the novel with my eyes wide open rather than blinded by romance, I would notice that Emma is a horrible snob who is caught out by her terrible meddling in the end. What's more, she is so short-sighted she almost loses out on the love of her childhood friend.

I don't know what she is trying to imply, but I am neither blinded by romance nor short-sighted, and I am certainly not a snob. If anyone is stuck-up, it is Aster, who is still determined not to darken the door of the Balfour wedding, this time citing 'frightful socialites' as her reason for evasion. They, of course, are the exact reason I am desperate to attend. Otherwise, the closest we ever get is Evangeline Balfour, who is as hideously irritating as she is beautiful, and Valentine, who hardly counts.

And, as for losing out on the love of my childhood friend, that is ludicrous. Freddy has never shown an ounce of interest in me romantically. It is all 'purpose' this, and 'calling' that and 'oh, you're all so grown up these days'. And, besides, how on earth can one fall for someone who has seen them dance a jig in their underpants aged seven? No, it is Margot whom I have in mind for him. If only briefly – as brief is all Margot ever musters. And as for me, perhaps I shall become a spinster.

Or perhaps – I have just thought of it – there will be something in this 'Buck'. Though if he is an acquaintance of Valentine, one has to expect the very worst, or at least assume he's of the Greek persuasion. And, much as it would amuse me to horrify Grandma, it doesn't help my plight to save the family fortune in the slightest.

FRIDAY 18 APRIL

Good Friday

9 P.M.

For once, the fates have smiled upon a Mannering. Either that or there is some sort of god, and one who is not at all deterred by bad language and unladylike behaviour. Though I am inclined towards the former, as they are women after all, and therefore more apt to be forgiving, unless they are Grandma, who could take a grudge to her grave. Anyway, the point is, there *was* something in Buck.

No: *is* something.

Something rather extraordinary. So extraordinary I don't quite know where to begin. Except, perhaps at the beginning.

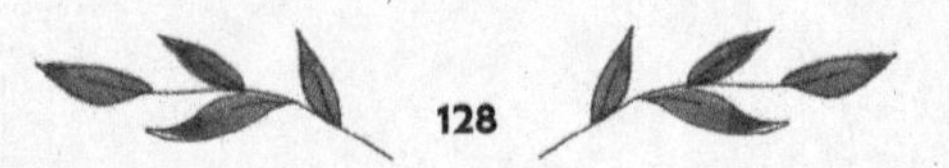

The day started an ordinary one, or at least as ordinary as days can be in the Mannering household: Mama occupied with Dinah's teething, which is keeping her and several of us up at night; Marigold occupied with Bad Harry and rabbits, and keeping them out of the reaches of Grandma and Hamilton (who were occupying each other with hard stares); and Aster occupied with who knows what.

Lunch was fish soup and a terrine, mercifully lacking aspic, with the promise of hot cross buns later for Margot, who arrived as planned on the 3.20 from Liverpool Street.

'Ickthorpe's awfully small,' she declared as Rapsey and I hauled her luggage (so very much of it: four valises and two hat boxes and she's only here until Monday) into the car. 'Far smaller than I remember.'

'You were ten, then,' I said (she had not returned to Radley since being thrown from Socks and landing in the brook, much to Mrs Forbes-Rawlinson's mortification; she was convinced Margot might be trampled on by cows or catch pneumonia and die, and so we have been, until recently, firmly out of bounds).

'Was I? I can't imagine I was ever ten,' she said. 'But I suppose I must have been.'

'I don't suppose you remember Freddy from then?' I said.

'Freddy?' she echoed.

'Spencer?'

'Oh, yes, you mentioned him! No. Definitely not. Though I do remember a drip of a thing hanging off Aster all the time.'

'Daphne,' I replied. 'Balfour.'

This elicited a string of questions. 'That was Daphne Balfour? The one engaged to Pakesy? Evangeline's big sis?'

'The very one.'

'Lucky Daphne. Pakesy's a bit of bore but Evangeline's a hoot! She's the queen of the spoof. Do you know she got herself into Novello's bedroom at the Ritz pretending to interview him for *The Sketch*!'

'Novello? The composer? Gosh,' I said, for want of anything better.

'And of course she won the scavenger hunt.'

'Scavenger hunt?'

'Oh yes! Didn't I tell you? We had one around St James's. It was all brilliantly thrilling. We had to fetch a dog, and a policeman's helmet, and a door plaque from an embassy.'

I tried to imagine such a hunt here. Us gallivanting round the village in pursuit of what? Ralph the post boy's hat? Mrs Gibberd would have our guts for garters. All of which only goes to highlight the desperate chasm between life in London and here in Ickthorpe. I hoped she wouldn't be so disappointed she failed to repay the favour.

'Where's Marigold?' she asked then. 'I thought she'd come.'

'Oh, in the village somewhere. Her and Bad Harry have taken to being detectives. They're determined to solve a murder.'

'What murder?'

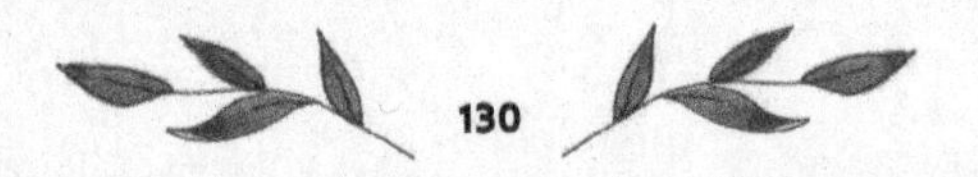

'Precisely. I rather think they're hoping to stumble upon one. Preferably the Launceston twins.' Though possibly their own if they start snooping around Mrs Gibberd's shop. 'Come on,' I said then. 'You can meet her later. And Freddy. Oh, and Valentine. He arrived not long before I left. Must have caught the train before. He's wearing the most ludicrous hat.'

Which he was. It was black and feathered and pulled so far down his head as to look as if a dead cormorant were nesting there.

'Hello, Val,' said Margot as we bustled in, as if they were old pals. 'Why on earth are you wearing that?'

'You know each other?'

'Oh, everyone knows each other in London,' Margot replied, delighted. 'So, what is it? Have you sprouted a second head?'

'What's wrong with it?' demanded Valentine. 'Anyway, it's all I could find.'

'But it's not even cold out,' said Aster. 'And you're indoors now. It's rude not to remove it.'

'That's church,' said Valentine, clamping a hand down on the cormorant.

'What's going on?' Grandma demanded. 'You're behaving awfully queer. Queerer even than usual,' she added pointedly. 'Take the thing off, for heaven's sake.'

At that, Valentine, solemn as he is tall, sighed and removed the hat to reveal a head of canary-yellow hair. Hair that should be, and had been until recently, the colour of pitch.

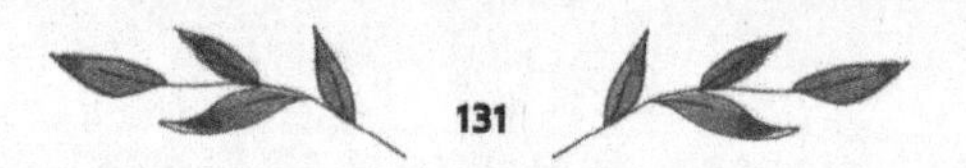

Grandma snorted. Hamilton (incredibly, on her lap, like a witch's familiar) hissed.

'Whatever possessed you?' asked Mama.

'It was for an audition,' he said defensively.

'Who are you playing?' asked Aster. 'Tallulah Bankhead?'

'Oh, ha ha,' Valentine retorted, then visibly slumped. 'Oh, God, it's awful, isn't it? I tried boot-blacking it, but that just got everywhere.'

'Not a one of you with any sense,' declared Grandma at that. 'Where you all inherited this idiocy from is a mystery.'

It is not at all mysterious. Both Daddy and Uncle James, Valentine's father, were prone to hare-brained schemes. It was only lack of funds, and then life, that prevented them indulging further.

'I can fix it,' came a voice from the corner.

We all turned to see Mabel hovering in the doorway, a plate of buns on a tray (the silver, now the gilt has been indelibly stained with dead rabbit).

'And who are you, you delightful creature?' asked Valentine, in an act of excessive generosity, as I feel safe in saying Mabel will never have been described as delightful in her life, particularly not in this household.

'Mabel,' she explained in unimpressed monotone.

'My cook,' Grandma clarified, then added, with a sigh, 'and housemaid.'

'And I does her hair,' Mabel blurted. 'Don't I?'

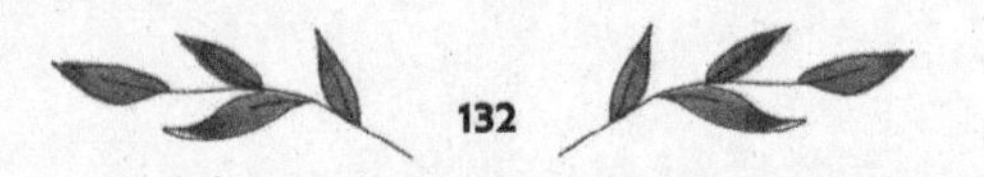

Grandma raised an eyebrow, but patted her pewter-grey coils. 'She does.'

'I used to work in a salon, I did. In Stepney.'

'What on earth made you come here then?' asked Mama.

'I thought I'd get to see some glamour, miss. What with her' – she nodded at Grandma – 'being a Lady.'

Grandma shuddered.

'Oh dear. How very disappointed you must be,' I said.

Mabel did not disagree.

Anyway, the upshot was that, within an hour, Valentine had been transformed, his hair both trimmed and, if not restored to its former inky glory, at least a more acceptable shade of brunette. And cut rather dashingly as well.

'Incredible,' declared Margot.

'Why, thank you,' said Mabel, in a voice the very echo of the one that addressed her. 'Oh, lawks, sorry,' she blurted quickly. 'I didn't mean no offence.'

Margot gaped. 'None taken. That is quite extraordinary.'

'Extraordinary,' agreed Grandma, frowning.

'Quite,' said Valentine, his face distant and thinking. Then, suddenly coming to. 'Oh, cripes, I've just realised the time. I have to go.'

'Where to?' I asked. Then, suddenly wondering, 'Why are you even here?'

'Didn't I say?' Valentine frowned. 'I'm meeting the new tenant.'

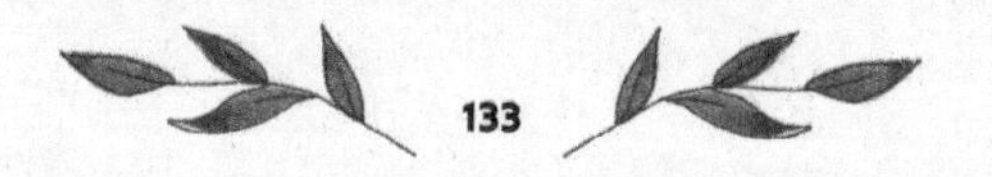

'Oh!' I exclaimed. 'Can we come?'

'Oh, yes,' agreed Margot. 'Can we, Val?'

Valentine seemed to pale. 'Absolutely not,' he insisted. 'I don't want to put him off.'

'Well, he's bound to meet us sooner or later,' I pointed out.

'The later, the better,' said Valentine, but kindly this time. Then disappeared off in a cloud of cologne and hair chemicals, leaving us to await our now severely delayed tea.

'I suppose someone had better fetch Marigold back,' Mama said then. 'Perhaps she can bring Harry now that we're one less for buns?'

Or someone else, I thought. And, struck with a sudden idea, or several of them, I spoke up. 'We'll go.' I nudged Margot.

'Will we?' asked Margot.

'Absolutely,' I said, ushering her towards the door. 'It's such a nice day.'

'Is it?' asked Margot doubtfully (she is not one for the great outdoors, unless it is cream tea on a Kensington terrace. Mrs Forbes-Rawlinson's paranoia has seen to that).

'Yes, come on.'

'Why the urgency?' said Margot as we scurried back into Ickthorpe. 'What's going on?'

'Freddy,' I said.

'Freddy?'

'Spencer,' I said. 'Remember. From my letter?'

'Oh yes! The scholar. And practically an orphan. How

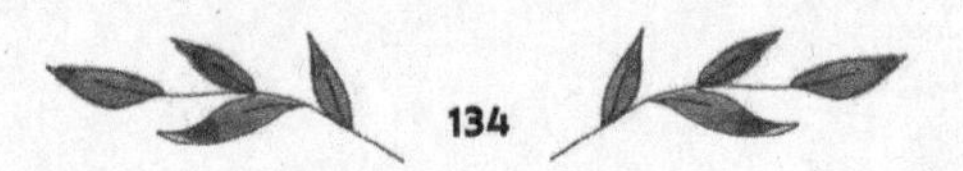

frightfully romantic!'

He was no more orphan than I, plus he had a wonderful stepmother, but I didn't correct her.

Margot fished for more information. 'Is he terribly dashing?' she asked.

'Oh, yes,' I said. 'Terribly.'

'Divine! And tall?'

That I could confirm without crossing my fingers this time. 'Terribly tall.'

This continued for several minutes until we arrived at Bridge House and I rapped on the door, bolder than I could have imagined, and crossing my fingers again, this time in hope that Freddy hadn't already had buns, or at least could manage another.

But when the door opened, it revealed not Freddy nor any other Spencer, but Marigold.

'What on earth?' I asked.

'Oh, hullo!' she said, quite sing-song. 'We're detecting.'

'I'm so sorry,' I said, as Freddy, followed by Bad Harry, finally appeared in the hallway. 'Have they been bothering you?'

'Not at all,' said Freddy generously. 'Father has been showing them bones. Real ones.'

'An actual dead person!' exclaimed Marigold, with hardly less delight and wonder than if she'd seen a live flamingo.

'And on Good Friday,' said Margot, speaking at last.

'Hello,' said Freddy. 'We haven't met.'

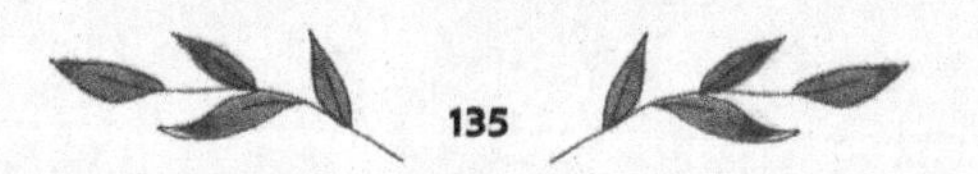

'Oh, you have,' I said. 'But she was ten and you eleven and neither of you will remember.'

'Not a jot,' admitted Margot. 'But hullo now.' This with less enthusiasm than I had hoped, though I put that down to the talk of bones and bodies.

'Anyway, come along, Marigold, it's tea. And Freddy, too, if you'd like?' I mustered as much nonchalance as I could. 'Just that we've spare now Valentine is gadding about at Radley.'

'Well, how can I resist an offer like that?' he replied. 'Let me fetch my coat. Pa can drop Harry home.'

And then, my plan working like magic, we were all walking home-ward, I with Marigold, and Freddy with Margot, by dint more of pavement width than design, but fortuitous nonetheless.

Marigold blathered happily about skulls and sockets and orbs, while I tried my hardest to ignore the macabre and listen in on Margot and Freddy, desperately hoping to have kindled some sort of connection already. Sadly, any flicker of desire was very much not taking. At least not yet. Instead, Margot was regaling her would-be suitor with stories of school, and my apparent habit of getting stuck in the stock cupboard (the door locked on closing and I always forgot to stop it open. Once I was trapped in there for several hours. I had even considered the indignity of using a paint pot as an emergency lavatory; private and painful information, which Margot, it seemed, was only too happy to share).

'Do you have to?' I swung round.

'Oh, it's charming,' said Freddy.

'Hardly,' I said.

'Resourceful, then,' he countered. 'Egg is always resorting to bottles when the lavs are occupied. I think he actually prefers it.'

'I weed in the sink once at Radley,' said Marigold. 'When Aster was in our lav and Mama's was blocked.'

'It wasn't blocked,' I said. 'It was tricky. And no one needs to know that anyway. Can we all stop talking about toilets?'

'What shall we discuss, then?' asked Margot. 'Oh, how about the Balfour wedding? Are you going? I'm not invited, bad luck. But you must report back with all the news of who's wearing what. You can be my personal *Tatler*.'

'I shall be wearing a sack at any rate,' I said. 'I don't suppose *The Tatler* will want to feature that.'

'Oh, I don't know,' said Freddy. 'I rather think—'

But I never got to hear what Freddy thought about me or the sack or *The Tatler*, because at that very moment an open-roofed motor car – silver and glinting – careened around the corner, perilously close to the kerb. So close, in fact, that Freddy was compelled to snatch me back as if I might be injured (not Margot, I noted with disappointment, though perhaps only because she was closer to the wall).

Even more surprising was the car's contents: in the passenger seat, Valentine, his hat abandoned, but his face the very picture of alarm; in the driver's seat, a man whom I had never seen before. Swept-back blond (of the real kind), a silk scarf that billowed behind him, and, pasted on his chiselled face, a smile that could charm the dead.

'Goodness,' I managed.

'Who on earth was that?' demanded Margot.

'That was Valentine,' I said. 'And someone I don't know—'

'Thaddeus Buchanan,' said Freddy, his voice painted with undisguised disdain.

'That's Buck Buchanan?' gasped Margot.

'Buck!' I exclaimed, remembering what Valentine had said about the tenant. 'And you know him?'

'Everyone knows Buck,' said Margot. 'He's infamous!'

'Even you?' I turned to Freddy.

'Unfortunately, yes,' said a pained Freddy. 'He was at Magdalen. Left last year with a poor degree and an even poorer reputation. But' – and at this, he even sneered – 'a wealth of notoriety. Incredible he wasn't sent down. Though I suppose it helps if your father is the Baron of Fleet Street.'

'Not a proper one,' said Margot. 'On account of being American.' Then, discarding *Debrett's* temporarily. 'But he's still rich.'

'Wildly,' confirmed Freddy. 'Though at the rate Buck spends it, it surely can't last forever.'

'He's a catch, anyway.' Margot practically swooned.

'A cad, more like,' countered Freddy.

'Oh, you're just jealous,' she chanted with a laugh, and danced after Marigold, who was chasing the car towards Radley as fast as she could go, leaving Freddy and I to plod back to the Dower House in silence, and not of the companionable kind this time.

His mood hardly lifted as, once back, all the talk at tea was of this Buck.

Marigold and Margot had failed to catch them, as the car had not returned to Radley after all – it had doubled back in a terrific spin towards the station (assumedly to drop Valentine off for the 5.45 – but that didn't stop the pair imagining they knew every small thing about him).

'He looked like God,' said Marigold.

'Don't talk nonsense,' said Mama.

'God has a beard,' I pointed out.

'Does She?' said Aster, only exasperating matters.

'Well, he's not a god, exactly,' said Margot. 'Rather a devil in fact. I hear he once trashed a suite at the Savoy. Just because he could!'

'Imagine having that much money,' I pondered idly.

'Imagine having that little sense,' said Freddy decisively.

And so it went on, all through buns and tea, served by Mama as Mabel had been let off early to meet Ralph as recompense for her hairdressing services earlier and Rapsey was otherwise occupied with securing Siegfried, who had spent the day, unbeknownst to all, in Mama's bedroom making his merry way through a drawer of socks. So that, when the bell went, it was I who stood up.

'I'll go, shall I?'

Aster eyed me. 'Well, you hover around the door in the morning as if expecting a prince to deliver the post, so surely you can do it now?'

I reddened, but arguing would only have worsened the matter given Freddy's presence. And so off I stomped, cross with Margot's disinterest in Freddy, and my own burgeoning one in Buck.

'Hang on,' I called as I wrestled with the handle. 'It gets stuck sometimes.' I put my body weight behind it and hauled, just as the person on the other side of the door must have leaned into it, hoping to be of help, but instead sending us both sprawling into the hallway as the door flung open.

And then, to add to my embarrassment, when we managed to stand whom should I be faced with but Thaddeus Buchanan himself.

'Buck!' I blurted.

The man frowned. 'Yeah, I . . . Sorry, do I know you?'

'God, no. I'm just . . .' What was I? Who was I? I'd lost all reason, floored by that accent, that hair, those teeth! 'I live here.'

'Well, I'm sorry to bother you. But can I speak to the— God, what do you guys call it? The master?'

'Master?'

'Or mistress? Your boss,' he added, as if that would explain.

It explained more than he realised.

'Oh, heavens.' I felt my face redden with shame. 'You mean

my grandmother. I'm . . . I'm not . . . staff. I'm a Mannering. Valentine is my cousin.'

'Oh, Jeez.' In his defence, he looked genuinely pained. 'I'm so sorry. It's the . . .' He gestured at my dress, as well he might.

But ashamed though I was, I wasn't cross. I could have forgiven him anything at that moment, even treason or possibly murder. 'You're not the first,' I said. 'And I doubt you'll be the last, not at this rate. Anyway, she's gone for a lie-down. Can I help?'

At this, Buck pinked a little. 'It's kind of embarrassing,' he said.

'We Mannerings rarely get embarrassed,' I assured him. 'We can't afford it.'

'Okay,' said Buck. 'Here goes nothing.' He took a breath. 'You know that lavatory off that red bedroom? I can't seem to get it to flush.'

'Oh, I see,' I said, now flaming as scarlet as Mama's old wallpaper. Why had I offered to help? Why couldn't I, for once, have kept my mouth firmly shut? And yet, I was about to blurt again. 'The trick is, you must pull the chain hard and fast, but hold it there for exactly two seconds. Then let go boldly and Bob's your uncle.'

'Bob's what?'

'Your uncle?' I flustered. 'Never mind. It's an English thing. Silly, really.'

'I see. Well, much obliged. I don't suppose you'd know where I can get a guy to do these kind of jobs in future?'

'You don't have . . . people?'

'I had someone to open up, supply furniture and things. And I have a valet,' he said triumphantly, as if he'd produced a rabbit from a hat. 'But he's from Chelsea. He's as much at sea as I am out here in the boondocks.'

'The where?'

'The boondocks. You know, full of devils and rednecks.'

I felt a sharp prick of shame to add to my embarrassment. Was that us? Rednecks? 'I –' I began.

But Buck interrupted. 'I'm sorry, I didn't mean—'

'It's quite all right. Just that we're not used to hiring servants, only having to let them go. But you could place an ad,' I said then, 'in *The Lady*. Or in the window at Gibberd's in the village,' I added, remembering Cook's success. Then, suddenly emboldened, seizing on an opportunity as if it were a gold chalice, 'But until then, you could just call here. By telephone, I mean. The number's Ickthorpe seven-nine-nine.'

'I would' – Buck smiled, and I swear I had to stop myself sighing out loud – 'but the wire seems to have been eaten?'

'Oh gosh. That'll have been Siegfried,' I said. 'Or rabbits, perhaps.'

'Rabbits?'

'It's another English thing,' I said quickly, rather than have to admit it was far more of a Mannering thing.

'I'll get it fixed then,' he said, as he backed towards the door. 'Or get a man to.'

I nodded.

'But, thanks for now,' he said, then waited, expectantly.

I gaped, as gormless as a fish.

'Your name?' he prompted. 'Or shall I just call you Miss Mannering?'

'Oh! That's Panther,' I declared, missing the chance to rename myself something sensible, or even alluring.

'Really?'

'Well, not exactly. But it's what everyone calls me.'

He paused in thought, before a grin as wide as the Nile but twice as enticing spread across his face. 'Well, I think "Baby" suits you better. Perhaps I should just call you that.'

At that moment he could have called me any name he wanted – Damson or Dobbin or even, dare I say it, the one I was christened with. 'Perhaps you should,' I replied daringly.

'Fine. Goodbye then, Baby.'

'Goodbye, Buck,' I said, barely managing to disguise my sigh.

Then, thank heaven for the solidity of the Dower House door, for I swear I practically fell on it.

Because Buck is everything I could have imagined in a man and more. I was right, there *is* something about him. Something dangerous almost. But he's been to Cambridge so he must be clever as well, whatever Freddy says. And, as Margot pointed out, Freddy's probably just jealous because he doesn't have half of Buck's money or charm. 'Buck': even the name conjures a Regency leading man. Why, he's a living, breathing Willoughby! A highwayman! A sheikh!

So now I lie in my twin bed, Margot snoring in Marigold's (Marigold has been sequestered to share with Mabel, about which she is wildly enthusiastic, and Mabel less so), not wishing away the spring months as I have done on so many evenings, nor imagining myself in London or Venice or indeed anywhere but dreary Ickthorpe, but, rather, wondering what glories they will hold.

Yes, this is going to be quite the season, I think.

And, what's more, right here at Radley.

So that, for the first time, I'm thankful to be poor, glad to be a girl. For if not, Buck would never have come.

And I would never have fallen hopelessly, irrevocably in love.

MAY

THURSDAY 1 MAY

11 A.M.

I am utterly lovelorn. It has been almost two weeks (twelve days, eighteen hours and forty-two minutes to be precise) and there has not been one smidgen of a sign of Buck since he departed the Dower House doorstep to fix the sticky lavatory at Radley. It is almost as if he never existed – was naught but a phantom or an apparition conjured by my own desperation. I almost wish he was – at least then there may be an excusable reason for his absence. As it is, there have been all manner of comings and goings at the manor – motorcars and small lorries and red-faced Ralph on his bicycle – all of which I am party to, what with our bedroom window overlooking the drive, but not once have I caught more than a glimpse of his shimmering

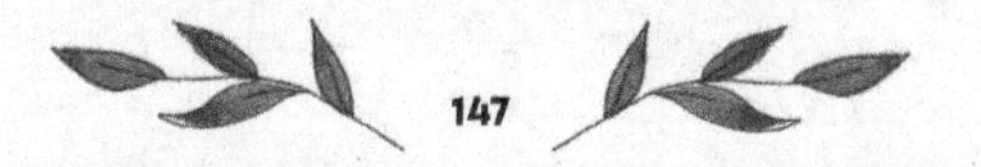

hair as it passes at speed with some unnameable passenger hooting with delight beside him. At the risk of sounding like a stamping six year old, I would like to hoot at whatever it is that is so very thrilling.

Aster, being Aster, says it is not love, it is infantile infatuation, borne out by the fact that I am not the only one going gaga for him. For a start, Marigold and Harry have moved him to the top of their rankings and he has now completely replaced Reg in their affections. They have been begging to go to the house on myriad deliveries – roses, Mabel's biscuits, a baby rabbit – and, more than once, Marigold has, I suspect, deliberately 'mislaid' Siegfried. Thankfully, Rapsey is back on sheep-rumbling form and has managed to extricate him from whatever bramble Marigold has stored him behind before she can march up the drive, haul on the bell, and embarrass us all.

As if that weren't enough, Margot is similarly smitten. Her three days here at Easter were spent on long, determined country walks and indulging a hitherto undeclared interest in Georgian architecture, of which, she pointed out, Radley is a prime example. I reminded her I had never once before heard her volunteer for a hike. In fact, I recalled her declaring she was practically allergic to exercise and the 'great outdoors', far preferring the comfort of indoor activity. She insisted it was all part of her new plan to be healthy, but the crimson of her cheeks suggested my initial assumptions were correct. Though I did not deny her, for of course I, too, was experiencing a sudden pressing need to tramp the manor grounds and stare at length at Radley's symmetrical fenestration.

'Of course, Freddy is an excellent prospect,' I tried on one such ambulation.

'Hardly.' Margot sniffed, before adding, 'He lacks glamour. All that earnest concern.'

I did not tell her this mirrored my own dismissal. Instead, I ploughed blithely on. 'But he's a solid sort. Terribly kind, and ever so clever.'

Margot stopped, all the better to take in Radley's transom window and side gables. 'Freddy is all very well,' she said. 'But he hasn't a motorcar, can't drive even if he had, and he's practically trade.'

'He's a doctor!' I protested. 'Or at least, he will be.'

'Precisely. I don't want someone who *does* something. I want someone who *is* something.'

Buck is something. Though what, I am not yet sure.

Perhaps I shall find out later, for we are off to Ickthorpe village green to watch Marigold and Harry dance gaily around the maypole with the rest of Mrs Bottomley's lot. I say 'gaily', though if Marigold's practice is anything to go by it will be leaden stamping accompanied by a frown of concentration and a metronome declaration of 'under, over, under over' until everyone is dizzy and quite sick of it all.

But, no, I must not allow pessimism to cloud this otherwise unblemished spring morning. There is something in the air –

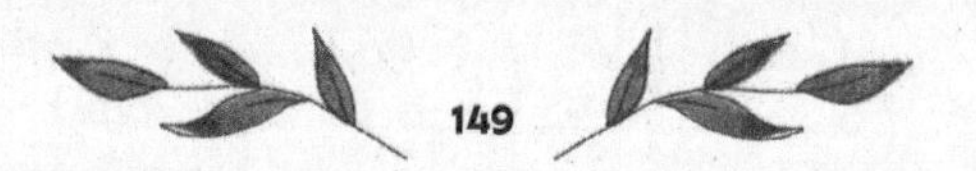

a tingle, or a mischievous jinking, like the hares on the hill up to Badger's Copse. And, more than that, my dress is pressed and relatively unstained, my hair is as tamed as it can get, and Margot is safely several score miles away at the Glasshouse Street apartment so cannot steal what thunder I may muster when Buck appears on the green, as surely he must. Yes, this will be a May Day to remember; one to tell Daddy about when we visit him. The anniversary of his passing is coming up in a few weeks, but I shall not dwell on that either. Not now, not yet. Today must be wonderful, I have decreed it!

4 P.M.

I honestly have no earthly idea why I thought decreeing something might make it so. I have no special powers of any sort, not to engender any kind of festival at any rate. Heavens, I can't even enforce decorum, not where Mannerings are involved.

It did not help matters that Grandma had decided that it was high time she accompanied us on an outing.

'What on earth for?' asked Aster, as well she might, for Grandma has not engaged in anything involving the village since before Grandpa died, on the grounds of 'germs'. The germs being of an unspecified and mainly imaginary nature. Rather more, she believes the villagers to be so far beneath her as to be practically animals, which, aside from the spitting Reg

Nesbitt, is horribly harsh and absolutely untrue.

'I need some air,' Grandma declared. 'Is there something suddenly wrong with that?'

'Not at all,' Mama admitted, though her tone suggested even she was hedging on the true purpose of Grandma's sudden calling.

'Good,' snapped Grandma. 'Rapsey will drive me and . . .' – she scoured the room as if picking a victim, rather akin to Hamilton surveying the hapless rabbits – 'you.' She pointed at me, and I felt my insides sink a little. 'The rest of you will walk, of course. It's such a nice day, after all.'

'Of course,' agreed Mama. 'Panther?'

'Of course.' I tried not to sigh, though what hope for an illicit rendezvous with Buck if I was to be in charge of a cantankerous septuagenarian and her cat, whom she insisted would be perfectly happy on her lap throughout proceedings, despite both my and Rapsey's protestations?

Hamilton was, of course, not in any way content to remain in Grandma's vicinity, let alone on her lap for any longer than a minute, and so Rapsey had to be dismissed to trail it wherever it may wander, lest it got lost or a 'commoner' took a fancy to it. Hardly likely, I thought, for who but Grandma could warm to the creature, or it to her? Which she swiftly went on to highlight by deriding every single villager who happened to wander too close to our shooting chairs. Mrs Gatwood was dismissed for being childless, despite not one but two husbands (the first died in the war, the second – his brother – of flu just months after the wedding, which was, disappointingly for Grandma, and assumedly for Mrs Gatwood, not shotgun after all). Celia Rigby's crime was smoking in the street, on top of which her heels were declared too high and her hats too vast. Whereas Joyce Goggins' only fault was that she remained Welsh despite ample opportunity to mend her accent and ways.

On the plus side, we managed to miss most of the maypole dancing, which was, as predicted, less than gay, though for once this was not entirely down to Marigold or even Bad Harry but to the Launceston twins. The terrible pair seem to have taken this opportunity to wreak revenge on Marigold for her declared sole ownership of Badger's Copse by determining to twine her in the ribbons so that she became the thing which they danced around, flailing like a trapped beetle or pinioned insect. It took Mrs Bottomley a good ten minutes to unravel her, and a further five to discuss Marigold's language with Mama, which, Mrs Bottomley declared, was more suited to a brewery boy than a young lady of breeding.

That, however, was not the last of the Launcestons. And I am beginning now to see why Marigold detests them so very much. For, within minutes of the maypole misdemeanour, they came rambling back to Grandma and I, bearing aloft an oddly contrite Hamilton and followed by flapping Rapsey.

'I couldn't stop 'em, ma'am,' he explained. 'They said it was theirs by right.'

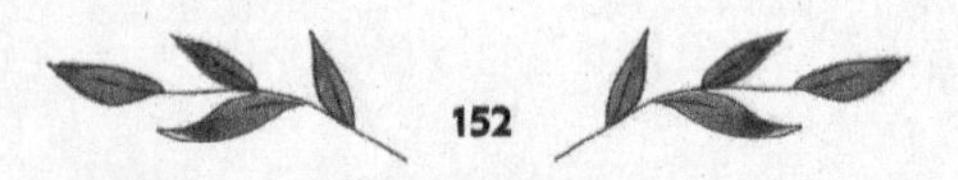

'What is theirs by right?' demanded Grandma, reaching for her cat, who remained glued to Hugo (at least I think it was Hugo; they are hard to tell apart. According to Marigold, Hugo's nose is fatter from the time she punched it, and this boy did have a fat nose).

'Bruce,' said the boy.

'Who on earth is Bruce?' demanded Grandma.

'She is,' said the other twin, Julian, jabbing the cat with no heed for his own fingers.

'She?' Grandma bore a look of complete perplexity. 'That' – she jabbed at the cat herself, though with the presence of mind to keep her hand several inches away – 'is Hamilton, and *he* is a *boy*.'

'Girl,' said Julian.

'Well, that's that,' said Grandma, 'because you can't call a girl Bruce.' As if that were the issue at stake here.

'Well you can and we did and she's ours.'

'If she's yours, why has she been living at the manor for over a year and the Dower House since?' I demanded, uncharacteristically backing Grandma, who, for once, was suffering through no fault of her own.

'I'll fight you for her,' declared Marigold, back from her trappings and telling off, and chewing some sort of rock cake with an air of grim determination that suggested Cook may have been behind it.

'No one need fight anyone,' said Mama, desperate, no

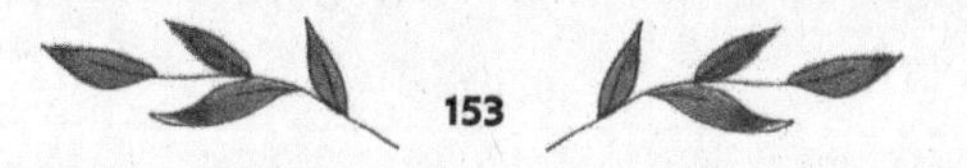

doubt, to keep Marigold in check, at least in public.

'Quite right,' said Grandma, 'because the cat is mine.'

'Mine,' shouted the Launcestons simultaneously, Hugo squeezing the creature so tightly I thought he might lose an eye to add to his once-injured nose.

'You could test it,' I said quickly.

Grandma looked dubious.

Aster, who had been regarding the whole charade with absolute disgust, rolled her eyes heavenward, though I have no idea why as she believes it entirely empty. 'How, pray, do you imagine you might do that?'

I thought quickly. 'Put it— I mean, her, in the middle of a circle,' I said, 'and see which way she decides to go.'

'*He* will come to *me*,' declared Grandma. As if she had any more control over a cat than I had over the Mannering family.

'Or me,' said Marigold, not wishing to be left out of any animal shenanigans.

'Or me,' said Hugo, glaring at his ten-year-old nemesis. Julian nodded in menacing approval.

'Go on, then,' said Aster. 'Prove it.'

Persuaded, Hugo put Hamilton/Bruce in the centre of a vague shape set out by spare sweaters and Dinah's blanket and Marigold's hat and then, baited breath, we all waited for it to decide its true ownership. Of course, being a cat, it regarded all parties with disdain and walked off in the general direction of Mr Gibberd, at which point Rapsey snatched her.

Anyway, the upshot is, Grandma agreed to pay Hugo and Julian two shillings each (or rather Mama had to pay them, as Grandma does not carry money on the grounds it is undignified for women to concern themselves with finances) so she can keep the cat, who is back to being Hamilton, and a boy, despite the Launcestons yanking up 'his' tail and pointing out the absence of 'knackers'.

All I can say is thank heavens Buck was not there to witness any of that. It could only concern him further as to my suitability. Only Freddy, inured to such absurdity and spectacle where we Mannering girls are concerned, could have borne it with fortitude. Though his tolerance for Marigold and Grandma is quite unfathomable. His tolerance in general, in fact. He sees the good in everything and everyone.

Except Buck, now I come to think of it. How very queer. For Buck seems the very advertisement of a man. You would not catch him making bets over a cat's provenance or inspecting it for testicles, of that I am certain.

On the plus side, Mama had no more money with which to buy the rest of us rock buns so our teeth were spared at least. And who knows what will happen tomorrow – it is an entirely new day, after all. And if not, then there's always the day after that, and the day after that, and the day after that. Because it's not as if I have anything else to do but wait around for someone to notice me. However long it takes.

SUNDAY 4 MAY

2 P.M.

The days are tocking solemnly on and still no Buck. But at least I have something else to occupy my waking hours, though one could hardly describe at as 'purpose': Mama's birthday is just weeks away and we have no means for a proper present and no earthly idea how to raise them. So pressing is this dilemma that I was forced to call a Mannering Meeting – that is, Aster, Marigold and I – to discuss an urgent plan of action.

At Radley, these infrequent summits were held in the morning room, where no adults had dared tread since Siegfried had been installed in there in a particularly drenching storm and chewed through the wiring, causing a minor explosion and some singeing to both Siegfried and the drapes. Here, with

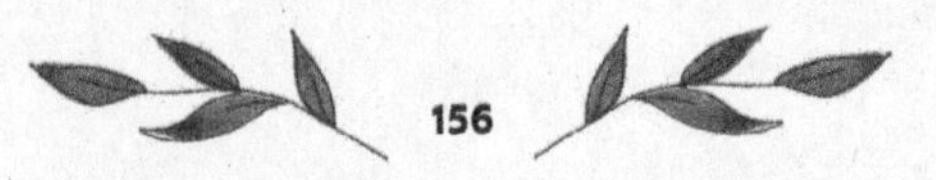

Grandma ever-present in the drawing room like a sort of awful, all-hearing schoolmistress, Mama and Dinah in the small parlour where Dinah cannot be seen or heard by Grandma, and Mabel liable to pop up in either at any moment, we are forced to resort to Aster's bedroom. Marigold was all for the airing cupboard to add an air of subterfuge, but having tested it Aster declared it cramped and 'rabbity'.

'Well, being eldest, I shall chair, obviously,' announced Aster, from the throne of the four-poster.

'Eldest doesn't mean most suitable,' said Marigold with an air of sulk that rendered her argument almost immediately obsolete. Though I have to say I agreed with her – one only has to compare flighty, pliable Margot with the far more dependable, tennis-playing Deborah to see the truth of that.

'Perhaps we should toss for it,' I suggested, mindful of keeping the peace lest Mama or, worse, Grandma, should be summoned by any racket.

'You can't toss a coin three ways,' Aster pointed out.

'Straws, then,' said Marigold, still angling for position.

'Oh, for heaven's sake, can we just get on with it?' snapped Aster.

It was clear her already bleak disposition could darken swiftly and so neither of us replied, rather awaited further instruction with ruffled impatience.

'Right. Whoever has funds must declare them now,' Aster began. 'And I mean all funds. Not just the ones you're willing to give up.'

At that, I bristled, for, though I had my shillings saved from *The Tatler*, I had been hoping to spend them on notepaper for the novel as I'm currently reduced to Grandma's Basildon Bond (lavender-scented), which, while plentiful, is hardly professional. Though perhaps it is fitting for its genre at least. But Mama was surely more important than the dignity of my prose. 'Seven shillings,' I admitted.

'Well, that's a start. Marigold?'

Marigold turned out her pocket.

'Tuppence, four peanuts and a button,' Aster observed with a sigh.

'The wretched hens still won't lay,' said Marigold. 'Otherwise, I'd be an egg baron by now.'

I did not like to point out one cannot become a baron with only seven hens and two ducks, one of whom is past retirement, and one of whom is male. She is, after all, so unrelenting in her determination. She and Bad Harry have taken to sitting with them in the run, reading them adventure stories. Grandma says it is a sign of madness. Aster is inclined to agree, though I think it is rather charming, if apparently unproductive.

'Anyway, what about you?' Marigold asked Aster. 'I thought you were going to sell paintings.'

'I never said anything of the sort,' said Aster, which I think is actually true, it is just that we assumed, for what else could she possibly do? 'Anyway, I've given up,' she added, finally admitting what we all feared.

'Why?' I asked, as softly as possible.

Aster looked down for a brief, but telling second. 'One can't paint without a muse.'

I thought then of Daphne, wondered what had happened to end their friendship; wondered, too if that was what Aster was thinking that very minute.

Marigold snapped us back to the here and now. 'I might become a muse,' she announced.

'Don't be ridiculous,' said Aster.

'Why not? I can't see it's hard. Just some sitting around looking frail or dead.'

Aster ignored this. 'Who on earth to?'

'I don't know.' Marigold was tetchy by then. 'Perhaps I'll look in *The Lady*.'

Aster's eyes went heavenward. 'One doesn't advertise for a muse. Or tout for the position. You just . . . are one. If someone finds you inspiring. Besides' – her face had reddened and she was flustering – 'you're far too young to be nude.'

'I don't see why,' Marigold protested, adding, quite matter of fact, 'It's just skin.'

'Why *do* they have to be nude?' I wondered aloud then.

'It's— you have to understand anatomy if you're going to capture it. If you don't know how it animates, how can you best render it? Or . . . or dress it, even.'

'I can dress myself quite easily without knowing,' I replied.

'I mean making the dresses in the first place.'

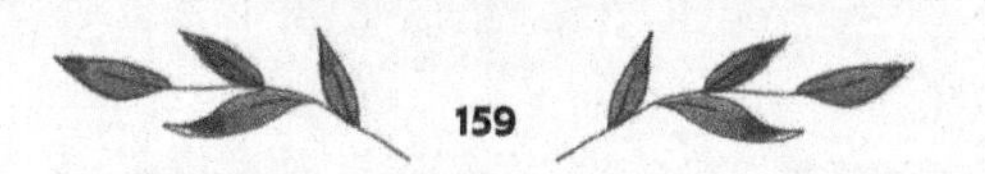

'Some people do it for fun,' said Marigold then.

'Do what?' I demanded.

'Dress in the nude,' she explained. 'Mabel said Ralph said Mr and Mrs Gibberd have a book all about it. It's not shameful, it's just nature. So they say. And only in the garden in private. But I wouldn't like it if they did that, I think.'

We were all silent in contemplative horror at that – for no one but Mrs Gibberd could possibly want to see Mr Gibberd in his birthday suit, still less doing the pruning. But, unpleasant though it was, it did give me an idea.

'You could paint portraits,' I said.

'In the nude,' added a dogged Marigold.

'No!' I blurted. 'I mean. Not if you didn't want. Just their heads. The vicar perhaps,' I added, remembering he had taken quite the shine to Aster.

'You'd get more money naked.' Marigold seemed quite the authority on this. 'Even a vicar. Although perhaps it's not allowed. By God, I mean.'

But, God willing or not, Aster nixed it. 'I'd rather die.'

'I'd rather die' accompanied every one of our suggestions after that, except my final, and quite inspired one, I thought, which was to go to Mrs Gibberd's, not for nude painting reasons, but to check the advertisements in the window for Help Required. Obviously, I don't for a second imagine 'half-hearted romantic novelist' will be among the cards, but perhaps there may be something for one of us. Otherwise, it will be a poor birthday indeed, with only seven shillings, tuppence, and a button.

4 P.M.

Mrs Gibberd's was not the cornucopia of employment I had hoped (if not exactly imagined), but rather a roll call of the menial and the borderline awful. Not a one of us could bring ourselves to either mind the Launceston twins once a week on a Wednesday evening when the maid is off and Mrs Launceston has bridge, or assist with the Sunday school, which also involves the Launcestons and isn't even paid. And we would all, frankly, rather die than housekeep for the Hendrys and their pigs. It is hopeless being born a woman to this class. We are lucky enough to be educated out of the realms of the manual but then expressly forbidden the roles to which we might aspire. As if to emphasise this sorry situation, our hopeless mission was interrupted by the arrival of Lady Balfour's motorcar – a gleaming black stallion of a thing – from which emerged her Odd Man, Fenton, to fetch something from the shop.

'Oh, heavens,' declared a paling Aster. 'Don't look.'

But it was too late, the window was wound down and Mrs Balfour's cemented head (her hair is immoveable) emerged, bearing a look that I recognised immediately as pity.

'Aster, dear.' She made a faint attempt to feign empathy

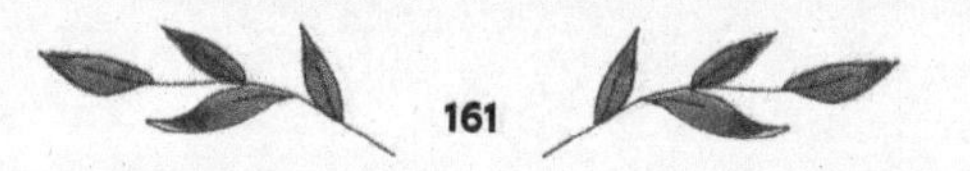

before launching into her true purpose. 'I'm so very sorry to hear about your sister. Dinah, isn't it? Such a . . . solid name at last.'

I felt myself bristle, my back up like Hamilton when Siegfried invades his territory. 'Why?' I asked. 'What's wrong with her?

'Oh, not being a boy, I mean. An heir. Thankfully, Nathaniel has already managed that.' She smiled, the snide cat with the cream. 'I'm sure Daphne will as well, not that it will matter.'

She spoke as if it would be an achievement. As if one can just put one's mind to it and ensure the contents of one's womb will come out be-penised.

And it didn't stop there. 'Are you quite well?' She peered at Aster. 'You look a little peaky.'

'She's fine,' I snapped, the devil in me suddenly. 'We all are. And so is Dinah. Even if she *is* just a girl. Now come along.' I grabbed at Marigold's jacket. 'We'll be late.'

'For what?' demanded Marigold as I half dragged her along the green.

'Never mind,' I said. 'Just – chop-chop.'

Aster didn't require herding; she had already stalked ahead, a walking black cloud. I didn't need to see her face to know she was crying.

'What on earth is wrong with your sister?' demanded Mama when we arrived back at the Dower House, breathless and red.

'Lady Balfour,' announced Marigold. 'And penises.'

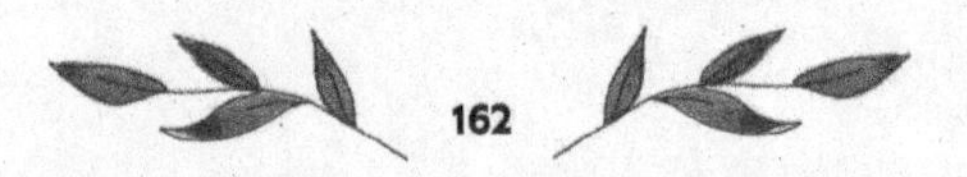

'My ears!' protested Grandma.

Mama frowned. 'Well, she is enough to send anyone into a grump,' she conceded. 'Though it is we who pay the price.' For indeed, at that very minute, the awful caterwaul of now two remaining catgut cello strings howled through the house as if Hamilton himself was being strangled.

I wasn't sure 'grump' sufficed but as I was no more in the know than Mama as to what, exactly, caused Aster such distress, I didn't correct her. Instead, I determined to fetch my Basildon Bond and put pen to lavender paper, for romance of the fictional variety was, it seemed, my only viable option. But, as Marigold set off for the hens with a paperback of unknown specification in her pocket, Mama called me back.

'I forgot; this came for you.' She held up a letter that had been propped on the hall table.

My heart seemed to pause before quickening and I had to temper my breath so as not to sound panicked. For this was it; this was from Buck, surely. An invite to Radley, or, better, Claridges. 'Thank you,' I managed, weakly reaching for the vellum envelope.

But as my fingers gripped the sturdy rectangle, as I focused on the flourish of my name in thick ink, I saw at once that I had been a fool again. This wasn't from Buck, nor even Freddy, who has not bothered to write since the motorcar debacle at Easter.

This was only from Margot. Worse, it was Margot with news of not one but two sightings of Buck, both in the Café de Paris, and both in the company, if not exactly on the arm of, Evangeline Balfour.

Those wretched people. It was a Balfour who upset Daddy so in Parliament, a Balfour who has done something dastardly to Aster (though what I am yet to fathom) and now I am blighted by one as well. It's not enough that they own half the county and a house that could put Highclere to shame, but they manage to lord it over us all as well. And as for Buck, why bother renting Radley at all if he's just going to run back to London at every opportunity.

And so the days at the Dower House shall tock on, it seems, and we Mannerings at their tedious mercy. If only we didn't live in the depths of Essex. If only Dinah had a penis.

If only Daddy hadn't died.

If only, if only, if only. The two saddest words in the language.

SATURDAY 17 MAY

10.30 A.M.

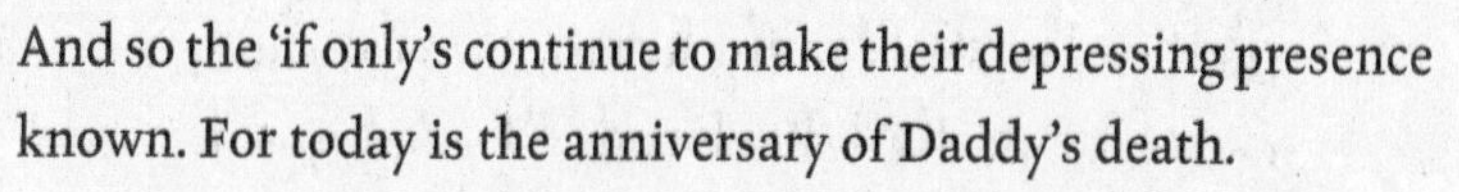

And so the 'if only's continue to make their depressing presence known. For today is the anniversary of Daddy's death.

Aside from Marigold, who has been in cahoots with Bad Harry since yesterday evening, we are all struggling to muster the courage to face the grave. After all, there is nothing good or useful to tell him. We are still pitifully poor, both Aster and I are without prospect, and now Grandma is barely speaking to any one of us because Siegfried got into the glass house, broke four panes and ate several raspberry canes and Rapsey's entire tomato crop. Marigold seemed entirely unperturbed by the incident and said Siegfried cannot be held responsible for behaving as sheep do, any more than the rabbits can be

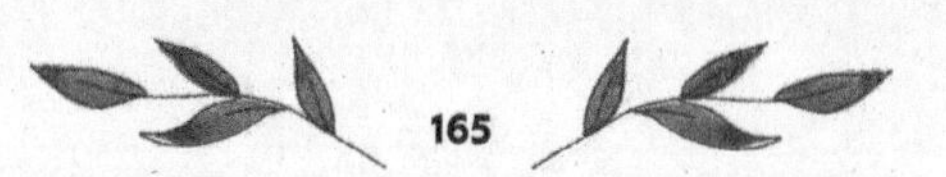

maligned for breeding. Grandma said she won't be so cavalier when we are living off tins come July but Marigold announced she has gone off tomatoes anyway and will eat only cheese and marzipan if it comes to it, and then went back upstairs for heavens knows what.

If I had only had word from Buck. Even just a passing nod from his car. I know it would hardly be a proposal nor a promise of anything but neighbourliness, but right now any mere morsel would do. As it is I shall probably resort to reciting yesterday's letter from Freddy. At least his life is mildly exciting.

Dear Panth,
I should have written sooner but Easter term is relentless I'm afraid – the lectures, the supervisions, and of course the balls. I wish I'd asked you to ours now – though perhaps you'd have baulked at a merry Egg staggering across the quad, bare-chested, sporting a cardboard crown. I prefer to observe – not that I'm Methodist about it, but someone has to make sure he gets back to his own room in one piece. If he wasn't so brilliant, I wouldn't take so much care, but he'll eclipse us all one day. 'If he lives long enough' I was going to add, but that seemed tempting fate, Perhaps I already have. Still, it cannot be

worse than anything he does to himself.

What must you think: me wittering on about a man you've never met? I was writing to send you condolences. Although that word seems meagre now I write it down. Insufficient for what I want to say, and how you must be suffering. It is a year, isn't it? I should have been there for you. I should be there now. Or perhaps you need your sisters more, and your Mama needs you. I am only an old friend after all. Gosh, I'm wittering again.

Just know I'm thinking of you – all of you.

Yours,

Freddy

On reflection, perhaps I shan't recite it. I'm not sure what to make of it, and heavens knows what Mama or Aster would think, let alone Daddy. All that bare-chested Egg nonsense, and then acting as if we are the very best of friends when we've only seen one another a handful of times in the past five years. And anyway, Grandma would likely have a conniption.

She has relented and is coming to the graveyard after all, which seems akin to adding insult to injury, though, as Mama has pointed out, Daddy *was* her son, and so she must suffer more than any of us.

Though surely she cannot feel as weak as I, nor as bitter or enraged.

Or as completely, absolutely lost.

7 P.M.

It is a strange sensation, finding oneself standing at the grave of one's father. More so now than on the day of his funeral, I think. As if I can't quite believe he is still dead. As if he might have joined me at any moment, peered down at the slab of granite, and asked, 'What's all this nonsense then, Pan?'

But he, of course, did no such thing. We stood, all five of us, six with Dinah, in abject silence, awaiting some kind of divine intervention. Eventually, I could bear it no more.

'What now?' I asked.

'Well,' began Mama. 'You may say something to him.'

'Like what?' asked Marigold.

Mama thought. 'Anything.'

Marigold frowned. 'Can he hear us then?'

'Perhaps. Perhaps not,' admitted Mama. 'And, anyway, maybe that's not the point.'

I wanted to ask her what she meant, but decided this mightn't be the time for a philosophical discussion. And besides, Grandma did not afford me the opportunity.

'Well, don't look at me,' she bridled. 'I don't talk to the dead.'

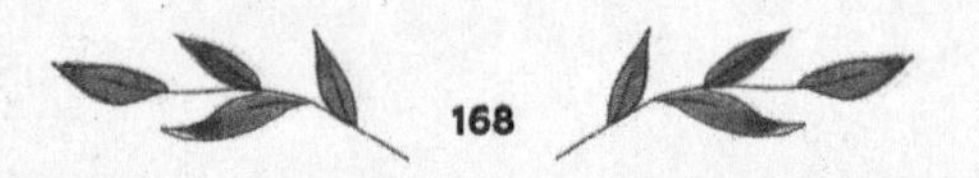

Which is rich, as I've seen her have words with the portrait of Great Uncle Hawsley before.

I could see Mama steel herself. 'Girls?'

'Don't you want to go first?' I asked.

She shook her head. 'I come often,' she said. 'So he's heard all I have to say already.'

This was news to me – to all of us I think. I supposed it must be when she takes Dinah out in the pram on one of her long constitutionals. Grandma says Mabel should take her but Mama pooh-poohed that as old-fashioned nonsense, much to Aster's delight, and Grandma's blackening fury.

'I'll go,' said Marigold then. And stepped up to the headstone. 'Hello, Farv,' she said plainly. 'There's ever so much to report. I have a verruca on my right foot, and am not allowed to take my stockings off ever in case I am infectious. Also, Mrs Bottomley says I am testing her patience on a daily basis but you know that from last year. What else? Oh, the rabbits are doing ever so well, you'll be pleased to hear. I counted seventeen yesterday and there would have been more only Hamilton had one and I think Rapsey got another for the pot. But there'll be more soon I expect. Anyway, I hope it's nice up there. Say hello to Uncle James for me.' Then she turned to Mama. 'Can I go home now? I've something to get on with.'

'Absolutely not,' snapped Grandma. 'This isn't a chore to tick off.'

'Oh, let her, do,' pleaded Mama then. 'She's only small.'

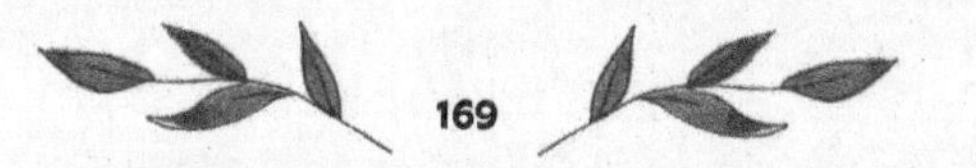

Grandma gave Mama a look that could have wrecked the Hesperus twice over but did not protest further and so off Marigold shot down the road in the direction of the Dower House, leaving Aster and me to take our turns.

Aster was brief and to the point, as always. 'I do miss you,' she said, and placed a sprig of her namesake on the stone, though it was sparse and, as they rarely flower until August at the earliest, could have been any piece of greenery. Though I suppose that's not the point. Anyway, that left me.

I stood for what felt like ten minutes, but must have barely been one, trying to think of something special to say, something fitting and important and just, just right. But in the end, it all just sort of blurted. 'We're a mess without you,' I said. 'A terrible, terrible mess. I wish you'd come home and sort everything out. I just want to go back in time and for this never to have happened.'

'Panther,' Mama comforted.

I stifled a sob. 'What? It's true, isn't it? We *are* a mess. An unsolvable mess.'

'We were a mess before.'

'What?' I turned to Aster.

'We barely had two farthings,' she said. 'Remember when we had to ration coal?'

'Oh,' I said, as I did indeed remember: the lumps separated into small piles for each day of the week, as we silently prayed for clement weather.

'And when we couldn't afford to fix the water and had to bathe Marigold in the trough.'

'Oh, gosh,' I said, a half-smile peering through the salt water at the memory.

'Well, really!' I sensed Grandma's hackles rising high as Hamilton's. 'If this is going to turn into a . . . a dissection of my son's money mismanagement then I won't stay a moment longer.'

'Mother, we weren't saying—'

But Mama's entreaties fell on selectively deaf ears and soon we were all trooping back to the Dower House, Grandma in a black cloud to match her mourning dress, the rest of us oddly lifted, as if the admission had given us licence to be as hapless with cash, with life, as we ever were.

But then we arrived back, and there, on the street, in front of the wall, sat Marigold and Bad Harry and what looked like a stall of bric-a-brac, or lost property, but which, I quickly realised, were Marigold's entire possessions.

'What are you doing?' asked Aster.

'We're having a sale.' She grinned, pleased as punch at her cunning.

'How horribly common,' said Grandma. She turned to Mama. 'Do something, Amelia, will you?'

Mama laughed. 'I've given up trying to make them do anything they don't want to, or stop them doing anything they do.'

Grandma's eyes narrowed. 'It's one thing if it's for charity, but this—'

'It *is* for charity,' Marigold insisted. '*We're* the charity.'

'Lord in high heaven,' Grandma exclaimed. 'What will Hermione Lightfoot think?'

Mama's bravado slipped a little. 'Oh, darling. But what do you need money for?'

Marigold crossed her arms. 'It's a secret.'

Grandma raised an expectant eyebrow. But Mama mustered again. 'Very well, then. How much for the china frog?'

'A penny,' said Harry, who seemed as surprised as we at her managing to say anything (if she ever talks, it is only to Marigold; usually she just stares menacingly).

Marigold stepped in to rescue her. 'Or you can have the jar of flies as well for tuppence.'

At that, Grandma stalked up the path and slammed the door of the Dower House pointedly behind her. But the rest of us, without even deciding it, or needing to, set up camp – a Mannering camp, with Bad Harry and Siegfried too (a penny to take him for a walk) for the rest of afternoon.

Customers were few and far between – Ralph bought a jar of marmalade that Mabel had made several summers ago, but which Marigold insisted would only improve with age; Mrs Spencer, who was passing by on her return from her sister's, bought a paperweight Marigold had made at school – an ugly thing, but Mrs Spencer insisted it would be excellent for Mr

Spencer's desk and all the correspondence he had to deal with; and the vicar, cajoled by Marigold, and no doubt encouraged by the presence of Aster, bought a bag of marbles and a feather quill for sixpence and then took a stubborn Siegfried up and down the drive for what Marigold insisted was two pennies because they took so long, thus depriving other potential customers of sheep-walking opportunity. Incredibly the vicar didn't complain once. Though I have a feeling Marigold may have hinted any funds would reach the collection plate, which as far from the truth as is possible to be. Still, I believe God, or someone, must have been equally oblivious, because he, or fate, deigned to smile upon me.

Because then – I can hardly write it – a miracle happened.

We were just packing the unsold clutter – Marigold, Bad Harry, Mama and Aster back in the house with boxes – when the unmistakable sound of slick motor on metalled road rang out from. My head flung up like a rabbit at the flap of a hawk – instinctive, knowing – and I was right: there, driving towards us, slowing down in fact, was none other than Buck Buchanan. And what's more, he was quite alone.

My heart, hare-like as well, sped up and I had to steady myself on the trestle table, which was less than sensible, propped as it was on a pile of old *Wisdens*, which promptly toppled, sending me to the floor under planks of rough pine and all manner of Marigold's shenanigans.

'Oh, for crying out loud,' I spluttered, flinging paperbacks

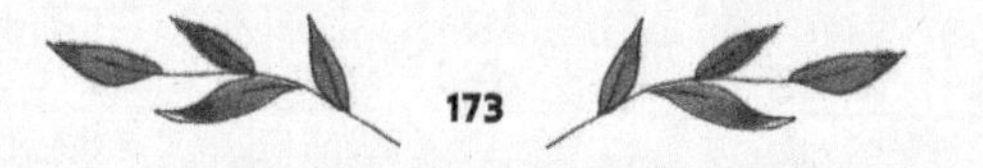

in every direction as I felt my face redden with heat and shame.

And something else.

For then a hand descended – smooth, manicured, manly – and offered itself, palm up, to me. And, defying my pattering heart, I took it and found myself expertly hauled from the floor and into the capable arms of Buck.

For a second, I let myself hang, enraptured, then I suddenly came to and snapped myself back, brushing the worst of the dust from my skirt. 'I'm so . . . gosh, what a fool you must think me.'

Buck stood back, hands on hips, his shirt perfectly tailored to his broad shoulders, slim waist. 'Don't worry about it,' he said. 'Accidents happen.'

'To me,' I said huffily, 'more than most.'

'It rather suits you,' he said.

My cheeks flamed again. 'Being so clumsy?'

'No.' He reached towards my cheek, then, fingers skimming my skin, plucked a single blade of grass from the mess of my hair. 'Being natural. So . . . unpolished. Unfinished. Real.'

For a second I brimmed with brilliance, but then remembered Evangeline – the hold she had on him, and how groomed she was, how elegant.

I didn't want to be real. I wanted to be beautiful. Only—

'I've been meaning to drop in,' Buck continued. 'Or drop something off, anyway – an invite. I'm having a party, you see.'

Oh, be still, my beating heart. 'A party?'

'At Radley. If that's not too weird.'

Too, too weird. 'Not at all.'

'Smashing. June twenty-seven, then.'

I nodded. 'The twenty-seventh of June.'

Buck turned to go.

'Wait!' I exclaimed, then, scrabbling for something to say, landed on Marigold, who had appeared behind me and stepped into the breach.

'Would you like to buy something?' she said.

'No!' I stared hard at her.

'Sure,' he said, his hand landing on Marigold's stuffed monkey (Albertine) atop the wreckage of the sale. 'A quid do?' He held out a crisp bill.

'Oh, he's not for sale, and that's far—'

'Thanks,' said Marigold and snatched the note.

Too much, I was going to say but instead stood rather gaping.

'June,' he reminded me, as he slipped into the creaking leather and revved the still-purring engine.

'June,' I managed, as dust flung into my face, and I descended into a coughing fit I am glad only Marigold had to witness.

*

Of course at that moment June the twenty-seventh seemed the very next day but now it languishes in the distant never-never of next month. Though Mama has hatched a plan to shrink this, albeit a somewhat botched one, at least in my eyes. She insists, you see, that we must invite him to dinner first.

'If you are to spend time with someone – especially a man,' she began, 'then it is only right that I meet him.'

She means vet him. Which should have been Daddy's job, I suppose, though I suspect she will be far more vigorous than he. Daddy always saw the best in everyone, which, now I can admit it, is half the reason we're so terribly poor. Mama is far more rational, while Grandma verges on the vicious.

'But he'll see how impoverished we are,' I protested.

'We're hardly impoverished,' snapped Aster. 'Have you seen the poor soldiers on the streets of the East End?'

I had to admit I hadn't, as *The Tatler* rarely ventures past Piccadilly. But, awful though the poor soldiers' plight may be, that wasn't the point. 'We are impoverished compared to Buck,' I said quietly.

'Frankly, he seems a frightful cad,' Aster carried on. 'I should run a mile. But if he *does* like you' – this said as if it were entirely an impossibility – 'he'll take you as you are, not wish you were richer or more beautiful.'

'More beautiful?' I yelped 'What's wrong with me?'

Aster sighed. 'Nothing. For heaven's sake, it was just an example.'

'Stop it, the pair of you.' Mama intervened. 'He can come next Saturday. Mabel can do her splendid Wellington.'

'But . . . that's your birthday,' I said.

'Good. It will take my mind off mortal thoughts,' Mama said decisively, and with the clear intention that this was to be an end to it.

And it is, but for this: a last word to my father after all.

Oh, Daddy. Something is happening – something good, and I believe it must be down to you.

I can't believe I ever doubted you for a moment. You have sent me Buck, and in return I shall be the dutiful daughter, and perfect – dare I say it – girlfriend.

Oh, I must write to Margot this very minute!

Freddy can wait.

SATURDAY 24 MAY

2 P.M.

Today is Mama's birthday. Her first since our eviction – and the arrival of Dinah, of course – which Aster says I would do well to remember rather than treat it as a sort of floor show before the headline act, i.e. Buck coming to supper! So, arduous though it is, when I find myself almost giddy at the mere act of writing his name, I shall endeavour not to mention Buck again, but rather detail the splendid celebration it has turned out to be – Grandma notwithstanding – when I think we were all imagining something eliciting pity rather than joy.

With the proceeds of the table sale, Marigold had bought her a box of chocolates with a rather dear picture of a lamb on the lid, which Mama said she would keep afterwards for storing

important things. This pleased Marigold no end, as did Mama immediately opening the box and allowing her to scoff several even though she had barely finished her fourth round of toast and marmalade. Grandma said Marigold would end up like Great Aunt Hortense if she carried on like that. I assume she meant with no teeth rather than dead, but Marigold's molars were too glued with nougat to answer back, for which I think we were all grateful.

I, of course, lacking Marigold's apparent talent for entrepreneurship, only had my *Tatler* shillings and had handed them to Aster to pool with whatever she had managed to conjure. When she brought out our package, I braced myself for Mama's 'delighted' face, of the kind that accompanies Marigold's daubings, or Hamilton's 'gifts' of dead rodents. So, imagine my surprise when Mama unwrapped the brown paper to reveal the most darling cream silk slip.

'Oh, girls!' Mama exclaimed, her smile guileless and wide. 'But where on earth did you get the money?'

I could not answer of course, as I was as in the dark as Mama for once.

'I made it,' Aster said, as if that explained anything.

'But the material,' Mama protested. 'Silk is ridiculously dear.'

'Ridiculous full stop,' added Grandma, unnecessarily.

'It was a leftover piece,' Aster said quickly. 'Mrs Booth let me have it at discount.'

Mrs Booth runs the haberdashery on the high street and is renowned for being as wanton a gossip as Mrs Gibberd and as ruthless a businesswoman. 'Why on earth would she give you a discount?' I demanded.

'Because . . .' Aster began, then trailed off as if she couldn't do it, say whatever it was she meant to say. But then I saw her seem to steel herself, take a breath, push her shoulders back and jut her chin. 'Because I work for her.'

Grandma's teaspoon clattered noisily onto a saucer. 'I beg your pardon?'

Aster, defiant now, continued. 'I've been taking in sewing.'

'Oooh, crikey,' said Marigold, gums unhelpfully unstuck now. Though she was only articulating what the rest of us felt.

Aster ignored her. 'Just alterations, repairing dresses,' she continued. 'Mrs Booth hasn't the eyesight any more and she had a card in her window and I so answered it.'

If Aster had hoped that was the end of it, she was sorely mistaken.

'Whose dresses?' asked Mama, with her air of kind concern.

'All sorts. Celia Rigby's for a start. And Hermione Lightfoot's–'

'I can never play bridge again!' Grandma threw her hands up. 'You may as well be trade.'

'And . . . the Balfours'.'

'Oh, Aster,' I cried, knowing how that must sting.

But if it did, she wasn't going to let it show. 'What?' she

snapped. Then dismissed it as if it were no more bothersome than a wasp. 'It doesn't matter. Anyway, isn't it someone else's turn?'

It was, of course. Grandma managed to recover her limited benevolence long enough to give Mama a vest (one can never have too many sensible vests apparently, unlike silk slips), while Siegfried gave her a sponge cake (Mabel helped, Marigold revealed, as if we might have imagined a sheep at the mixing bowl) and the rabbits the portrait of their dead relative that Marigold had helpfully painted when the Attleseys came to tea.

It was at that point I decided it was high time to depart and stood, admittedly rather noisily as Bobby happened to be behind my chair hoping for toast and I inadvertently stepped on his foot.

'Where are you going?' Aster asked.

'I thought I'd have a bath,' I said, as nonchalantly as possible.

Not even Marigold was fooled. 'She's getting ready for Buck.'

'For heaven's sake,' said Grandma. 'It's barely eleven. Besides which, I don't know why you'd want to bring an American into the house in the first place.'

'Oh, mother,' Mama began, but what she said after that I have no idea, as I took the opportunity to slink out, as did Aster, fortune having shone on her own misdemeanour by eclipsing it with the terribleness of Americans.

I proceeded to lie in the brimming slipper tub, into which I'd vengefully emptied half a jar of Grandma's bath salts, for the

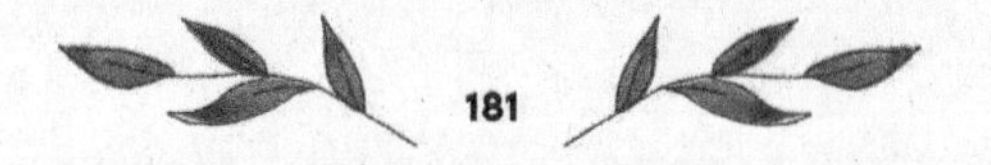

rest of the morning. By the time I got out the water was grey and opaque and I was quite the raisin.

'How revolting,' said Aster as I hurried through her room to get to ours. 'Lying in your own filth for all that time.'

'How dirty do you think I am?' This was a rhetorical question, flung over my shoulder before I closed the door. I know baths are few and far between in the Mannering household, but I'm not like Marigold, who often has to have a second dip to wash the dirt off from the first. Particularly since she took to bathing with one of the ducks. Grandma is still oblivious to this, though Mabel is not, and is not in any way happy. Though nor was she happy with my lengthy soak, as apparently there's no hot water left for anything, and on my head be it if she can't wash enough dishes in time for supper. It will be bound to be on my head anyway. Or Marigold's. It always is.

Anyway, I smell heavenly now (lily of the valley) and I shall look at least vaguely presentable. I'm wearing one of Mama's old dresses – a draping, emerald crepe. Aster has taken it up so that it no longer drags on the floor, and put in a generous panel at the back, to allow for my 'endowment'. It's actually terribly clever, hidden under a sort of train that she ran up from the excess hem, so you can only see it if you peer hard, and, according to Margot, men are not known for peering hard at the back of dresses, only the front.

I can understand why people are paying Aster to sew. She's as good at dressmaking as she is painting. If only she didn't deride them both as beneath her, somehow. At least she has a sort of purpose now, even if she considers it unworthy. I wish I had the luxury. Still, I'm not sure Buck is the type of man who wants a woman with purpose, or indeed a job of any sort, not if his acquaintance with Evangeline Balfour is anything to go by. Indeed, my only purpose now is to better my own acquaintance with him and eject Evangeline from his affections for good.

So, wish me luck, dear diary, for these next few hours are crucial. Not only for the fortune of my family, which was my initial aspiration I admit, but now, for my own hopeful heart.

11 P.M.

Heavens! Where to begin? I shan't bother with details of dinner itself, because, thanks to Mabel, for once in the history of Mannering dinner parties the food was quite delightfully edible, and most of the meal passed without incident. Buck presented Mama with a jeroboam of champagne, which was quite the most fabulous thing I've seen, and too, too generous, which we all said, but Buck would have none of it. And conversation was only momentarily awkward, and when it was, rescued by the most gallant man I think I've ever met, bar Daddy of course (though not even Daddy ran to Moët).

He even seemed to charm Aster.

'What do you like to do?' Buck asked her.

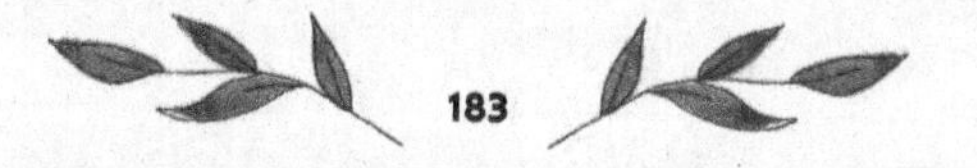

'I sew clothes,' she said, diffident.

'And she paints,' I added. 'Really ever so well. You should see her portraits of Daphne Balfour.'

'That old harridan?' Buck guffawed. 'If you can make her look like a work of art then you must have skill.'

Harridan is harsh – Daphne is merely plain – but Grandma began to thaw at that. And Aster, whose eyes had flashed with anger at his words at first, steadied somewhat when he apologised for being 'brutish'.

'You should try a self-portrait,' he added. 'Now that would be a masterpiece.'

Before she could say anything, he turned his attention to Marigold, who was only too willing to receive it, seeming to bask in the glow of him like her namesake in the sun.

'I've got seventeen rabbits most days and a sheep called Siegfried,' she blurted. 'Do you want to see them? Do you want to see my hens? You can read to them if you like. It helps them lay. They haven't yet, but I think an egg is imminent.'

Buck laughed again. 'What are you reading to them, kid?'

'*The Sheikh*,' she announced.

Grandma paled. 'Amelia,' she pleaded, referring to Mama.

'What?' demanded Marigold. 'They like it.'

'I don't think Buck wants to spend time in the hen house,' I said hastily. 'But perhaps a walk in the garden. Alone,' I added for Marigold's benefit.

I think I surprised even myself at my sudden gumption, but

I was in danger of being swamped by my brilliant sisters and being shown up for the unremarkable middle sibling I am.

'I'd love to,' he said, to my relief, and then immediate regret and trepidation. For what, I thought, shall we talk about?

Roses, at first it turns out. Though I was clueless and wished sincerely I'd listened to Daddy when he explained the varieties and the soil types and the ways to keep off blackfly. Buck was obviously unimpressed, both by the subject and my pitiful witterings and so, grasping at straws, I remembered my first conversation with Freddy this year – that fateful day when Dinah arrived – that prompted so many more.

'What do you want to do?' I blurted.

Buck, hands in his trouser pockets, polished Oxfords scuffing the lawn, paused in his perambulation. 'Do? When I'm "grown up", you mean?'

I felt myself flail; I'd said the wrong thing; a stupid thing. 'I– I'm sorry. That was facile.'

But Buck shook his head. Shrugged. 'God knows. I'm not fit for anything. What *does* a guy do when he has no real ambition or talent?'

For a moment I thought he meant me and shrank under his exacting gaze. 'I don't . . . ' I began. 'That is to say, I . . .'

But he wasn't asking, not properly. It was rhetorical, or reflexive anyway, referring, absurdly, to himself.

'But you can't mean you,' I protested. 'You've been to Cambridge.'

'Going isn't the same as succeeding,' he conceded.

I thought of Freddy then, and Egg – brilliant men, I'd reckoned. But at least Buck saw his flaws, could admit them.

'There must be something,' I said.

'Not according to my father,' said Buck.

I wanted to squeeze his arm then, to comfort him, as Freddy had done once for me, but it didn't feel possible – that foot of summer air between us as unbreachable as his own country's Grand Canyon. Instead, I seized upon a subject about which I was at least vaguely informed. 'Of course, your father's a newspaper man,' I said with some authority (thanks to Margot's investigations.)

The response was less positive than I'd hoped.

'Yes, *The Herald*,' Buck said, slipping his hand inside his jacket pocket and pulling out a silver cigarette case. 'Quite the magnate.'

He flipped the case open, offered it to me.

I shook my head. It may be the height of sophistication to smoke, according to Margot, but neither Mrs Forbes-Rawlinson nor Mama agree, and so we have avowed never to try it, at least not until we're married and out of their jurisdiction.

'What's he like?' I asked.

Buck took out a cigarette, snapped the case shut and slipped it back in his jacket, then took out an ivory lighter, which he flicked with a flourish and lit the thing, taking a long, satisfied, swoon-worthy drag. I instantly regretted my resolve.

'Tough. Stubborn.' He exhaled, a plume of smoke unfurling into the bright sky before dissipating like mist on an August morning. 'Disappointed in me,' he continued. 'Thinks I should have had to fight against the odds. Work all hours. Walk a mile in a poor man's shoes. Like he did.'

'Oh,' I said, unable to imagine a papa who wasn't indulgent of their children's whims. Daddy let Marigold have her menagerie, let Aster paint, let me . . . well, I'm not entirely sure. Perhaps he just let me be me.

'I've let him down,' Buck continued. 'So he says. You've read the rag, I suppose?'

'Oh, yes,' I said, pleased to be part of things again. Though in fairness, I'd only read it in Mrs Gibberd's when she wasn't watching (Grandma has barred it for backing Ramsay MacDonald) and even then only for the gossip column. 'I like "Cad About Town",' I admitted. 'Though it's not half as good as *The Sketch*.' I was eager, you see, to align with Buck against his father. 'Whoever writes it has no concept of nuance.' I paused, suddenly fearful I may have gone too far. I lowered my tone. 'Who does write it?'

Buck grimaced. 'I do. At least of three weeks ago.'

I reddened. 'I'm so sorry—'

'Don't be,' said Buck, taking another drag of the cigarette before stubbing it out on the west wall and throwing the butt into the dahlias. 'That's my point. I'm no good at anything really. And that column is my last-chance saloon. So I guess

I'm about to get kicked out of the bar. I couldn't write if my life depended on it.' At that, he seemed to brighten, as if realising what he thought was an old penny was pirate's gold. 'In which case, I shall just have to loaf.'

'Loaf? I asked.

'Dawdle. Dilly-dally. Isn't that what you say?'

I nodded. Then frowned. 'But how will you get paid for it?'

'Why would I need to get paid? I'll just move back to the States.'

At this, I was reminded of Margot and her 'someone who *is*, not someone who *does*'. And I wanted to believe her, but something in me – something to do with fathers and needing to please them – couldn't let this lie. Also, I needed Buck around, didn't I? Not dilly-dallying back in America. 'I can help,' I suggested. 'Only if you want, of course. But if it kept you in your father's good books, then what harm?'

Buck stared at me. Only this time I didn't shrink, but rather tipped my chin, Aster-like, daring him to doubt me.

'Help how?' he asked.

'Help you edit,' I said. 'Or write it, even. I'm good with words. At least, Daddy once said so.'

'You write, then?'

'A little,' I lied.

At that Buck smiled. 'And I thought only the strange or desperate put pen to paper.'

I didn't bristle, for I knew he included himself in that.

Instead, I went on with suggestions. 'For example, last week, that bit about Deirdre Beeton.'

Buck nodded, doglike. He was actually listening to me. I was actually doing this. 'Well, instead of "awfully tall" why not say she was "blissfully willowy"?'

Buck smiled. 'Clever,' he said.

'Not really,' I replied.

'No, it is, you're brilliant.'

Emboldened, I listed off another three improvements off the top of my head. 'And that's only this edition,' I ended, excitedly.

Buck gave a single snort. 'No need to rub it in,' he said.

I flinched. 'Oh, no . . . I didn't mean—'

'Hey, hey.' Buck put his hand on my arm, stroked it gently, the chasm forded at last. 'It's all good. You're good.'

My heart skittered like a moth caught in a slice of sunlight, my arm trembling under his touch. 'I can start next week if you like.'

'It's monthly now,' Buck said, his words fat with failure, 'after last time. And May's done, but June, perhaps? After the party.'

I nodded, somewhat gormlessly.

But if Buck saw he didn't care. 'Then it's settled.'

And the moth in me soared.

*

Buck left soon after – he had to run up to London – but that

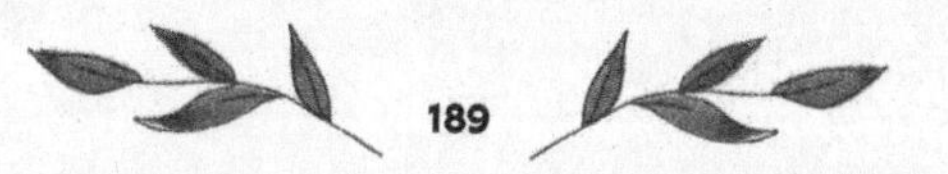

didn't stop all after-dinner talk centring on him, or rather, his countrymen in general.

'Terribly strange, the Americans,' was Grandma's opening gambit. 'Accents unfathomable of course.'

'What rot,' I replied. 'You understood every word. Anyway, I think it's charming.'

'You would,' said Aster.

'I didn't see you complain when he compared you to a Botticelli.'

'Flannel and flattery,' she said swiftly. 'Men are all the same. And Americans are the very worst.'

I ignored her, though the accent – the very lexicon – is odd. Jam is jelly. Jelly is Jell-O. And Battenburg cake must be entirely baffling to them. And when they eat, they cut everything up at once and then discard their knife as if it has served its only purpose, swap the fork to their right hand and shovel the food in as if it's a spade.

'Practically savage,' said Grandma when I said this.

'Practically,' I found myself agreeing.

But maybe it is this savagery I find so fascinating.

*

'Don't worry,' I said to Aster when the unsavoury habits of all foreigners had been exhausted as a topic and we were getting ready for bed. 'About the sewing, I mean. It won't be for long.'

Instead of snapping, she seemed weary this evening, as if she had conceded some sort of defeat. 'How do you know that?'

I'd been longing to tell her since the minute we got back in from the garden, my forearm still warm – tingling it seemed – from Buck's touch. 'Because Buck is going to fall hopelessly in love,' I blurted, words tumbling out of me as I were an unstoppered bottle. 'And it won't be thwarted or doomed or unrequited, as I couldn't write a more dashing hero if I were E.M. Dell herself. And we'll get married and then we can all move back to Radley Manor and be rich and happy ever after.'

Aster, plaiting her lengthy tresses, raised an eyebrow. 'And what will you do in this happy ever after?'

'Well, obviously I've not worked out the precise details,' I admitted. 'But if you're in love then nothing exactly matters, does it.'

'I hope it works out for you,' she said, and turned, and I thought that was the generous end of it, but then I heard, almost under her breath, 'better than it did for me.'

But right now I don't have time to wonder about Aster's past. It's my future that counts. And that future is Buck Buchanan. Even Mama agrees.

I asked her, in the drawing room after supper, if she had had a happy birthday, after all.

Marigold put down her paperback (*The Sheikh* again, I note, despite lacking the excuse of the chickens) and leant her head against Mama's knees. Then, with Dinah on her lap, Mama held out her palms, one for Aster, one for me.

'Don't you realise yet?' she said, grasping us and squeezing

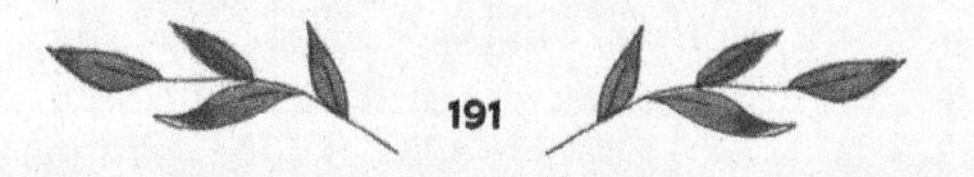

our bitten-nail fingers in her own pale, manicured hands. 'If you girls are happy, then I am happy.'

And I *am* happy. I truly, truly am.

JUNE

SATURDAY 14 JUNE

10 A.M.

June! How I adore the hum of this month. The very gateway to summer, it unfolds before me like a bolt of gold cloth, or the fabulous landscape of Radley itself – rose-scented and sun-dappled and every inch of it studded with life, life, life!

The cherry atop this cake is Buck's party, of course, though that is still an interminable fourteen days away. But – hoorah! – my pestering of Margot (or more likely my access to one Buchanan) has paid off and she has invited me to the Glasshouse apartment in the week before the party, while Mrs Forbes-Rawlinson is otherwise occupied with Deborah and her tennis (they are decamping to the Chalfont-Latimers' for the duration of Wimbledon, as not only does their balcony

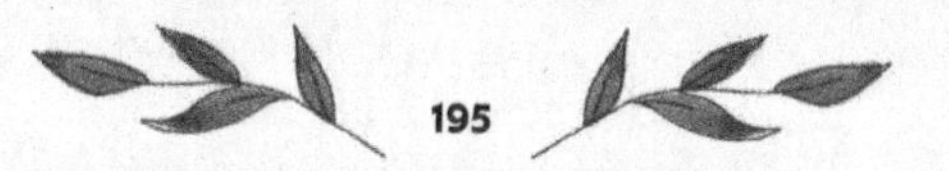

practically overlook Centre Court but Mr Latimer knows René Lacoste and Mrs Forbes-Rawlinson is keen to impress him with Deborah's nascent forehand skills). What is more, Margot has promised to take me to the Button Club so perhaps I shall get to meet the infamous Brilliant Baker at last. Though her fascination has waned somewhat in recent weeks, and it is 'Buck this' and 'Buck that'. I have not told her of my feelings for him, nor of his for me, as I don't want to seem as if I am boasting. But she will see it for herself anyway as he is bound to turn up at the club (according to *The Tatler* and *The Sketch*, he is everywhere every night). And, of course, there's his own column. He's bound to want a private meeting to discuss my edits. Perhaps it will be at Radley. Or, better, his suite at Claridges!

Anyway, I shall stop daydreaming as that is not for a week at least and today heralds another pressing engagement: at two o'clock Lady Daphne Balfour is marrying cheese-faced Nigel Pakenham, and all Mannerings are attending, even Aster, though this is under duress on her part (the alternative was spending a day playing canasta with Grandma, who has excused herself on the grounds it will be overrun with 'ghastly arrivistes' – I do hope so!). Though I will say, Aster has pulled a rabbit out of a hat (metaphorically, though the other is always a risk around here) as far as garb goes. Not only has she darned and darted Mama's and Marigold's and my dresses, but she has sewn one of her own as well. It is quite the sight – slender and silken and draped low enough at the back one can see the entire arc of her shoulder blades as if they were the wings of an angel.

Grandma has declared it an abhorrence and told her she will be shaming the very name of our family if she shows up at Balfour Hall in that state of undress. Aster said nothing, but her look suggested this was the exact intent. Mama is just relieved she is coming at all, so has only demanded she at least wear a shawl in church, though she has couched it in 'you don't want to catch a chill' terms, which is terribly clever. Besides, if anyone shames our name it will be Marigold who has already been informed twice that Siegfried is not a suitable wedding guest, not even with a hat on.

Aster is up to something though. I am not sure what, exactly, but I worry it won't turn out well for her, and I'm not sure the cello can take any more of her moods.

9 P.M.

I was right about Aster! Though it is not a single one of the things I had imagined (which I admit at one point included an attempt to seduce Lord Balfour and blackmail him for enormous amounts of money – Miss Ince always said my imagination was too vivid for my own good). But I shall come to it in good time, as it is too enormous to just blurt out, and there are other less tremendous but still significant things I must chronicle first.

First, Buck, whom I sought the moment we entered St Ignatius's. Just my luck to be so late (Marigold; I can't even go into it) as to be several rows behind him. Still, my unusually loud rendition of 'The Lord's My Shepherd' paid off with a sudden swing of his brilliant, brilliantined head, and a wink – a wink!

Next, though, Evangeline, who, the moment we left the shade of the nave, was glued to my suitor like a barnacle on a slab of granite. Though I concede he is quite the slab and she the most beautiful barnacle. Everything about her shimmers – her dress, her legs (which seem to be twice as long as mine), her hair, which is a neat, gilt cap where mine is a waist-length mess that may as well have been skinned from one of Marigold's rabbits. She is a veritable orchid among cowslips now, which is a far cry from her childhood, when she was decidedly less elegant. At school they cruelly called her Bunty after her pony, but the laugh is on the others as she has eclipsed us all; Margot and I the first to be bypassed.

Then there was Balfour Hall itself, which is rather more macabre than I remember. Half of Epping Forest now hangs on the walls, or is stuffed and mounted in display cases in various states of absurdity: stags and badgers and even a poor dear otter, now permanently surprised at the perch welded to its left paw. No wonder Daddy so loathed Lord Balfour. Grandma thinks Daddy's aversion to blood sports was a 'horribly modern attitude' he picked up from political colleagues, but Mama says he was always completely squeamish about such things and I believe her. He once told me he passed out when first blooded and always feigned stomach ache on the Sunday hunt after that. No such queasiness at the Balfours', who seem to have gleefully garrotted every creature that had the audacity or misfortune to wander onto the estate.

But most significant of all was the groom himself. Or rather, he is so significantly insignificant. Honestly, it is hard to see what Daphne can possibly admire in him. Even Marigold, at ten, can tell.

'He is no Reg Nesbitt,' she declared sagely, once we had returned to the Dower House (Dinah was fractious and Lady Balfour more so, mostly at the very fact Mama had thought it acceptable to bring a baby to a wedding).

'He does seem an utter dullard,' I agreed. 'What will they have to talk about?'

'There is nothing to discuss with boys.' Marigold sighed. 'If I can't have Reg I shan't bother. Or I shall marry Harry.'

'You can't marry a girl,' I said, not without a little wistfulness, as the idea does have its merits.

'Why ever not?' asked Marigold. 'If you wanted a baby, you could just borrow one. Or have rabbits.'

Which is when Aster, who had been tight-lipped and diffident all day, finally broke into sobbing and ran upstairs.

'Oh dear,' said a distraught Mama. 'What can be the matter with her?'

'Jealousy,' said Grandma with more than her usual air of doom. 'That girl needs a husband like a rose needs water.'

But that, it turns out, is the very last thing Aster wants.

*

I ran after her – someone had to; Marigold would have only irritated and Mama was trying to persuade Dinah not to slap Hamilton (though I suspect letting her carry on and try it would teach her this lesson more successfully) – and found her prone on her four-poster, her wet eyes ceiling-ward and riven with distress.

'Go away,' she said, without shifting her gaze.

'I shan't,' I replied. 'Not until you tell me what's going on.'

She turned on her side to face the wall, and the gaping door to my own room.

I sat on the very edge of the bed, tentatively. 'Did you have a crush on him?' I asked. 'On Nigel, I mean. Is that it?'

'Nigel?' She half laughed, half sobbed. 'I'd rather die.'

'Alfred Mackerell then?' (Hooked nose, aggressive moustache, something in shipping.) 'Or that Lezard chap. The one with the dicky limp?'

'Please stop it! I don't love any of the men! Not a single useless one of them!'

'Who then? Oh—'

And then, it didn't dawn on me so much as flood, like so much sunlight when the drawing room drapes are flung back on a bright spring morning. Suddenly the evidence was

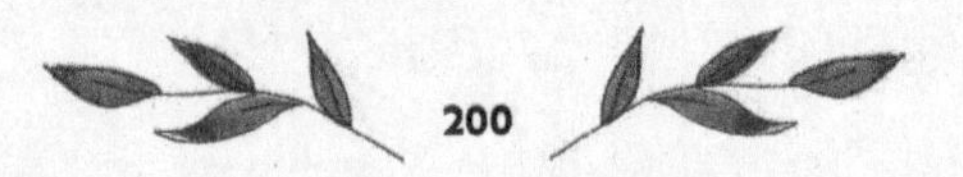

everywhere my mind's eye sought – the paintings, the late-night whisperings and giggling, the summer when they'd barely ventured back to Radley, remained locked in the folly for hours – nights – on end. 'It's Daphne, isn't it?' I blurted in wonderment. 'That's why you fell out. Not Nigel at all. You have a crush on Daphne.'

Aster covered her face with her hands. 'Not a crush,' I heard her mumble.

My heart swelled for a second, then sunk for my poor sister at this second revelation. 'You mean you loved her?'

She said nothing, but nodded.

'And . . .' – oh, this was too much, but it had to be true – 'did she love you back?'

'I thought so.'

'Oh, Aster,' I cried in empathy.

But then, as if thwarted love was not enough, another, more awful thought occurred to me. 'Aster, did you sew Daphne's dress? Her wedding dress?'

Aster nodded.

My heart cinched inward now, a jolt of shared pain. How dreadful that must have been; almost as bad as sewing a loved one's funeral robe.

'I'm so very sorry.' I placed a hand on her shoulder; instead of flinching, she seemed to sink into it, let her hands fall from her face. We stayed like this for several seconds, in taut but warm silence.

'It doesn't matter,' she said eventually. 'It's not as if anything could ever come of it.'

I thought for a moment. 'But there are people,' I said. 'In London. Margot says so. And what about Valentine?'

'Valentine has to sneak about. I don't want to live like that.'

'But–'

'No.' Aster snapped now, sat up, my hand dropping to the quilt like a withered limb. Then she turned to me, and glared harder than she has ever done. 'You're not to say a word, do you hear? Not to Mama, not to Marigold, not even to Valentine.'

'But–' I repeated, thwarted and doomed romance dancing in front of me, enticing as firelight.

'I mean it.'

I slumped. 'Fine,' I said. 'I won't tell a soul.'

And I shan't. Except here. And only to say that this is yet another great shame of mankind: that we cannot love whom we choose, but whom we are told is suitable. I just thank my lucky stars that Buck is in possession of that vital organ.

Not that I want to see it or go near it – not just yet. But at least it means the future may ring with proud wedding bells rather than the shameful clang of a beggar's.

SUNDAY 22 JUNE

10.30 A.M.

It has been eight days since the wedding and Aster hasn't breathed a single word about Daphne in all that time and nor, I am proud to say, have I, although the temptation to beg for even scraps of detail is immense. Did they kiss, for instance? Or have 'relations'? What do 'relations' even involve when there isn't a penis to be wielded? Because really, it sounds rather a relief. And, more importantly, does cheese-faced Nigel know? Or Lady Balfour? But I am having to swallow all these and more down, of which Aster is fully aware, and the tension at the Dower House is thus utterly unbearable. Not to mention, Marigold has taken to Grandma's piano and I am not sure which is worse: Aster's two-string cello or the thunderous

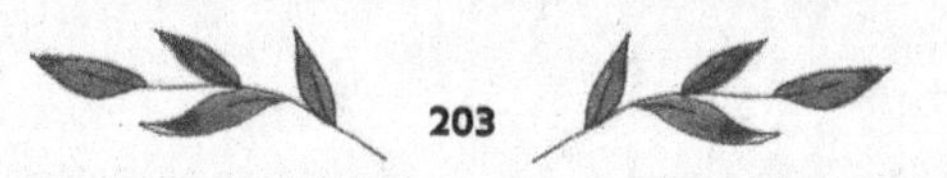

clunking of Marigold murdering 'Oh, Praise Him'. It is a relief to be leaving for London tomorrow, frankly.

But also an absolute thrill.

'But what on earth will you *do* there?' asked Grandma at breakfast, as if it were impossible one might find things of interest in the village let alone the capital city.

'Zelda Fitzgerald rode down Fifth Avenue on the bonnet of a taxi,' I said.

'What are you proposing?' asked Aster. 'To mount Buck's Bentley and careen through Piccadilly?'

I am ashamed to say that the thought had occurred to me.

'No,' I replied. 'And anyway, who said Buck would be there?'

'Buck is always there.'

I knew this, but I did not give Aster the satisfaction. 'Actually, we're going to a seance.'

'Whatever for?' This was Mama, who had hitherto been trying to persuade Dinah that porridge was to be eaten, not worn, and had now, evidently, given up.

'Margot says he can predict husbands. And also "apport stones onto one's person".'

'Whatever use is that?' snorted Grandma. 'Conjuring up stones, I ask you.'

'I don't know. He just can. Perhaps they're precious gems.' (I knew for a fact they were not; they were pea gravel. Not that that dissuaded Margot of his supreme skill).

'Harry can make wasps die with just her mind,' announced

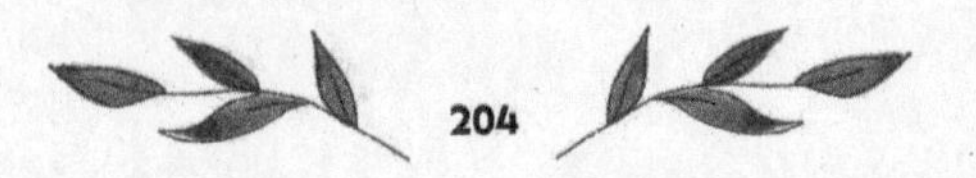

Marigold with fanfare.

'No she can't,' I replied.

'She can. She mesmerises them. Flies too. She's been practising.'

'Perhaps Rapsey can hire her,' Mama suggested, I assume in jest.

'For heaven's sake!' snapped Grandma. 'Don't encourage her.'

Marigold shook her head sadly at that. 'You can't deny the powers,' she said. 'She's going to try something bigger next.'

'Then I should keep the rabbits out of her way,' I said as I stood.

'Where do you think you're off to?' demanded Grandma.

'Oh, sorry.' I sat again. 'Please may I leave the table?'

'Of course,' said Mama, frowning over Dinah's oat-spattered cap. 'You must have things to do for London.'

'I do,' I admitted, clattering to my feet again. 'Lots of things.'

*

What things, though, I dared not tell her. But the fact is, I cannot go to London looking like a female Reg Nesbitt (I don't spit, it's the excessive hair I refer to). I need to be glamourised in every aspect including – Oh! I can hardly believe I shall do it – bobbing my hair!

I would rather it were not left to me, but Mrs Higginthorpe in the village refused, citing the wrath of Grandma as her excuse, as did Aster, who would quite like to incite the wrath of Grandma, but said she was not ruining her dressmaking shears

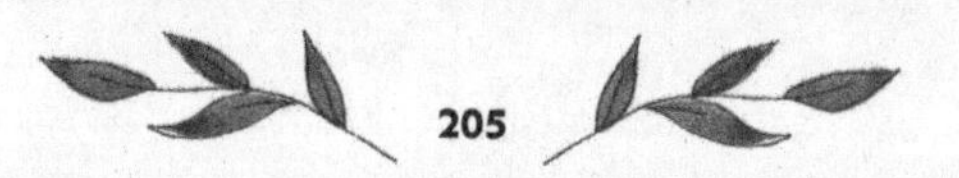

on my wiry mess. Marigold offered with some glee, but I have seen the results when she tried to give Siegfried a trim and it was quite alarming, so it is me or nobody.

Also, I am going to pluck my eyebrows! Margot said it is all the rage (i.e. *The Tatler* says, which is more verifiable than the Bible) and I cannot possibly be seen in the Button Club with my beetleish ones. She insists it is perfectly easy, but that I must make sure they are symmetrical or I will end up looking like Clifford DeWinter, whose older brother pinned him down and shaved one off in a fight, and he has never looked the same since.

How hard can it be, anyway? It's not as if one needs qualifications to be a hairdresser or beautician. Though I admit I am giddy with thinking of it. Like a chrysalis about to hatch into a glorious butterfly, or the ugly duckling into a swan: by the time I am done I will be every bit as gilded as Evangeline Balfour.

Yes, I will be quite the Bright Young Thing! Mama will barely recognise me, and Buck?

Buck will fall at my feet.

2 P.M.

I am not the Bright Young Thing. Buck will not fall at my feet. And, as for Mama not recognising me: I barely recognise myself.

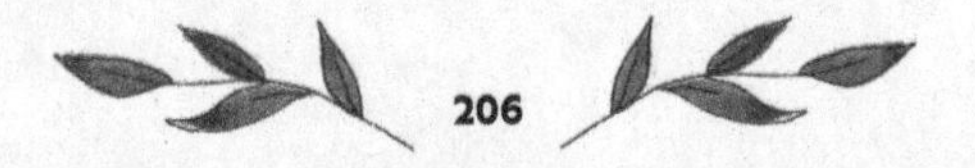

The hair is terrible. Who knew it was so difficult to cut a straight line? Well, hairdressers, I expect, but really, this is the sort of thing that should be taught at school, rather than French conjugation and chemical elements, neither of which I shall have any use for in life. And as for my eyebrows, they are so thin as to be non-existent, because every time I plucked a hair from one brow, the other seemed to be slightly bushier, so I plucked one from over there, and then that brow seemed too fine in comparison, and so it went on until I was down to about ten hairs on either side and a look of permanent surprise/ extreme illness. I cannot be seen outside my bedroom, let alone at the Button Club, unless it is to join a circus. Which is actually looking like quite a bright option right now, being that my only viable alternative is lying on the bed and sobbing.

4 P.M.

I am ashamed to admit I chose lying on the bed and sobbing. I did weigh up the circus option briefly but decided my riding abilities were negligible, and I am not fond of tigers either.

It was Aster who found me.

'What is the matter with you?' she demanded of my prone body.

I didn't have to answer. I just turned, red-faced and shorn, to face her, and saw her clap a hand to her mouth, to stifle a

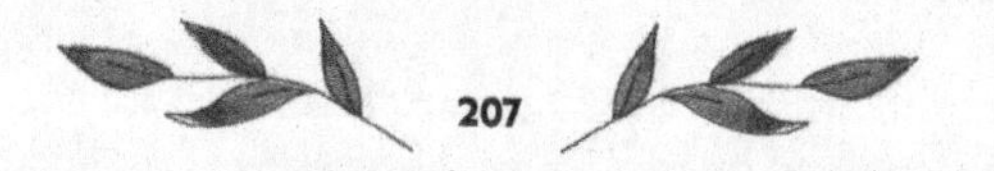

laugh. Though that, thankfully, swiftly segued to sympathy.

'Oh, Panth,' she said. 'Whatever possessed you?'

'Well, you wouldn't do it.' I sniffed. 'And now look.'

'You can hardly blame me,' replied Aster. But her voice, for once, wasn't scornful, rather riven with pity. 'Though I suppose I shall have to fix this somehow.'

'How?' I despaired. 'My train is in two hours and I resemble a scarecrow and a bad one at that.'

'You do look rather like something Marigold has drawn.'

'See!' I resumed noisily sobbing. Though, in retrospect, there *was* something of Marigold's wonky oeuvre about my appearance: I resembled an object seen in a distorting mirror.

'Wait here!' she instructed. 'And stop making that noise. You sound like Siegfried.' And she swept out of the room with more purpose than I have seen in weeks, while I continued to bleat, though rather less plaintively.

What is she fetching? I wondered. A hooded cloak? A balaclava? Mrs Higginthorpe under duress?

It was none of these.

'All right, miss.'

Mabel. And then it came to me: Valentine's white knight, or knightess, in shining uniform. She'd been a hairdresser, hadn't she, and she read *The Tatler* front to back so must know her trends in everything from dresses to eyebrows.

I sat up and wiped my nose. 'Can you help me?' I begged.

She peered from under her bonnet, as if sizing up a heifer

at auction, or a slab of ham at Goddard's. 'There's things I can do,' she said at last. 'Won't be easy, mind, not with that bugger's muddle.'

'I'm sorry.' I was. Truly. Though for myself more than her.

Mabel shrugged. 'I've seen worse,' she said, before adding, 'amateurs,' with more than a hint of a sniff.

And perhaps she had. And I wonder now what miracles she whipped up for those poor unfortunates, as the one she performed for me was mighty indeed – the work of a magician – for in less than an hour she had my hair neatly levelled with my chin, and my eyebrows, though not at all 'normal', were at least 'there', with the aid of a small brush and palette, which she has pressed upon me along with what seem like easy instructions. Though I am hoping, if I don't wash too often, these versions will at least last until the club, and Buck.

Not that the farewell party assembled in the hallway was impressed.

'Oh, Panther!' cried Mama. 'Your glorious hair!'

I touched a hand to the nape of my neck, stubbled now but soft as the nap of a velveteen rabbit. 'It'll grow back,' I said. *If I want it to,* I added silently, for now that Mabel had worked her wonder, I had come to rather like the feeling of fresh air on me, the freedom it afforded. No clips, no pins, no plaiting ever again.

'You look absurd,' said Grandma, never one to mince words.

'Or a boy,' said Marigold, though not without some admiration. 'Can I have it done? Can I?'

'No,' said Mama and Grandma in uncharacteristic unison.

Aster was oddly un-Asterish too. 'London won't know what's hit it,' she said. And I know she meant it well, for, as she handed me my case at the station, she added, 'Do be careful, won't you? Don't do anything stupid. Or ruinous.'

'I shall try not to,' I said.

But that, I am afraid was a lie, for what is the point of London in season if one doesn't do at least one stupid and ruinous thing?

The cherry on the cake of it is, how will they ever find out?

WEDNESDAY 25 JUNE

8 P.M.

I am back!

Two days early, which I will explain later, but – oh! London was exactly as I imagined: sordid and glorious and far, far from the city I visited all those months ago. At night, it is as if some invisible wizard clicks a switch and suddenly, from Glasshouse Street all the way down to St James's, everything becomes spangled and jazz-rackety, shoes clattering on cobbles to a frenetic tempo, with a story or a scandal around every corner. Far too much to write down in fact, and I am not sure words can do any of it justice, especially not in my state of exhaustion, but I shall try to capture a little of it – the important parts. Or people.

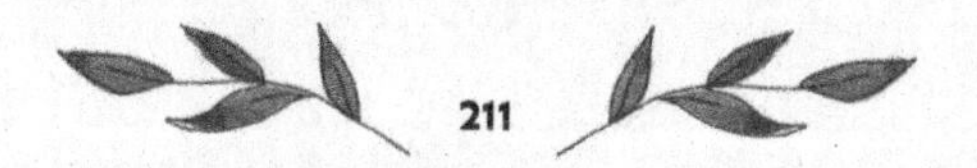

The first evening was a rather tame affair, not aided by the fact that Mrs Forbes-Rawlinson had 'popped back' from Wimbledon to Lillywhite's on an urgent mission to fetch Deborah a third racket as her second had been damaged in an incident with a ball boy. Thankfully she had left Deborah in the charge of the Chalfont-Latimers so we were at least spared comparisons, in which both Margot and I would inevitably emerge less favourably. She did, however, insist on staying the night, so instead of creating fabulous ballyhoo at the Button we sat awkwardly in the drawing room listening to Brahms until Margot yawned demonstratively and decreed it was definitely time for bed, at which point we gossiped energetically until gone one in the morning.

The next evening, however, was the ticket. The bee's knees. The absolute cat's pyjamas!

I picture now a whirl of images: the hair setting (Margot thrilled at my transformation), the dressing, the accessorising – Margot with a tiara and I with a peacock feather borrowed from Deborah's nature collection; our table at Alfonse, candlelit and gingham-checked, where Margot ate snails, but which I, having seen one of Marigold's hens consume several by hacking into their shells, declined and opted for something called onglet, which was, categorically, the most delicious thing I have ever eaten, even beating Mabel's beef Wellington; her cousin Jonty and his friend Ginger Wyndham (of eel-tongue fame), our erstwhile escorts whom we abandoned the very second we made it through the door of the Button Club.

For of course we went to the Button. For there, we knew, would be Brilliant Baker (who I am slightly sad to report is both as glorious as Margot described, but also quite clearly of Valentine's persuasion, and is no more amorously interested in her than she in Ginger, me, or our malodorous waiter, who had more oil in his hair than Cook used to cremate bacon). And there, too, I was sure of it, would be Buck.

But first – the club! It is hidden, as all the best places are, down a thin, rickety staircase leading to what one would assume is a dingy cellar, but after knocking three times in the right rhythm on the black-painted door, opens into a vast cavern of velvet chairs and gilt ceilings and walls covered with the most glorious art – from ballerinas to cancan girls to brazen nudes, not caring one jot they're naked but gazing straight at the painter – at us! Grandma would have had a conniption, though Aster, I imagined, would at least see the technical merit.

Anyway, it is not the chairs, nor the ceilings, nor the walls that really interested me, but the life inside. People of every colour, dressed in every colour – teal greens and mustard yellows and cherry reds that seemed plucked from nature herself and spun into clinging silk and kitten heels – and every inch dripping with bugle beads or scattered with sequins or feathered, like elegant birds, and so very far from the Ickthorpe Village Dance as to be comparing custard with caviar. And the drinks! Margot made me try a vivid pink thing with unidentifiable lumps of

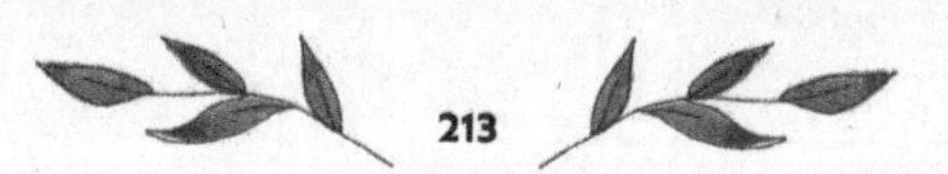

fruit floating in it. Margot declared it to be pineapple but I remain unconvinced.

And the people! Margot knew everyone, or, rather, knew *of* them.

'Who's that fellow with the odd eye?' I asked.

'Boy Huxley. And it's glass. Apparently, he'll take it out to show you if you're lucky.'

'No thanks. What about the glorious woman with the awfully short shingle?' I touched my own hair again, wondering if I dared go even further.

'Topaz Attlesey. Brandon's big sis.'

So *that* was Topaz. It seemed impossible that she should be related at all to Brandon, still less to Lady Melcham, but there was no explaining inheritance. Look at the contrast between Aster and I.

'I hear she had a you know what,' Margot hissed.

'I don't know what.' I had not an inkling.

'An' – she lowered her voice; tricky given the racket – and hissed out, 'abortion.'

'Oh!' I exclaimed, feeling a wash of shock and horror and, I was surprised to find, absolute admiration.

'Silly to be caught,' said Margot, at full blast again. 'And of course he didn't love her.'

'Of course,' I repeated dumbly, still steeped in wonder. I snapped to. 'How about the one in the cravat?'

'That,' she said with some satisfaction, 'is Sassoon.'

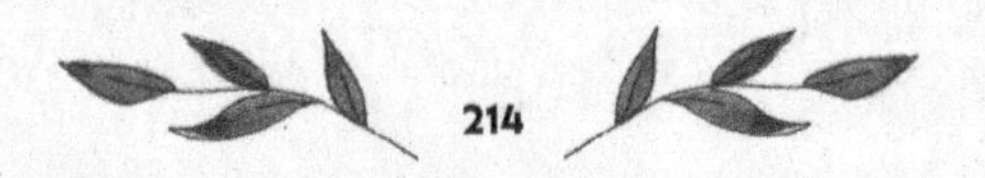

Sassoon! In the flesh! *Just wait until I tell Margot,* I would have said at any other time, but here we were, the three of us, breathing the same deliciously stale air, dancing (badly, I might add) to the same furious beat. I felt as if I may have gone to sleep and woken in a fever dream, or died and gone to a version of heaven in which the devil presided benignly.

But I never got to speak to Sassoon, because that was the very moment the cellar door swung open again and in stalked Evangeline Balfour, and, behind her, shirt Jermyn-Street-new, hair slicked but eyes wild, Buck.

And both of them striding straight towards me.

'Darling.' Evangeline kissed some air in the vicinity of my cheek before smiling briefly and acidly at Margot then turning back to inspect me. 'Interesting hair.'

'Thank you,' I said.

'Quite . . . startling. I was so sorry to hear about your sister. Diana, is it? Though I've always been grateful to have been born a girl of course. I do so like having someone to look after me.' At this she flicked a glimpse at Buck. 'I pity the suffragettes. Though one can't blame them. It must be hard being left on the shelf. How is dear Aster?'

Throughout this monologue my back had arched and my hackles risen as if I were Hamilton and she the wretched tom from next door. 'It's Dinah, not Diana. And Aster is well. Better than,' I added. 'So very talented, of course. She doesn't really have time for such trivial things as men and babies.' I didn't know where the words were coming from, but out they spilled like vomit or venom.

Margot gasped.

Evangeline stared at me; an unspoken dare was set. 'Well, must fly,' she said. 'Come along, Buck.' And she slipped into the crowd, all lithe and pliable and irritatingly nymph-like.

But Buck, it seemed, hadn't heard her.

'I've been hoping to see you,' he said. 'My column's due soon.'

'What column?' demanded Margot.

'Nothing,' I said quickly. 'Boring really. Can we catch you in a moment? I think I saw Brilliant blow you a kiss.'

Margot's head swung to the stage and without a moment's pause she pushed her way forward, all the better to catch any more kisses that might be flung her way. Leaving Buck and I alone.

'Well played,' he said.

'I'm used to it,' I said. 'I have sisters, and secrets.' Gosh, I was on verbal fire tonight!

'Do you, indeed?' He smiled, and touched a hand to my now springing ginger curls. 'I think it rather suits you.'

My stomach leapt, my onglet threatening to make a dreadful reappearance. 'It was a whim,' I said.

'I like whimsy,' he replied. 'Forethought and forward planning makes Baby a dull girl.'

I thrilled to that name again. 'I completely agree,' I found

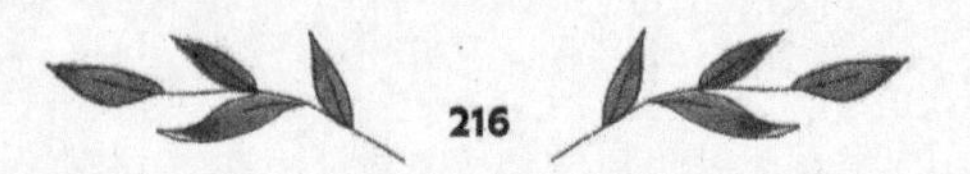

myself saying. 'And Buck a dull boy.' Who was this version of me? I rather liked her.

He nodded at my glass. 'Another?'

Of course. I had had courage. 'I should say so.'

*

The Button Club dispersed in riot, Margot and I, pink-faced and beaming, and hanging off Buck, to the hoots and catcalls of passers-by and the flash-flash-flash of cameras. It was quite the most exciting moment of my life.

The night, though, ended rather less splendidly, with Margot taking a sudden turn for the worse and having to be escorted home (by Ginger Wyndham – Buck having been snatched from my grasp by the wretched Evangeline and dragged off for breakfast at the Belvoirs', more's the pity) before she retched endlessly into the sink. It was not, as one might assume, the alcohol (we had only two each) but rather, a rotten sausage. As with all clubs, the drinking of alcohol at the Button is vigorously policed to ensure it is served only with food, to which end the owner (Mrs Cartland, all cleavage and cologne) – keeps an old sausage on every table as a decoy. Margot was so panicked at the sight of uniforms she ate it, for which gallantry she is still paying the price.

As am I, as I have been forced to return to Ickthorpe as Margot says there is not a hoot of a possibility of her going out later, plus my manic jabbering about Buck was apparently only adding to her awful nausea.

But, and this is the best bit, I don't even care. Because I, Panther Mannering, erstwhile spinster of this parish, am snapped in *The Tatler*!

Ralph handed it to me just as I arrived back with Rapsey, and took great pride and length in showing me exactly the page and location and there it was – or rather there I am – right there, in our bible, in black and white – my hair a quite charming halo, my dress fashionably tangled and carried far above my ankles (though only in order to walk), my arm tight in Buck's. Admittedly, I am described as 'unknown girl', but still this is too, too thrilling. Poor Margot will be distraught of course, though one can catch a glimpse of her forearm to the left of the shot if one peers determinedly (she was momentarily distracted by a pigeon) but I shall remind her of the sanctions that would be imposed if Mrs Forbes-Rawlinson happened upon a copy. As it is I am going to have to secrete ours out of reach of Grandma. I shall tell her it got eaten by snails, or, better, Siegfried, who once ate the entire *Times* before Daddy had even got near the front page.

This, though, was not Ralph's only surprise. Buck, it seemed, had written his column in mere minutes, and mailed it straight to the Dower House from Claridge's. I had hoped he would invite me to Radley and ensconce us in intimate privacy in the morning room, or at least call here in person, but an envelope is better than nothing. I shall despatch it back with Ralph when I'm done. I have already glimpsed one thing begging for amendment: he has described dear Margot as a 'green want-to-be'. However accurate, it is insult on top of the *Tatler* injury. I shall change it to 'fresh debutante', which is at least kinder. Also, there is a letter from Freddy, but I shall save that for when I have time.

Though when that will be I do not know – for, what with *The Tatler*, and *The Herald*, I have far more important organs to occupy myself with than correspondence with the doctor's boy. And then there's the party at the manor on Saturday.

Oh – what a whirl my life is. And how happy am I.

And how thankful that Dinah was born a girl, and that Valentine let Radley to a ghastly American after all.

FRIDAY 27 JUNE

10 A.M.

But what to wear to the ball tomorrow, that is the question.

Thankfully, Marigold has the answer and I the raw material. We are going to dye a pale georgette that Aster made moons ago a daring ruby red so that I will be a veritable jewel – as vivid as the women in the Button Club. Aster has already tailored it to skim me without clinging too much to 'bits' and I have run the bath ready for the grand transformation. Heaven knows where Marigold got the dye from but she insists it is 'good results guaranteed'.

2 P.M.

'Results guaranteed' would have been slightly more accurate. The dress is now a very definite red. But so is the bath enamel, both mine and Marigold's hands, and two pillowcases, several antimacassars and every pair of school socks, which will no doubt distress Mrs Bottomley no end. Marigold was very keen on dying Siegfried as well, but Mama put her foot down at this. As it is, she had had to rescue her own apron and one of Aster's handkerchiefs before they hit the tub and she already has enough explaining to do about the antimacassars. If we were schooled in that sort of thing, we could crochet new ones but alas, my knitting is limited to a scarf with more dropped stitches than actual ones. We will just have to hope Grandma has an unlimited supply of spares (likely, given her disapproval of oily men) or is fond of crimson. How we are to explain our hands, however, is another thing. It looks as if we have done bloody murder.

Though, perhaps it will wash off by the morning.

In fact, I am quite sure of it. Nothing seems to faze me now – I am bathed in joie de vivre. It is quite invigorating being endlessly happy.

Even if it does irritate poor Aster.

SATURDAY 28 JUNE

8 P.M.

I knew my newfound joie de vivre could not last. It never does in the Mannering household. There are far too many traps and catches, and the greatest of all is Grandma.

She has found *The Tatler*. Or rather, Mabel found it, and was so overcome with excitement at my appearance (in every sense) that she ran through the Dower House flapping it above her head as if it were a marathon baton before handing it to Grandma's snatching claw. Then followed much face pulling and several strange noises before the issue of her final decree, which can be summed up thus: a woman of note should only appear in the press three times – birth, marriage and death.

'Four,' said Marigold.

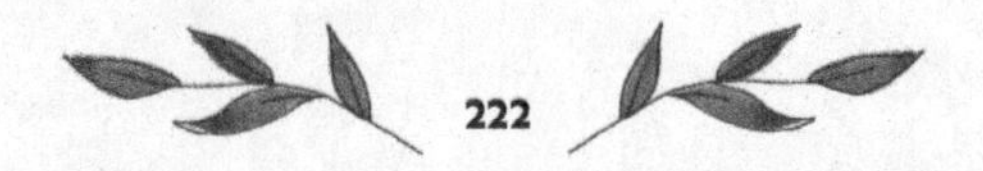

Grandma's eyes narrowed. 'Four?'

'When she has a baby.'

'I suppose,' conceded Grandma, generous as ever.

'Or when she swims the channel or circumnavigates the globe or invents gold,' carried on Marigold.

'That is quite enough,' Grandma snapped.

Given swimming the channel was barely deemed acceptable, being drunk at a nightclub on the arm of a known American was obviously out, and comparable with thievery and vice of the dastardly kind.

'And where was Mrs Forbes-Hamilton?' Grandma hooted. 'Where the chaperones?'

I tried to explain about the cousin and Ginger Wyndham, but she is not keen on the Wyndhams in general – it is something inexplicable to do with pheasants – so this was no sop at all.

Even Mama was perturbed.

'I really thought you had more sense,' she said.

That was a worse blow than anything Grandma could have uttered. Or even Aster, who took great pleasure in hissing 'ruinous' at me several times. Only Marigold pointed out the obvious.

'They don't even know who she is.' (So harsh.) 'So perhaps no one will find out.'

But too late, as apparently Hermione Lightfoot got round to her copy with her sable biscuit and Ceylon blend at four and was straight on the telephone to Grandma demanding sordid details, which thankfully Grandma could not give, having refused to discuss the matter with me (which I suspect she is now beginning to regret) except to confirm that, yes, the 'green want-to-be' described in the *Herald*'s gossip column was likely Margot.

I can only assume Buck didn't get my notes, and hope Margot is still too ill to read it in any case.

But none of this is the worst thing. Nor is it the fact that my hands are still a very visible pink.

Oh, no. The very depth of awfulness is that I have been barred from Buck's party tonight unless I can find a responsible chaperone, and Valentine does not apparently count. Obviously, I have begged Aster several times but she says she would rather eat Hamilton's supper than accompany me, and that is saying something (it is invariably raw liver or rabbit innards). And who else is there, bar Freddy Spencer? And he, according to his missive, is in Italy again.

But I shall be Ickthorpe-bound soon, he writes. *Perhaps we can see each other? I'll treat you to tea at Gilder's!*

As if lardy cake or scones are of any consolation or even interest.

I don't want confectionery or baked goods. I want ridiculously pink cocktails, and sole in brown butter, and snails even! I want to stay up until four and sleep until noon and wake still feeling as giddy as if I'm being danced across a chequered floor under a glinting chandelier. I want ballrooms and basements and Life with a capital L!

Instead, I have sent myself to bed feeling quite sorry for myself, though I have told Mama it is stomach flu.

'Caught from that American, I expect,' said Grandma.

I did not argue, rather groaned and thanked Daddy for my already pale complexion, then exited stage right to no applause at all. Thankfully, Marigold is at Harry's for the night so I can wallow in my own self-pity as much as I like without idiotic interruption. Though I am quite glad of the rabbit she has left, which is snuffling in a comforting way at my feet. Perhaps I shall name it Margot in honour of my poor fallen friend.

Or Buck, in honour of my triumphant new one.

Oh, Buck.

I shall sleep and try to dream of you, dancing and laughing and lighting up the long hall with your wit and brilliance. Before glimpsing me, and abandoning your adoring audience to slip your hand down my silk-draped back and whisper 'Baby' in my ear, and with those both, claim me as your own.

Heavens. *That* is going in the novel.

9 P.M.

I cannot sleep.

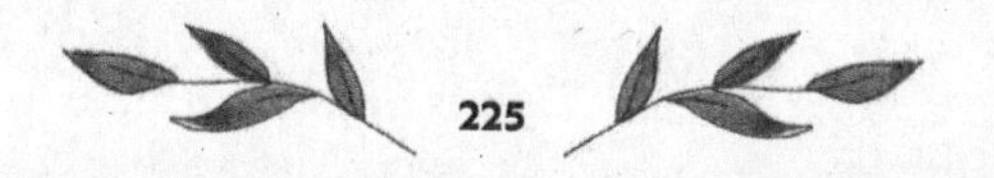

10 P.M.

I cannot sleep. Cars keep passing the house in honks and hoots and whoops of pre-party glee on their merry way to Radley Manor. It is too, too sickening. Also, I cannot persuade Buck to turn his head to catch my eye in the crowd, and instead Evangeline Balfour is dazzling him with her jangling bangles and hip-skimming dress and generally symmetrical eyebrows. Why are even my daydreams so defiantly unpliable?

11 P.M.

This is useless. I shall just have to stay awake all night and content myself with reading Marigold's *Farming Times* (*The Sheikh* is now firmly in the possession of the hens and no one has seen *The Highwayman* in weeks, chief suspects being Marigold and Mabel, who clearly has unsuitable romantic ambitions of her own).

11.10 P.M.

Unless . . .

But no. That cannot happen.

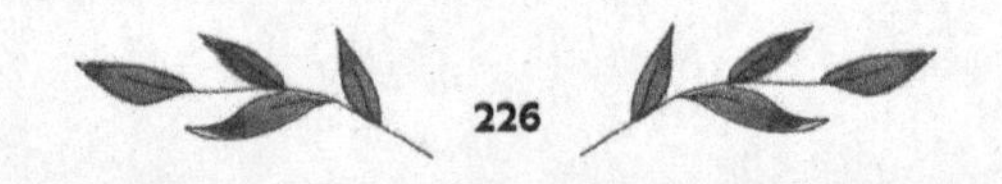

11.11 P.M.

Unless I were to somehow sneak out of the house and run to Radley. Just quickly. Just to glimpse Buck through a window – check he's not clamouring over Evangeline. If anyone asked, or if I was caught, I could say it was work. I could insist we must discuss the column and its misprint as a matter of urgency.

It's plausible. Isn't it?

And purposeful. And purpose is something I must have, according to Freddy. So, if even *he* agrees, then there is nothing for it.

Like Cinderella, I am going to the ball!

(Only with slightly more suitable footwear, pink hands, and possibly no eyebrows as it is awfully dim in here and I cannot put the light on for fear of alerting Aster.)

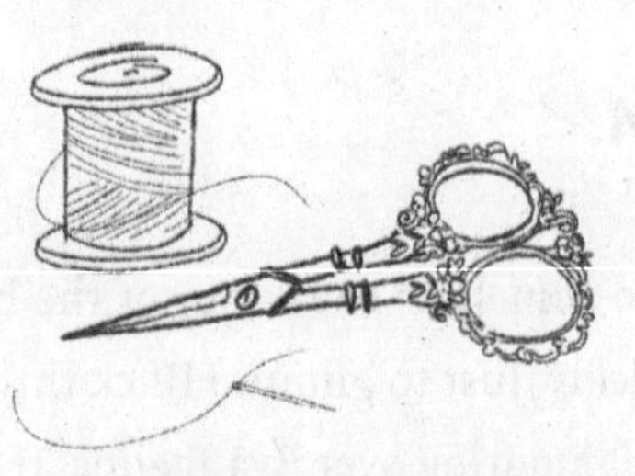

SUNDAY 29 JUNE

7 P.M.

It has taken me this long to be able to hold a pen steady enough to be able to write, and to be able to assemble my memories into something resembling discernible events. As it is, I am writing this from bed, with the window wide open for air, and Siegfried's galvanised bucket next to me in case I have to be sick again.

I do recall that climbing out of a window is not nearly as easy as it seems in romantic novels, especially not in red georgette and evening shoes, even modestly heeled ones. But that, I am afraid to say, is the last really vivid thing I remember. The rest is rather blurred at the edges by the who-knows-how-many coupes of champagne I consumed, on what I now recall

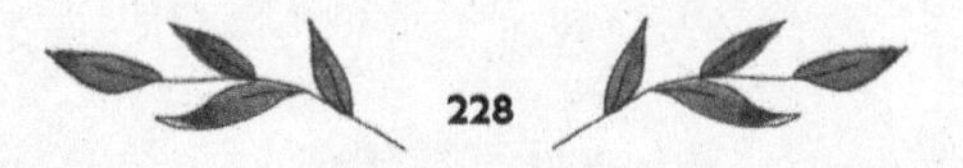

was an entirely empty stomach as I had refused supper on the grounds that I may have stomach flu. Oh, the irony!

There are, though, flashes of accuracy.

I recall reams of people. Coteries of bright, shimmering men and women, behind every door, lounged on every stair and chaise, and in every manner of dress and undress.

I recall the pop of bottles, the clink of coupes, the ring of laughter and talk and gossip being passed and pocketed and created anew.

I recall snapshots of faces: Valentine – FLASH! – straight from the stage, eyes ringed in kohl like Mata Hari and tan arms flung to the heavens as he danced the Charleston; Evangeline Balfour – FLASH! – descending the stairs with the best of the debs; Buck – FLASH! FLASH! FLASH! – holding court with the Old Boys, pouring Bollinger as if it were water, handing out his expansive happiness like candied peel at Christmas.

And did our eyes meet across the crowded floor?

Yes.

Did he smile and stride straight towards me as if to pluck the prize poppy?

Yes.

Did I remain aloof and alluring, pretending he were no more worthy of my attention than a bothersome moth while batting my eyes and willing him to kiss me?

No.

Instead, I rather fear that, fuelled by champagne, I

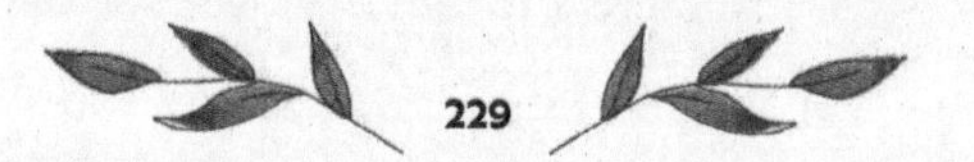

immediately buttonholed him about the column, accusing him of riding roughshod over my editing abilities as well as my feelings.

'You don't understand,' he said. 'It's all about colour. And truth. Isn't truth one of your crusades? You women?'

I wasn't sure to which women he was referring, and argued my point. 'Sometimes,' I think I told him, 'truths are better left unsaid, or at least glossed a little. Especially where women are concerned.'

'Then it's not journalism.'

'So says Jack Buchanan,' I said, intentional in my cruelty, knowing that invoking his father was rather like conjuring a terrible nemesis – someone to do battle with.

'So says Buck,' he retorted, fired up, eyes flashing with something.

I felt a brief pang of guilt, recalling an argument with Aster in which she'd decried 'Cad About Town' as barely being worthy of the 'journalism' tag.

'Half of it's hearsay and the rest downright lies,' she'd declared.

I'd defended it then, but now, in front of Buck, I was ready to go to battle, sword hand swinging.

But before I could parry, he pulled out his pistol. 'You're really quite beautiful when you're angry, you know that?'

And my defences melted, as surely he had known they would. And then someone handed me another glass of champagne, and at some point I stepped out of the long hall for air, and stepped straight into Topaz Attlesey.

'I know you,' I said, as green as can be. (How I shudder now.)

But Topaz, her inky hair slicked down like a man's, her ears glinting with diamonds, smiled. 'Well, I don't know you.' Then she arched an eyebrow (expertly plucked and in stark contrast to my own). 'And I absolutely must, you deliciously crimson thing, because you're frankly dazzling. Is it a Hartnell?' she asked, stroking a swatch of my dress.

'No,' I replied. 'It's a Mannering.'

'Haven't heard of him. But I should, clearly.'

'Her. Aster. I can introduce you one day if you'd like.'

'Oh, I would! Where is her atelier?'

'Her pardon?'

'Where does she work from? Bond Street? Savile Row?'

'Oh, no,' I said. 'The Dower House.'

'Haven't heard of it, either,' she admitted. 'But I'm sure I shall.'

And so convinced of this and everything was she that she took me by the arm as if we were the best of friends and marched me to the morning room, which is now something else entirely, and, even more alarmingly, hung with Aster's nudes, which I hadn't even known were left behind, let alone on display.

'But that's her!' I blurted.

'Who?'

'My sister. Aster!'

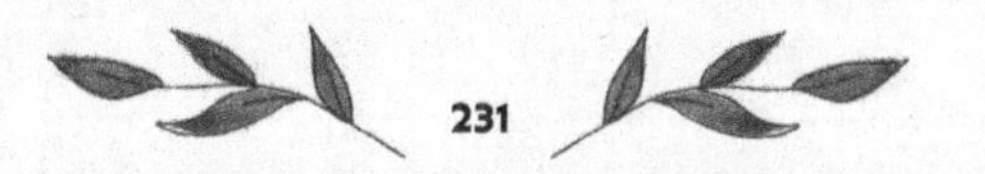

'The dressmaker?' Topaz peered closer at one clearly daubed in the folly. 'She doesn't look at all like you.'

'Oh, no. I mean my sister painted it. The model is Daphne Balfour. Or rather Daphne Pakenham now.'

'Poor woman,' said Topaz. 'His face is so . . .'

'Cheese-like,' I finished for her.

'Yes!' Topaz cried. 'How clever a description. You are clearly quite the talent.'

'Oh, no,' I insisted, 'Aster is far cleverer than I.'

'Then you are both complete geniuses,' she replied and she whisked me off for hot jazz and cold cocktails, plural.

And everything after that, I am afraid to say, is a giddy, sickening blur.

*

It seems mere minutes later that Aster was dragging me out of someone else's bed (whose bed? Not Buck's – he is in Mama's old bedroom. Nor even the one that used to be mine. I think it must have been Aster's room, though it was hard to tell with the gaudy wallpaper and my blurred vision).

Anyway, what looms largest is not the wallpaper, but Topaz, who had hitherto been passed out in a chair, and the positively seething Aster.

'At least it's not Buck's bed,' I drawled as I was dragged unceremoniously from under the covers.

'How do I know he didn't ravage you then abandon you?' She swung me upright, and propped me while I waited from the room to stop its whirligig round.

'Well, he didn't.' More's the pity. I sighed. 'Anyway, what kind of woman do you think I am?'

'A foolish one.'

That was when Topaz thankfully intervened. 'Do be kind,' she urged. 'I think it's her first.'

Aster turned to notice her. And something in her slipped, it seemed. 'First what?' she asked, significantly less bristling.

'Hangover,' replied Topaz. She stretched, languid as a cat. 'Aster, isn't it?'

'What? Yes, I . . .'

But at that moment, my insides all seemed to surge and gurgle. 'I think I might be—' I managed, before dashing to the window, throwing open the casement and heaving what little I'd eaten onto poor Daddy's begonias.

'Revolting,' muttered Aster.

'Poor thing,' said Topaz.

I whimpered in reply. It was all I could muster. Though my presence was suddenly, and thankfully, not the focus of the room.

'So, *you're* the artist,' I heard Topaz say.

'Pardon?'

'I saw your nudes. Of that Pakenham gal. You painted her well. With the eye of an admirer. Or lover, even.'

She paused, and I held my breath, the room pin-drop quiet.

Topaz went on, and air released a little, but only a little. 'Though she's not half as beautiful as you, of course.'

Was Topaz sapphic? What was I witnessing?

'Beauty is in the eye of the beholder,' said Aster, without the snap I expected.

'Clearly.'

Their eyes were locked. It was mesmerising, even in my weakened state. This woman was as different from her pock-marked, mumbling brother as a pea from a peppercorn – or Evangeline from Daphne or I, indeed, from Aster.

'I . . . Well . . .' stammered Aster.

It was almost lucky I chose that moment to be copiously sick again or who knows what would have happened?

*

Aster was back to being Asterish all the way home. She demanded to know what I had been thinking, sneaking out like that, and, without waiting for an answer, said I was lucky she'd been woken by the bleating of Siegfried, who had got himself wedged in a corner in the kitchen. (Marigold and Grandma could sleep through cannon-fire, and Mama is busy being alert to Dinah's manifold cries, so cannot be expected to be rallying for animals as well.) 'And I can't believe he's put a billiard table in the long gallery.'

On she went, listing the ridiculous and irredeemable things Buck has supposedly done to blacken Radley's reputation as a house of standing. I did not dare point out it never had one in the first place.

It was then I noticed something, clutched in her hand.

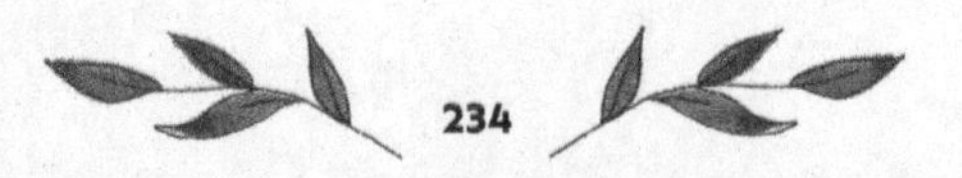

Ragged and filthy and limp. 'Why are you carrying Marigold's monkey?' I asked. 'Did you bring him with you?'

She held him up, as if only just remembering he was there. 'Albertine? Don't be ridiculous,' she snapped. 'I found him. In the hedge just past the dead elm.'

'But . . .' I remembered the table-top sale. 'But he's Buck's. He bought him.'

'Well, he can't have thought much of him if he threw him away like that.'

I felt queasy and seasick again. This was strange. Wrong. 'It must have been an accident. Perhaps he was flung from the car – it swerves ever so much.'

Aster gave me a withering look, and opened her mouth, but then seemed to stopper up whatever she wanted to say. 'Just hurry up, for heaven's sake,' she urged in the end. 'And straight to bed before anyone sees you. Otherwise I shall jolly well tell all.'

And that is what I did.

*

When I awoke, ten hours later, it was to Mama perched on the edge of my bed, her face etched with concern.

'I'm sorry you're ill,' she said, her cool hand resting for a second on my brow. 'And for not letting you go to the party. There will be others though.'

She didn't know. Aster hadn't blabbed.

'Yes,' I said, contrite as possible. 'Thank you.'

'Ring the bell if you need anything.' She rose, patted down

the rumpled sheets. 'And don't even think of getting up until you're better.'

I nodded.

And she left.

And here I am. Giddy, still; sick with acid champagne, with guilt (though I didn't do anything ruinous at all this time) and with something else – a sort of awkwardness, vulnerability.

To think all those brilliant people – all those Bright Young Things – had been there, draped over sofas in our old drawing room, clattering down the staircase, gavotting across the long hall. For a second, then, I felt a wash of disappointment, that Radley wasn't ours, not any more, only by distant association. And a weird feeling that I shouldn't have been there at all – I was a fraud, an imposter, a foolish village girl who thought she could play with the grown-ups when all she is really fit for is cribbage with her sisters and tea at Gilder's with the solid doctor's son.

But then I remembered how Topaz had said I was dazzling, how Buck had declared me beautiful, how I'd laughed and spun and even sung at one point and suddenly nothing mattered any more – doesn't matter.

Because now – now I am one of them.

JULY

SATURDAY 5 JULY

7 P.M.

It is all very well going to smart parties, but if there is anything to remind one that once a Mannering, always a Mannering, it is Marigold.

Today is her eleventh birthday, a milestone that should be accompanied by some sort of transformation, a putting-away of childish things and embracing of sense, or at least fewer catastrophic tendencies.

Instead, she has stolen a penguin.

I suppose it was almost inevitable. Ever keen on expanding her menagerie, all talk lately has been of monkeys. Apparently, someone called Evan Tredegar has a cage of marmosets halfway up the stairs and Sassoon has a golden thing who wears a

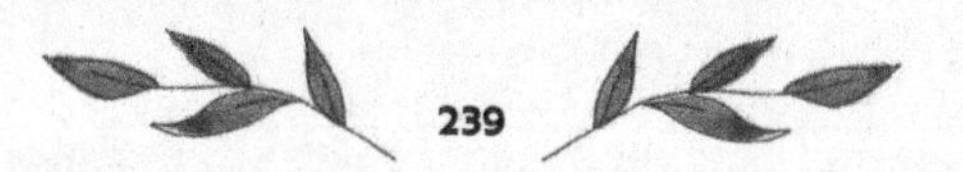

waistcoat and dances a jig, which Marigold did agree seemed rather cruel, but suggested that, if she *were* to get one, hers wouldn't have to dance at all unless it chose to. Thankfully, Grandma immediately vetoed any simian immigration on the grounds that Marigold can barely control Siegfried and he is limited to the things he can climb on. Imagine a monkey that could swing from doorjamb to lamp to mantle, outdoing even Hamilton's feats of menacing trapeze.

Mama said Marigold would just have to settle for a visit to the zoo. I was hoping for Regent's Park as an excuse to see Margot (recovered from the sausage incident but not from the fact that Brilliant Baker has sailed home to Chicago with his trombonist) but Mama, quite astutely, deduced Buck was in London this weekend and vetoed that as well – she does not agree with Grandma's 'three times only' press assessment, but does want to keep the peace. So, instead, we were to troop to Mole Hall, which is short on lions and tigers, but has several snakes and penguins and a solitary otter, and has the advantage of being a short drive away and rather less dear. I was commandeered to accompany the party, about which I did complain. However, Mama said it was hard enough to corral Marigold alone but with an accomplice (Harry was joining us) one needed forty pairs of eyes to keep track. Which I had to admit was true: individually they are quite problematic, but together they form one unstoppable force of tomfoolery. It is a shame leading reins are frowned upon above the age of four. I did briefly suggest Aster as she is far beadier-eyed and better at controlling things, but apparently she was busy in the back attic doing heaven knows what and we were not to disturb her.

This was clearly a mistake.

For a start, once we arrived at the zoo, Mama was mainly occupied with Dinah, and trying to stop her licking the cages. (Her latest thing is to stick her tongue on anything – animal, vegetable or mineral – for as long as she is allowed. Which, given the many distractions at the Dower House can sometimes be minutes.) So, that left only my eyes to follow Bad Harry and Marigold wherever they roamed, which was extensive, and at lightning speed. Every time I managed to hold one in my sights, the other would disappear behind a refuse bin, or awkwardly placed privet hedge. And this was before the incident with Mrs Gibberd.

What Mrs Gibberd was doing at Mole Hall I do not know, unless she is a secret snake-fancier, but she somehow manifested outside the reptile house (more of a wooden hut really) and started asking all manner of questions about my *Tatler* appearance as apparently there has been 'talk' and 'everyone' is 'all ears' to know whether Buck and I are a) courting (Hermione Lightfoot) b) engaged to be married (Celia Rigby) or c) secretly already married and expecting (Joyce Goggins, with whom I am furious as c)i. I have not been in the vicinity of any penis, let alone Buck's and c)ii. I did not think my stomach was quite so big as to resemble pregnancy). I said that none of these things were in fact accurate (more's the pity in cases a and b) but that he was merely the new tenant at Radley and so it was more an act of neighbourly friendship. Of course, *that* elicited an inquisition into what he'd done to the manor (rumours include an aviary at the tamer end of things, and a Turkish bath in Cook's old pantry at the more outlandish). Clearly none of them have ever seen Cook's pantry.

By the time I had dissuaded her of the birds and the Turkish bath, as well as several other bizarre and unlikely additions, I had completely lost track of both time and the children. It was Rapsey's frantic honking from the entrance that alerted me to the fact I had been buttonholed for over an hour, and who knew what havoc Marigold and Harry might have wreaked in that interlude.

I suppose I should have had my suspicions in the car. The pair were clearly in cahoots: Harry clutching her school satchel as if it were the Ark of the Covenant itself, and Marigold asking loud and manifold questions about the workings of the universe, which I now know were a calculated distraction but at the time seemed standard Marigold randomness.

'But what is at the end of the universe?' (Ask Mama.)

'But which bit does God live in and does he share it with Allah?' (Ask the vicar.)

'But why does the world even exist?' (Ask Grandma. For amusement purposes only.)

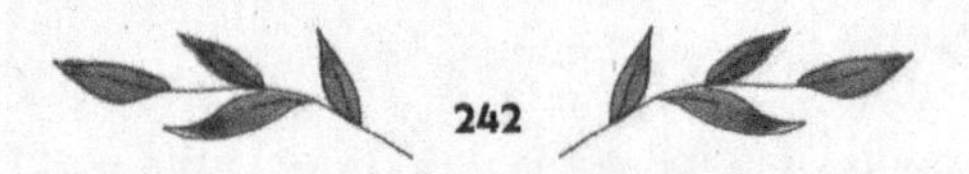

Then followed a long monologue about stars only shining because they are dying and whether Siegfried might be about to die and how would we know. All of which was so sad and baffling and exhausting that no one thought to wonder about Marigold's frantic clapping when we arrived back at the Dower House, or Harry's refusal to relinquish her satchel to the hatstand, or the pair running upstairs and locking themselves in the bathroom and immediately turning on the taps. I admit I just thought Marigold's new maturity had engendered a sudden interest in cleanliness.

More fool I.

The only clean thing among them is the wretched penguin.

We were alerted to the 'situation' by Mabel's yelp, then arrival into the dining room with a complexion paled to the colour of whey, and an inability to articulate anything beyond 'Ugh!' and odd pointing.

Mama, sensing catastrophe of the Marigold-made kind, said she would deal with whatever it was, and I, sensing this was a two-woman situation, and possibly very much my fault, scuttled after her, only to find the creature (a dear thing really) swimming disconsolately in pink-tinged enamel.

Marigold, called upon to explain herself, admitted she and Harry had lured it from the Mole Hall pond with an egg sandwich.

'He was awfully keen to come,' she insisted. 'It wasn't thievery.'

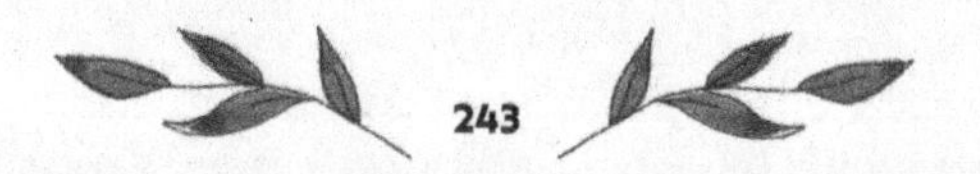

'But it *is* thievery,' Mama tried to explain. 'As he's not really yours.'

'But animals are their own beings,' Marigold continued with mustered authority. 'He can live with whomever he chooses.'

Mama, however, never one to be stumped for long by Marigold, countered cleverly, 'And what if Siegfried chose to live at Mole Hall?'

It was Marigold's turn to pale then; she agreed to the penguin's immediate return, which was scuppered only when we realised the hall was closed until Monday. So Marigold's birthday wish is granted, for two days at least, and she is merrily playing with her temporary penguin (now named Hector), having fed it half a tin of sardines, a slab of Battenburg and a piece of cheese. (It has rejected both the Battenburg and the cheese, which are now soggily floating in the pink-tinged enamel quite revoltingly. As are several of Hector's emissions.)

I only pray Grandma does not require a bath for the foreseeable future but limits herself to the sink in her room and the lavatory on the landing. As it is, we are in her black books for the dye and have had to agree to an IOU to be determined once Derek Nesbitt (uncle of Reg, Essex flyweight champion, and sometime plumber) has assessed the situation. Any recompense is pie in the sky anyway as, aside from Aster, whom I assume is beavering away with a needle in the attic, we are still woefully impoverished and it is Grandma who pays for practically everything. Which is why I need another invite to

Radley, and soon, as I fear I squandered the last being dazzled by flappers and wasted by champagne.

Next time I shall be the very epitome of polite, refined society.

Or, at the very least, I shall be from a penguin-free (if not beast-free) home.

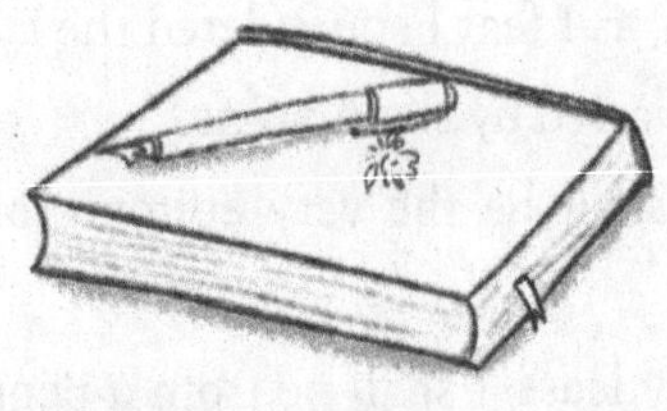

MONDAY 7 JULY

10 A.M.

Marigold managed to keep Hector's presence a secret from Grandma for precisely twenty-four hours.

The Dower House, and possibly the entirety of Ickthorpe parish, was alerted to the discovery yesterday afternoon when Grandma, deciding she might be coming down with something and, in the absence of Mabel, who was spending her afternoon off going to look at Ralph's geraniums (I do hope this is not a euphemism but fear it may well be), saw fit to run herself a bath, only to find it already occupied, smelling of sardines, and most of her lily of the valley bath salts missing (though that, I suspect, was me in pre-Buck preparation).

There was much wailing (Grandma), flapping (Hector),

and protesting (Marigold), until eventually Grandma was ushered to bed with a hot, restorative beef tea; Hector was confined to the pantry with a bucket and a rollmop herring; and Marigold was forced to add the cost of a bar of Pears soap, the rest of the bath salts (upended in the kerfuffle) and several towels declared beyond wash or repair to the enamel damage. Marigold is bereft as she had been hoping to raise her own flock, however this argument is moot, as, while we have no idea if Hector is male or female, he or she has not laid an egg, and is being returned to Mole Hall this morning in any case.

Of course, the task has been left to Rapsey and me, Marigold being otherwise occupied with the necessity of school and the horror of Mrs Bottomley, and Aster still doing heaven knows what upstairs. Some of it, I believe, is sewing, as the distant crank and rattle of Mama's old Singer is a constant accompaniment to all activity, but how many dresses can she be mending? What are these women doing to cause such rents? (I am quite sure Grandma has an opinion, especially if any of the gowns belong to Hermione Lightfoot.)

Anyway, Rapsey has the motorcar already turning over, while I have Hector shut in a Fortnum's hamper (this was the only suitable receptacle other than Grandma's old meat safe, which one of the hens – Captain, a sort of hen overlord – has claimed as her own and will fight for her right to defend it).

Pray for me, dear journal, for returning a stolen penguin

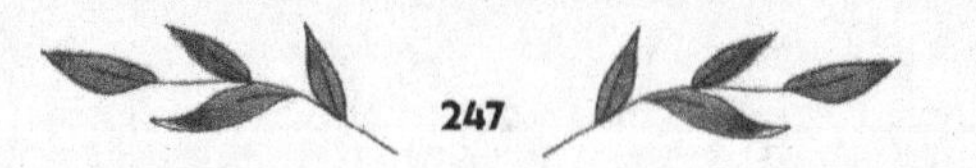

cannot be without mishap. Not when there is a Mannering at hand.

7 P.M.

I am not sure if this entirely counts as mishap, or more, wilful neglect. But the simple fact is the motorcar is dead, Rapsey is taking a week off for his nerves, and Hector the penguin is back in the pantry.

I shall spare you the mechanical details; suffice it to say we had barely left the Dower House when smoke began pouring out from somewhere (the engine I presume) and, temporarily blinded, Rapsey swerved and hit a lamppost, upon which impact more great billows erupted and I was flung unceremoniously on top of Hector's hamper, which burst open, releasing its excitable contents straight out of the window, past Mrs Gypp and her King Charles spaniel and onto the village green.

Of course, I was thankful none of us was injured, not least the spaniel, who, had he been several seconds later in his urination, may well have never urinated again. And thankful too that he and Mrs Gypp were our only witnesses. Which is when it began to unravel further. Or neatly stitch itself up, depending on your viewpoint.

Because that, of course, was the moment that Buck showed up.

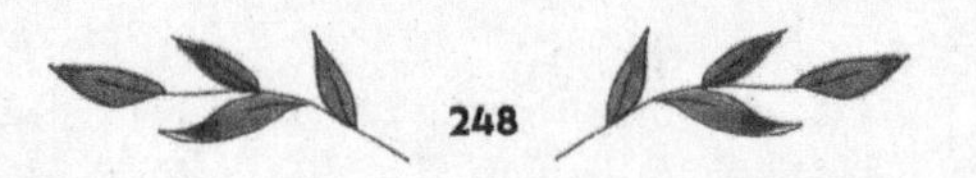

'Baby?' His motorcar had pulled to a graceful, smokeless halt next to the wreck of our own.

I flushed, feeling not only his wide eyes, but Mrs Gypp's narrowed ones on me. 'Buck.' I hurriedly dusted myself down, praying it was only feathers stuck to my sensible dress, and wishing I had thought to wear something more becoming.

'In trouble?'

'I . . . you see . . .' Perhaps I was in shock.

'Can I give you a lift somewhere?'

I peered across the green to where Rapsey was giving chase to a determined penguin who had undoubtedly spied the duck pond. Should I help him? Or would I just be a cumbrance? He was rather masterful with all the Siegfried practice after all.

I was suddenly seized with something. Perhaps it was the emancipation I felt with my new hair, or just the whimsy of a summer day, but I knew I couldn't let this opportunity pass. 'Actually,' I said, 'that would be splendid.'

And with that, I tossed my bob, set back my shoulders, and slipped into the passenger seat as if I were Evangeline herself. Abandoning the old Panther on Ickthorpe Green, along with Rapsey and the penguin.

*

Of course, I could have asked Buck to take me home. Should have. I could have alerted Grandma, or mustered Mama and some extra hands to wrangle the wildfowl, but you have to understand what a thrill this was, to be beside a man, and a handsome one at that, careening along the Larkham road, the wind in my hair and my cares, for now, dispelled on a gust of summer.

It was enervating. Emboldening. I went with it. 'So where are we going?' I asked.

Buck looked across, his whiter than white smile widening. 'To see your cousin, actually.'

I started. 'Who? Valentine?'

Buck laughed. 'That's right. We're going to London, Baby.'

*

It transpired that Valentine had a business proposal for Buck – some sort of investment potential, which sounded improbable as Valentine rarely invested in anything, rather frittered it on this and that and nothing in particular. As evidenced by his flat, where we went to fetch him.

Mama would have a conniption. I cannot work out if it is down to appalling taste or none at all, but it was all rather eclectic and garish, as if the collected antique dealers of St James's had deposited their entire stock in the three rooms, with no thought to what might suit, or even fit. Profusely carved tables rub up against vast cloisonné vases and a marquetry vitrine, while the walls are flock-papered, and gilt-painted, and smattered with parrots and toucans at once. Not to mention the several overflowing ashtrays and questionable stain on the chaise. The effect was quite nauseating.

'Sorry, I've not cleaned up,' he lamented. 'Maid's off.'

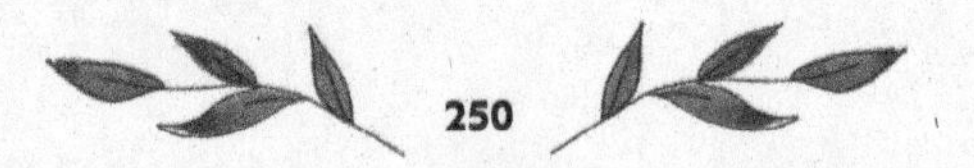

Which is rich as I knew very well the maid left for Sorrento with Aunt Valentina. But I said nothing of course, and just prayed Buck found it bohemian as opposed to a slum. In any case, we were barely there for minutes as Valentine had somewhere he wanted to show us.

'It's a theatre,' he said as we wound our way through a rather insalubrious corner of Soho. 'Little place but with big potential.'

He wasn't wrong. The Pippin lived up to its name, barely seating a hundred and fifty, and tiered at such a rake as to be dizzying, all the better to fit into the postage stamp of a plot of land on Beak Street. Meanwhile, the curtains were moth-eaten, the stage splintered and worn, and the fire safety all but non-existent. But there was something magical about it, even for me who has never thrilled to the smell of greasepaint or roar of anything.

'This way I can put on what I like.'

'And cast whom you like?' Buck questioned.

'Well, I . . .'

The fact was, Valentine was failing to get the meaty roles, and was having to make do with duds or the understudy. Not for lack of talent, I like to think, but for fashion perhaps. In any case, I suppose this made sense. And I knew Valentine needed it. And that mattered more than rightness to me.

'You'd be like Barnum,' I gushed suddenly. 'Or . . . or the other one. An entrepreneur in any case.'

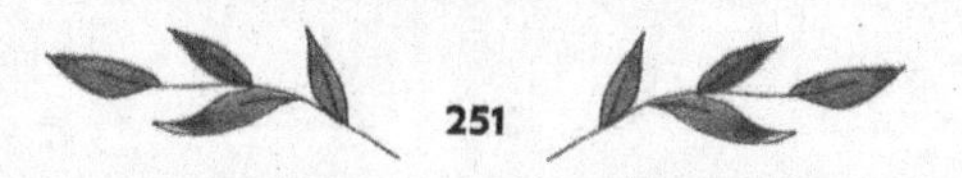

Buck shrugged. 'Not sure I have that kind of collateral.'

'You could ask your father,' I pushed.

Valentine nodded, rather too desperately.

'Sure,' said Buck. 'Sure.' But his face twitched a little, and I saw him stiffen, just slightly.

*

'Will you?' I asked later, as we sat in Claridge's (Claridge's!) awaiting beef sandwiches with horseradish sauce.

'Will I what?'

'Ask your father.'

Buck shrugged. 'Not sure he'd listen. Not sure I should anyway. That Valentine' – he paused to light a cigarette – 'he'll end up in Reading.'

'Reading?' I questioned. Then flushed, realising my naivety. Reading Gaol, like Oscar Wilde, famous playwright and infamous homosexual. 'He's careful,' I said. 'Not that he should have to be.'

Buck frowned. Then, as if caught by something dazzling, flashed a smile. 'Anyway, enough about your cousin. It's you I want to talk about.'

I felt weak, both in need of those sandwiches and not sure I could even eat one. 'Is it?'

'Yes.' He tapped his cigarette into engraved silver. 'I'm having a thing. A party. On the nineteenth.'

A hum ran through me. 'Like last time?'

'More . . . intimate. Dinner. Just five or six of us.'

'Who?' I asked, begging for clemency guest-wise. I was to be strangely blessed.

'Well, you and I. And Evangeline—'

At this my heart sunk. Of course, Evangeline. Why would I assume otherwise?

But Buck, it seemed, had yet to finish his sentence.

'—and this new Frenchie of hers. Gaston something.' He spat the name out as Grandma might.

'DuPont?' I asked, remembering the assumedly now-abandoned Cynthia Chivers. So Evangeline had a man. Interesting.

'That's the cad. And Topaz. You know Topaz?'

'I do,' I replied, delighted with that, too. 'She's marvellous.' Then I felt my stomach slump. 'But . . . I'll need a chaperone, or I shan't be allowed.'

'Then bring your sister.'

This was no tonic. 'I doubt she'll agree. She doesn't . . .' *Approve,* I thought. 'Do parties,' I said.

'So, call it dinner.' Buck's eyes flashed at me and I swear I felt it – whatever *it* was – in my very bones.

'Very well,' I said, trying to dampen my ardour, muster some of Hamilton's disdain. 'I shall ask.'

*

But that, I confess, is a task I have, as yet, avoided, having been occupied since my return with explaining myself, at length, and several times, as to my absence, apologising to all and sundry

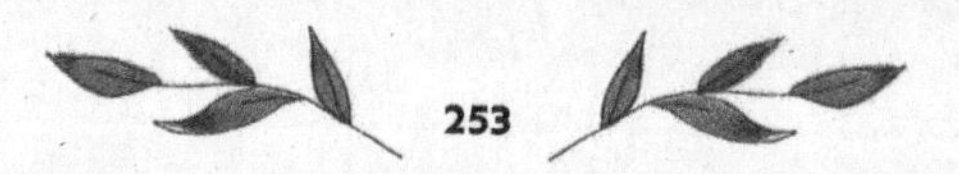

for the abandonment of Rapsey, and agreeing to walk the wretched penguin back to Mole Hall tomorrow myself.

I would ask Aster but as Hector is now in our bedroom (much to Marigold's delight), and quite vocal about it, I fear any more penguin menace may only succeed in her refusing to talk to me at all.

As for me, I could happily put up with a whole colony of penguins if it meant another night with Buck. I could barely eat at luncheon, could barely breathe in the car on the way home, as his hand brushed my thigh – quite deliberately, I believe. And when he dropped me at the Dower House door, I was sure he was leaning in for a kiss.

I closed my eyes, felt a finger touch my forehead, then – oh – tuck a wayward curl behind my ear. But my disappointment, though palpable, was brief.

I opened my eyes to see him smile.

'You really are something, Baby,' he said.

I felt my insides wilt and swoon. Then remembered myself. Mustered. 'I rather am, aren't I,' I said.

And with that, I climbed out of the car, clunked the door behind me, and walked into the Dower House without even looking back.

How daring of me!

Maybe Panth is gone after all, left on the bedroom floor with the rest of my hair. But I am glad, because, whatever Mama says about loyalty, I like this new me.

And what's more, it's as clear as the Ickthorpe river that so does Buck.

SUNDAY 20 JULY

2 A.M.

I can't sleep. I can't think.

But I can write. So I shall. And tell you everything – beginning with my sister.

*

It took several days for me to brace myself enough to face Aster and beg for the favour. My legs almost trembled as I ascended the attic – as well they might, as she had forbidden anyone to venture near it, including Marigold, her many rabbits, and Hamilton.

Should I knock? I wondered. Would heralding my entry lessen the injury? Or better, should I just barge in and blurt the words and thus leave her no choice but to hear me out? In

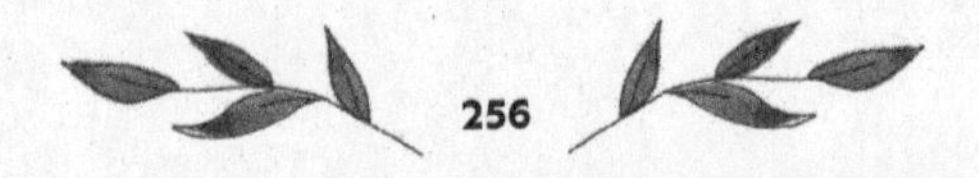

the end I opted for the latter, turning the handle in my damp hand and clattering into the room in what seemed to be one precarious movement, eliciting, as predicted, a howl from a gape-mouthed Aster.

But that was the moment any plan I may have had went awry as there stood my sister in a state of some dishevelment, not sewing – though there in the corner was the Singer and there next to the window several dresses awaiting repair – but painting.

And oh, what a painting! I recognised it – her – at once. Mannish and feminine and entirely sexual. Alive with it.

It was Topaz Attlesey. Doe-eyed and slick-haired.

And naked as the day she was born.

'I . . .' But words would not come.

Instead, it was left to Aster to fill the dust-mote silence. But not with scarlet rage, or even snippy vitriol. But instead, with a soft, heavy, desperate edge, 'Please don't tell,' she begged.

'I shan't,' I promised, still mesmerised by the portrait. And then, spoken as if in a dream. 'She'll be at dinner at Buck's on Saturday. Will you come?'

At that, Aster's body seemed to come to life, her eyes brightening to match her wild hair, and gratitude practically snapped from her. 'Yes,' she answered. 'Yes, please.'

*

So that is how we found ourselves tonight, seated in the long hall, I between Buck and Evangeline's moustachioed Frenchman, and Aster between he and Buck.

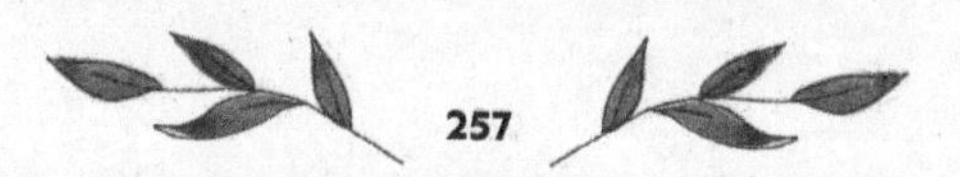

But opposite her, rendering Evangeline a washed-out sketch or mere line drawing, sat Topaz. The very personification of a goddess. Skin like an alabaster statue, lips like vermillion pillows, hair and cheekbones as precise as a geometry lesson. At one point I found that my fingers were reaching out on the verge of touching her. Only Aster snapping, 'Panth!' made me snatch them back and remember it is not etiquette to manhandle other guests.

I would say it is a shame that Aster doesn't quite match up. I'm not claiming she isn't without good looks but they had previously seemed in a different league to those belonging to Topaz. Aster is classically handsome. Beautiful, in her own way. It's just that her way is so very far from that of Topaz. At least I thought it was. But tonight, Aster seemed to glow with something, as if bathed, haloed even, in warm light, which rendered her a luminous beauty all her own. And Topaz, I knew, saw it too. She sat, gazing, as rapt in Aster as Aster in she. Questioning her about her dress (the low-back thing she'd worn to rattle Daphne at the wedding), begging Aster to sew her a version. Aster could barely speak, but managed to stammer out that mauve wasn't quite Topaz's colour, but a deep green would be the thing, if only Mrs Booth could get hold of some.

They seemed to match, somehow, despite their many differences. Something fitted, clicked, slipped into each other like pieces of a jigsaw puzzle. And I wondered then about Buck and I, if that might be – was – us. I knew I didn't measure up when standing next to Evangeline. She was born to his gilt-edged world, while I hung at the fringes. But wasn't difference all part of it? Look at Daddy and Mama, after all.

And Evangeline and the Frenchman – he has two decades on her at least, and all manner of strangeness, but she seemed smitten. Or at least she played that part to perfection – it is never quite clear which with her.

And the night itself was different. Not the rackety, spangled glamour of the last party, but something thrumming anyhow, busy with the electricity of six Bright Young Things, or youngish in one case. And with something else.

Love.

*

It is as if I knew it was coming. I could sense it through dinner, could feel his need to get me alone as he eyed the Frenchman with irritation, with his endless, incomprehensible sentences that all seemed to end in him cupping Evangeline's delicate face in his swarthy hands and declaring her his 'amour'. I am glad Margot wasn't there as she would have swooned within minutes. He is everything she wants in a man: too old, foreign and possibly dangerous.

Not Buck, though. Buck may be American, but he has manners, youth and money on his side.

'Shall we walk?' he asked, after we had demolished coffee and chocolate (which had sent my already skittering nerves zinging).

I remembered myself in time and painted on the new, improved me. 'Shame to waste such an evening.'

And what an evening – starlit, still warm, and heaven-scented thanks to Daddy's legacy. It's not that I didn't appreciate it before – I did. But now I saw it anew, felt it anew, because I had Buck's eyes to see it through, his everything with which to sense it.

We walked slowly, side by side, Buck's hands thrust in his pockets, mine dangling, waiting, wishing. For hours it felt like, though it can only have been minutes – each one of them thick with intensity. For then we were standing on the little bridge, staring at the folly, where Aster and Daphne had stayed, where Freddy and I played, and now . . .

'What *is* that thing?' Buck said at last. 'I keep wondering. It just seems so . . . pointless.'

'It's just . . . a folly,' I replied. 'It's not *for* anything. It's just meant to look good.'

Buck turned to me, his hair gilt, his face glimmering silver in the moonlight. 'Like me?'

I felt myself weaken. 'You're not pointless.'

'My father thinks so.'

'Maybe he just wants you to do some good. Don't you crave . . .' – I heard Freddy in my head – 'purpose?'

'Purpose?'

'You know – a reason for being here.'

Buck shrugged. 'What's yours, then?'

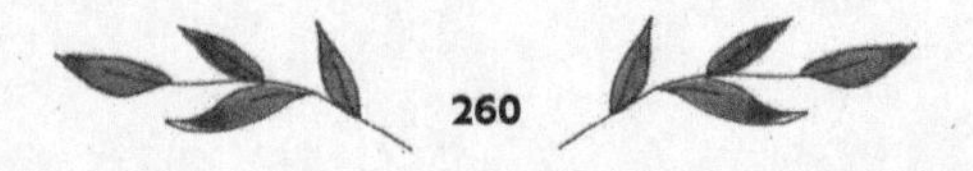

'I . . .' What would I do, I wondered, if I had all this at my feet as Buck had? But my thoughts were interrupted.

'Be beautiful.'

I bloomed, my cheeks red as peppers, thankful for the shawl of night to hide them. 'Pardon?'

'That's your purpose. To decorate my world.'

I should have refused to be flattered. I should have mustered a calling to suffrage or medicine or at least teaching. But something was happening and I found my words stoppered, and emotions – devilish, reckless – taking over.

'The stars,' I blurted, to hide the wildness I felt in me.

'Stars?' Buck looked up.

I clutched for something else. 'You know they only shine when they die. Stars, I mean.' Oh, gosh, what was I saying?

'How very depressing.'

Alarmingly, I did not stop. 'It's their death rattle, I suppose.'

Buck paused. 'But what a beautiful death.'

And at that he turned to me. And I knew what was happening. He was going to kiss me, and in that second I felt life had begun and could end happily on this bridge, in the depths of Essex.

Then our lips met – I was being kissed for the very first time – and I would like to say violins played and the world tilted on its axis. But actually, it was oddly clinical. I could taste the beef we'd had at dinner. Hear the clack of his teeth. Feel the eel-ness (Margot was right) of his tongue pushing at mine. And all the time worrying, wondering, if I was doing it correctly. Or if it was my fault that something was missing.

But then I did feel something: a surge in the trouser area, something urgent and pressing itself against my dress.

'Oh, Baby,' he moaned.

It was a penis! An actual penis!

Oh, God. It was both horrifying and strangely empowering that the inside of my mouth could make *that* happen.

I pulled away. 'I . . .'

'Baby, come on.'

What to do? We were alone, too far from the house to raise an alarm, no one to check with that this was natural, desirable. Though I have to say I did feel it, in me, I mean. A sort of quickening, contracting inside at the point where he pushed so. Was this what the sheikh's women so gasped about? It wasn't entirely unwanted, just so very . . . new. And now.

'Buck, I–'

But I did not need to say another word. For at that moment came an unexpected sound. Not human. Not ours. But, from the inside of the folly, the unmistakable bleat of Siegfried.

I had never been happier to see that sheep.

'I'll have to take him home, of course,' I blustered.

'What? Now?'

'Yes, now. This minute. Or he may eat cement again and who knows what might happen.' I didn't know what might happen, probably nothing, but Buck was not to know that.

'Have you a piece of string, or a scarf, or something?'

'No. But you have.'

And at that he held my waist, and, eyes still fixed on mine, unravelled the length of organza that Aster had rustled up to cinch my dress.

'I . . . Oh, well done.'

I looked away, still flustered, both by man and sheep, and tied the pale peach material around the recalcitrant animal.

'I'll send Aster after you,' he said. 'If Topaz will release her.'

He wasn't coming? 'But . . .' And try as I might, the new defiant, mighty Baby was gone and clamouring Panther back. 'When will I see you again? Tomorrow?'

Buck frowned. 'Didn't I say? We're off to Paris in the morning. Last week of the Olympics. Gaston's driving us all.'

'All?' Did he mean me? Oh, how I wished, but–

'Gaston, Evie and yours truly.'

My balloon of hope was well and truly pricked.

'Then the Riviera for the rest of the season. Gaston has a villa in St Paul de something or other.'

'St Paul de Vence,' I finished, picturing it: all dramatic lavender and honeyed light and cocktails at Cannes.

'So, August sometime. The end, I expect.'

'What about your column?' This was my last gasp – surely he'd need me to edit, check, even write the damn thing!

'I'll send it over – telegram, I guess. You don't mind, do you, Baby.'

It wasn't a question but I answered anyway. 'Not at all,' I lied. Then, 'You'll miss my birthday.' I hadn't meant to say it aloud, it just came out of its own accord.

'Your birthday?'

'But it doesn't matter,' I corrected myself quickly.

'Of course it does. How old will you be?'

'Seventeen. Practically ancient.'

'Practically.' Buck laughed. 'When it is it?'

'The twenty-third,' I admitted.

'Then, if I don't see you, happy birthday, Baby.'

And then he kissed me again, full and hard, on the lips. And this time something in me shifted, though it may well have been the beef.

'Baby,' he repeated, and then the pushing again, with the thing!

'Buck,' I muttered. But then a yank on my hand and a strong smell of livestock reminded me. 'I must go,' I said, and this time with an air of lament. Maybe I did want this – it – after all.

But before I could even consider shutting the sheep in the folly, Buck was gone, across the lawn towards the carousing Evangeline and Gaston, and . . . who knows what Topaz and Aster were doing.

Not I, for it's now half past two and she's still not home, and, frankly, who can blame her? I don't feel in the least bit sleepy either. I just can't stop thinking about it. That hot, hard urgency. It's not like the animals I've seen at it or Marigold's clinical descriptions. But highwayman-like, sheikh-like after all. Hungry and heaving and needy.

And the kissing? Well, that will get better, won't it? It just needs practice, I think.

It's just a shame I have to wait so many weeks to begin my lessons.

But when he does come back, I'll be seventeen. Practically an adult. Ready for anything.

Ready for love.

AUGUST

SUNDAY 3 AUGUST

2 P.M.

What began as boredom has segued into torpor. August is not a bolt of gold cloth but a vast, featureless landscape stretching inexorably in front of me. No flood of wondrous blooms studding the verges, no intriguing pathways and turn-offs, just blank, flat pasture and stubbled fields, muddy and dusty and horribly hot.

My days are taken with lolling under the apple tree plucking petals from a daisy: 'He loves me, he loves me not.' Or on the drawing room floor with a deck of cards, gambling on a hand of patience: 'If this comes out, Buck will love me.'

Aster, predictably, thinks I am being terribly fey and pathetic; Marigold is too busy grooming Siegfried for the

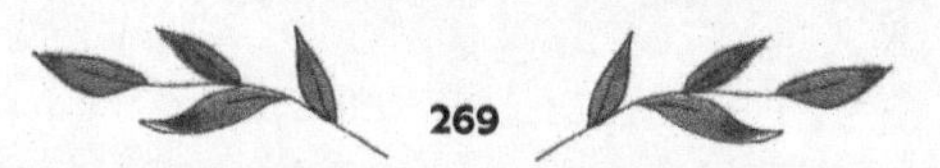

Ickthorpe Show (a pointless and thankless task as once one has finished it almost always requires starting again as he has inevitably rubbed on something or run through something or sat on something. Painting the Forth Bridge would be easier); and Margot is summering in La Napoule at some dreadful tennis camp of Deborah's, so every letter is taken up with the trials of her life. I suppose I should think myself lucky I'm not forced to thwack balls at every Felicity (or Marie-Claire) in a five-mile radius, but at least that might take my mind off Buck, or rather the lack of him.

Ever since that night, and his departure, it's as if the air around me has slackened around the gap he has left. Days are shapeless. Baggy and flaccid when I require them spangling and taut as a tripwire again. Even Grandma is exasperated and has said I am in danger of becoming boring (not as inconsiderate as French or American, but still an offence in her capacious book).

It is for this reason she has insisted we girls swim. That, and the fact that Marigold's sheep-leading practice is playing havoc with the lawn, as well as her hearing (there is much loud complaining, from all sides). Plus, there is always the risk that we'd dye something else through sheer boredom.

Aster, of course, has excused herself on the grounds she is usefully employed. Grandma was set to argue about the word 'usefully' but Aster swept back upstairs to her Singer and her easel, and her own version of purgatory. Topaz is on the Emerald Isle, appropriately, at another Attlesey mansion. It is a shame the Mannerings only ever had Radley. But I suppose at least we know where to call home.

Or we did.

Anyway, I suppose I shall have to find my bathing suit. Heaven knows if I even packed it. And I can hardly rap on the door of the manor and ask to check if it's stowed in the cellar or at the back of some wardrobe. Half our lives disappeared the day we left, literally and metaphorically. But with Buck, I feel like I have gained something again. And not just access to Radley, but to a brilliance that has been missing since Daddy died.

Not that Buck is anything like Daddy. (Thankfully. That would be beyond even any book of Margot's.)

Perhaps just one more hand of patience.

If this comes out, Buck definitely loves me . . .

11 P.M.

I found my bathing suit – a dishevelled thing at best, handed down from Aster and to her from Mama before that, but now, after two decades of overuse then benign neglect, moth-holed and fraying. And, with Marigold charging around in nothing but a pair of pants, begging that Bad Harry might join us, no time for Aster to patch it. There was nothing for it, of course, I would have to join Marigold in her alternative swimwear and take the plunge, quite literally, in vest and knickers, though

both were of the sturdy sort so it was not too imperilling a venture. Besides which, I decided, who would be likely to see me? Only Ralph, perhaps, who has to walk that stretch of the river to reach the Hendrys' farm, and who is notoriously short-sighted, and Mr Hendry, who only notices pigs. I was thankful, for once, that Buck was far away in France, for surely a glimpse of my immense gym knickers would be an end to his interests.

But someone saw.

And that someone was not myopic Ralph or pig-witted Mr Hendry.

But Freddy.

*

I was wet from the green silk of the river, slick as an otter, if not as graceful, and stretched out on the bank in the sunshine, picking wistfully at a daisy again while Marigold and Harry splashed in the shallows or scavenged the banks for frogs and toads and anything else they might befriend and take home.

'Hello, stranger,' I heard, and felt the whump of a muscular body dropping down next to me.

I shot up, clutching Marigold's towel to my chest (mine was under me, and sodden).

'Freddy!' I spluttered.

'Stranger is right,' he went on. 'Look at your hair!'

I clutched a hand to it, as if not knowing what to expect. But, of course, it was short. Mabel had trimmed it again, and even closer this time, so that my neck seemed to stretch almost swan-like. Almost. 'You don't like it?'

He shook his head. 'I didn't say that. It's just different, that's all.'

I bristled. 'Maybe *I'm* different.'

Freddy laughed, his teeth white against the Italian tan. 'You'll always be Panth.'

An image flashed into my head then, of me, kohl-eyed in crimson, sipping champagne from a coupe. Baby, then. To Buck.

But not to Freddy. Never, I supposed, to Freddy. We were doomed to be the girl from the big house, and the doctor's boy.

'Want to get wet again?' he asked then. 'Too bloody hot to sit here and not.'

'I . . . yes.' If I was in the water, I fathomed, he wouldn't be able to see me.

And I wouldn't be able to see him.

Because, as he grinned, and said, 'Great,' he hauled off his shirt, and I saw, for the first time, that Freddy was a man.

'Like old times, isn't it?' he said as we floated, starfish, or boatmen, on the surface of the water.

'Yes,' I agreed. 'Just like it.'

But it wasn't, not at all. Everything had changed, and not just my hair. There was something odd now, something awkward. Before, we'd dipped in the river like cherubim, or Kingsley's water babies, naked and unashamed, our bodies barely differentiated but for 'down there'. Now, though, I felt a spasm of embarrassment at my attire, at the shape of me under it – my breasts swelling under the knit of my vest, my hips wide in my knickers.

And of him.

I was aware, suddenly, of every bone in him. Every stretch of flesh. Aware of his own underwear, slippery and see-through as a moon jellyfish, and aware as well of the tangled darkness that hid beneath. I remembered Buck then, swelling and pressing into me, and a surge of something ran through me, followed by more shame, and I knew I could not look at him, could not be in the river with him, instead hauling myself out of the water, and snatching up a towel again.

Of course, he followed me.

This was no good. No good at all. I needed a shield, not a towel; a suit of armour.

And then it came to me. I had one: Baby.

It was like a swig of champagne, steeling me. I leant back on my elbows, pushing myself out, wild, defiant. 'Do you swim in the Cam?'

Freddy lay back on the grass, his eyes closed. 'Only accidentally. If I fall off a punt.'

'Punting, how darling,' I said. I was channelling Topaz now, or Evangeline perhaps, borrowing their lexicon, their bravado.

Freddy opened one eye and, shielding his face from the bright slice of sunlight that fell on us, asked, 'Darling?'

'You know.' I smiled, as I imagined a cat might – patronising, with guile. 'Too, too dear.'

Freddy ignored me, closed his eye again and flopped back down. 'I owe you tea.'

'Do you?' I was Panth again for a second, wrong-footed, confused.

'I said, in the letter.'

'Oh, that.' I snatched at it with relief. 'You don't need to keep to that. I thought nothing of it.'

'Nothing?' Freddy echoed.

I felt a needle of guilt I was sure Topaz or Evangeline had never experienced. 'Well, I just mean . . .'

But Freddy rescued me. Again. 'I'd like to,' he said.

I couldn't be sure if he was oblivious or gallant. But I could hardly say no, could I. 'Very well.'

'How about Saturday next? I'll call round, shall I?'

'Yes— no.' My diary was as bleak and featureless as August itself, but I needed to at least seem in demand. So, I did what any sensible and desperate girl would do: borrow her sister's fixtures. 'It's the Ickthorpe Show,' I blurted. 'I'll be busy. With Siegfried, you know.'

Freddy, now sitting up, and, thankfully, shirted, frowned. 'I didn't think a village show was your sort of thing. Not now, anyway,' he added pointedly.

'Oh, it is,' I insisted. 'And I'm quite fond of Siegfried, really. And Marigold, of course. She needs support, you see.'

We watched her merrily flinging mud at her friend, looking like the last thing she required was any sort of back-up.

'Quite,' said Freddy. 'Well, maybe an ice-cream there instead.'

'Maybe,' I replied.

But right then I wasn't sure if it was Baby or Panth answering, and I wasn't sure who I wanted it to be.

Freddy stood, turned his back to me as he pulled on his trousers, leaning so I could see the crease of him. I didn't look away this time.

'See you there,' he said.

I nodded. 'See you.'

*

'Good swim?' asked Mama when we returned, one eye on a sweaty Dinah who was crawling across the lawn testing anything in her path for edibleness (she has the makings of another Marigold).

'It was fine,' I lied.

'Fine?' Mama pursed her lips. 'Is that all? Really?'

I shrugged. 'It was . . . I don't know. Freddy was there.'

'Was he? How lovely.'

I shrugged again, disconsolate as Hamilton, who dislikes this weather as much as Grandma and sulks alongside her on the chaise, drapes drawn and Rapsey fanning them intermittently. 'I suppose.'

I could tell Mama was about to raise issue with my attitude

when mercy came in the form of Marigold, who deposited the contents of her bucket at Mama's feet. 'Frogs!' she declared with untrammelled happiness. 'Can I keep them?'

'Well, you probably should have left them in the bucket for a start,' said an exasperated Mama as the lawn became alive with amphibians.

'Oh, they're awfully easy to catch, frogs,' said Marigold.

'It's keeping them that's the problem,' said a voice.

I looked over to where Aster now stood under the wisteria, ethereal in the late afternoon light.

'And working out which is prince,' she continued, slyly, 'and which just creature.'

I felt a shiver in me, cold as the riverbed. 'I don't know what you mean.'

'Of course you don't,' she said in a tone that implied I very much did.

And the thing is, I did.

I do.

But I couldn't admit it, couldn't say it out loud, and thankfully I didn't have to say anything, for at that moment Dinah decided to test her theory and not just kiss a frog but try to eat it and all manner of hell was let loose as Mama tried to rescue Dinah, and Marigold the frog.

Only now, here, in bed, can I allow myself to reflect on it.

And my question is this: what if I chose the wrong frog? What if I kissed him, and he isn't the prince at all?

SATURDAY 9 AUGUST

10 A.M.

I just read back what I wrote a week ago. What hogwash I was talking! What rot! What nonsense! Of course Buck is my prince.

The sun must have got to me. I was out in it for at least three hours after all, quite pinked as a lobster by the evening in fact, so that Mama had to calamine my shoulders as if I had chicken pox. Of course, Marigold begged for some as well, though hers was so she could masquerade as a ghost, which is, in her case, impossible, as she is brown as a berry from all her outdoor activity and far too clattery to be able to jump out and spook anybody. She succeeded only in rattling Grandma, who was more concerned about smears on the velveteen than phantoms of any persuasion.

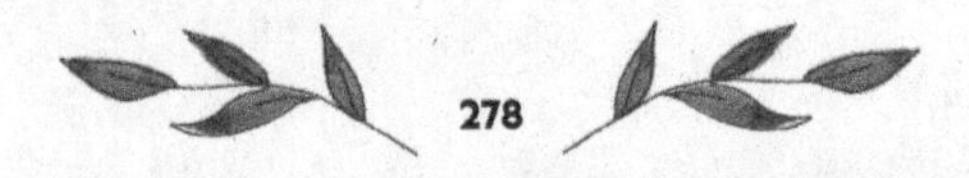

And frogs of course. Of the original seven, only two remain – Harold, who evaded Dinah's ravenous clutches to croak another day, and who resides mainly in a bucket in the scullery, and Andrew, who is indistinguishable from Harold as far as I can tell, but is Marigold's new familiar, and whom she has taken to carrying everywhere with her in an old jam jar. The rest have been lost to Hamilton, Bobby or possibly one of the more adventurous or desperate rabbits. However, even the jam jar has been abandoned today, I believe. For today it is Siegfried's turn to shine in the annual pastoral extravaganza (or annual celebration of appalling mediocrity, according to Aster) that is the Ickthorpe Show.

Marigold is highly confident that he will win in both his categories, i.e. 'Best Ram', and 'Pet the Judge Would Most Like to Take Home'. But, as I have previously mentioned, the judge is Mrs Gibberd, so this is as unlikely as me being picked for possible marriage by the Prince of Wales, or even for the first hockey eleven by Miss Pickersgill (swarthy, short, impressive moustache). Marigold is not to be dissuaded though and has already made space on her wall for the rosettes she is confidently expecting, as well as a possible place on the mantel for the Best in Show trophy. She will never get that. It goes to Mr Hendry every year for one of his stinking pigs, as well she knows. But one must admire her self-belief, and indeed belief in her sheep.

Though, for a sheep, even I have to concede Siegfried is

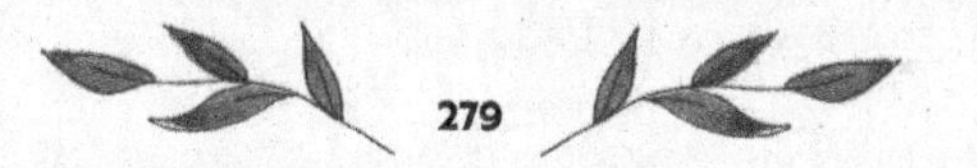

looking his best. Admittedly, this is not necessarily prize-winning, given he usually resembles something that has been lying happily in its own faeces for days, but he is at least clean, and smells less hedgy than usual. And his new collar (adapted by Rapsey from a saddle strap and painted red by Aster) is decidedly natty and dandyish.

It is a shame not to have proper transport in the form of some sort of horse box, but Marigold says the walk will give him extra practice at being both obedient, and gawped at by admiring crowds. I haven't the heart to disavow her. Instead, I shall just have to be extra vigilant that his usual penchant for destruction and defacement cannot be indulged. For, of course I am going. I told Freddy I would, so I shall. Otherwise, it would be awkward tea and scones in Gilder's and that just won't do. I rather wish he'd just go back to Cambridge, or had never come home in the first place. It's just a distraction, and an irritating one, reminding me how stuck I am, and how much I miss Buck.

Perhaps he won't even come, though. Animals are hardly his thing after all; it's humans that interest him, and broken ones at that. And while we may not be exemplary in achievement, the Mannerings' health can hardly be questioned.

5 P.M.

I take it back.

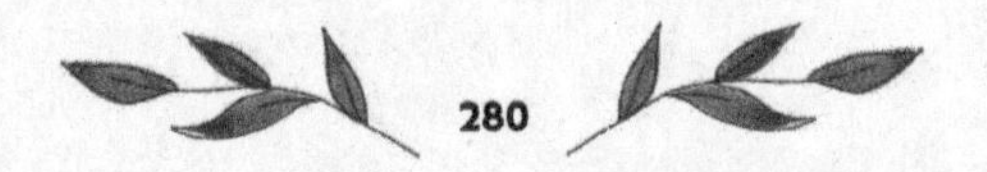

Thank heavens for Freddy!

He may not have Buck's breeding, or standing, or money, but one cannot say he does not know how to wrestle a recalcitrant sheep who is about to play merry hell with the vegetable section. If it weren't for him, Mr Gibberd's prize-winning marrow would be mere pulp by now, or entirely digested, and as for Hermione Lightfoot's fruit cake (commended) and Celia Rigby's damson jam (unplaced due to a rogue stone) I quite dread to think. Although Grandma (a surprise addition to the party) had already declared the cake a travesty anyway.

'Everyone knows she doesn't bake herself,' she hooted. 'It should be disqualified.'

'You think *everyone* should be disqualified,' I reminded her.

'Oh, they should,' agreed Grandma, 'for even entering in the first place. Wanting to enter is a sign of complete foolishness, therefore they shouldn't be allowed. Don't they have better things to do with their time?'

Neither Mama nor I mentioned that Grandma spent swathes of the day doing precisely nothing and perhaps jam-making might be an exciting diversion, because that was the precise moment that Freddy appeared, again as if by magic, materialising at my side like a tanned phantasm.

'Not entering?' he asked.

I shot him a look I hoped was suitably filthy. 'As if I would,' I retorted. Hoping he would think it was because domestic duties were beneath me, rather than the truth, which was that my kitchen skills were as woeful as most of my other ones.

'Dad's got some runners-up for "Best Bean",' he added.

'What makes a bean the best bean?' I wondered aloud. 'Aren't beans beans?'

Freddy shrugged. 'I have no idea,' he admitted. 'Not even fond of them myself.'

'It all seems rather mercenary to me,' I went on. 'Like a beauty contest for things that don't even have a choice about entering.'

'You don't approve?'

'No,' I said, realising the truth as I said it. 'I'm not sure I do. Although perhaps I don't like competition in general.'

'I don't think I do, either,' said Freddy. 'I tend to secede gracefully.'

'I don't think I even manage the grace,' I said. 'I just bow out, often before I've begun. I was always awful at sport.' Words seemed to tumble out: things I didn't like to admit, even to myself.

'As was I,' said Freddy, proving his grace. 'Still am, really.'

'Miss Ince said everyone excelled at something in life, I just hadn't quite found my area yet. Perhaps it's jam after all.'

Freddy, who had been admiring – or pretending to admire – an outsize turnip up until that point, turned to face me. 'Panth, believe me when I tell you that jam is not your calling.'

It sounded funny, a joke, but he wasn't smiling. He meant it.

'I . . .' But I couldn't find the right words suddenly. Honesty

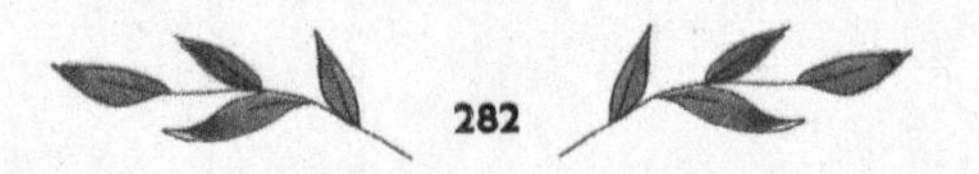

had dried up and I was brittle-limbed and stiff-tongued again. 'I should . . . Marigold,' I managed.

'I'll come,' he offered.

And, unable to think of a reason why this was unnecessary, or unwarranted, I just led the way from the stifling bell tent, Freddy sauntering behind me, and Grandma behind him, her look of perpetual disapproval still firmly painted on, Mama and Dinah presumably lost to the cake table, and Dinah's appetite.

*

The ring is the very epicentre of the Ickthorpe Show, festooned in improbable bunting, and fenced by a rope over which hang grown men and small children alike, their faces etched with the kind of worry worn by world leaders, their white knuckles clutching the lead ropes of livestock as if their very existence depended on it.

'How very undignified,' Grandma announced.

I was minded to agree with her until I saw the men entering, hair slicked down, shirts precisely buttoned, and realised how much it mattered to them, to all of them, Marigold included. Even Rapsey was dressed for the occasion, his buttons polished, his boots blacked.

'How much longer do you suppose they will be?' Grandma went on. 'It's all very well for those with sturdy constitutions but some of us have knees that have seen sixty.'

I did not dare correct her.

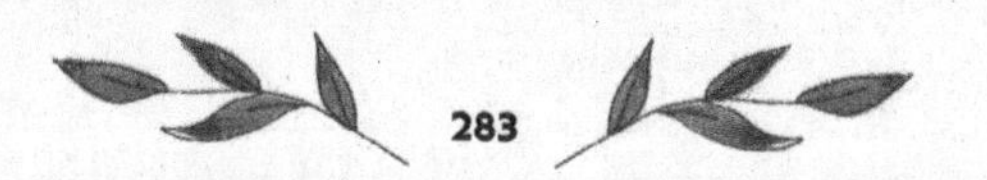

'Would you like to sit down?' offered Freddy instead. 'The refreshment tent is close. I can take you, if you like.'

Grandma eyed him as if he were decidedly foreign. 'I'm not an invalid,' she snapped. 'If I "like", I can very well take myself.'

Which, thankfully, she did, as I did not want her lack of enthusiasm (verging on the aggressive) to in any way taint Marigold's potential moment of glory. As it was, I could see her getting quite agitated in line, arguing with Rapsey over something while Bad Harry (entering the Guinea Pig class at 4 p.m.) watched on eagerly, and the Launceston boys with their ram, 'Hercules', rather less so.

And this where it all went rather haywire, I'm afraid.

Marigold says it's the Launcestons' fault for letting Hercules get too close to Siegfried, smell the air of victory that he emanated and kick him in jealousy.

The Launcestons say it's Bad Harry's fault for nudging Hercules with her knee so that he lashed out and accidentally kicked Siegfried, who probably deserved it anyway as everyone knows red collars aren't standard and thus should be banned.

Bad Harry says she didn't nudge anyone, she was just scratching a bite on her leg, which was probably a flea from Hercules so if it's anyone's fault it's his for not cleaning himself properly.

Whoever's fault it was, though, is moot, as the next thing we knew, there was an enormous bellow from Siegfried, who pulled loose of his lead, cantered (do sheep canter?) across the ring, shot under the fence, and headed for the flaps of the Produce Tent.

Rapsey, Marigold and Harry set off in hot pursuit, but were hampered rather badly by Harry, who was carrying her guinea pig and Marigold, who had Andrew the frog in his glass jar (a last-minute entrant to 'Pet the Judge Would Most Like to Take Home') as well as the fact that Rapsey is older even than Grandma. Thankfully, one spectator was young enough, and carrying nothing but his wits and an athletic streak he'd only minutes previously denied.

I watched in awe (mouth gaping as if I were catching flies, I'm sorry to report) as Freddy Spencer, a streak of white shirt and cream linen Oxford bags, raced across the packed field just steps behind the runaway before diving heroically to the floor, no thought for inevitable grass stains and worse, to snatch Siegfried's lead in his hands and bring him to a sorry halt just inches from the visibly fraught 'Best Bean' considerations and potential crop devastation.

The crowd, dear journal, went wild. Even the Launceston boys cheered, though this may have been in anticipation of their rival now being definitely disqualified for poor behaviour. However, the judge (Mrs Hendry, don't even ask) deemed Siegfried's actions to be 'spirited' but not criminal, and thus he was allowed to take his place in the ring, and his blue rosette for second place (losing to Mr Hendry's 'Garth'). I think Marigold may ordinarily have been on the verge of arguing nepotism (which it obviously was), but the fact that Hercules went unplaced must have made up for it as she conceded defeat without complaint in this and Siegfried's second category, in which Andrew took a coveted 'runner-up' slot for 'excellent temperament' and 'strong croak'.

'Best in Show' went to a dog called Norbert, with a quite surprising hairdo. But I think no one there would have minded had it been awarded to Freddy Spencer.

'I'm so sorry about your trousers,' I offered. 'I can let Mabel have at them, if you like?'

But Freddy shook his head. 'I'm sure I can manage. Now, about that tea I owe you.'

*

So, in the end we did share Earl Grey and scones. And it was not at Claridge's, nor even in Gilder's, but on a picnic rug on a scrap of grass amongst hysterical children, an overindulged sheep and a frog in a jam jar.

But the odd thing was, I wouldn't have had it any other way.

THURSDAY 14 AUGUST

10 P.M.

I will admit that I now rather regret declaring August a month of torpor and boredom, as it seems to have worked in rather the opposite way: willing mishap after ridiculous mishap upon the Mannerings (as if we didn't suffer disproportionately already).

Today, though, the incident is not mere mishap, but rather more tragedy, for our poor dog Bobby has died. Mama found him behind the green chair this morning, stiff as a broom and quite, quite cold. Worse, he may actually have been dead since yesterday. But, as usual, no one bothered to note his whereabouts when we went to bed. The fact is, he was summarily demoted in our affections with Siegfried's arrival, and now, what with Hamilton and Andrew and the excess rabbits it's as if he barely

existed but for the lingering smell at the end of the chaise.

I pity him, really, being outshone by a dim-witted sheep, but Marigold has always been fonder of the unconventional in pets. He was Daddy's dog, of course. And for that reason alone, we should have loved him more in life. But, as Marigold has pointed out, at least we can honour him in death.

Grandma pulled a face at that. 'Whatever do you mean?'

'A funeral,' explained Marigold. 'We must all dress in black, with veils.' The 'veils' spoken with a mixture of aplomb and menace. 'And sing a hymn and I shall recite a eulogy.'

'How lovely,' agreed Mama with expertly feigned false jollity. 'Perhaps something rousing like "Mine Eyes Have Seen the Glory".'

'No,' replied Marigold. 'It will be "For Those in Peril on the Sea".' She did not go on to explain why and no one dared question her thinking, for it is never straightforward and she never changes her mind.

'And where do you think you're going to inter the creature?' Grandma went on, her alarm becoming more apparent.

'Next to the yellow rosebush,' declared Marigold, matter of fact. 'That was his favourite place after the chaise and we can hardly bury him in the drawing room, so it is only right.' At that she dug out her eager-to-please face and smiled maniacally.

'Absolutely not,' said Grandma, who is as unaffected by winning smiles as she is by logic and plaudits. 'If you must bury the thing then do it at the bottom of the garden where I don't have to be faced with the maudlin on a daily basis. And make sure you do it properly. At least two feet. I don't want foxes digging it up.'

It's more likely to be Hamilton not foxes, though I did not say this, for fear of aggravating both Grandma and the cat, who are now one combined force of perpetual disapproval. And now, of course, Hamilton has the complete run of the house. Not that he didn't lord it over Bobby before. In fact, he is suspiciously pleased with himself, and if I didn't know better, I would suspect him of plotting Bobby's downfall and carrying out the deed with some sort of poison and a dollop of gusto.

'Rapsey has a large box,' Marigold went on. 'For a coffin, I mean. And you must all come.'

'I–' began Aster.

'Of course we will,' I cut in. 'We can even be coffin bearers.'

'Oh no!' snapped Marigold. 'It has to be men.'

'No it doesn't,' I said, but then an image flashed into my head of Valentine and Rapsey and several Balfours bearing Daddy aloft. 'Does it?'

'I don't see why,' said Aster. 'We're perfectly capable of carrying a dog in a box. We don't need a penis to do it.'

'Aster!' snapped Mama.

'Coffin,' corrected Marigold. 'And I don't care about penises, I just want men. It is the Thing!'

'What men though?' demanded Grandma, who is now as inured to penises as the rest of us. 'We don't have any!'

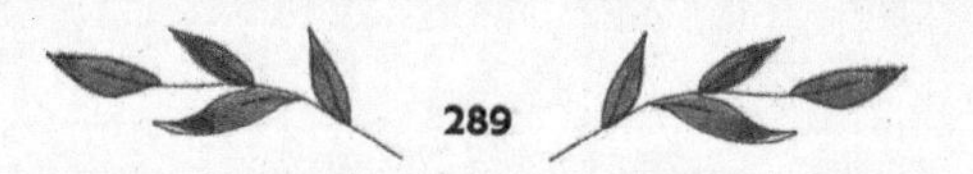

We all knew, of course, that this was the root of everything. But none of us wished to concede ground to Grandma and so began mustering men and conscripting them into our scheme, willing or no.

'We have Rapsey,' said Marigold.

'And Ralph won't mind,' added Mabel.

Grandma shot her a look that was part-scolding for talking out of turn and part-surprise she was even in the room at all, though Mabel is rather like Bobby in that respect – always there but mainly noticeable only by smell. Though in her case it is the pleasant scent of baking, not something old and rotten.

Aster sighed. 'You could always ask Reg Nesbitt,' she said. 'If you were desperate.'

Marigold's eyes widened, possibly in anticipation of wooing him with her desperate and tragic stance and loud singing. 'Can I? Can I really?'

Mama nodded. 'If you like.'

'And Freddy,' I blurted. 'He'll do it, I'm sure.' The words were out of my mouth before I'd thought about them, but I knew I was right. He would do it; of course he would, for Freddy was practically family – practically my brother. And for once I was glad he was the one here in Ickthorpe, and not Buck, who would have been appalled at the whole sorry affair.

'Well, there you go,' said Mama. 'Four is plenty for a dog, I think. Any more and it will be a little cramped around the box–coffin, I mean.'

'Dog funerals. Whatever next?' muttered Grandma. 'Sheep weddings, I suppose. Frog christenings.'

'You're only giving her ideas,' said Mama.

I looked at Marigold, whose face did, indeed, suggest, she was pondering possible brides of the ovine variety.

'I think a funeral is plenty to be planning,' I said quickly. 'Come along, Marigold. Let's fetch the men.'

'And Harry,' she added, leaping to her feet with the sort of glee not usually associated with death.

Which is how I found myself knocking on Freddy Spencer's door at eleven on a Thursday, and asking his father if he wouldn't mind calling him down for us.

'Another swim, is it?' asked the doctor. 'Fine day for it.'

I felt my cheeks heat a little, wondering what Freddy had said.

Marigold spared me my blushes. 'No,' she replied for me. 'It's so he can carry our dog's coffin aloft properly like at an actual funeral.'

Dr Spencer, bless him, did not flinch or fumble for a moment at this. 'How jolly thoughtful,' he said. 'Have you enough mourners?'

'Mourners?' asked Marigold.

'Oh, yes,' Dr Spencer went on. 'I think a dog like yours deserves a good turn-out, don't you?'

Marigold nodded, wide-eyed and grateful.

'Then it's settled,' said the doctor. 'We'll come, all three of us, to pay our respects. What time does the ceremony commence?'

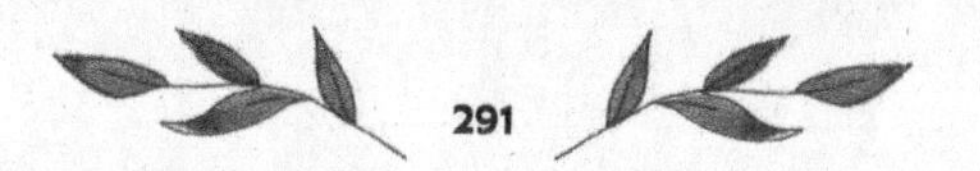

'Four,' said Marigold decisively.

'Four it is,' said Dr Spencer.

'Thank you,' I managed.

He smiled at me, then – the kind of smile Daddy always gave: wide, with that variety of generous concession only vicars and fathers seem able to make. 'It is the least we can do.'

We left before he could see my tears, and they were quite dry by the time we arrived at the forge.

'Go on,' I said, shoving my sister towards the door a little.

'No, you ask,' demanded Marigold, scuttling back and shoving me in turn.

'Heavens,' I said, as I braced myself. 'This is not in the rulebook for sisterly duty.' Though, even if it existed, I'm not sure anything pertaining to Marigold would make the pages.

The forge itself was orange with heat, and Reg sweating. 'Mr Nesbitt?' I asked.

Reg looked up from the hot metal of a large horseshoe, the Launcestons' Shire, Florence, patiently waiting in the wings. 'Arr,' he replied.

I took this to be a multi-functional sort of retort, here meaning, 'yes, what is it?'

'I don't suppose you're free at around four this afternoon?'

Reg spat, quite spectacularly, into the flames, sending an impressive hiss into the blistering air. ''Oo wants to know?'

'I . . . my sister.' I nodded to the door, where Marigold lurked earnestly.

'Oh, that one,' he said. 'I seen her afore. Always round, she is. What she want?'

At that Marigold sprang forward, her nerves forgotten in his acknowledgement of her mere existence. 'My dog died!' she cried.

'Oh, you want him burning, do you?' Reg nodded at the fire.

For a moment, Marigold looked worryingly keen on this idea.

'Heavens, no,' I said quickly. 'We're burying him. Properly. We just wondered—'

'Will you carry him?' asked Marigold. 'Like a proper pall bearer.'

Reg laughed then, revealing a missing tooth, which I knew would only endear him further to Marigold, who regards missing teeth in the same manner she admires missing arms and legs in pirates: a badge of honour and suggestion of thrilling mystery.

'En't you got your family for that?' he asked.

I bristled. 'No,' I replied. 'We obviously do not. Or we wouldn't be asking.'

'Oh, arr,' said Reg again. 'I remember now. Well, 'appen I'll be off by then, so I'll see what I can do.'

And with that, he spat a second impressive time and went back to Florence and her size nines.

Harry was far easier to enlist – Mrs Ponsonby obviously used to Marigold's random requirements. She even lent her a black veil and cloak, for dramatic effect. The pair of them

agreed to share both, as long as dibs on Reg Nesbitt were also doled out equally, with one marrying him for a week, then the other. (It is best not to argue with them in these circumstances, because how can one counter absolute nonsense?) And so we returned to the Dower House, with a full funeral party on the cards (Ralph agreed readily, clearly willing to do anything for Mabel, and Rapsey gets no choice in this or any matter).

The affair itself passed without major incident. The four men (dressed in black, bar Reg Nesbitt, who wore his habitual stained vest and brown trousers, tied with twine, and smoked a cigarette throughout) led the procession, carrying Bobby aloft in a Fortnum's hamper (the box snapped under Bobby's considerable weight) from the scullery to the compost heap with a sort of dignity, followed by Marigold and Harry at the head, then Aster and I, Mama and Dinah, Mabel, Mr and Mrs Spencer, and Mrs Gibberd and Celia Rigby, who had overheard Ralph discussing it in the shop and turned up of their own accord to 'pay respects' (nose over Grandma's roses). Grandma and Hamilton watched with notable disapproval from the drawing room window.

We sang a verse and chorus of 'For Those in Peril on the Sea' (no one could remember any more than that), Marigold recited her eulogy (surprisingly moving) and Harry her poetic dedication (unsurprisingly less so): 'Oh no, the dog is dead. What will the other animals do? They will weep and then eat their tea.' Then Reg, Freddy, Ralph and Rapsey lowered the

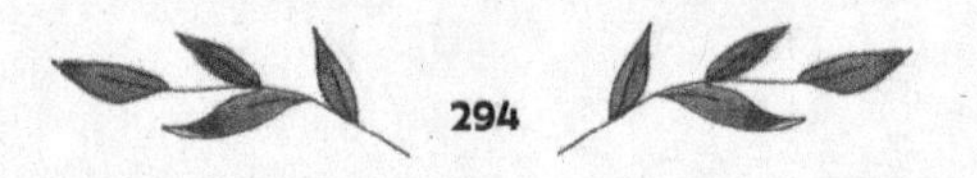

hamper into a massive hole behind the hydrangea, dug, it turns out, by Mama and Aster – an act, I think, of tremendous love.

'Daddy would have been proud,' I said.

Mama touched by arm. 'Of all of you,' she replied.

Then we ate Mabel's egg sandwiches on the lawn and discussed nepotism at the Ickthorpe Show, the dos and don'ts of manure as fertilizer, and whether or not we would have an Indian summer or rain by the twentieth.

'I hope not,' said Freddy. 'Rain, I mean.'

'Why?' I asked. Then, daring myself, 'Will you swim?'

He smiled, and I thought – I thought I saw a flush of something on his cheeks, though that may have been the heat, and the exertion of carrying Bobby, who was heavier in death than in life, and he was fairly leaden then. But, 'I meant for your birthday,' he replied. 'The twenty-third, isn't it?'

I nodded, vacant as one of Marigold's frogs. 'You remembered?'

'Of course. Are you having a party?'

'I— no, I . . .' We couldn't afford a ball. Nor even dinner, for anyone other than us Mannerings, really. 'Tea, I think. You could come,' I added, a sudden something seizing me. 'It won't be special. But . . .' I struggled for justification. 'You're practically family.' I managed.

'Family.' Freddy nodded, almost solemn for a moment. Then snapped to, his mouth broadening into a smile. 'I'd like that. Thank you.'

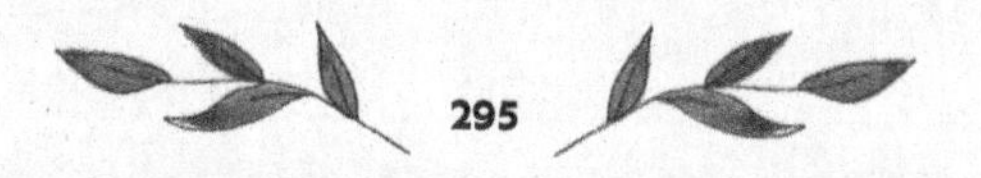

*

And so it shall be: I shall spend my seventeenth birthday not in Paris, nor London, nor on the Cote d'Azur, but here in Ickthorpe. And not with my suitor or a coterie of bright young anythings, but with my calamitous family and a boy who was almost that.

I should have been disappointed, and I know on the twenty-third, or even tomorrow, I shall be, but right now, I am not.

Just as I am not disappointed that Aster ruined a dress that I had my eye on with the digging.

That Mama insisted on burying a pair of Daddy's socks with Bobby (he was fond of chewing them).

Or that Marigold's last words before she went to bed were, '*Now* can I have a monkey?'

SATURDAY 23 AUGUST

4 P.M.

I know I predicted disappointment at my location and lack of man (or specific man), but it is impossible to be entirely disappointed on one's birthday when one is surrounded by ridiculous sisters, a darling mama, and a menagerie of animals of which the Zoological Society would be proud.

I was awoken alarmingly early by Marigold, who had determined that she must be the first to flourish a present.

'But it's not even six,' I protested.

'But it can't wait,' Marigold jabbered, adding, mysteriously (and with an air of foreboding I should have detected then). 'It can't stay wrapped for much longer.'

It was a frog. Of course it was. Not Andrew, who is living in

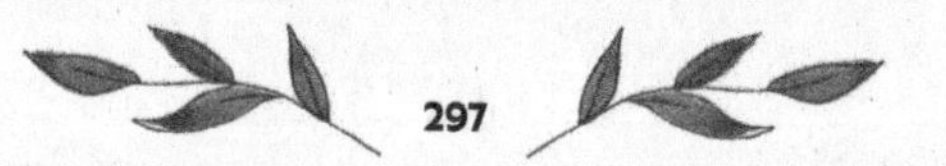

luxury between his jam jar, the bathroom sink and a bowl in the garden, but Harold, who has until now resided on shelf in the scullery in a bucket where Hamilton cannot get to him easily.

'You must guard him with your life,' she urged.

'Of course,' I agreed, with a look that I suspect was somewhat dubious. 'Though perhaps,' I suggested cautiously, 'it might be better if we made him and Andrew a pond?'

'Grandma says absolutely not because Hamilton might drown.'

I did not think Hamilton capable of any such thing, given his wiles, but knew there was no truck to be had with Grandma over Hamilton or her precious lawn. 'What about the pond on the green?'

'Oh no.' Marigold shook her head solemnly. 'The muscovy ducks are too fierce, and besides, Mr Gibberd fishes in there and what if he hooked Harold?' (This said with much horror and an air of admonition.)

'I suppose.'

Marigold frowned, and pouted – her party trick ever since she were three and refused a biscuit. 'Don't you want him, then?'

'Of course I want him. He's darling!' I lied. 'I am just worrying for him already, that's all.'

Marigold perked up at that, and lectured me lengthily on his various likes (flies and worms) and dislikes (cheese and music). Rapsey is, apparently, in charge of supplies so at least am let off the onerous task of fly-trapping.

I was relieved when I heard Dinah's waking mewl and announced I must rush to Mama for it was she who had birthed me on this auspicious day after all.

'Take Harold!' Marigold yelled after me.

'Oh, do be quiet!' Aster, still trying to sleep, replied for me as I thundered past, allowing my escape.

She had cheered, though, by the time we sat down to breakfast, before which no present-opening was allowed, on Grandma's strict instruction.

'Only the lower classes cannot wait for things,' she added. 'A lady is glacial in her wants.'

Marigold's eyes widened at potential discovery – at Harold or not being a lady, it wasn't clear. But I shook my head – I would keep our secret.

'Seventeen,' Mama announced, as if I had no idea of my own age. 'I remember my seventeenth quite clearly.'

'Had you met Daddy by then?' demanded Marigold.

Mama smiled. 'I had. And it was on that very day he asked me to marry him.'

Grandma snorted.

Marigold 'ooh'ed.

I, on the other hand, felt my heart speed to match Harold's small one. (Assuming, of course, that frogs have hearts. I recall a biology class in which we were required to dissect said creature but Margot was sick on her shoes and so I had to take her to Nurse and thankfully by the time she was clean and able to speak the sordid task was over.)

'How did he ask?' I blurted, though I knew the story by heart – we all did. But I needed to hear it again, and urgently.

'It was written on a card inside my present,' she said, addressing a bemused Dinah, who was new to this of course. '"Will you marry me?"'

'What was the present?' asked Marigold, clapping her hands in anticipation.

For a moment, Mama disappeared somewhere, far away, but happy, I think. Then she shook herself. 'It was a dress,' she said. 'I didn't have many and he knew that. It was so he could take me to dinner. I'd said I couldn't, you see, on account of not looking the part to be on the arm of an earl. He said he didn't care if I was naked' – at that, Grandma hooted in alarm – 'but *I* cared, and so then, of course, he cared. I think that's so often overlooked when it comes to love,' she went on. 'The simple act of caring.'

I should be marking her words, I knew, but my head was filled with images of that card, slipped between silk and sheets of tissue paper. What if Buck had something like that planned? What if a card arrived now with those very words – 'Will you marry me?' – written in his lackadaisical hand?

But the post was yet to arrive and there were other matters at hand.

'Now, your presents, dear Panth,' declared Mama.

'Thank heaven,' said Aster, who had always shrunk at the mention of love and seemed to show no sign of growing out of it, not even with Topaz on the permanent periphery of her vision.

I shan't recount the entire ceremony, which was lengthy, and interrupted on several occasions by animal-related emergencies. But I received the following:

- From Grandma, a copy of *Vanity Fair* by William Makepeace Thackeray, which she told me Mrs Gibberd had advised her might be the sort of 'colourful' saga I admired
- From Margot, a copy of a new novel called *She Danced All Night*, which looked far more like the sort of colourful saga I might admire
- From Valentine, a scarlet lipstick of the sort worn by the 'wrong sort of woman' (according to Grandma) and the very best sort of woman, according to me
- From Rapsey, a quarter of mint imperials
- From Mabel, a hair clip (I insisted she shouldn't have, but she said she got it cheap off her aunt in Stepney who ran the salon, and so I mustn't be worried she was out of pocket, and besides which Ralph owed her half a crown over a bet. I did not ask on what for fear it might alarm Grandma.)

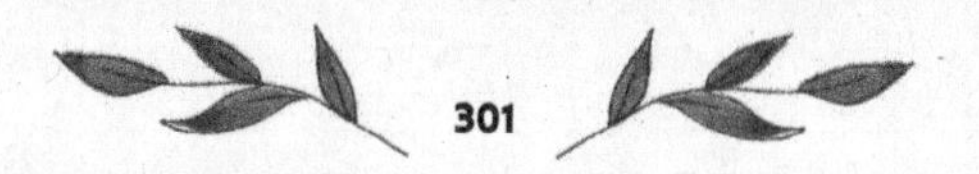

- From Marigold, a voucher to walk Siegfried once a week. Grandma said this didn't seem like a very generous gift, at least not for the receiver, but I said Marigold had already bestowed kindness on me this morning, and who would not want to spend time with such a prize-winning specimen? (If there was one thing living with Grandma was teaching me, it was how to lie and lie well.)

But it was from Mama and Aster that I received the most generous gift of all.

'What is it?' Marigold demanded as they brought in the fat packet.

Mama laughed. 'Well, give her a chance to open it and see.'

For some reason I knew it was special before I even slipped a finger under the pleat of brown paper wrapping. Of course, anything from Mama was to be treasured, but this was from Aster as well; they'd been in cahoots. And for that to happen it held a new kind of importance, and my opening a reverence I'd never yet mustered.

It was warranted. For there, sitting amid its stretch of paper and string, was a bolt of oyster-coloured cloth.

Not just cloth, but satin – duchesse – of the highest quality. And so very much of it. It must have cost a small fortune.

'I . . .' I began, but words would not come.

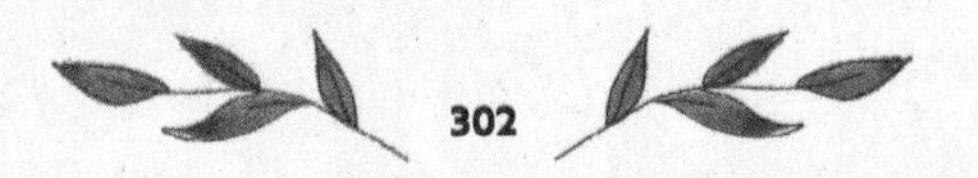

Aster found them for me. 'It's for the season,' she said. 'For coming out. I know it's too late now. But next year, perhaps, you'll be able to go.'

'But where did you get the money?' I managed at last.

'Never you mind,' said Mama, smiling. 'And Aster got a good discount, so please don't be thinking of that.'

'And I'll make it, of course,' added Aster. 'That's my gift, really.'

I was wordless, still; witless. 'I don't know what to say.'

'"Thank you" would suffice,' Grandma snapped, never one to be lost for words, or to mince them.

'Of course!' I cried. 'Thank you!' And I wrapped first Mama and then my sister in a tight embrace.

'All right,' said Aster, stiffening, then succumbing briefly.

'What a birthday,' I declared, cat having let go of my tongue. 'And still the post to come!'

'Why, what are you expecting?' Grandma raised an eyebrow, sharp as a pin. 'A proposal? I wouldn't hold your breath.'

My swelling hope popped like a soap bubble. 'Nothing of the sort,' I said.

*

If I had hoped for that, even for a second, I would have been a fool.

While the sole envelope was indeed from Buck, it was his column, largely detailing the splendours of Evangeline Balfour, which I decided I would take my blue pen to later with relish.

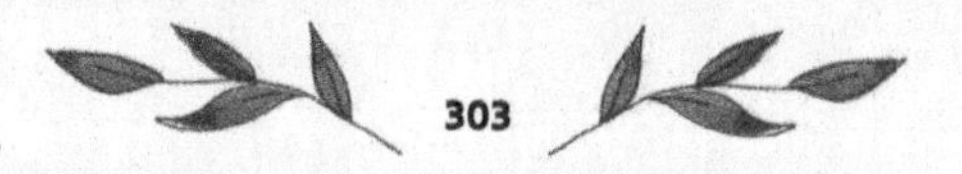

Though it also mentioned Margot, and this time not entirely in an unfavourable way, though what she was doing at Gaston's house in Cap d'Agde, or how she even got there, I have no idea. I shall write to her later, of course and demand plain answers, and nefarious detail.

Oh, I feel a wash of cold water over me all of a sudden. I am fooling myself, I realise, at times like this. I am just an Ickthorpe girl. No Cannes or Paris glamour puss, no bright anything.

I'm not anybody's Baby, not really.

Just plain old Panth.

*

But I must muster, of course.

I have my family. I have my health. I have a frog in a bucket, and a bolt of cloth waiting for one day in the future when something might be made of me.

Until then I have tea, and cake, and my old friend Freddy due any moment.

That will do, I think.

It must do.

For, now I have the maturity to reflect, I wonder – isn't that what we must say of life? That 'this is enough'? 'This will do'?

And so I clip my hair in place, and straighten my dress, and paint on a face that says just that.

8 P.M.

I take it back.

It is not enough to make do.

It is never enough to settle.

And to think I was settling for Freddy being the highlight of my seventeenth birthday!

Not that he wasn't as delightfully Freddy-like as ever. He had brought me a gift – more ink. For 'the novel' he told me. I didn't like to tell him I'd quite forgotten the novel, given how real life had rather taken over in the romance stakes. But I feigned gratefulness well, and anyway, I shall use the ink, even if only to continue this journal and write to Margot (who is consumed with adoration for her tennis instructor, Sven. Sven is twenty-eight and married, but that has not deterred Margot in the slightest. She says she is definitely in love, as evidenced by her inability to eat. I suspect this will only induce her to faint on court, but perhaps that is the effect she is hoping to engender).

He has also generously offered Marigold and I use of Dr Spencer's ornamental pond as a sort of frog accommodation. Marigold was reluctant at first, but the picture Freddy painted of the plethora of readily available flies, and recreational activities of the sort one supposes frogs enjoy, was quite the image and she is escorting Harold and Andrew to their new home at this very minute.

I would have gone with them but something too, too wonderful happened.

Heavens, I can barely believe it so I am going to have to write it all down (in Freddy's ink) in the hope that black and white will set it in my head.

We were midway through cucumber sandwiches (of which the frogs, rabbits and even Siegfried, fed through the window, approved) when there came a knock at the door.

Mabel, sighing, left the teapot and went to answer, upon which we heard a yelp.

'It's for you, Miss Panth!' she called, bustling in, bearing a parcel. 'Ralph had a phone call all the way from Paris. Can you imagine? Saying it had to be delivered today. Even though it come too late really and should have waited 'til the morning. But Mrs Gibberd, she said—'

'That's quite enough!' Grandma interrupted. 'I think we get the picture.'

'Sorry,' said Mabel not looking it at all and showing no signs of leaving until she had seen the parcel's very contents.

'Ooh,' said Marigold, her third or fourth of the day. 'What do you think it is?'

'Paris,' said Aster inscrutably.

Paris, I thought, my face hot and my heart fast.

I touched my fingers to the box, slipped them under the rim of the lid. For despite the lack of return address, there was no doubt who this was from, and it was not Evangeline Balfour.

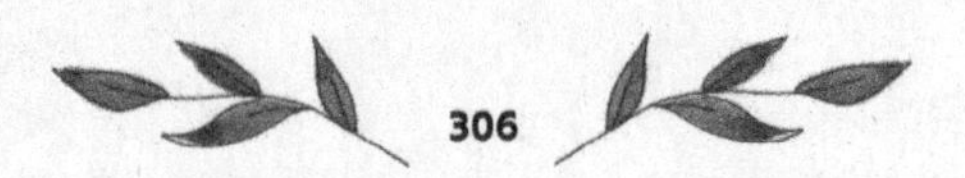

I trembled as I lifted it, as if I were opening Pandora's box itself. Then gasped, as did Mama, Marigold, Mabel and even Aster.

For there, nestled in tissue, was a sliver of peach silk, trimmed in bugle beads and fringed with delicate feathers.

'It's a dress!' said Mama.

'It's a Vionnet,' breathed Aster, who never normally 'breathed' anything, let alone to do with dresses. Of course, it meant nothing to me but I could tell in her world, in Mrs Booth's, in Evangeline's even, that was something.

'Who's sent you a dress?' asked Freddy, an edge to his voice.

'There's a card!' yelled Marigold triumphantly.

I could hardly bear to pick it up, Mama's story still sitting in my mind. But pick it up I did, and turned it over.

'My Baby,' I read. 'Happy birthday.'

'Baby?' asked Freddy.

'It's what he calls her,' said Aster, drily.

'Who?' demanded Freddy.

'Buck,' I said. For though he hadn't signed the card, nor even written it, it was his, I knew.

And though there was no proposal, no suggestion of anything proper, I didn't care, because he had declared intent anyway. I was 'his' Baby. His.

Not anyone else's. And nobody else could take my place. Not now.

Not in that dress.

'I wonder what he expects in return,' mused Aster.

Grandma snorted.

'Aster!' snapped Mama.

'S-E-X.' Marigold picked up Aster's theme blithely. 'Or you could loan him your frog.'

I ignored her. I ignored everyone. I can hardly recall the rest of tea, or what Freddy said as he left with Marigold and the jam jars. It was something, but probably nothing important.

Because Buck had remembered.

Buck had sent me a dress – a dress he means for me to wear on his arm at a party.

Buck loved me. I was *his*.

I *am* his.

His Baby.

Seventeen and ready for anything. For love. For marriage.

And even, yes, for his penis!

SEPTEMBER

SATURDAY 6 SEPTEMBER

10 A.M.

September has crept in on a whisper of chill breeze, and with it has slunk an awful sort of sinking feeling: a sense of an ending – to the season, to summer, to freedom perhaps. Though I cannot fathom why that might be as among us only Marigold has had to return to the classroom. Much to Mrs Bottomley's disappointment, who was rather hoping she might be sent to Hedingham to board, but no chance of that of course. Though Bad Harry is suitably thrilled as, with the absence of the Launceston twins, who have been packed off to Harrow (God help Harrow), they will now be free to lord it over the small ones with their hideous schemes to get rich quick, the latest of which seems to involve selling on lucky 'four-leafed' clovers at

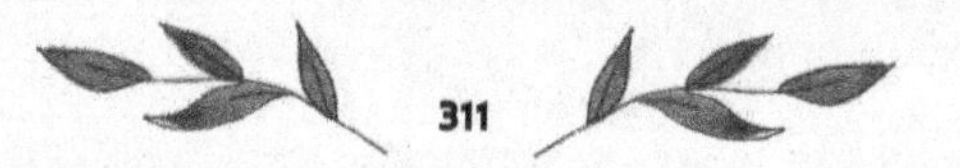

an extortionate profit (the only expense being a few minutes on the lawn and the glue from Mrs Gibberd).

Aster disagrees, of course, and insists September is a beginning. A New Year of sorts. This is only because she and Topaz are permanently in cahoots. They are either in the attic doing who knows what, or in London doing who knows what else, given there is no Grandma there to lend her air of menace to anything. Meanwhile, I am left to languish with *Vanity Fair,* my Siegfried voucher, and the Vionnet, which hangs pointlessly on my wardrobe door like a jester with no king.

There is still no physical sign of Buck. He must be back in the country by now, but has yet to set foot on the Radley estate. I know this because I have walked past on a daily basis, on the pretext of exercise, but have so far spotted only Ralph delivering quantities of post (bills, according to Ralph, and final demands at that), Rapsey removing Siegfried yet again from places Siegfried should not be, and a man from Chipping Midbury who had taken a wrong turn at Little Wyndham and had been going round in circles for four hours. I gave him a mint imperial and sent him right towards Larkham at the end of the drive.

My only highlight is the post, but that has been sharply lacking in the Buck stakes as well. Plus, it does necessitate extra helpings of Ralph.

Oh! There is the door now. And with it my foolish heart flutters, bright as a butterfly, only to be swatted, moth-like,

I expect, when it turns out to be nothing but a bridge invite for Grandma or the butcher's list for Mabel.

5 P.M.

For once, I am glad to be wrong, as I have not been moth-like at all since Ralph's call, but fluttering triumphantly like a Painted Lady or a Chalk Hill Blue. For though there was still nothing from Buck, and though I still had to endure Ralph's description of Mr Hendry's pig difficulties (one had got into the house and eaten the cat, which frankly makes Siegfried look benevolent, although may be a solution to Hamilton) and Mrs Gypp's new hat (too large for her face, and the wrong colour, being red), there was a prize at the end of it all in the shape of a stiff, thick envelope, addressed to Aster and I in the sort of handwriting that heralds its presence, all loops and curls and 'look at me!'.

I knew it once it must be from a Balfour (the return address rather a giveaway) but my surprise was which one, for this was not from the steel-hearted and helmet-haired Lady Balfour, nor from plain-Jane Daphne – Mrs Cheese-Faced Pakenham, now – but glamorous Evangeline who was, it seemed, hosting her very own ball!

Come in disguise! it urged. *Be whomever you dream of being!*

'How vulgar,' declared Grandma.

'How exciting!' countered Marigold. 'I shall be Joan of Arc.

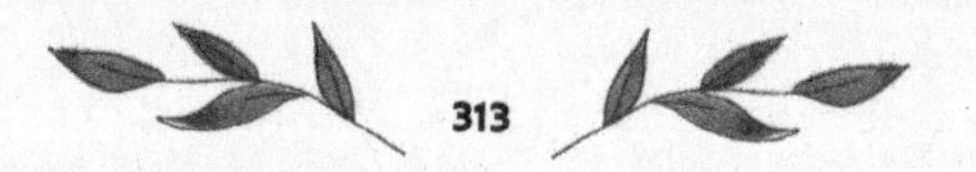

Or perhaps Jesus. Does Jesus have a sword? Or I could be Mr Hendry. Or . . . or Reg Nesbitt!'

'You shall be no one of the sort, darling, as you're not invited,' Mama replied, but not without kindness. 'Though the Balfours must be hunting,' she added. 'Surely they won't allow Evangeline the run of the house without suitable supervision?'

Grandma, for once, was spot on with her snort. 'That is precisely why she will have sent out invites,' she declared. 'I never liked that one. Far too forward for her own good.'

'Awfully pretty though,' said Mama.

I bristled, then, recalling Buck's words in his last column: 'the star of the South' he called her, 'radiant as the sun's rays' (which I doctored to 'another of London's shining stars' on the pretext of ineptitude – one cannot be the sun and a star, and rays are already radiant, are they not? Plus, she is not Tallulah Bankhead, however much she wishes it.) But then I remembered the peach Vionnet, waiting patiently, resplendently, for its first outing, like a gelding at Epsom.

At last, my chance!

'May I call Margot?' I blurted.

'What for?' demanded Grandma, mindful of the price of Margot's gabbering.

'I thought I'd invite her to stay? Aster can chaperone us,' I added quickly, as remarkably Aster, while tight-lipped about her costume, had agreed to attend, assumedly because Topaz had.

'You may have four minutes and I shall time you,' Grandma decided.

She wasn't lying, but sat with one hand on Hamilton and the other following the tock of Grandpa's old pendulum as she counted down the seconds with which I had to garner from Margot not only a yes to the party but all the salacious detail of her summer with Sven (and, apparently, Buck).

Margot, however, made a mockery of Grandma's precise timing by only engaging in the briefest of conversations before hanging up with more than two minutes to spare.

'What on earth is the matter with her?' asked Mama, who knows Margot of old, and knows she cannot be prised from the telephone with love nor crumpets on a normal day.

'I think it must be Sven,' I said.

'Sven, Sven, Sven,' repeated Marigold oddly and shook her head. 'They are all Svens in the end.'

'Who is Sven? demanded Grandma.

'Who indeed?' replied Marigold even more bizarrely.

'What are you up to?' I asked her.

'It is grown-up conversation,' Marigold said plainly, as if I were the strange one. 'Harry says we have to do it, now we are the eldest at school, so that everyone will think us mysterious and respect us.'

'Well, they will certainly think you mysterious,' I agreed.

'*You* could go as Joan of Arc,' Marigold said then. 'I bet I could cut your hair to look the part. And there's a helmet in

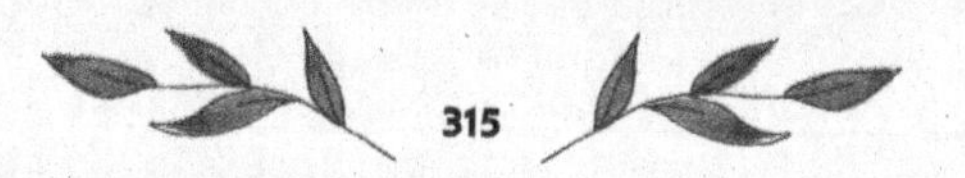

the garage. It has a chicken in it but I can put her in the meat safe with the others if you want it.'

'That's too kind,' I lied. 'But I think I may pick someone else.'

*

The question is, who? Who do I want to be?

The list, I think, is endless.

I want to be Tallulah Bankhead, Adele Astaire, Zelda Fitzgerald.

I want to be Diana in *The Sheikh*, Becky Sharpe in *Vanity Fair*, any of Austen's Bennets.

I want to be someone whom Buck will see and realise is the one, the answer to everything, the Cleopatra to his Antony, the Beatrice to his Benedict, the Juliet to his Romeo.

Oh.

That is it.

I shall be Juliet! For who could be more romantic, more beautiful than she?

And she would wear peach silk. I think, if she were here now.

And perhaps a feathered headdress.

And she would give herself to her lover that very night, for if it is true love (and she, with the gift of that dress, knows it must be) then it is surely the only course of action?

Now all I need is to find out how.

SATURDAY 20 SEPTEMBER

5 P.M.

Just seven days to go, and I have tirelessly dedicated the last two weeks to the study of the finer details of love-making (as novels invariably describe it), or sexual congress (the preferred term in Daddy's medical manuals) and am still none the wiser as to what, actually, it will feel like and how, importantly, not to get pregnant. The acts seem to differ vastly not only in descriptive terms but also in technicality. In novels, there is much ravishing, and romping, whereas in medical manuals once the thing is in place (how does one ensure it gets in? Is there an etiquette as to who directs it correctly?) no one seems to move at all, rather they just wait until the thing erupts, Vesuvius-like, which signals the end.

Older sisters are supposed to be helpful in such matters of education but of course mine is not inclined to anything in the penis area, while Margot's experience is limited to Sven standing too close to her in the luncheon queue. And I can hardly ask Mama. As such, after a week's ceaseless and fruitless pursuit, I decided to focus on the second part of the equation, that is to say not getting pregnant. Partly because, having witnessed Dinah's entrance, at least in audible form, I don't believe I am ready for such human brutality, and partly because, much as Grandma would like to see me married off, I don't think a shotgun wedding is quite what she has in mind.

Again, Aster was strictly off limits, and I did try Margot when Grandma was briefly out at bridge but she was still on the odd side.

'Oh, just don't, Panth,' she begged when I told her of my plan.

'Whyever not?'

'It's . . . it's just not all it's cracked up to be.'

'Sven?' I gasped.

'No! I mean, it's no one in particular. I'm just told. I think . . .' But she trailed off into suspicious sniffing and then claimed she could hear her mother coming back from Harrods.

Well, the last person I needed being party to my prospective sexual congress was Mrs Forbes-Rawlinson so we both hung up. I don't know what happened to Margot on tennis camp but she is clearly a reformed character. Either that or she has some sort of flu. I do hope it's the latter, as her lust for fun, for men,

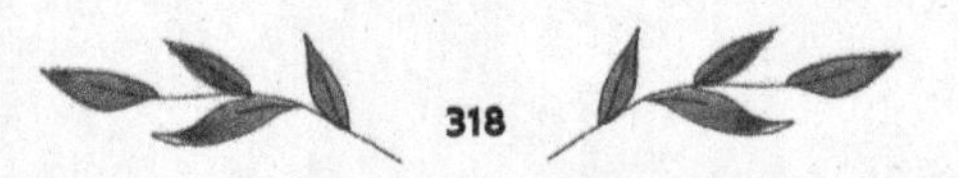

for life itself, was wholly invigorating, even if it did tend to get one in a spot of bother every now and then.

It was at this point that I decided to enlist the wisdom of someone whom, I firmly believed, despite her station in life, had seen far more of the world than either Margot or I, and probably enjoyed it: Mabel.

I was right, of course.

'Is Buck the lucky one?' she asked, as she continued to attempt to coax a rabbit out from under the butler's sink (I had cornered her in the scullery). 'He's ever so handsome.'

'Isn't he!' I blurted, able at last to share my enthusiasm. 'Only, what to do? When, you know.'

'Oh, he'll do all that for you, you don't need to worry. Flaming hell!' (This to the rabbit, not me.) 'I bet he's done it a fair few times, and with a fair few girls and all.'

I blanched. 'Yes, quite. But I meant . . . to not . . . I don't want to—'

'Oh, I get it. You don't want a bun in the oven.' She nodded sagely. 'I can only imagine what her ladyship would say.'

Except she did not only imagine, she proceeded to mimic her with the alarming accuracy I had witnessed before, ending with a hard stare that quite set me on edge.

'Well, yes, that,' I managed.

'What you really want's a Dutch cap,' she said, thankfully Mabel again. 'Marie Stopes is all for them. Drab sort of woman. But means well. Only you can't get hold of one that easy if you

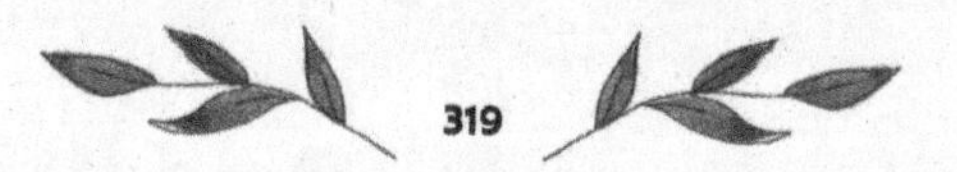

ain't already married, which seems the wrong way round to me, but there you go. So, either you'll have to hope he's already got a little something for the weekend–'

'A whole weekend?' I interrupted. 'I only want to do it the once.'

'I mean a sheath, don't I. Condom, if you like. It's either that or you'll have to do what I does.'

I braced myself. 'And what's that?'

'Get him to pull out before it goes off.'

I winced, not only at her description, but at the entire act, which had gone from something dashed romantic or at least reassuringly medical, to the awfully sordid and, it seemed, potentially messy. And then there was the question of who, exactly, she was doing this with. I did not ask; the less I imagine Ralph in any state of undress the better.

'I wish I was coming.'

'Pardon?' I asked, a vision of Mabel watching us perform from the sidelines hoving horribly into my head.

'To the ball, miss. I'd only poke my nose in, you know. Only, I thought I'd see more of them, moving here to work for yer grandma but the closest I get'll be dressing you.'

'Oh, I–'

But that was the end of the conversation as the rabbit took the opportunity of our distraction to make a bolt for the door and head to the drawing room, where Grandma was residing with Hermione Lightfoot who, like Grandma, approves of few things, and lagomorphs given the run of the Persian rugs is not one of them.

I breathed a sigh of relief, not least because the whole sex endeavour was rather moot as there was – is – still no sign of Buck yet and with less than a week to go.

6 P.M.

I have come up with the most brilliant wheeze to a) prove to Buck that I am his ideal bride by besting Evangeline at her own game of spoof and b) cheer up poor Mabel: I am going to bring Mabel herself to the ball! It is costume after all, so we can pop her in a gown and with her brilliantly faked accent no one will know she isn't eligible for *Debrett's*, or at least a mere marriage off it.

Mabel is entirely behind the ruse, needless to say; her *Tatler* addiction is as strong as mine, of course, and her devotion to the details of the private lives of society far beyond even Margot's.

'She can do the voice,' I told Aster. I turned to Mabel. 'Go on,' I urged. 'Show her.'

Mabel proceeded to give a pitch-perfect imitation of Topaz.

'Bizarre,' said Aster.

'Absolutely fabulous,' said Topaz. 'We must do it! You can be' – she flapped a hand in the air as if snatching a name from the ether – 'Minty Brigthorpe, fourth daughter of the third earl

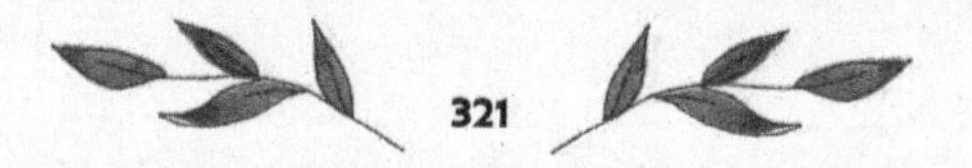

of – I don't know, anywhere. Throw in enough numbers and they'll be too baffled to calculate the truth.'

'But—' Aster began to protest.

'Oh, please,' begged Topaz. 'Live a little. Aren't you always saying you wished you could?'

'Well, yes, I suppose.'

'Then it's settled.' Topaz, seated at our dining room table, leant back triumphantly, one arm over the back of her chair, as bold as any man. 'Minty Brigthorpe you shall be.'

'But who does Minty Brigthorpe want to be?' I asked. 'It is a costume party after all.'

'Good point.' Topaz leant forward again, a strand of her sharp, shingled hair falling elegantly over one eye. 'I think Agatha Carew is coming as Botticelli's Venus. Enormous shell and not much else. And Valentine a Lyon's waitress.'

'Why would he want to be a waitress?' asked Mabel. 'If he can be anyone.'

'Good point,' said Topaz. 'It is rather odd. Though perhaps it's just the cap.'

'I could make you Medusa,' Aster said then.

Mabel frowned. 'Who's that?'

'From the Greek myths,' I explained. 'She had snakes for hair.'

'Or Ariadne,' added Aster quickly, sensing, I think, Mabel's unease. 'She was Greek as well, a beauty. No snakes though. Or Tinker Bell, from Peter Pan? I could fashion wings then. And no snakes for her either.'

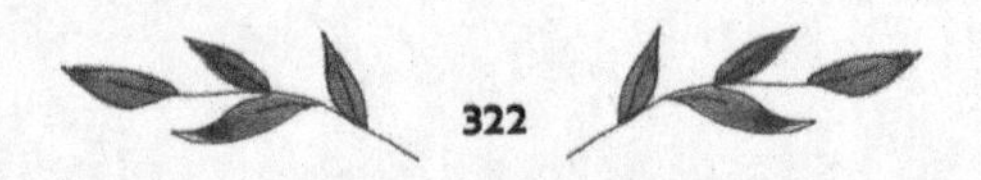

'Thank Christ for that,' said Mabel. 'It's bad enough with rabbits. Not that you must tell Marigold. Only, I'm a maid not a flaming zookeeper, and I certainly don't want no snakes on me head. I'll be Tinker Bell then. Always fancied being a fairy. Surprised Valentine didn't pick her. He does love a costume.'

And with that chip of wisdom, everything was settled. I was to be Juliet; Mabel, Tinker Bell; and Topaz, Cleopatra (she had the hair of course, and the unquestionable beauty). Aster would not give up the secret of her own costumed longing, saying we must wait until Saturday, but she promised it would be surprising. I am sure it will be, given her dressmaking. Perhaps she has bagsed Ariadne for herself. Or Helen of Troy even, though given she was the woman who launched a thousand ships that is stretching it a bit.

Saturday. Only three days away but it seems eons now.

Though each day is a day more likely that my own Romeo will return and claim his Juliet.

In every sense.

Oh, golly, I keep thinking of it 'going off' and the mess.

I do hope one doesn't need a bucket.

SATURDAY 27 SEPTEMBER

8 A.M.

There is no sign of Buck.

10 A.M.

There is no sign of Buck.

2 P.M.

There is still no sign of Buck and Aster says if I am going out again then next time can it be to the village because she has run

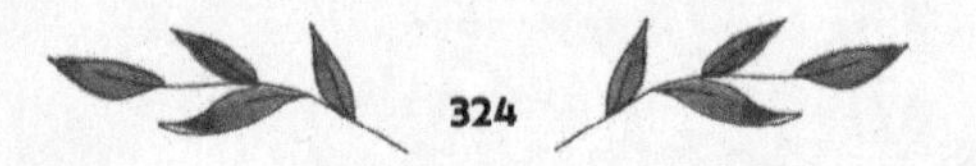

out of glue for Mabel's Tinker Bell wings and Mrs Gibberd will have some, only not the cheap cow gum, the other sort. I have agreed, if only to give me something to take my mind off the Buck subject. Though even this distraction is not without peril.

'I shall come,' announced Marigold immediately.

'Whatever for?' I asked. 'I'm only fetching glue.'

'I want to see my frog,' she replied. 'At Dr Spencer's. And you can see yours.' This said with pointed accusation, as if I had been neglecting half of my birthday gift. She had a point.

I made a quick calculation. Freddy had said he would back at Cambridge at the end of September but did that mean Monday or was he already there? Not that it should matter – Freddy is Freddy after all – but still, one likes to know where one is with these things. 'Very well,' I said, having decided he would indeed be in Cambridge, no doubt up to something with Egg at this very minute. 'Glue and frogs it is.'

And if we detour back via Radley, then no one is to know but Marigold and I.

2.10 P.M.

And Siegfried, who is coming on the walk too, as Marigold says I am yet to use up my voucher and he is very disappointed by this state of affairs. I did not bother to argue.

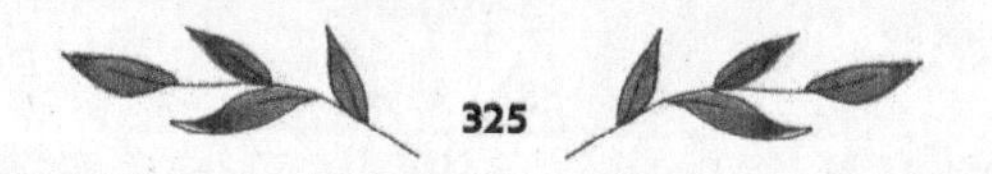

6.30 P.M.

There is so much to tell and so little time to tell it, which is mostly down to Siegfried falling into Dr Spencer's pond, which is rather the doctor's fault for welcoming him into the garden in the first place when he could have quite happily been tied up on the green with Derek Nesbitt's goat. But the doctor insisted that 'no Mannering must be left behind' and so into the garden I verily hauled him, whereupon he spent several minutes trying to destroy poor Mrs Spencer the Second's gardenias, before bolting for the pond (or rather Marigold, who was busy dipping with her jam jar in the hope of hauling up Andrew from the murky depths). So enthusiastic was he, and so already teetering she, that they both fell in with a terrible yell and a kind of tidal wave that surely sent several fish and both frogs into Mrs Gypp's next door.

'Oh, for heaven's sake,' I despaired. For I could hardly ask the doctor to pull either of the fools out, but I was already bathed and my hair set and pond water is not a look or smell I think becoming of anyone, let alone Juliet. Although Millais' Ophelia drowning did spring to mind momentarily before my wild thoughts were interrupted by a loud 'halloo'.

I turned and something in me both sunk and flourished.

It was Freddy Spencer. Not at Cambridge at all but here, in Ickthorpe, in rolled-up shirt sleeves, and striding toward the water as if he were Poseidon himself.

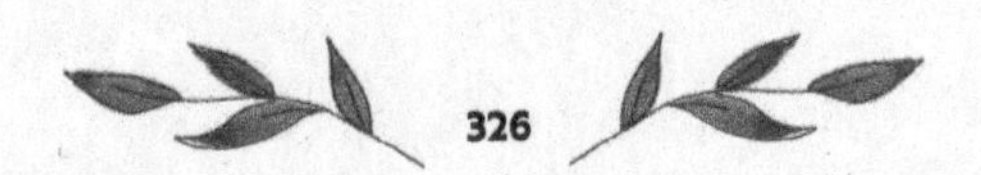

'Don't!' I cried.

But it was too late. Freddy was waist deep in weeds before I could think of something more convincing to say, grasping Siegfried by the collar (again, thank heavens for Rapsey) and hauling him shoreward. If that sounds senseless, rescuing sheep before human, let me assure you that Marigold, a fearless swimmer, was already sat on the side in her sodden frock, cheering them both on.

Within minutes, Siegfried was back where he should have been all along – tethered to the railings on the green – and Marigold was in the kitchen wrapped in a Welsh blanket and being given cocoa and a jam tart by a jovial Mrs Spencer (the doctor had offed to his study to find Marigold some book on the anatomy of amphibians).

Meanwhile, Freddy stood on the back verandah, dripping still with pondwater and yet somehow appearing none the worse for it.

I watched a drop trickle from his clavicle towards the golden hairs of his chest where it was trapped, glistening, for a second. Feeling myself flush I looked away. 'I'm so sorry,' I said. 'We should never have brought him, but Marigold rather insisted and you know what she's like when she insists on something.'

'It's nothing,' he said. 'I've been in before. You have, even. Remember?'

I shook my head as I met his gaze – peering at me, willing the image to spring from the well of my memory. 'I don't . . .

No, wait, was I chasing a ball?'

'A kite,' he replied. 'We made it, from dowelling rods and an old piece of curtain.'

'That's it! Orange, wasn't it?'

'Hideous. No wonder Mummy had taken the curtains down.'

We both paused at that, caught in the snare of remembrance, and the snap of loss, for it had been the first Mrs Spencer who had taken down the drapes.

'You look . . . dressed up,' he said then, breaking the spell.

I looked down at my rumpled summer frock. 'Hardly,' I said.

'I mean the hair and . . . I don't know. Something about you.'

I touched a hand to my Marcelled waves. 'It's for the ball,' I said. 'At the Balfours'.'

He shrugged and I felt a prick of guilt. He'd not been invited. Of course he hadn't.

I covered my embarrassment by blathering again. 'It's a costume party: masks and everything. So you could come anyway and no one would know. We're taking Mabel. She's Minty Brigthorpe for the night. Fun, isn't it?'

He shrugged. 'And who are you going as, then?'

I felt ashamed to say it then. But why shouldn't I tell him? Why couldn't I be her? 'Juliet,' I announced, my chin tilted, as if waiting for the blow.

It never came.

'You'll look beautiful,' he replied. Then frowned. 'Though I think they had different hair then.'

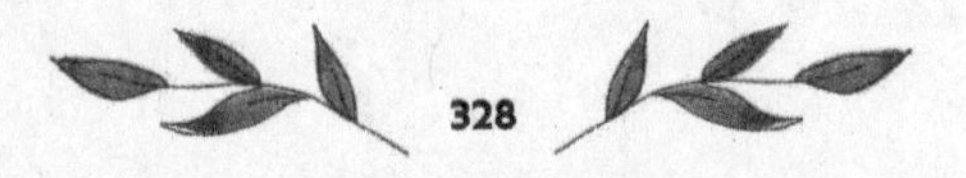

I felt myself give. 'I know. But I so wanted this style and to wear that dress. The one Buck—' I stopped, knowing I'd gone too far.

'Buck, eh.' Freddy plunged his hands into sopping wet pockets. 'Well, tell him he's a lucky man.'

I felt myself flush, unsure what to make of an obvious compliment, or what to say in return. 'I would,' I replied finally. 'But I don't think he's even coming.'

Freddy was quiet then, inscrutable for a moment. Then, he smiled, only the kind that doesn't light anything, rather concedes something. 'Oh, he's back,' he said. 'I saw him drive past – swerve really – an hour or so ago.'

I opened my mouth to say something, anything, to let out the butterflies that had fluttered suddenly in my stomach, but Freddy went on.

'But if he doesn't turn up for you, then he's a bigger fool than I thought,' he said. And with that, he turned on his heel and walked back into Bridge House, a series of wet footprints trailing him up the wooden stairs.

I didn't have time to ponder what he meant by anything; my heart hammering like Rapsey at the garage roof, I mustered Marigold as quickly as I could, thanked the Spencers awfully for their pains, and retrieved Siegfried from the green where he had cornered the goat and was making advances of the amorous kind, which was not only cross-species, but same gender, much to Marigold's delight.

'We don't have time for that kind of shenanigans,' I explained. 'Come along.' And, hauling on his collar I dragged the sheep back to celibacy, and myself to possibly the opposite.

And now I am about to descend the stairs to join Minty Brigthorpe, Topaz and a spectacular Aster, who has tailored herself not a slip of silk nor a crinolined ballgown. Nor a dress at all. But a suit. A man's suit.

'A woman's, actually,' she corrected.

'But . . . who are you?' I asked.

'I'm me,' she said.

'I don't understand.' I didn't.

She stuck her hands in her pockets, an echo of Freddy. 'A seamstress may not change the world,' she said. 'But I can at least alter the way women dress.'

I had a sudden flash of clarity and nodded in ascension. I knew exactly what she meant. We may be mere women, but there are tiny changes we can make, while we are on earth, that will rock this enormous boat and send ripples far into the future. I was only ashamed not to have done the same.

Grandma, however, was unimpressed. 'You look like Prince Edward,' she said. 'And not in a good way.'

'I think it's dashing,' countered Mama. 'And daring as well.'

'Thank you,' said Aster.

'I still don't know why I can't be Jesus,' protested Marigold. 'No one would even know if I had a beard.'

'Jesus wasn't four foot tall,' Grandma said, putting an end

to things, as she so often does. It was just a relief she hadn't yet seen Mabel, who was not on her evening off at all but secreted in the scullery in a tutu and wings, ready for the flight to Balfour Mansion.

It is only minutes away now. And then, with the toot of Rapsey's horn, we shall leave the Dower House as already altered people – Cleopatra, Tinker Bell, Juliet and my true, luminous sister – and return, perhaps, unrecognisable, even to ourselves.

For we shall have danced.

And drunk.

And done bright, defiant things that will seem debauchery when we reflect on them in the half light of a hungover Sunday.

But not tonight.

Tonight, we will do what we wish and be whom we wish and with whom we wish.

And I wish for nothing but Buck. And, as Freddy has already said, now that he's back at Radley, my wish is set to be granted.

SUNDAY 28 SEPTEMBER

11 A.M.

There is again, much to say, but I am not yet ready or able to say it.

2 P.M.

Nor yet.

5 P.M.

Nor yet.

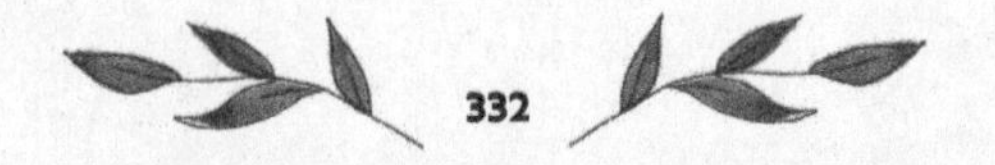

But I realise I must say it anyway, scribe it in indelible ink, as a warning to the me in the future who may have buried the memory and lapsed into foolhardiness again. To remind myself of every sliver of indignity to which I was subjected, or, rather, allowed myself to be subjected to.

But I shall set the scene before I get to the dreadful denouement.

So, Saturday night, Balfour Hall.

It was as every bit as glittering I could have wished, and everyone who was anyone (apart from Margot Forbes-Rawlinson, more of whom later) was there. A Sassoon, a Tennant, a Mitford sister; Valentine in full Lyon's uniform, and our very own maid as a fairy; Topaz as Cleopatra and her version of Antony in Aster.

And then there was the hostess herself in so little material she seemed veritably naked.

'Who is she supposed to be?' I hissed at my sister.

'Eve, I think,' she replied. 'In the Garden of Eden.'

'I wonder who her Adam is,' mused Topaz, scanning the expanse of marble onto which were crammed more bodies than a Renaissance painting. 'I can't see Gaston.'

'I don't see how you can tell,' replied Aster. 'Half the men are in masks.'

This was indeed the case, as, shy of full pantomime regalia, several guests were in the penguin shades of dinner dress but with the poster-paint faces of peacocks or foxes or cats, so as to become a strange but indistinguishable Greek chorus.

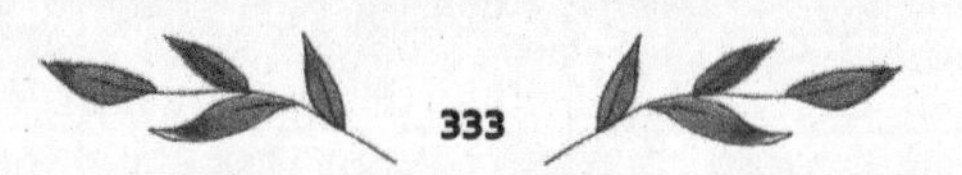

'Darling!'

I found myself suddenly pressed against flesh (or rather, bone – hard and wiry); breasts barely more than bee-stings buried under my own somewhat blancmange wobbles.

'Evangeline,' I replied.

'You look marvellous.' She held me at arms' length, assessing my form like a horse. 'Who are you?'

I felt the revealing heat of my cheeks. 'I . . . Juliet.' I held out my tattered copy of the schoolbook Shakespeare as if in explanation.

'Right. Well, jolly good. I don't suppose you've seen Buck, have you?'

My shimmer of shame segued swiftly into indignation. 'No. Why, should I?'

Evangeline considered me. 'No, I suppose not. Well, do have a good time. I see your sister is making quite a spectacle of herself. Thank heaven Daphne isn't here to witness it.'

And with that, she glided off through crowds that seemed to part as if they were the Red Sea and she some almost-nude, effeminate Moses.

I looked back at Aster – hands casually in her pockets, head tilted to listen to the animated Topaz, a smile glimmering on her lips – and I thanked heaven Daphne wasn't there either, to ruin it with old Cheese-Face, and heaved a sigh, just as two hands slid down my hips and a pair of lips skimmed my neck, whispering, 'I knew it would suit you.'

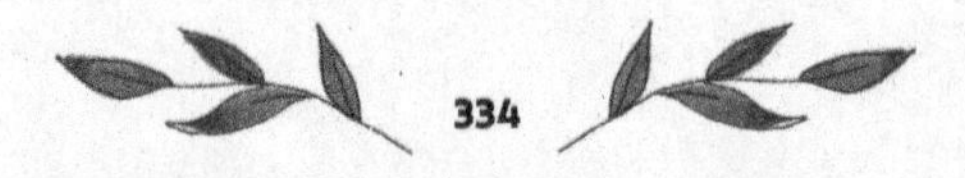

I spun and found myself in the arms of a man in a dragon mask, its teeth bared, its tongue forked and curling toward me. I should have gasped. I should have beaten my fists against his stiff shirt front. I should have made my escape. But this, I knew, was no fierce beast.

This was Buck.

He pushed the mask up a little, exposing his generous mouth. 'Did you miss me?' said his lips, so ridiculously pink I might have thought they'd been painted on if I didn't know better.

'Every second,' I said, my heart beating harder, louder as if to prove it true.

'Good,' he replied. And then, without another word, he pressed those blushing pilgrims to mine. Though these were no innocents. These were hungry, devouring, wolfish in their appetite and size.

'Buck!' I gasped, breaking free.

He smiled. 'There are rooms,' he said. 'Upstairs.'

I jinked, startled as a hare. 'But it's . . . it's barely seven.' I said, playing for time. 'Later.'

'You promise?'

I nodded.

He smiled, then lowered the dragon back into place. 'So, I'll come for you then.'

*

I needed Dutch courage, and a lot of it. And it wasn't hard to find. I suppose that was where it all started to slip. I must have drunk a bottle's worth of Moët, less the sloshes that fell down my dress as I skipped and skittered through the throng, a childish Juliet indeed, before I stumbled from the ballroom into a side corridor and saw them.

Topaz, one arm slung round the neck of a man, one disappearing into the fabric of his trousers, her lips on his, as he moaned in pleasure.

No, not his. For this was no deep, guttural thing. This was soft, breathy, a different gender.

This was Aster.

It was all I could do not to drop my glass, hear it shatter on hard marble and break their beautiful spell.

But I really didn't want to do that. For I knew then what I was feeling. And I wasn't shocked, still less appalled.

I was jealous.

A fiery spike of it shot through me, hot and enervating as alcohol, envious green as Absinthe.

I wanted Buck and I wanted him now.

My mission crystal but my vision swimming, I flailed my way back through the ballroom, eyes flicking from one penguin to the next as I sought out that dragon.

Then I saw him, deep in conversation with Eve.

Of course he was.

Well, Eve may have corrupted Adam, but this Juliet knew her Romeo when she saw him. I stormed forward and grabbed him by the hand.

'I'm ready,' I said.

If I was expecting a fight, he didn't offer one. Instead Buck indulged me. 'Right now?' he asked.

'Right now,' I replied. It had to be. I couldn't dither. I couldn't lose my nerve.

And with that, I led him – I led *him* – up the sweep of the staircase to whichever one of the twenty-seven bedrooms was closest and empty.

And I let him undress me.

And then, my mouth dry, my legs trembling, I lay down on the bed and waited for him to begin.

He began with a hand. Clamped down on my breast, kneading it as if it were yeasted dough or clay to be moulded into a better shape.

I wasn't sure what I should be feeling, other than a slight twinge of pain and another of shame. I squashed them down, refused to amuse them.

His tongue licked a nipple then, as if he were feeding. A giant Dinah. Was this right? It didn't feel right.

But that was nothing compared to what came next. The hand that had held my breast released it suddenly and slid down to my hip, then inward, brushing the electric red of my pubic hair.

I stiffened swiftly, my legs closing unbidden. I willed them open, to let him do what he wanted to do, but they seemed rigid, as if rigor mortis had set in. Wasn't I supposed to melt

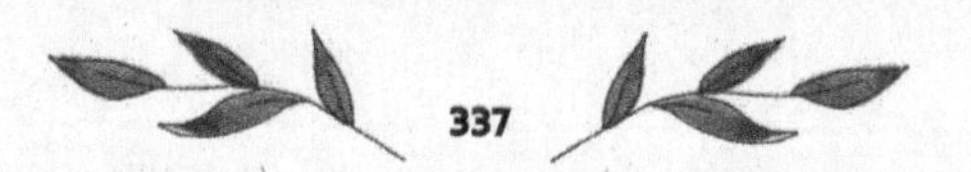

with desire? Though perhaps that came later.

His fingers thwarted, he bade me 'relax'. As if he could command me, Aladdin like, and with 'Open sesame!', I would spring wide to reveal my riches.

But my secret cave remained stubbornly shut.

This was no good. I must muster, I thought.

I conjured images in my head: Aster as Antony and her Cleopatra. Tinker Bell and some Lost Boy she had danced the foxtrot with, locked in enthusiastic embrace.

Juliet and her Romeo.

But still I could not do it.

'Stop,' I blurted and sat up suddenly, clutching the sheet to cover my shame.

'What the hell is wrong with you?' Buck stood, pushing it – that thing, turgid and purple – back into his trousers, buttoning up.

I suppose I should be grateful for that.

'I . . . I just . . .' But I couldn't get the words out. Couldn't explain anything. That I wanted it but didn't. That I was both ready and not. That I loved him, and yet . . .

And then he said it.

'Frigid bitch. I should have stuck with your idiotic friend. At least she knew what to do with it.'

It took a second, but only a second, and then, heavy as a freight train, it hit me with hard, damaging clarity: Margot had made love to him. Not Sven or any of the tennis men.

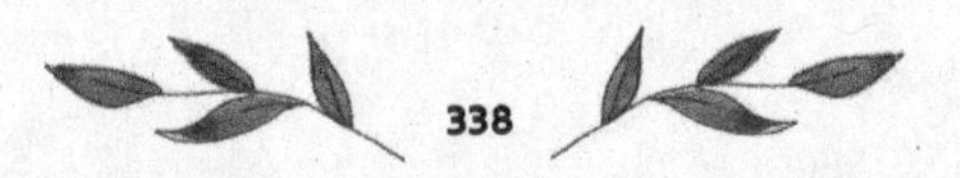

She had made love to Buck. Knowing how I felt about him.

Only, it wasn't just her betrayal, though hers was certainly worse. Buck had made love to *her*, after calling *me* his Baby. After sending *me* the dress.

But I wasn't Buck's Baby, was I? I was just another target: a doe to be shot, a bird to be bagged.

'You never intended to marry me, did you?' I said it aloud as I realised it.

Buck's face, red, ugly now I looked at it, screwed up. 'Marry you? Are you mad? Why would I marry you?'

I shook my head. 'The dress. This dress.' I grabbed it, yanked it on, not caring about the sharp rip I could hear as I pulled it down, the bugle beads that scattered on the floor like rice at a wedding. Wedding. Ha! 'And you said—'

'I said nothing.' Buck was already making for the door. 'You're hardly the marrying type anyway. Far too . . . feisty.'

That word! Used almost exclusively for cats and difficult women. Why was that?

'And poor,' he added, unnecessarily.

'Did you even love me?' I asked as his hand turned the beehived knob of the door.

He softened then. 'Baby . . .'

And I could have too. But that word had done for me. 'Don't,' I said. 'Just go.'

And go he did.

Five minutes later, I did too.

I can't begin to think of the state I must have looked, stumbling down the stairs, one shoe abandoned, like a drunk, downmarket Cinderella. I just wanted to get out of Balfour Hall, to get back to the Dower House, even in all its insipid dreariness and promise of spinsterhood.

I knew I should find Aster or Mabel but I didn't want to ruin their nights. So, forgetting my fur, I launched myself at the door and out into the dimming light, into the chill of late September air, autumn taking the stage now, winter visible in the wings.

'Panth?'

A man.

I swung round in panic, my ankle collapsing on the gravel and I after it, a sob, finally, escaping my crimson-smeared lips. And then I did what any girl would do. I closed my eyes and prayed for the ground to swallow me.

Of course, it didn't oblige, for the ground and God never listen. Instead, seconds later, I felt my body born aloft and opened my tired eyes to find them level with two bright, blue ones, blinking above a surgical mask.

'Dr Spencer?' I asked blearily.

'Not yet,' said Freddy. 'Though at least the costume is clear.'

'Freddy,' I murmured. 'You came.'

I could have been affronted. Could have told him to stop manhandling me like the other one had. That I was no damsel in need of rescue by a white knight or surgeon of any sort. I had rescued myself. In the end.

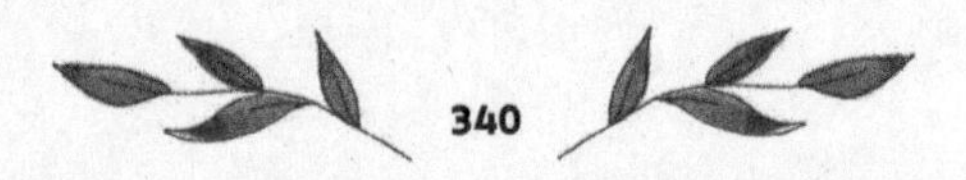

But this was Freddy. And I was hurt. In every sense. And so I flung arms around his neck and clung on as he carried me, without once complaining, from Balfour Hall a mile back to Ickthorpe and thence to the Dower House, where he explained quietly to Mama that I had had one too many glasses of champagne but I was otherwise fine, and that his father would be round in the morning to check my leg.

'Not you?' I remember asking.

'I've got to go to Cambridge,' he said. 'But you're in safe hands. I promise.' Then he leant in, his lips almost on my ear. 'He can't get at you again.'

I teetered, not remembering what I'd told him on the way, worried I'd said too much, glad I'd said something.

'Thank you,' I said. 'And I'm sorry. I'm so—'

'Nothing to be sorry for,' he said quickly, saving me again.

And that, aside from me being sick on the hallway floor, necessitating Mama, a mop, and a bucket, was the last thing I remember before waking the next day to the cold wash of morning, the knowledge one's life is ruined, and the conviction that I never want to see a penis again as long as I live.

*

Dr Spencer did come. And my ankle is healing quickly – I can walk on it now without wincing. But my heart, and hope, I fear, will remain bruised for far longer.

Not that you will have to hear about it.

I have decided that as nothing short of a fairy godmother

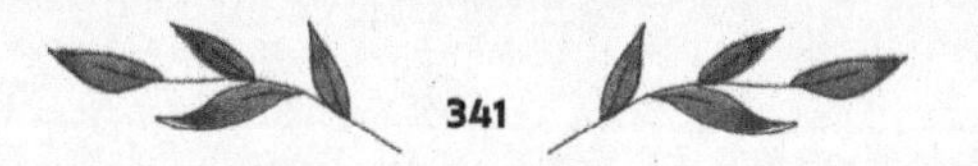

and a magic wand can sort this story out, I may as well stop now.

For the downfall of this Mannering, at least, is complete.

OCTOBER

WEDNESDAY 1 OCTOBER

10 P.M.

In my defence, I didn't think they would publish it. In my defence, it was meant as a sort of warning shot, an 'I know all about you' ransom note with its implicit demand to stop. For you see, the thing is, I did write something else.

I wrote Buck's column. Telephoned the editor, feigned being Buck's 'secretary' and dictated the copy, assuring him it was 'the corrected, final version' so that whatever Buck had mustered in the meantime would be binned.

And today it appeared, in all its awful glory, on page three of *The Herald.*

I'm not entirely sure how it happened. Well, that's not true. Obviously, I know how the writing bit occurred: I was ravaged

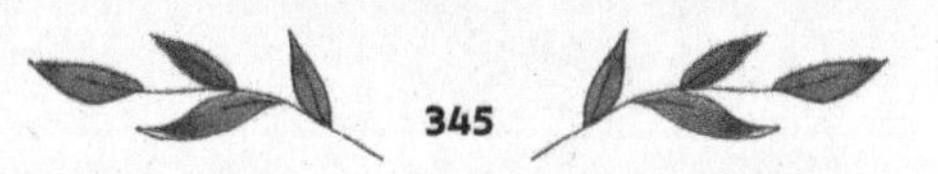

by anger and felt the need to humiliate in turn those who had humiliated me and so I put pen to paper. I had thought it would be cathartic. Admonishing Evangeline for wearing barely anything. Ruining Buck the way he had almost ruined me – saying he had been seen in several bedrooms with several women, none of them the 'fresh debutante' he had bedded in France. Revealing Margot to be as naïve as everyone always said she was while I, the fool, defended her.

Only now, of course, all I feel is the needle of shame at stooping so low and a swamping, horrible guilt for the bruising injuries I must have caused.

Oh, I can hardly bear to think of the slices I bade my pen take to my friend, and such low blows all of them: her morals, her mother, her thighs. Even the words with which I described Buck seem brutal and cruel now I see them in stark serif type. Though there is no doubt he deserves them, every one.

I cannot fathom what the editor must have been thinking. Does he not understand that Jack Buchanan, who owns the very press on which *The Herald* is printed, is Buck's father? Or perhaps he has no insight into society and so cannot see through the pseudonyms I used. He certainly cannot own a copy of *Debrett's* or he'd know that the 'delicious nymphette' Minty Brigthorpe doesn't even exist.

Worse, he had acquired a photograph – a paparazzo, I presume – to accompany the pitiful piece. But not of Buck, nor even Evangeline, but of Topaz and Aster, the former described (not by me this time) as 'sapphic society scourge' and the latter, my darling sister, as a 'man-hating gender bender'. I mean, there is a little truth in that, I suppose, but where I see it as something of which to be proud, *The Herald* clearly thinks it a disgrace. Though whoever captioned it did compliment her couture, so there is that.

But there is something far worse: I mentioned Freddy. I said the only person of worth at the whole affair was a 'local nobody', a medical student 'playing peacock' for the evening.

In my defence, I was only trying to sound like Buck, and thought the 'worth' might balance out the 'nobody' in Freddy's – or anyone's – eyes, but again, in print, it seems to loom large and unforgiving.

Of course, there is nothing on the page to undo me; not a word to reveal the true identity of the author, and in any case, everyone who's anyone knows the column belongs to Buck. But that has not assuaged my guilt in the least, however many times I have read and reread it, checking for revelation.

To make matters worse, Aster and Mama are coming in and sympathising with me by the minute. Mama, because she is worried about my ankle and my lack of appetite; Aster, because she knows very well my ankle and appetite are only the half of it and that I am covering up something far more untoward.

It is true, though, that I have barely eaten a thing since Saturday. Not even now Mabel has ditched Minty Brigthorpe and is back, plain-faced and accented, and aproned as a maid again. My throat is too tight to swallow and my stomach a hard knot of a thing that would refuse to let food in anyway. It is all I can do to suck on the last of the mint imperials, and stroke the rabbit Marigold has left on the bed with me as comfort, coming in every now and then to remove its droppings and offer both of us carrots (the rabbit has mine, of course).

Perhaps I shall die of shame.

I wonder if that's possible.

I almost hope it is.

THURSDAY 2 OCTOBER

8 P.M.

Aster says it is not possible to die of shame but I may well perish on account of my idiocy if she has anything to do with it.

She forced me into confession. Quite brutally, and through the judicious use of soup. She said if I did not confess immediately, she would pin me down and force feed me cream of asparagus, as if I were a suffragette and she Asquith himself, as heaven knows those women had reasons for their hunger strike but I wasn't fighting any battle of import as far as she knew, and so deserved it.

I didn't think the words would come. At first, they wouldn't. And, the soup looming in a milk jug, I snatched up this journal,

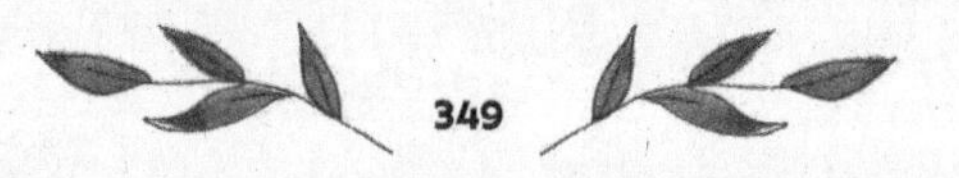

opened it to the relevant page and handed it to her, head bowed in shame.

Then I waited, my shrunken stomach cramping in agony, my heart fair breaking with pain, while she read every word of the whole sorry story, from my drunken thrusting at Buck, to being shamed and naked, to the damning indictment of society that flowed as easily as syrup from my very own pen.

'Well, well, well,' she said as she snapped shut these very pages.

I waited for more. For the stream of invective; for the 'stupid' and 'useless' and 'black sheep of this family'; for the dismissal of me as her sister, even.

But instead she sat next to me on this bed, taking the rabbit from my lap, which I admit I may have been clutching rather too harshly, and my cold, trembling fingers in her own.

'You've been a fool,' she said at last. 'But it is Buck who is the devil here, not you.'

It was as if a stopper had popped in me, and the words I had longed to say burst from me at last. 'I'm so sorry,' I wailed and repeated my apology between sobs.

But Aster still refused to admonish me, instead holding me to her shoulder as I wept out days', even weeks' worth of worry and upset, and then begged for penitence for wasn't she pictured too, and in such unflattering terms? A man-hater! A gender bender!

'Oh, Panth,' she said, and held me tighter still. 'I know

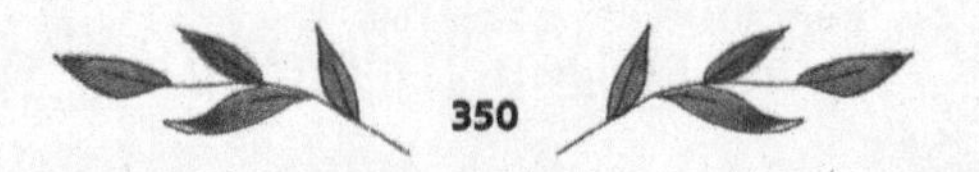

you didn't write that. And perhaps I am a man-hater. Is it any wonder, given what you and countless others have been through?'

'I...'

'And the caption has hardly harmed me,' she continued. 'Do you know, I've had four calls this morning alone for new gowns. And one for a trouser suit. From a *Miss* Allingham.'

I wiped my eyes, and nose, I'm sorry to say, on the sleeve of my nightdress (I had not bothered to get up, for what was the point if one was going to die any moment).

'So, you don't need to say sorry to me,' she said. 'But there are several people you do have to apologise to.'

'Mama?' I asked.

'The less Mama knows the better,' Aster replied. 'But you must write to Margot and Freddy and Buck at once.'

'Buck?' This was too far, surely.

'Yes, Buck. What he did was wrong, but your writing about it does not make up for that. And he rents from Valentine, remember. You don't want to jeopardise your own cousin, do you?'

At that point, I rather did. In fact, I would have liked nothing more than for Buck to pack his bags and move out of Radley Manor for good. But as Valentine's fortunes were so tied up in our own, I conceded defeat, and Aster left me with my pen, a writing pad, and the jug of soup, which, my secret out, I found I now had a little room for after all.

And so the letters are written, and have been despatched via Ralph, who came round to have a loud but annoyingly muffled argument with Mabel in the back pantry.

Now all I can do, I suppose, is wait, and hope that Margot and Freddy – my once truest of friends – will take the letters in the sense of contrition with which I wrote them. And accept them as a sort of olive branch, albeit it a lavender-coloured, and slightly tear-smudged one.

And as for Buck, I hardly care what he thinks.

Well, only for Valentine's sake. And for Radley's.

My heart does not beat for him any longer. I am not his Baby. Nor anyone's.

Ever again.

MONDAY 13 OCTOBER

7 P.M.

There has been no reply from anyone. Not Margot, not Freddy and not even Buck, whom I know is at home, as I have walked past Radley Manor no less than five times, and I can see his motorcar on the drive as plain as day, which I was almost tempted to tell him to garage, given the inclement weather, but then decided against it as the ruin of his calf-leather seats is no concern of mine.

Aster said I was torturing myself and she should know as she walked to Balfour Hall almost daily just to stare from the gooseberry thicket up to Daphne's window.

'I know,' I said.

'You knew?'

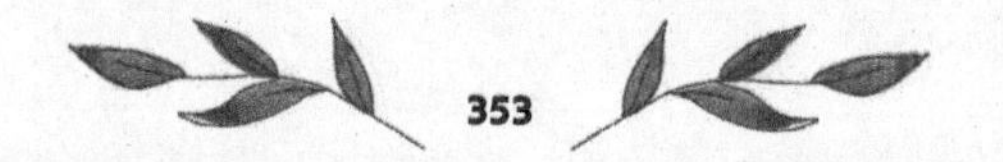

'Well, I guessed.'

'You know, the best revenge is to be fine without him,' she said then.

'I am,' I said. 'I don't want him any more.'

And it's strange, but until I had said those words aloud, I don't think I believed them. Only now they were almost a freedom cry, a battle rally. I really didn't want him. Nor any man. Not that I was going to follow Aster. Just that I wasn't ready for men. Not yet. Maybe not ever.

All that mattered – all that should have mattered before – was my friendship with Freddy and a rapprochement with Margot. For though she had to forgive me, I had still to quite forgive her, and while I longed for a letter, even a word, there was part of me that couldn't bear to hear what she had to say for herself.

'Perhaps I could come with you,' I suggested to Aster then. For she was off to London to meet this Miss Allingham – on Grandma's bidding, who was tired, she said, of strange women 'trooping in at all hours and undressing unnecessarily'. It was worse, she said, than the rabbits or the frogs.

But Aster refused. 'London will do you no good,' she said. And I knew it was true. 'Find something to occupy you. Read or sew or write, even. Haven't you a book to complete?'

I nodded. The romantic novel was half written – well, there were a hundred pages or so of notes. But how could I muster enough courage, enough hope, to go back to romance? After all that had happened.

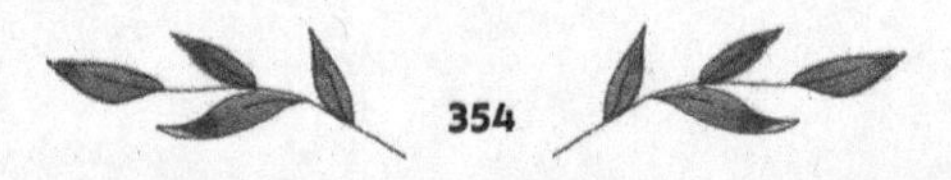

Papa always said the best cure for gloom was noble deeds. But there are no damsels to rescue but myself. There is not even a cat up a tree aside from Hamilton and it just sits belligerently in the uppermost branches of the oak howling pitifully, then the minute you get within grasping distance bolts off as if scalded and leaps to triumphant safety, leaving you looking quite the fool.

So, for now, it is back to staring from the window.

Waiting on Ralph.

And for my pitiful existence to crank into something like life again.

FRIDAY 17 OCTOBER

There is no word from anyone.

MONDAY 20 OCTOBER

There is still no word from anyone.

TUESDAY 21 OCTOBER

2 P.M.

There is *still* no word from anyone. But Buck has left Radley, at least for now.

I know this not because I have been stalking the ha-ha again, but because Rapsey told me he saw the car tear down the drive and swerve left towards London at about eight this morning, when I was still asleep, and he was dealing with Siegfried who was somehow jammed in the back seat of our motorcar and was trying to make himself at home. (There is no 'somehow' about it. Marigold has been letting him in as she says it is more comfy for him at night. She usually lets him out again on her way to school but must have forgotten this morning, in the excitement of a visit to a toothpaste factory.)

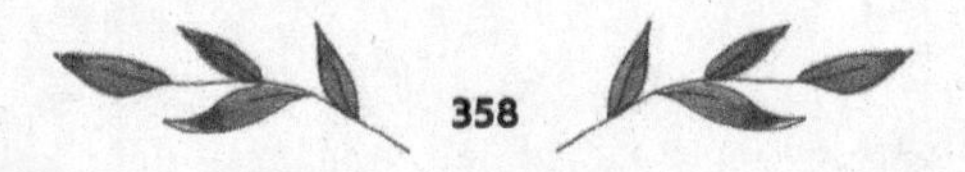

I think perhaps Buck may have telephoned to let me know. Or tried to. For someone rang just before lunch, and then hung up.

I have no idea what is happening with Margot or Freddy either. I suggested to Aster I should write again but she said I have said my piece and it is down to them now, however long it takes.

She is wise. Wiser than I ever gave her credit for. Almost Mama-like.

I only wish I had Mama's patience. But I shall try.

I shall wait. Patiently. And with grace.

WEDNESDAY 22 OCTOBER

There is still no word from anyone.

THURSDAY 23 OCTOBER

There is still no word from anyone.

FRIDAY 24 OCTOBER

3 P.M.

There is still no word from anyone. Though, yet again, the telephone has rung, only to offer up a lightly menacing heavy breathing and then the dull buzz of nothingness once whoever it is has rung up. Grandma insists it is a pervert. She has been warned all about them by the wireless (which she has decided is not an instrument of devilment after all, but a useful tool with which to gain a grip on political and pervert proceedings, and thus beat Hermione Lightfoot 'at her own game'), and they are everywhere, apparently, the telephone only their latest medium of terror. I suspect it is more likely to be a shy client of Aster's, who does not know quite what to do or say when greeted by Grandma's harsh bark. That or Buck, who likely feels the same.

Though, as Aster points out, I must not start to feel sorry for him, for that is the beginning of the end again. Rather, I must sever him from my affections as if ripping off a scab, or a sticking plaster. Marigold said Mama had said that ripping off a scab was foolish, as it will only scar. Aster replied that her advice was metaphorical, as well Marigold knew, and in any case Marigold had hardly heeded Mama's initial warning, as evidenced by the pink constellations peppering her knees and elbows.

I do not feel sorry for Buck in any case.

I just feel a little sorry for me.

SATURDAY 25 OCTOBER

8 P.M.

No strange telephone calls today, which is almost a shame as Marigold and I have hatched a plan to toot Uncle James's old trumpet loudly and repeatedly down the speaker to shock the caller into confessing all. Aster says at seventeen I should be above such childish things, though when I reminded her it might be a pervert she relented somewhat and agreed a little trumpet might be a suitable punishment.

In any case, though, I am not too horribly bothered about the lack of pervert as there is far more pressing news: Freddy Spencer has written.

Ralph delivered the letter along with a lengthy treatise on the problem of voles, with which Ickthorpe is apparently

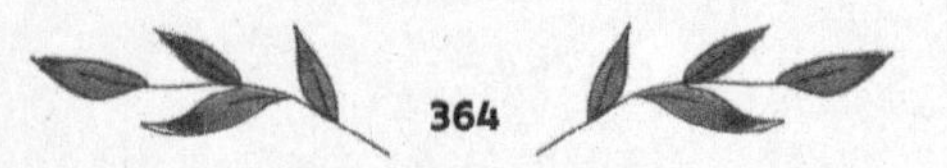

inundated, and the myriad irritating hillocks on Mrs Gibberd's back lawn. After several both boring and fraught minutes, during which I had to actively prevent my fingers tearing open the envelope, it transpired he meant moles, and I sent him round to see Rapsey, who is quite the mole-catcher. (His method involves bait and a spade and Marigold's assistance, about which she is morbidly thrilled, and has begged me join her. Naturally, I have declined.)

Then, the door closed firmly behind me, and ensconced in the deserted drawing room I began to read, trying not to mind that I am no longer 'Panth' in his eyes.

> Dear Panther,
> I am sorry it has taken so long to reply to your heartfelt plea. It is only because I have been trying to decide how best to address it. While I cannot say your words didn't hurt me, I don't believe there is any merit in punishment by me or suffering under your own self-flagellation. You were upset and rightly so and lashed out. I may have done the same. Although I like to think that, if I were a woman, I would have the wit not to fall for the charms of someone so obviously on the make.

At that, my stomach slipped a little, for these were harsh

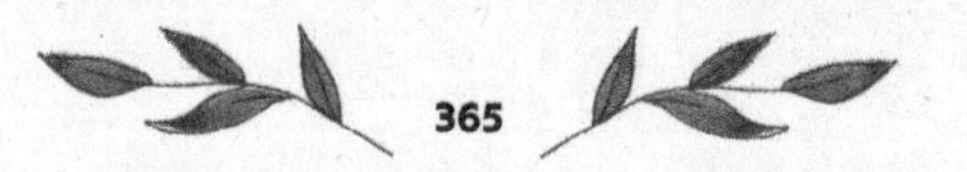

words, by Freddy's standards. Though I accept also fair. But then he went on.

But perhaps not. It is easy, at seventeen, to be dazzled by the flash of camera bulbs, by a glittering smile, by gleaming notoriety even. So of course I forgive you. And you are already older and wiser, I warrant. Though I urge you not to let yourself believe that all men are so terrible, that love itself is so brutal.

However, I hope you will forgive me too if I remain a little more 'distant' now, and ask you to do the same. It is nothing you have done, I must assure you that; rather it is something I feel, and should not be feeling, I fear.

But, be assured that I remain, forever, your friend,

Freddy

I felt the same wash of nausea I had suffered in those early days after the party, the article. For though he insisted his desire for distance was nothing I had done, he was surely only sparing my feelings while suffering his own, whatever they are.

What are they? Is it shame as well? Embarrassment? Or . . . something else? No, I mustn't think about that, and I can hardly ask him now as he has forbidden me contact him. Nor can I pester Margot for answers as she is presumably not speaking to me at all, given the absolute lack of correspondence from either Suffolk or the Glasshouse Street apartment. Not that I should want to allow her to be privy to my secrets, not after she trampled all over my confidences by bedding Buck.

And yet, I do so miss her.

What a terrible mess this season has been. This year, even. However is one to rescue it?

*

At least Grandma, emerging from the morning room minutes after Freddy ended everything, is in buoyant mood.

It is not pervert-related but because, according to the wireless, Labour Prime Minister Ramsay MacDonald has lost a vote of no confidence so there is to be another general election. Usually she despises such things, but now that she has the right to vote (being both landed, and ageing, which is a start, but surely not the end of suffrage, for why should she have more say than Mabel?) she is rather looking forward to putting the country back in the hands of the Tories, which is, according to her, its rightful place.

I would disagree but, as I can see precious little change for me or any woman since MacDonald got in, it all seems rather relentlessly depressing. Aster says if there were more women in parliament beyond the seven or so who have managed to wheedle their way into the heavily male chamber it would be a different matter, which perhaps it would. Though, going by

Grandma's attitude, perhaps not after all.

Not that it concerns me anyway, given my age and land, or lack of it. I cannot change the world. I cannot even keep hold of my friends. I am, currently, neither use nor ornament, and feel myself torn between the well of self-pity and bitter anger.

Perhaps there is merit in mole-catching after all. Brandishing a spade might furnish me with a sense of import.

Yes, I think I will join Marigold and Rapsey after all.

Who needs Freddy Spencer or Margot Forbes-Rawlinson when one has perverts and several dozen moles to despatch?

FRIDAY 31 OCTOBER

11 A.M.

Grandma is jubilant on two counts. Firstly, Ramsay MacDonald has lost the election, which one would think were down to her singlehanded voting efforts, although Hermione Lightfoot is apparently also claiming victory for herself. There is, it seems, no end to their snide rivalry, despite evidence of unity – if only they could see it. In fact, it is trumping Hermione Lightfoot that has led to Grandma's second triumph, which is that the pervert is back and has been loudly and firmly tooted.

He telephoned at just gone seven this morning, at which time no one but Mabel is usually up, but today Grandma had risen in a fit of panic because Hamilton was not in his usual place at the foot of the bed, guarding her from all manner of

midnight menace, and Grandma had gone to track him down lest he be trapped, lost, or stolen by animal rustlers (Marigold has given her the heebie-jeebies because all talk in the village is that someone has kidnapped Mr Hendry's prize Tamworth so Grandma thinks it is only a matter of time before Hamilton is earmarked for thievery and enforced breeding).

When she answered the telephone, it was in full expectation that it would be the police, or, worse, the rustlers themselves demanding a ransom, but she was met instead by the same breathy nothingness. In absolute anger she picked up the trumpet and gave the pervert four loud blasts herself before hanging up.

She is now back in bed after all the alarm, being comforted by Mabel, and Hamilton, who is not yet the victim of thieves (nor ever likely to be, given his own menacing tendencies) but was instead in a stand-off with Siegfried over ownership of the scullery. Siegfried is back in the garage, and the rabbits (also quietly claiming scullery territorial rights) are in a new chicken-wire run fashioned by Rapsey. Marigold is likely to protest when she gets back from school, but Mama says it is only right, and she is tired of picking up rabbit droppings before Grandma sees them, as well as dealing with Dinah's endless evacuations before Grandma smells them.

This, I think, is another nail in the coffin of motherhood as an option, for who would choose such a station when its main function seems to be waste disposal?

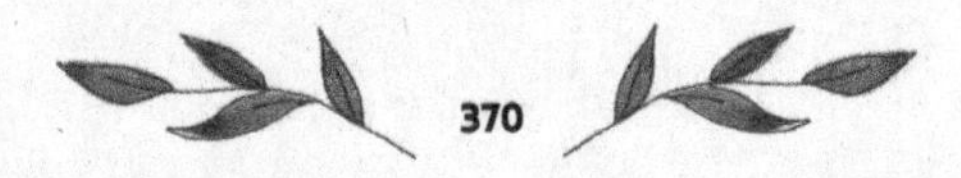

Oh, the telephone is ringing again. Perhaps the pervert is not despatched after all! What larks! I do hope the trumpet is still in position.

11 P.M.

It was not a pervert. It was not even a man.

It was Margot.

Thank heaven Mabel had moved the trumpet or I should have given the poor girl another deafening shock to add to her already tortured state, for it was she who had rung at seven, and on several previous occasions, but been unable to speak.

And no wonder.

'Panth?' came the voice, weak and reedy, and as unlike the usually blustering, jolly Margot as junket from jam.

'Margot?' I asked, for I did not yet know it truly to be her.

'Oh, Panth!' she cried, and then fell to several minutes of incomprehensible sobbing, before she could finally articulate anything of use.

'I need you,' came the entreaty. 'Please, Panth. Something terrible has happened.'

I steeled myself. It was bound to be Buck, or another man. And I was not to embroil myself in matters of the male persuasion, however they presented themselves. And yet, poor Margot seemed so distressed.

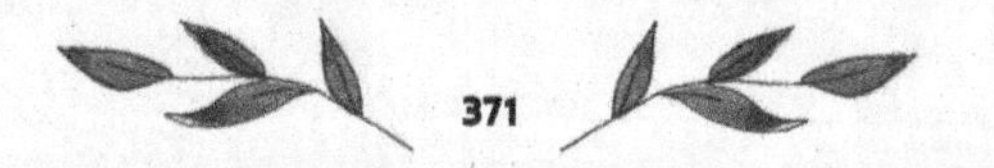

'What?' I asked, as glassily as I could muster.

There was a pause. Then a stuttered uttering. 'I'm p–pregnant,' she said.

For a second, the world seemed to still – no clocks tocked, no beams creaked, no rabbits scampered down the hallway runner. This could not be possible, could it? And yet, I knew it could.

'Oh, Margot,' I managed, relieved to even speak.

But there was worse to come.

'Or, at least, I was.'

My stomach knotted. 'What do you mean?'

'I've . . . I've done something dreadful, Panth. Something awful. And I think . . . I think I might be dying.'

At any other moment, I would have dismissed this as mere 'Classic Margot'. But I knew from the edge of desperation in her voice that these were no histrionics. And I knew, too, what she meant when she said she had 'done something'.

And then a strange air of calm descended, and a strength such as I have never felt, and possibly never will again, seemed to seep into my very bones.

'Where are you?' I asked.

'Glasshouse Street,' came the whimper.

'I'll be there as soon as I can.'

*

What followed seemed to play out at the painful pace of cold molasses on flat ground, but now I see must have been mere feverish minutes.

First, I telephoned several people, all of whom I trusted neither to judge nor to blab. Valentine, Aster – who was with Topaz in Marylebone, and then Freddy. I did not know, given his wish for 'distance', if he would come, nor even get the garbled message I was forced to leave with the college porter, but he was the closest thing I knew to a medic bar his father, and I could hardly ask Dr Spencer to attend.

Then I explained to Mama that there had been an emergency with Margot.

'But what sort of an emergency, darling?'

I have never wished harder for Daddy, who would have let me go without question. 'I can't tell you, because I'm not precisely sure,' I explained, hedging on the edge of truth at least. 'But I fear it's something rather rash. Aster is coming too,' I added quickly, knowing Mama would feel safer with her sensible head at any scene.

Mama paused, then clasped my hand in hers. I felt the cool calm of her, the strength. 'Go,' she urged. 'A friend in need is more than a suitable excuse.'

'It's probably a pervert,' snapped Grandma from the drawing room, her hearing momentarily and conveniently bat-like. 'London is packed with them.'

Mama, out of sight if not earshot, rolled her eyes. 'Go,' she urged. 'Rapsey can take you. Tell him I said so.'

And with that, I flew from the door, with only my coat and

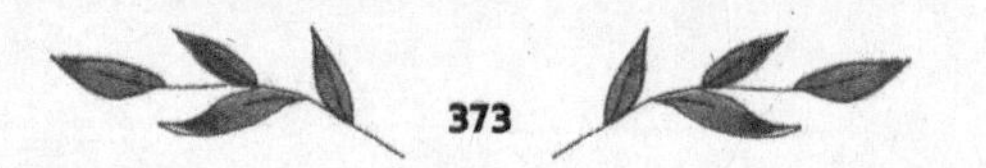

a ten-shilling note that Mama had pressed into my hand for an 'emergency'.

*

Rapsey clattered up to Piccadilly as spectacularly as a racing driver at a Grand Prix; I abandoned the car at Glasshouse Street and hammered on the door of the apartment, which was flung open by a wide-eyed and pale-faced Valentine.

'Thank heaven,' he said. 'She's been asking for you.'

Without reply, I hurried behind him down the salmon-carpeted corridor (such a sickening colour – like being inside an intestine) and, pausing only mentally to brace myself, burst into the bedroom.

The sight was both worse, and less terrible than I had imagined.

There was blood, so very much of it, and not the vivid crimson one imagines but a darker, more worrying colour, tinged almost brown. And people. So very many of them. Topaz and Aster and Valentine and – yes! – Freddy Spencer, in deep discussion with another man, a shock of rust-coloured curls sprouting from his head like wayward gladioli, and a frown above a crop of freckles and the ruddy tan of a farmer. And Margot herself at the centre of it, her face pale as milk pudding but her eyes open, and widening as she saw me.

'Oh, Panth,' she breathed.

'Margot.' I felt a pain in my chest, a flood of something. 'You're alive.'

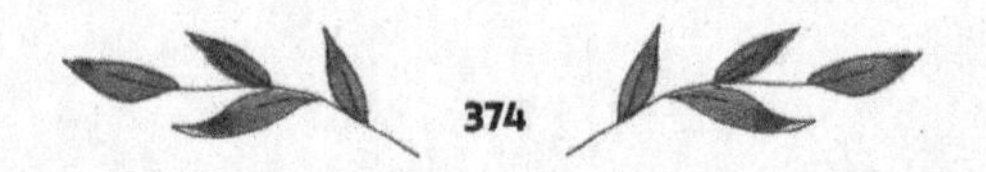

The words had seemed at first to stick in my tightened throat like gobstoppers, but now forced out, opened the floodgates to a stream of tears as, with no regard for my clothing, I flung my arm around my friend.

'I'm sorry,' I sobbed. 'You poor, poor thing.'

'Steady on,' came a voice. 'She's out of the woods but weak as all hell.'

I looked up to see the farmer fellow frowning down at me. Remembering myself, I sat up, then stood, pointlessly brushing down the brown stains that now dappled the camel coat.

'Of course,' I said. 'I'm so awfully sorry. Thank you for coming, Doctor . . . I . . . I don't know your name.'

The man let out a blast of a laugh, which seemed highly inappropriate given the situation, and yet somehow in keeping with his demeanour.

'I'm Egg,' he said. 'And it's not me you want to thank. I only drove. It's old Freddy here who's done the dirty work. Sorry.' He turned to Margot at that, his face surprisingly kind. 'Didn't mean to offend.'

I looked up at Freddy, ready to beg for anything. 'I . . . I didn't know who else to call,' I admitted, then for want of anything better apologised yet again. 'I'm so sorry. You're the only person I could think of. The only person who might . . .' But at that I trailed off. Not sure what I thought he might he have been able to do and unclear as well as to what he had actually done.

His gaze on me was steady, but unreadable. 'You did the right thing,' he said.

'But will she . . .' Oh God, I could hardly bring myself to say it. 'Will she be able to have children?'

It was Topaz who answered. 'I think so,' she said, smiling at Margot. 'She's luckier than I.'

Aster took her hand then, and I saw her fingers tighten around it, as if to say, 'I love you.'

And in that small gesture I saw everything that was missing from mine and Buck's – I can hardly say 'relationship' – dalliance, perhaps: a sort of equality. (Not that I am sapphic. I have tried to get excited by women. By Tallulah Bankhead's hips or Topaz's lips or even Margot's thighs. But I confess, not without sadness, that I have never felt a single thing.)

And I wondered then if it was even possible with a man. To feel equal, on an even footing.

Not that I was courting that any more, and even less so now, seeing Margot.

I sat again on the bed, but gently this time. 'Does . . .' I glanced up at the others, wondering how much I could say. But they, I decided, had seen everything now, and so I said it. 'Does Buck know?'

Margot, whey until now, flushed with something like indignation. 'Oh, yes,' she said, 'I called him weeks ago. He said it was my problem.'

'The absolute brute,' I replied.

'He is rather,' she admitted. 'Mummy would have had a conniption, can you imagine? Pregnant by an American. As it is, I don't know what she'll say to this catastrophe when she gets back.' She indicated the sheets, which were beyond redemption.

'I'll see to those,' said Valentine.

'And then you must come with us,' said Topaz. 'Marylebone's minutes away, and we can get you all better before your mother gets back.'

'I'll drive you over,' said Egg, eager to please.

'Where is your mother anyway?' I asked.

'Oh, Deborah's backhand is all shot,' Margot replied. 'Mummy says Sven has ruined it with his Swedish ideas and now she's having to get it fixed by a man in Hampshire. She won't be home for a week. Jonty is supposed to be chaperoning me, only I haven't seen him in two days. I think he's with the Wyndhams.'

'Men!' blurted Aster. But then caveated herself. 'Present company excluded.'

I smiled, trying to catch Freddy's eye, but he looked away quickly.

I felt myself slump a little, before remembering that it wasn't about me, and healing my fractured heart, it was about Margot.

'Can I have a moment,' I said then. 'With my friend.'

The others trooped out dutifully, leaving me to nestle on

the bed, tentative again, mindful not to undo whatever mend, whatever magic Freddy had woven for her.

'Can you forgive me?' I asked.

'Can *you* forgive *me*?' she asked back.

'Oh, Margot.' I felt myself melt further. 'There's nothing to forgive.'

Margot nodded. 'Buck is awfully . . . persuasive.'

I felt a jolt and a wave of nausea as my mind flashed back to the night of the Balfour ball, him pushing at me, brutally. 'He didn't . . . he didn't force you, did he?'

Margot shook her head. 'No. So I am entirely to blame—'

'You're not to blame!' I interrupted. 'Buck is culpable.'

'Have you seen him?' she asked.

I shook my head. 'Not since . . . that night. "Cad About Town".'

'That's gone too,' she said.

'Has it?' I hadn't checked, hadn't dared in case he'd taken revenge by disgracing me. But it had gone and, strangely, I felt no guilt. He didn't deserve it; his words had never been worthy of print. And what he does now without Daddy's money is hardly my concern.

'There's a column about beekeeping now,' Margot went on. 'Too, too dull.'

'But better than idle gossip,' I tried. 'And outright lies.'

'I daresay you're right.' Margot sighed, her fingers, thinner than I'd ever seen them, clutching at the soiled sheets in which she still lay, propped on pillows. 'I don't suppose anyone will want me now. Now that . . . you know.'

Her eyes pooled with tears and I realised it was the first time I'd seen her cry since I arrived.

I took her hand – damp, hot – in mine. 'No one will know,' I said. 'Only us. And best friends don't tell.'

I felt Margot's fingers close around my own. Romance be damned, I thought. For what better than friendship?

'It's really not like in books, is it?' she said.

'No,' I replied. 'It really isn't.

*

A few minutes later, I watched as Topaz and Aster bundled a blanketed Margot down the stairs to Egg's motor, and Valentine stripped the bed and remade it, so appallingly it necessitated Freddy and I redoing the whole sorry lot.

Freddy, in contrast, knew exactly what he was doing with sheets and blankets and eiderdowns, and I wondered then if it was something his stepmother had taught him, or if he had stoically taught himself.

'Thank you,' I said, as he smoothed down hospital corners. 'I really am sorry though.'

Freddy shook his head but did not look up. 'I said it was all right. You saved her, calling like that. I'm only glad that Egg happened to pass the porter seconds later and came to fetch me.'

'He seems a good—' I stopped myself, only just realising the joke. 'Of course. That's where it comes from: Good Egg.'

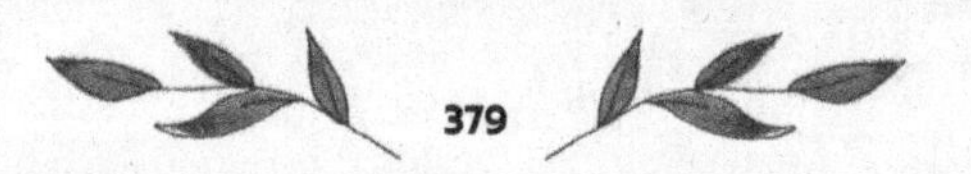

'He may be a gadabout,' said Freddy. 'But he's kind.'

'He was kind to Margot,' I said. 'That's all that matters.'

'So were you.'

He looked up finally, and my heart skittered and stumbled, fawn-like. 'I . . . I didn't do anything.'

'You kept your head,' he replied. 'That takes courage. And you put B— that cad aside in favour of your friend. That takes heart.'

I found I couldn't bear to look at him then, couldn't listen to what that insistent heart was telling me. 'I meant what I said in the letter,' I told him, picking at a tuft of lavender candlewick. 'I was a fool.' I waited but no reply came and so I went on. 'And I understand about you wanting to keep your distance, and I shouldn't have ruined it, but—'

But I didn't finish because his hand reached across the bedspread to still my fingers, and the words seemed to dissipate into nothing but a small gasp.

'I shouldn't have said that,' he declared. 'It was cruel and . . . and stupid.'

'No!' I protested, but Freddy, still pressing his hand on mine, ignored me.

'I could never stay away,' he said, more passionate than I had imagined him capable of. 'You're my . . . my Panth. And I don't know what that means, truly. But I know I want you in my life. Always.'

And then something odd happened. As it had done with

Margot, my heart seemed to steady itself and my head cleared of mist to be pin-sharp and decisive. 'And I want you,' I replied. 'And I don't know how, exactly. And perhaps we shall never fathom that. But I can't imagine a future without you in it.'

In a book, this is, of course, the moment we would kiss. But, as Margot had so incisively divined, life is never quite like it is in books, is it.

Instead, he lifted his fingers and I pulled my hand away, and then he plumped the pillows and I made a check of the floor for anything untoward. Then, turning off the lights behind us, we left the apartment and at Glasshouse Street turned our separate ways: he towards Marylebone, and I towards Liverpool Street station, my ten-shilling note the only crisp and clean thing about me.

*

And now I sit, and I ponder Margot's words again. 'It's really not like in books.'

But what, I wonder, if it were? Or rather, if the books were really like life?

For I believe I have something to write about now. A romance of sorts, but without the hearts and violins and doves, the handsome aristocrats and fainting ladies, the poorly painted foreigners, villainous simply because of their skin.

Instead, it will be the truth, as I see it, of love in the modern world. Brutal and tender, and messy and precise, and favouring, always favouring men. But still, I think, something to strive

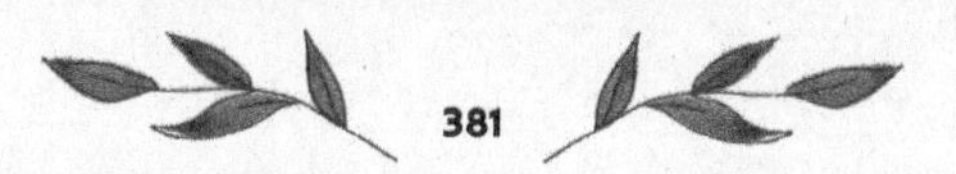

for, if only we can make it work a little better for us, give more detail as to . . . how to do things.

I doubt anyone will publish such a thing, still less read it. But in all the chaos of today – the bitter disappointment of this year – I have found a thing that might, just might, be worthy of calling a 'purpose'.

And so, starting tomorrow, that is what I shall do.

NOVEMBER

SUNDAY 30 NOVEMBER

11 P.M.

I wasn't sure I could do it. Not at all, let alone in a month. But it transpired I had rather more notes than I had remembered, and rather more to say on the subject of love than I thought.

And a rather more supportive family than I have ever given them credit for.

Mama checked in on me several times a day, opening and closing windows where necessary. Marigold dried (by the worrying method of blowing) and stacked finished pages and ran to fetch fresh ink from Mrs Gibberd when I ran out, which was often. While Aster, darling Aster, paid for it, and paper too.

'We may not be Emmeline Pankhurst or Nancy Astor, either of us,' she said. 'But we can make a difference.'

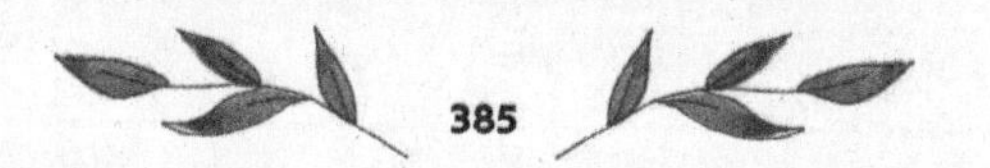

Whether her words will turn out to be true or foolish remains to be seen. But no one can say I haven't tried. Not even Grandma, who has, in fact, proved a useful proofreader, catching several errors of punctuation, grammar, and anatomy besides.

The result is *The Essex Skipper*. The title was Mama's idea – a play on the butterfly, and the bolting nature of the novel's villain. For of course my book has a villain. I could hardly glorify Buck, could I? Not after what he has done. So, it is a romance, of sorts, but a tale of love not unrequited, nor thwarted, but doomed by the ruinous tendencies of both parties: he arrogant and she naive, as she has been schooled to be by generations before her, and countless novels besides.

I shall deliver it to the publisher's – Creed's – myself tomorrow. They are not far from Margot, after all.

She is recovering well. Not least because Buck was spotted in the Button Club sporting not one but two black eyes.

'Who?' I asked her. 'Not Egg?'

'Bless him,' she replied. 'He offered, the darling. But no, it was your cousin. The dashing Valentine by all accounts.'

So, Valentine has proved himself the very best of men. I almost wish I could tell Grandma. Though she is far more concerned with apparent lapses in Mabel's catering than in the merits of 'theatrical types' right now.

I expect it is the terror of the festive season creeping in. For advent is but a day away and then, before we know it, it will be

Christmas with all its inherent chaos, and then another New Year to ring in and Grandma is determined to mark it with a party this year, just to smite Hermione Lightfoot, who has cancelled her annual do after a row with her husband Bertie over cheese.

I only know this because, as well as ink, Marigold has been delivering every snippet of information she has gleaned from Mrs Gibberd, Ralph, and Grandma herself. Though I am not entirely sure she has not been elaborating on it for theatrical effect, as I don't think even Grandma would use the words 'bleeding sheep'.

Though I suppose I, for one, should know that life is always more brutal than fiction, which is prettied and parcelled up neatly for convenient digestion.

On which note, I shall just check over the manuscript once more before I box it.

To see that I really have told it how it is for women.

So that perhaps, just perhaps, it may not be like that always.

DECEMBER

THURSDAY 11 DECEMBER

8 P.M.

It is a shame *The Essex Skipper* is not yet published as, after several days in London, I can report that Margot is quite restored; in fact she is more emphatic than ever about the promises of romantic love, and with one man in particular: Egg.

I suppose it was inevitable: he, the white (or rather ginger) knight; she, the damsel in evident distress. I would press Freddy for assurances that she will not be merely the latest in his 'string' of women but, for obvious reasons, we are not in contact. Neither of us knowing quite what is happening. Or what we want to happen. If anything at all.

In any case, there is no time to be thinking about such mundanities, when there is quite the hoo-hah going on at the

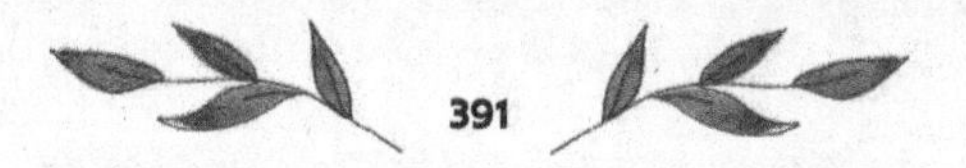

Dower House. It seems that Margot was not the only female to fall foul of man's wicked ways this summer, for it is not the festive season that ails Mabel so, but morning sickness!

It is Marigold who worked it out. She has been reading *Gray's Anatomy* again, and the *Mirror*, no doubt, and remarked upon Mabel's seeming need to vomit several times a morning.

'She can't be,' I said in reply. 'Can she?'

'Oh, she can,' carried on Marigold, practically. 'It's probably Ralph's. They do it behind the garage you know.'

'Marigold!' I admonished.

'What? I didn't watch. At least not for long. It's not like cows at all you know. And it takes such an interminable age for it to be done.'

I said nothing, not wishing to think of my own brush with such proceedings.

There was nothing for it though. We would have to confront the sticky situation and quickly. Or rather *I* would, as there was no knowing how much exactly Marigold had seen and might repeat.

Though Marigold, it turns out, may not have seen the cause of the awfulness at all.

*

'I'm sorry, could you repeat that,' I said. 'You think it's whose?'

'The Prince of Wales.'

I hadn't heard wrong. But this was impossible. Surely.

'But where did you meet him?'

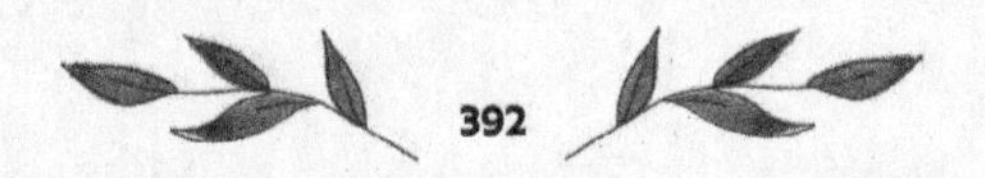

'At that party.' Mabel, confession having unstoppered a wash of tears, sniffed into a handkerchief, then blew her nose loudly. 'You know. When I was all done up like a kipper.'

'The Balfours'?' I ventured.

She nodded.

'But . . . I don't think he was there. In fact, I know he wasn't because *The Tatler* had him in Scotland. Evangeline was apparently horribly angry with her daddy for bagging him.'

'Oh.' Mabel deflated further.

I wanted to laugh, but empathy prevented me. 'You honestly thought you might be carrying the second in line to the throne?'

Mabel nodded sorrowfully. 'He looked like him. Said he was him and all. But I s'pose he could have been anyone.'

A sudden image of Buck sprung into my head. It wouldn't be unthinkable. I had stormed out after all, and he had been plain as day that any . . . receptacle would do.

For a moment I almost wished I hadn't finished the novel as that would have been quite the subplot.

'But it could be Ralph's,' I said, hoping beyond hope that Marigold had not got this wrong.

Mabel shrugged. 'Might be. We do it every Sunday. Behind the garage' – so Marigold *had* seen everything; I shuddered – 'or sometimes in the morning room if you're all out. Don't tell your Grandma though. She'll have my guts for garters if she knew.'

I had no intention of anything of the kind. 'Well, that's something anyway.' I thought for a moment, grasped at the

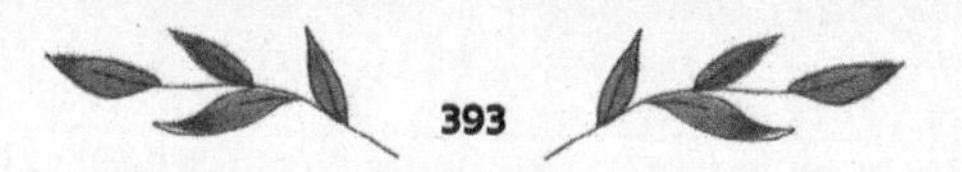

obvious, if depressing inevitability. 'Perhaps you can marry Ralph then.'

But Mabel shook her head. 'I've already said, ain't I. But he says his ma says he can't get married to me 'cause I'm common. And now I've only gone and proved it. What a scandal!'

'Oh, Mabel.'

Of course, it is quite the scandal, given she is unmarried, and an inconvenience, given she is in service. Though I don't see why it should be either. Mabel is quite capable of raising a child alone, as Mama is proving, and we can all muck in with the cooking. And in any case, until public opinion and medical provision are improved, this is surely better than the alternative as explored by Margot.

I had to check, of course, that she wasn't going to attempt anything that foolish. 'Then what will you do?' I asked. 'You won't . . . you won't try to get rid of it, will you?

'Oh no, I can't do that. I'm Catholic.' She blew her nose again. 'Don't tell your grandma.'

I wasn't sure if she meant the pregnancy or the Catholicism, but the former was an impossible secret to keep and even Mabel had to admit that in the end.

Grandma was predictably apoplectic.

'Well, she can't have the thing here,' she protested, Hamilton gripped in her lap like a child's comforter. 'What will Hermione Lightfoot say? Or Lady Balfour for that matter.'

'Who cares what Hermione Lightfoot says?' I replied.

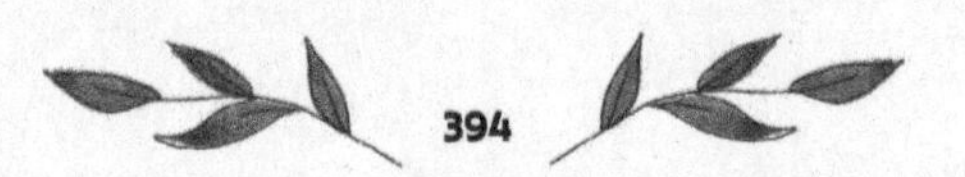

The answer was Grandma. But, it transpired, she had a plan. 'Valentine,' she announced, as delighted as if she were a conjuror pulling a rabbit from a hat.

'Pardon?'

'He needs someone to "do" for him. And he has the room.'

Having seen his flat, and his bed-making abilities, I could only concur.

'You must telephone directly,' Grandma continued. 'I can have nothing further to do with it, of course.'

'In case Hermione finds out?' I ventured.

'Well, precisely!' Grandma agreed, finally releasing Hamilton who bolted across the room as if shot from a pistol.

She is already in a viler mood with Hermione than ever. This is because Hermione has seen fit to send us a goose (alive and loudly so) for the Christmas table.

'As if we are no better than the Cratchetts!' Grandma reeled.

Siegfried is equally alarmed. Though I am rather less surprised at this as he has been replaced in Marigold's affections by a honking monstrosity and so has every right to be put out. The only consolation for everyone is that it will be dead and eaten within a fortnight.

Anyway, back to the point. I have telephoned Valentine, who went very quiet, but did not disagree entirely with the idea, which is a start. He says he is coming to visit tomorrow and will discuss it with everyone, including (thankfully) Mabel, then.

'You should see Dr Spencer in the meantime,' I said to her.

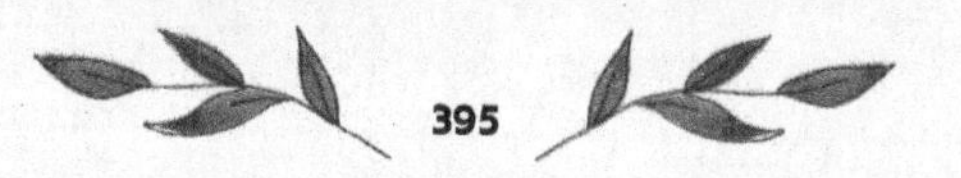

'To check the baby's healthy and . . . whatever it is they do.' What did they do? And how? I didn't want to think.

'Oh, I 'ave,' she replied. 'Well, Freddy, anyway.'

My heart stilled. 'Freddy's home?'

Mabel frowned. 'Has been since Saturday last,' she said.

I felt a flicker inside me, found myself flushing.

Mabel went on, oblivious. 'I know he's not a proper doctor or nothing yet, but he only used his stethoscope. Didn't put his hand up there or anything. And he only did the stethoscope 'cause I begged 'cause I only 'ad ten minutes and the doctor weren't back.'

My pink cheeks deepened at the thought of that, and of Freddy being the one to administer it.

'Well, very good,' I managed. 'All's well then.'

'Oh, yes,' she replied. 'All's well. I only hope he's wrong and it's not flaming twins.'

*

What absurdities life sees fit to fling at us.

Whatever unlikelihood I, or any writer, could manifest in months from the vividest of imaginations, the world outdoes in as many seconds, smiting fiction with the slap of reality and all its consequences. Though we have, at least, managed to assuage the worst of these, I think. Or rather, surprisingly, Grandma has.

I hope Mabel will be happy with Valentine. I hope for her sake it's not twins but a single, healthy child.

And I hope, in either case, none of them are Buck's.

FRIDAY 12 DECEMBER

1 P.M.

Well, the world really has outdone itself this time. Not even a Drury Lane pantomime could equal this most ridiculous of plot twists. In fact, I can only think of one playwright worthy of such a melodrama: Valentine. And he was, of course, the mastermind. For not only has he agreed readily to Mabel moving into his Caxton Street flat, but he has taken it all one enormous leap further and offered to marry her!

'Why not?' He shrugged, as if this were nothing less casual than offering to drop off a parcel or pick up some sausages from Goddard's. 'I need some sort of heir and I'm never likely to get one the traditional way. Besides,' he added, shrugging again though this, I suspected, was for effect, 'we both need . . . protecting.'

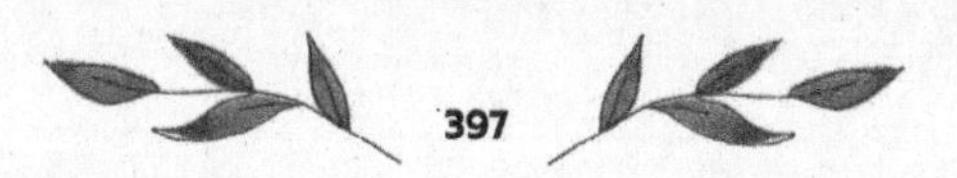

I knew what he meant. Not physically but from prying eyes and wagging tongues and stupid, foolish rules.

'You do know it's likely twins,' I said.

But even this did not deter him. 'Twice the chance of it being a boy then,' was all his retort.

Nor, oddly, did it Aster, despite the evident potential of Mabel's children inheriting Radley one day. 'The rules are all wrong,' Aster said. 'Inheritance is a menace; we should all have to work for what we have.'

I found myself agreeing, which is, perhaps, evidence of character growth, or purpose (though nothing yet from the publisher).

The wedding, rushed of course, is to be in three weeks. On New Year's Eve at the church in the village. Valentine and Mabel are at St Ignatius's with the vicar this very minute as the banns must be read on Sunday with no objections for it all to go ahead. Grandma is, of course, already objecting, and loudly, not least because it has put paid to her Anti-Hermione party. But as Valentine was her plan in the first place she can hardly complain when it backfires. Though complain she has.

'At least she's not French,' said Marigold. 'Or American.'

'But she's . . . she's . . .'

'What?' I asked. 'From London.'

'You know very well that's not the point I am trying to make.' Grandma's lips narrowed as to almost disappear. 'She's just not . . . suitable.'

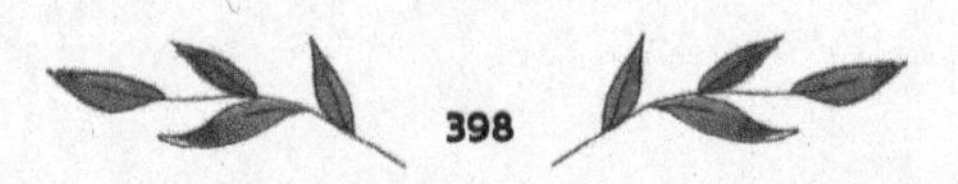

'Neither is he, according to you,' said Mama. 'And he's only doing it because of rules that forbid him love who he must.'

Grandma put her fingers in her ears at this point as if to make clear she was deaf to all declarations or entreaties.

Probably for the best, as what followed would only enrage her more.

'I'd like to give her a present,' I said to Mama. 'Mabel, I mean. If you'll allow me.'

'Allow you?' Mama asked. 'Why? What could it be that I would have to allow it?'

'You and Aster.' I turned to include my sister, who nodded at me to go on.

'I'd like her to have a dress,' I explained. 'A decent one. And I don't suppose I'll have any use for it any more as I shan't be coming out' – the very thought sickened me – 'so I thought—'

'The oyster satin,' Mama finished for me. 'I don't mind a jot.'

I looked to Aster, beseeching her clearly, prepared to beg if I must. But I didn't have to utter another word.

'Of course I'll make it. I'll start this afternoon. As soon as she's back.'

'In that case,' said Mama, 'you and Marigold can start on the invitations.'

'What?' exploded Grandma, fingers out again. 'You can't be thinking of letting the children write them.'

'I am thinking exactly that,' said Mama. 'Although one

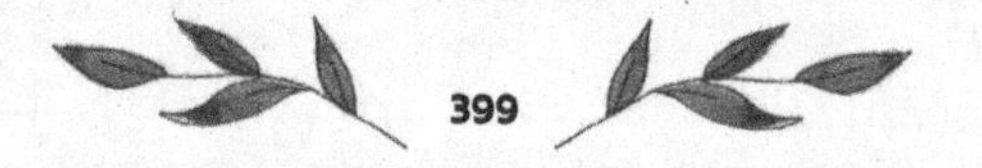

has proved herself more than grown-up today.' She smiled at me. 'And the other' – she raised an eyebrow at Marigold, who was outside on the lawn trying to persuade the goose (now worryingly named Bobby Two) to jump a puddle – 'well, she could use the handwriting practice.'

'Irredeemable,' declared Grandma at that. 'The lot of you. What would your father say?'

'He'd say "jolly good",' snapped Aster. 'And you know it.'

Grandma did not reply to that, but Mama's smile mirrored ours, and Dinah, until now occupied with a wayward curl, saw fit to add her glee to proceedings with a delighted yelp, which I think we all took as affirmation of Daddy's kindness.

And so it is all decided. Aster is busy with cloth and pins and scissors, Marigold is washing goose and sheep and mud off her hands before she is allowed to pick up a pen (this takes quite a while as she will be sent back at least five times for lackadaisical soaping) and I am off to Mrs Gibberd's for card and to collect the post (Ralph has been refusing to deliver since the baby debacle).

I did suggest sending Marigold but Mama said she would get waylaid by sheep or geese or Reg Nesbitt, and, besides, hadn't I avoided Freddy long enough?

I had no reply. For I could hardly deny it. I *was* avoiding him. Still am.

Though this, I know, is pointless, for what I need to avoid is myself. My thoughts. My wants. My treacherous feelings.

And I try to turn a blind eye, try to deafen myself to them, like Grandma, with my fingers in my ears. But still they press in on me, whisper their secret, tell me they're there.

Definitely there.

And there is nothing I can do to stop them.

4 P.M.

Ralph's one-man wildcat postal strike is all very well under the circumstances but is already having a devastating effect on matters pressing and otherwise. It transpires that I have received a letter from Creed's (or rather, I received it several days ago), summoning me to Grosvenor Square 'at my earliest convenience, should I still be interested in publication'. Which, obviously I still am, and am delighted, but heaven knows when will be convenient as the wedding is definitely going ahead.

The vicar is, apparently, thrilled with the prospect as no one else has seen fit to get engaged since Daphne Balfour and he was beginning to take it personally. Also, card has been acquired for Marigold and I, and Mabel is upstairs awaiting her first fitting. At least with only three weeks to go she cannot inflate too much.

I am, however, hoping three weeks will be long enough for me to muster up some gumption as I am now apparently rendered so insensible by whatever it is I am feeling about

Freddy Spencer that I can barely form a sentence in his presence.

I decided, against my better judgement, that the best way of banishing these – whatever they are – was to face up to them and then face them off. In other words, I would call for Freddy and invite him, nonchalantly, to the wedding. As a friend. Which, he said himself, is what we are.

But nonchalance, living up to its name, refused to attend the scene and instead sent stammering inadequacy, who is always willing to step in, I find.

'I . . . Hello. That is to say . . .' I trailed off, hopelessly distracted by Freddy's presence in the doorway.

He was fully dressed, quite buttoned up in fact, but seemed, somehow, as half naked as he had been the day we went swimming. The day I first felt, or rather refused to acknowledge, that there was anything more to him. To us.

'Panth,' he said, as awkward as I. 'Do you . . . do you want to come in?'

I knew he didn't mean it and I couldn't have borne it and so declined. 'I just wanted to say . . . there'll be a wedding.'

Freddy, his Italian tan already paled, seemed to blanch further. 'I—'

'Oh, it's not me,' I blurted, then cursed myself. 'Not that you were worried about that I expect.'

'I . . .' But he couldn't finish that either. 'So, who is it then?'

'Valentine and Mabel,' I said, decisive about this at least.

'Really?'

'I know. It's a long story. But . . . would you come? And your parents, too.' I was blathering now, all the better to disguise my fright, I decided. 'There'll be a proper invitation.' I brandished my card at him, as if it were a weapon. God, what a sight I was. 'But I was just . . . checking.'

'That's . . . quite all right.' He was frowning now, as if pondering what a horrible mess this all was. Which of course it was. 'When is it?'

'New Year's Eve,' I said. 'At two.'

'Of course,' he replied. 'Panth, are you sure you won't come in, you're shivering.'

'I'm just excited,' I lied. 'About the wedding.'

He smiled then, and leant in such a way against the door frame that I found myself pathetically unsteady.

'You are funny,' he said.

I flinched. 'In a bad way? Like a clown?'

'No,' he said. 'Like *you*. And that's . . . that's good. Very good indeed.'

And then, unable to say a single thing more, I left.

Honestly, if *The Essex Skipper* is published, I shall reread it myself immediately and remind myself of my own advice. For, while not all men are terrible, romancing them is a trap, I think, changing one's nature, altering one's stance, gait, very breath, until one has become someone else entirely. Someone unrecognisable.

No, better to stay away. Remain friends, or, if that is not

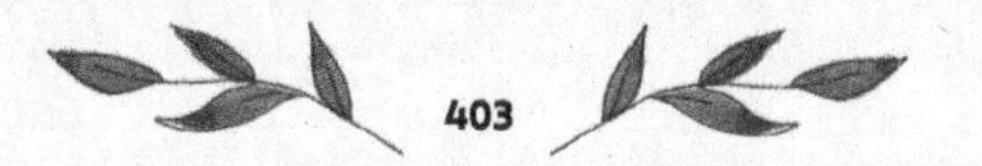

possible, cut them out of one's life altogether.

Though now, given my rash invitation, I shan't be able to do that until after the first of January either.

THURSDAY 25 DECEMBER

12 P.M.

I take back everything I have said about Grandma. She may mean ill a large part of the year, but she has braved this somewhat inflated festive season at the Dower House with, at worst, resignation and, at best, bravado.

The contrast to last year is stark. Then, Radley, and we were deep in mourning, the empty space at the table the most significant thing about the day. Today, while Daddy is still a palpable absence, the Dower House feels fit to bursting. The hallway is festooned with Marigold's ham-fisted paper chains, the table set with hastily polished extra silver for Valentine and Topaz, Mabel and the Rapseys, and everyone's pre-wedding jitters only adding to the rather fabulous, cramped chaos.

'It is all very . . . *Little Women*,' Grandma concluded as Marigold gave a rather painful rendition of 'O Come All Ye Faithful', accompanied by Aster on her restrung cello, Dinah and I on percussion (she is quite accomplished at hitting a pan with a spoon), and Bobby Two the goose on intermittent honking (for, of course, he has been spared the table, though largely through his antipathy towards Rapsey rather than Grandma's benevolence. I think she may just be hoping to send him back to Hermione in twelve months' time).

'Isn't it,' agreed Mama, though with rather more appreciation in her tone. 'I do like a busy Christmas.'

Grandma eyed Dinah, who was now merrily hitting the chair leg. 'At least more . . . progeny are out of the question.'

Mama smiled. 'Oh, I don't know,' she replied. 'Perhaps Valentine and Mabel will bring their child with them next year.'

Realisation, and with it, obvious horror, washed over Grandma. 'Perhaps I shall be dead by then. I suppose you will all hope so.'

I knew what she was doing, and so did Mama. 'Oh, don't be absurd,' she replied. 'I wouldn't miss seeing you cope with that for the world.'

I changed the subject before it descended further into self-pity versus sharp wit. 'What are we having for lunch then?'

'What do you think?' asked Mabel. 'Rabbit pie.'

8 P.M.

To extend Grandma's observation: 'Christmas wouldn't be Christmas without any presents.' And, despite our diminished means and circumstances, there were presents aplenty.

New shoes for Marigold, as she has outgrown hers twice in the last year and has been forced to wear gumboots to school, much to Mrs Bottomley's irritation. Not that Marigold has minded: it has given her extra leverage in the playground hierarchy as not only an elder, and a brave one, but an oddity.

For Aster, there were the cello strings, and new badger-hair paint brushes. For Dinah, a hat and a dress with matching jacket (all fashioned by Aster). And for me a new pen and Indian ink, and, in a separate parcel, bound with a deep burgundy ribbon, a leather-bound notebook embossed in gold with my name, all of it this time:

PROPERTY OF
AGAPANTHUS MANNERING

It was a shock to see it written down, for only Daddy ever used it really. But I thanked everyone for their generosity. 'It's beautiful,' I said, truthfully, turning over the butter-soft brown leather. 'Where did you find it?'

'Oh, that's not from us,' said Aster. 'It was delivered yesterday.'

I frowned. 'I thought Ralph had stopped coming.' And in any case, who, then, had sent it?

'It wasn't Ralph who delivered it, darling.' Topaz smiled, her china-white teeth glinting jewels in the flickering candlelight. 'It was Freddy.'

I felt the room shrink to a pinhead and at the centre of it, this present. I opened the cover, turned the thin tissue of the first page to get to the vellum.

There it was, in such familiar loops and precise lines I felt myself take a sharp gasp of breath.

'*To Agapanthus – rather, my Panth. Christmas 1924.*

May you document another year in this, and may I hope, a little, to be in it.'

I slammed it shut.

'What does it say?' demanded Marigold. 'Has he pledged some troth?' (She is very keen on pledging troth since Valentine and Mabel's engagement, and is readily hoping Reg Nesbitt may pledge his to her or Bad Harry or, preferably, both, any minute.)

'No,' I said quickly. 'He just says it's for another journal.'

'Of course he does,' said Topaz, nudging Aster.

'I'm not even sure I want to journal any more,' I retorted, ignoring her. 'It's such a . . . a commitment.'

'Another novel then,' said Topaz. 'With a happy end this time.'

'I . . . I . . .' But I was flustered and struggling, completely thrown by this gesture, by Freddy's intentions.

'You're ever so pink,' added Marigold.

'It's the wine,' I lied. 'I'm just not used to it. I think I may need to lie down for a while.'

And before they could interrogate me further I hurried upstairs and flung myself on the bed, leaving them to beetle and whist and the dregs of the sherry.

And now? Now I am calmer, I think. Rational. And can regard the gift as nothing more than what it is: a notebook, albeit a fine one.

Whatever Freddy's intentions, I am clear on one thing: this year *has* been rather too much. I would like a quieter one, I think. And that, I suspect, won't be journal-worthy. And so New Year's Eve – the wedding – will likely be my last hoorah.

I do hope it's a good one.

WEDNESDAY 31 DECEMBER

10 A.M.

It is still 1924, and only early morning really, but already it is all-change at the Dower House.

I suppose it was inevitable, with Mabel leaving for London and a new life entirely, but quite who Grandma would choose to replace her could not have been predicted even by one of Margot's mesmerists or mind-readers.

It is Cook!

Apparently, she could not suffer the Balfours any longer ('Monsters! The lot of them!') and has since been unemployed bar a brief and unhappy stint at Hermione Lightfoot's, marred by Hermione's unappreciative attitude towards kippers, and her endless bickering with Bertie. It was Hermione who

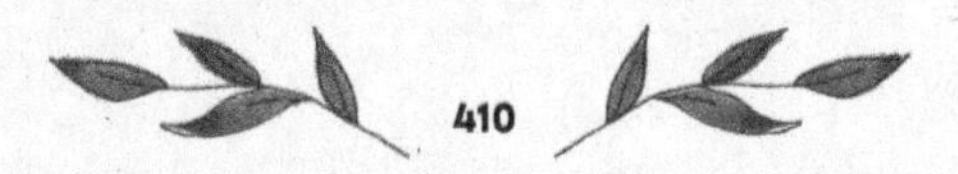

recommended her to the Dower House (revenge, no doubt); Grandma, apparently, not recognising the woman whose malt loaf could extend the Great Wall of China. I suppose I should not be surprised.

Though I suspect Grandma will be in for a shock when the wedding breakfast is served: a buffet affair, given the numerous guests and the rather less than voluminous dining room. Grandma was not at all keen, but Topaz said it is 'all the rage in London' and will put her 'streets ahead' of Hermione Lightfoot. I have never seen her acquiesce so rapidly.

Anyway, it is too late to regret her decision; Cook has signed a contract of employment and we are stuck with her for another twelve months.

I, for one, don't mind. Food is only fuel, after all, as Marigold is often explaining (in graphic detail) Siegfried's and now Bobby Two's behaviour (having been sworn enemies, the pair have united to form an unstoppable force of all-consuming idiocy) and I appreciate her stalwart presence.

Especially on a day as potentially fraught as this.

12.10 A.M.

Technically this is the first of January 1925, but, while everything does feel brand-new, our lives all shifted, it is so tied up with what has gone before that I am keeping it under the umbrella of 1924.

First, the wedding (though this, for me at least, was the smaller part of it).

The scene was set: the congregation (peers of the realm and Stepney hairdressers alike) crammed into the pews at St Ignatius's; the dress splendid, down to the last bugle bead and periwinkle stitch; the bride's swelling belly disguised by generous drapes of lace and the glimmering duchesse satin. The groom was customarily hungover, but his feet, clad in polished calfskin, were not a jot cold. And the bridesmaids – Aster, Marigold, and I – wore fur capes and bright smiles, and carried winter quince in place of roses. Even the vicar had gone as far as to shave his beard, rendering him strangely naked but putting him back in Grandma's good books, as far as vicars can ever be at least.

All was clockwork, in fact, the Wedding March bringing a tear to the eye of all those with hearts (and several without, as Mrs Gypp was in Guildford until the fourth and so we had to make do with Mr Hendry, whose organ skills are as fine-tuned as one might expect from someone who greatest experience is with pigs). But then, just as the vicar was about to ask if anyone had any objection (and Aster and Topaz clamped Grandma firmly, one on either arm) the oak door at the back of the nave swung open and there stood Ralph, red as you like, and gasping as if he'd run from Balfour Manor, not his mother's terrace two yards down.

'I do!' he yelled.

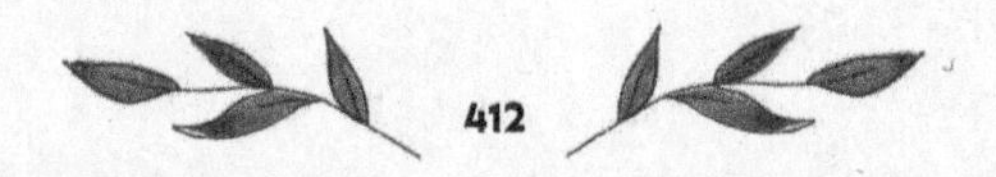

The congregation turned.

'That's to say,' he continued, his breath in staggers, 'no you mustn't marry that Valentine. You got to marry me!'

'Ralph!' yelped Mabel.

'Mabel!' called her lost lover.

And then, her veil flapping, her train catching on ankles, the bride left her elegant earl and scampered back down the aisle into the heftier if poorer arms of the postman.

Mrs Gibberd was mortified.

Marigold was delighted.

Topaz was practical, and asked the vicar if he couldn't perhaps marry the new happy couple then and there, but apparently there are rules. Grandma gave the vicar a look suggesting she did not approve of said rules but the vicar retreated farther into his cassock and cited God's wishes and not even Grandma can battle God, as much as she might like to.

So, the result is Valentine is still an unwed bachelor, without heir or prospect. And Mabel is still very much pregnant, engaged to Ralph, and moving in with the Gibberds as I write this. I hope she won't regret it too quickly. Or Ralph, if the baby turns out to be less than Gibberdish. Still, it is one less woman at Dower House.

And there is to be another loss: Aster is to move to Topaz's flat in Marylebone.

'It just makes sense,' she explained. 'I can't expect clients to keep traipsing to Ickthorpe. Not in this wretched weather.'

Grandma insists she is relieved (though I think she is rather taken with Topaz, whatever she claims), while Mama is awfully sad about it, but understands. 'Life moves on,' she declared. 'And it is high time you older girls found a new one.'

I ignored this, as it is enough that Aster is striding ahead right now. Marigold has already bagsed her room of course. I should have argued to toss a coin for it, but her resolution for the New Year is to keep lizards and bees, and I do not want to wake with either of them in my bed. Though I don't rate the lizards' chances against Bobby Two and Siegfried, nor the bees against Hamilton.

Mama asked us all for our resolutions after that. Hers, she announced, is to get a job. A proper one, in a shop, perhaps.

'But what about Dinah?' Grandma snatched at excuses. 'And what will Hermione Lightfoot think?'

'Cook will look after Dinah,' replied Mama. 'And perhaps your resolution should be ceasing to care what Hermione thinks.'

Grandma bristled. 'Only if she resolves to stop taunting me.'

'Then there is no hope for either of you,' said Mama. She turned, resolutely. 'Aster?'

'Oh, mine is to make a go of it in London.' She smiled. 'You know that.'

'And mine,' Topaz added, grasping Aster's hand briefly, and squeezing it, 'is to make a go of us.'

I am not sure if Grandma understands exactly what Aster

means to Topaz and she to Aster, but the rest of us knew in those words, in that gesture, what this was, and we welcomed it. But what of our cousin? Jilted at the last minute, and now heirless and maidless again.

'I'm going to sell the house,' he announced.

'What?' I blurted. 'Radley?'

Valentine nodded.

'But . . . you can't,' I said. 'It's not legal.'

'And it's wrong,' added Grandma. 'That house has been in Mannering hands for centuries.'

'It may be wrong,' replied Valentine. 'But it's legal, or will be. The law is changing. And what choice do we have? None of us can fund it. And I have . . . plans.'

The theatre, I remembered. The Pippin in Soho. The one Buck was supposed to back. At that I snapped my mind shut, stayed rooted in the room.

'Perhaps a change will do us all good,' I said, stoically. Buck at least would be gone, of course.

'As long as it's not another wretched American,' said Grandma.

On that, I think, we all agreed.

'Panther?' Mama was looking at me now. 'What will you do differently this year?'

I thought back to what I wanted this time last year: to do a season, to fall in love, to marry a man with money and standing.

I wanted none of that now.

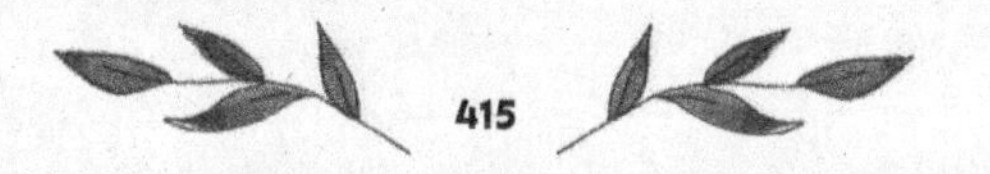

Then there was the letter, from Creed's. Perhaps another novel may be in the offing. But I wasn't sure.

Thankfully, at that point, the door went.

'Who on earth calls at this time?' Grandma snapped. 'It's as if we're all heathens. Or French!'

'I think I know,' said Aster, catching my eye. 'And Daddy would approve.'

My heart bloomed. For I knew who it was, and I knew Daddy would approve. And so I rose to answer it, and, more than that, face up to something. Something I have known for a while, and felt for longer.

*

We stood, gone eleven, Freddy and I, on the landing, looking over the land to Radley Manor, its lights a-blaze, its rooms full, I knew, of Bright Young Everyone.

Everyone but us.

'Do you wish you were there?' he asked.

I turned slightly toward him, smiled. 'Not one iota,' I said.

'Did you know iota is the smallest letter of the Greek alphabet,' he replied. 'That's where it comes from. I'm blabbing, aren't I? I'm sorry.'

'Don't be,' I said, and meant it. I liked his voice, his proximity, the smell of him even – lambswool and blankets and something baked – it all felt so . . . familiar, so safe. And yet wonderfully new and experimental too.

'I talk too much,' he said.

'But I like talking to you. It . . . matters.'

He laughed. 'Iotas and such.'

'Not that. Just' – I remembered his question, the night Dinah was born – 'purpose. You asked me once what mine was.'

He nodded. 'And do you know?'

'Not exactly,' I replied. 'But I'm clearer, I think. I'm just struck by the unfairness of it. Life, I mean. For women and . . . and men like Valentine. The wrongness of it is so vivid to me. And I'm tired of complying or even stamping my feet.'

'You want to do something about it,' he surmised.

I nodded.

'A lawyer, then.'

'Perhaps,' I replied. 'Or perhaps something bigger.'

'A politician?'

'I think so,' I said, realising the truth of it only that second. 'Though I'm not sure how, as yet.'

'Then we'll find out. You'd make a fine one.'

I smiled, felt his eyes on me, but not like Buck's – roving and gloating – rather, appreciative, taking me in; not just my figure, but all of me.

'What do you want to change?' he said then. 'What kind of world do you want to live in?'

'I want to live in a world,' I replied, 'where a woman has as much right to inherit a title as a man. You?'

'I want to live in a world where there are no titles to inherit.'

'Touché.'

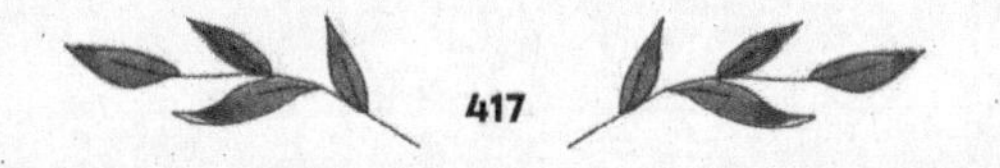

'What else?'

I thought back to the ball at the Balfours'. The end of Buck. And the beginning, I think, of this. Back then I wanted to be a flapper, a fictional princess; Juliet, who dies for her love.

Not any more.

'I want to be Emily Davison, running in front of a horse,' I said, my fervour building. 'I want to be Nancy Astor, striding into Parliament. I want to be someone who can show the world it is not a curse to be born a girl.' I paused for breath, to gather myself for this bit. 'It isn't a curse. I'm glad of it, in fact. It might be harder, I know. But I'm ready for the fight. For the climb.'

Freddy stared at me, his smile gone but his warmth not. He had something to say. Something I had waited for, I now realise, for longer than I can remember.

'I'm awfully glad you were born a girl as well.'

'Are you?' I asked.

'Yes,' he said. And his hand cupped my face in exactly the way I might write it.

'Me too,' I replied, my words barely more than a breath.

And then he kissed me. And it was everything I had ever hoped for in a kiss and nothing I expected. Soft and pressing and urgent and slow at once and all the while it wasn't just our lips that seemed to meet but our hearts, our minds, our very souls.

*

A year ago, Aster would say I was writing claptrap, but I think even she believes in love now. And I don't know what this year

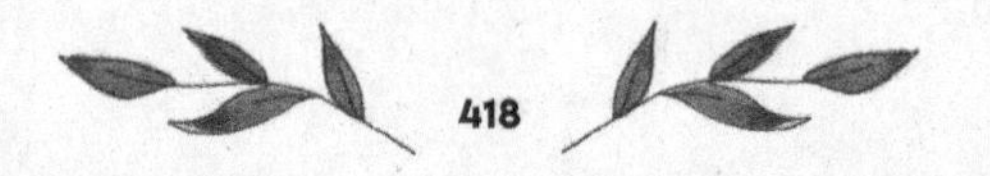

will bring. But I shall chronicle all of it. The grand and the small. For all of it is worth remembering. There are lessons to be learned everywhere. Not necessarily for anyone else. But for me. And for all of us calamitous Mannerings.

To remind us that, while we miss Daddy every day, we don't need men to fix anything. We can patch up our small world ourselves very well, thank you.

But sometimes, just sometimes, one man comes along who is worth letting in.

Not to make everything better, to take charge, take the wall, take over.

But to walk beside us. As peers. Equals. Lovers.

Friends.

ACKNOWLEDGEMENTS

This book was written during lockdown in England, and I am grateful to Panth and her sisters for keeping me occupied and optimistic. Gratitude also to my real world 'sisters' who do that for me through times happy and hard: Helen, Catherine, Annika, Anna, Jude, Nic, Rosh, Wendy, The Placers, and so many others. Thanks too to my agent Julia, editor Emma and publisher Hazel. What brilliant women all.

IF YOU LIKED THIS, YOU'LL LOVE . . .

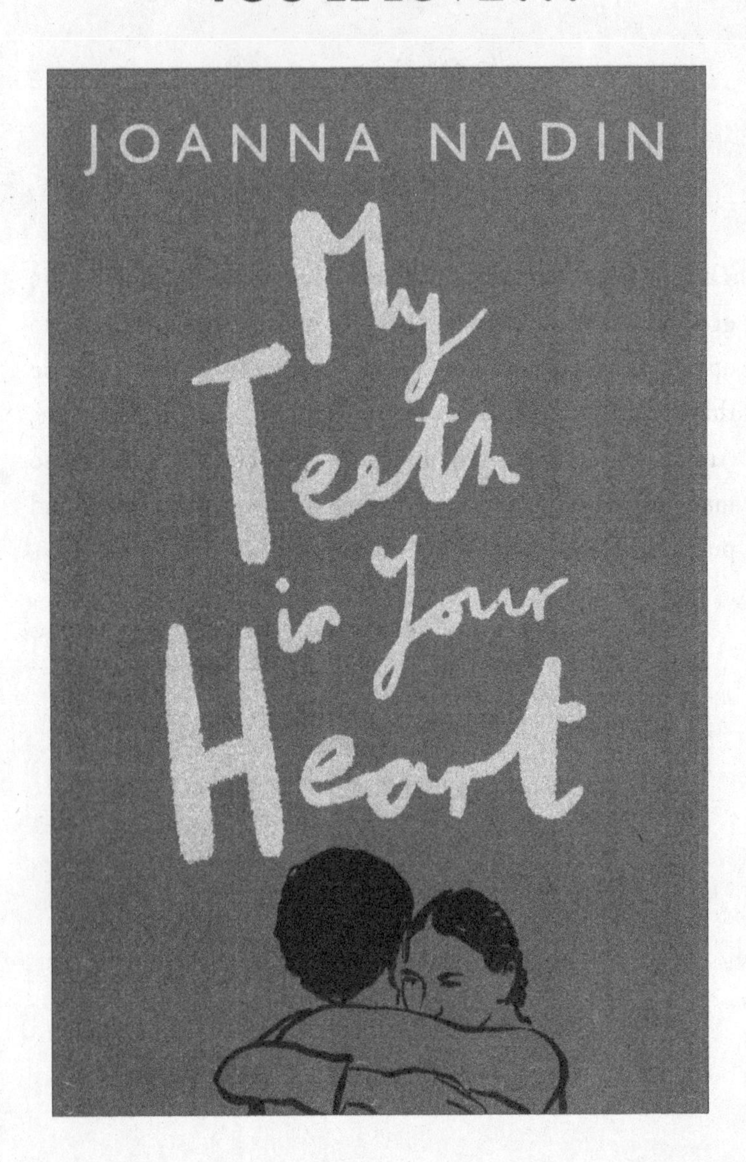